kissed by chaos

MAGIC WARS: HER IMMORTAL MONSTERS
BOOK 1

KEL CARPENTER

AURELIA JANE

RAGING HIPPO

Kissed by Chaos

Kel Carpenter and Aurelia Jane

Published by Raging Hippo LLC

Copyright © 2022, Raging Hippo LLC

Edited by Theresa Schultz

Proofread by Dominique Laura

Cover Art by Jay

 Created with Vellum

Kel Carpenter and Aurelia Jane are the hilarious team behind the international bestselling series, A Demon's Guide to the Afterlife.

They pride themselves in being absolute weirdos, spending hours on the phone coming up with detailed worlds, and laughing about crazy ideas for torturing characters. While they believe they each have the personality of a rabid badger, people still seem to like them okay.

They share a love of coffee, travel, and tacos, and they've made some adorable tiny people with their equally weird husbands. Best friends and work wives, Kel has the audacity to live in Maryland while Aurelia lives in Texas, but they try to see each other as much as possible.

"We never see in ourselves what others do," he muses, his words striking a chord. "Maybe that's because they only see the skin we're in and not the demons writhing beneath the surface."

COMPEL, CANDICE WRIGHT

For all the women out there that are just fucking tired and want to feel appreciated for who they are. Enjoy the escape. You've earned it.

Family sucked. Mine more than most.

I hadn't seen them in years, but it took all of a minute for me to realize coming to my childhood home was a mistake—and in true Le Fay fashion, they made me pay for it.

I'd been gifted a sleeping spell to knock me out cold and had bruised ribs to show how little they cared. I already knew they didn't give a shit what happened to me. Joke's on them. The feeling was mutual.

I'd only come because I knew they had information on where Lucifer was being held. The devil himself was missing, and I needed to intervene before they went through with whatever cockamamie scheme they'd planned. I figured I'd play the game, bullshit them a bit, and stroke a few egos so my best friend Piper could snoop around while I held their attention . . .

Joke's on me for this one. My mother saw the ruse immediately and put me under a sleeping enchantment before my partner in crime could even leave the room.

Now Piper was gods-know-where while I was safely

tucked in the dusty basement that made my allergies run haywire.

Face pressed against the dirty floor, I could feel my sinuses filling up, nose becoming stuffy, and eyes watery. Those assholes knew I had horrible allergies and they tossed me down here anyway. If I wasn't already annoyed, I would have been then.

My back ached as I rolled over and blinked.

Sconces lit the storage room in dim yellow light, bright enough to be jarring but not so much that I winced.

That was a good sign.

It meant the odds of a concussion were slim.

Slowly I turned my head, taking in every inch of the basement where I'd spent many, many nights in my youth. Both when my mother wanted to punish me for being useless and thought I needed time to 'think' about my shitty magic, and when my oldest sister Carissa decided tormenting me was going to be her favorite pastime.

Fear touched me as I remembered those difficult times, but I pushed it to the back of my mind, focusing on the present.

I lifted my arm to wipe the corner of my mouth with the back of my hand and winced. My ribs might be more than just bruised. It felt like someone took a baseball bat to my side. I swallowed hard, licking my dry lips in an attempt to soothe the cracks already forming from the acrid underground.

"How long have I been out?" I croaked without looking at my cellmate. I'd seen him in the periphery on my initial sweep of the room. Before I was captured and separated from Piper, I might have been thrilled that we found him so we could get the hell out of here.

Now? Not so much.

"Four hours," Lucifer rasped, his voice equally gravelly. Judging by the hundreds of cuts on his skin and shackled arms within the pentagram confining him—I'd guess my family had already spent a good bit of time draining him. It was the only way to kill a demon. But he wasn't dead, which meant that wasn't the end goal. "Maybe five. It's hard to know exactly without a window or clock."

I nodded once, the motion causing a sudden pain to explode at the back of my skull. It spread like hellfire all the way to my left temple. I put a hand to it and let out a grunt. Maybe I'd been too quick on that concussion assessment. "Did they drop me on my head?"

Despite the discolored skin where he was bruised on top of bruises, dried edges of blood that decorated his chest, or congealed blood that pooled around him—the devil smiled.

More of a smirk than a smile, really. Even a breath away from death, he was still mischievous. The light in his golden eyes failed to go out until it was well and truly over.

I could respect that, even if it was so unlike myself.

Don't get me wrong; I had a solid pain tolerance, thanks to my fucked-up childhood with these assholes. But the severity they'd beaten him? Cut him? Bled him?

I'd rather be dead than in that much pain, and I sure as hell wouldn't be smiling. If that made me a pansy, so be it.

There was no award for toughest bitch before entering the veil. I had nothing to prove.

"One of the women kicked you in the head. I believe she was a relative of yours."

"Carissa," I surmised. "She never liked me."

That was an understatement that nearly bordered on a lie, but my family was a can of worms that I'd rather not open in front of company. That type of misery was saved for when I was home, alone, with a hot cup of jasmine tea.

In other words, not now, and honestly? Not ever. I didn't waste my time on them anymore.

"Why?" There was a line on his neck where I suspected someone had already slit his throat once, but he spoke surprisingly well despite it.

I touched mine without thinking.

Yup. Definitely a pansy.

We needed to get out of here.

I pulled myself up off the dusty floor, pausing only to sneeze and then internally cursing Carissa to never have a day go by where she doesn't step on a Lego.

Taking a deep breath, I pressed my back to the wall for support and pushed the loose strands back that fell out of the messy bun I'd worn here.

It hurt like a bitch, but I was sitting. That meant I could stand. Mentally I worked through my different options of escape while answering Lucifer. "I'm different. Weird. My magic sucks, but instead of apologizing for it, I moved on. I became my own person, and I think, at the heart of it, that's why she doesn't like me. Even with shitty magic, I made a life for myself, and she's still just a pretty puppet on a string."

I wasn't resentful or angry about it. I wasn't even sad. Carissa was an awful, bratty child who grew into an awful, entitled adult. There wasn't anything to be done there. I didn't need her forgiveness or approval. I never had.

"You don't seem very upset for someone who was kicked in the face," he mused. The curiosity in his voice made me want to turn, to give him my attention, to feel that coldly beautiful gaze on my face. Even dying and looking like shit, he still held allure. Being a demon of desire gave him that power. At least that's what I told myself.

"There's no point in getting angry," I answered, taking in the four brick walls and bound pentagram. "Angry people lash out. They make stupid, rash decisions. My family drugged me for a reason, and it probably has to do with you, which means I need to find a way out of here. Getting angry won't help me do that."

"There isn't one." He sighed. So sure of himself. So arrogant.

I had a love-hate relationship with that trait in men. On one hand, a part of me loved to be choked and bound by arrogant men with dirty words.

The other side of me couldn't stand being underestimated. Sure, it happened all the time and it benefitted me in many ways, but it was still frustrating.

Instead of telling him he was wrong, I passively answered, "We'll see."

Out of my periphery I saw him narrow his eyes. My chest thudded hard, and I told myself it was the adrenaline of being trapped. It was. Mostly. "Do you know of one?" he asked.

My lips curled upwards in a smirk. "You do realize this is my parents' basement, right? I played in these tunnels as a kid and hid in them when I wanted to get away as a teenager. Few people, if any, know them as well as I do."

Technically it was the truth, if 'play' meant running from a demented older sibling that lit my hair on fire for fun.

I did hide in them later in my life, but only because I realized I'd get thrown down here anyway when they found me. It was better if I disappeared before that could happen.

"One would think your family knew this before putting

you down here, seeing that they didn't bother to secure you," he pointed out.

I wanted to laugh. Much like the devil, my family was too arrogant for their own good. They assumed I'd be a terrified mess, drowning in PTSD or bawling over what I was fairly certain were cracked ribs.

Like everyone else, they underestimated me.

I braced myself for the sharp twinge on my side as I climbed to my feet, using my hand against the wall to support some of my weight. I hobbled around the edge of the circle, toward the wall opposite of me.

"If you step into the circle, it will alert them—"

"I know this may come as a surprise to you, but as nice as your voice is, I'm going to need you to be quiet so I can think."

A tight inhale of breath was his only response. That was fine by me.

I needed to flip through memories I rarely accessed so I could recall the right pattern. It had been a little over three years ago when I'd last used this passage . . .

"Are you and Piper in a relationship?"

"What?" I couldn't help my surprise. It was such a random thing to ask.

"Your hearing is quite good for a witch. I know you heard me. Are you two fucking?" His line of questioning left me debating if saving him was really worth the trouble. The gravity of our situation was heavy. He got caught by a coven of black witches—my family—and now I was stuck here with him while he was bleeding out. Now wasn't the time to ask about my sex life.

I closed my eyes and exhaled once. "No, Piper and I are not *fucking,* nor are we in a relationship. Piper's my . . . friend." She was an asshole. I'd be the first to say it, but she was *my* asshole. It wasn't just anyone that would walk into an entire coven of witches, and not just witches—black witches—and claim to be my familiar so we could stop my family from doing what they did best. Ruining someone's day. Probably mine. Definitely Lucifer's. He may have had it coming, being the devil and all, but my family having a hand in it made it a hundred times worse. With them, death wasn't just death. It was *more*. Death was a means of accessing incredible power to do truly twisted, evil things. Which is why I was here. To prevent that. Or at least that had been the idea. Getting captured obviously wasn't part of the plan. My only real shot at getting us both out of this was hiding in the tunnels beneath the Le Fay mansion while Piper 'demoned out' on my asshole relatives. Maybe Ronan—her mate, atman, whatever—too. He'd been trying really hard to impress her and consummate their mate bond. Nothing says I'm in it for life like the skulls of your enemies, yeah? "Besides, I'm fairly certain it's only a matter of time until her atman wears her down."

The pensive expression on his face amused me when it probably shouldn't have. I chuckled at the cluelessness he showed despite being really, really freakin' old.

I know that I'm brilliant and have an eidetic memory, but c'mon. I was only twenty-two and this shit was obvious.

"What are you laughing at?" Lucifer asked, narrowing his golden gaze on me once more.

"You. Them." I chuckled again. "You're all very predictable. Take you, for instance. You don't shut up until I bring up Ronan and Piper. There's so much unnecessary drama between the three of you. You fucked this up by trying to force a bond on her using magic, and you barely survived it. You're the reason we're here right now. Really, you should all just bond and fuck, and then everyone can move on with their lives. But no. You all have to make things difficult." I rolled my eyes and his brows furrowed.

"Demons don't share."

Nice way of saying I'm too much of an 'alpha' to play nice.

"Yeah, well, Piper wasn't born a demon—she was made."

Her basic human morals made her incapable of ever loving him when she viewed him as the reason our world went to shit, but I wasn't his therapist and going to spell it out. I'd already shared my thoughts on the matter, and that was more than he deserved. I started tapping bricks with my knuckles as I recalled the correct pattern.

"Even if sharing was an option, she wouldn't have done it. Piper isn't like that," he said on a tired sigh.

Maybe he did understand. He just didn't want to admit it.

Fair enough, I suppose.

One final tap was all it took for the bricks to tremble. Dirt and mortar slid free, falling in chunks to the ground. They pulled back, one by one. The bricks receded into the wall, shuffling to the side in a wave that spread outward until it revealed a gaping hole a little smaller than the size of a door frame.

"That's true," I said, a slight smile pulling up one corner of my mouth while I patted myself on the back for my handiwork. "Piper isn't like that. If it makes you feel better, between you and Ronan, I don't think you ever stood a chance. They have something, and if she can ever move past her issues, I think they'll be good together. Or maybe not, but at least the sex will," I said, turning and crossing my arms.

"I—you—what are you doing?"

"At a loss for words," I murmured. "Now there's a first. Don't worry, though, I won't tell anyone that the devil needs relationship advice."

The silent opening and closing of his mouth was priceless.

I may not be the strongest witch or the savior of anything, but I was pretty sure I was one of only a handful of people that had ever made Lucifer speechless.

I didn't mind having exclusive membership to that club.

"I don't need advice," he said in a rush, golden eyes flaring brighter for a moment. "I want to know why you're not leaving. You're the one who spent the last five minutes telling me that Piper and I aren't right together. I'm trapped in this circle with no way out, when you clearly aren't in the same predicament. I've only ever been horrible to you and your kind . . . so why aren't you leaving?"

He wasn't wrong.

Most witches would leave him for dead. Cut their losses and call it even for all the bad juju he sent our way over the years. Everything from the Salem witch trials to the witch camps to the subsequent Magic Wars.

But two wrongs didn't make a right.

Yeah, he wasn't exactly a friend to witches, but neither was I.

We couldn't choose the life we are born into, but we can decide the one we want to lead. And for as crap as the world was, when I took my last breath—whether that was today or in sixty years—I wanted to be involved in making it a better place.

"Because I can't leave," I admitted quietly. "You and Piper would be awful together. She would never be able to fully forgive you, but regardless of that, magically forced or not, you share a bond. You are some bastardized form of her atman."

"She has another one," he pointed out. He was oddly ambivalent for a man that not long ago wanted Piper as his atma. Sure, her strange magic was partially why, and his marbles being a little lost didn't help, but that was a choice he'd made. He seemed ready to die on that hill, and now . . . I didn't know what to make of it.

"It doesn't matter," I said softly. "Tell me, Lucifer, is it true all supernatural bonds are merely weaker imitations of the atma bond?"

He studied me intently and I watched him right back, cataloguing every twitch, blink, and breath.

"I can't attest to if they're truly weaker. I've never experienced one. But they do come from the atma bond. Magic seeks balance. Without it, we all lose to chaos."

I nodded. His answer was very neutral, but still held the truth. Magic corrupted. Not instantly, but over time.

It was the reason he wasn't exactly all there and thought Piper was his atma. It was the reason Piper's body was struggling to contain her magic. It was the reason that witches went crazy in their prime, just as werewolves went feral, and vampires descended into bloodlust . . . Magic corrupted, and the only way to stop it was to find your other half and complete the bond.

For demons that was their atma.

For wolves their mate.

For vampires their bride.

And for witches, we had psychic bond mates. Not necessarily romantic in nature, but people whose magic grounded our own and kept us sane. Balanced.

Even if they didn't have a traditional bond, if something happened to Lucifer, it would do untold damage to Piper.

Demons didn't survive the loss of their mates usually. They hadn't completed it, but still . . . I wasn't willing to take that risk.

I stepped into the circle.

"Don't—" He tried to protest, but there was no point. I'd already triggered it.

"As you said, we all lose to chaos," I said, crouching at his side. "Which is why I can't leave without you. If you die, so will part of Piper. I won't do that to her."

Air hissed between his teeth as I placed my hands on the chain linked to his right wrist. The metal turned red hot and began to burn. His jaw clenched. The smell of burning flesh made my stomach churn.

"If there was a way out of these chains, don't you think I would have done it?" he said. "It's impossible. It's—"

"That's not true. Nothing is impossible. It's simply very difficult, and you're not being helpful right now. You said yourself they'll know I'm in here. Maybe they'll come down. Maybe not. Either way, I'd rather be long gone by the time my parents figure out what happened. So are you going to help me, or am I on my own for saving your ass?"

He jerked under my harsh words. I had no doubt the chains hurt. They were being used to contain what little of his magic remained. Mind you, 'little' was still a lot when talking about demons. All magic on earth came from their kind.

"These chains were made specially for me." Lucifer sighed. "They used my blood. It might not be impossible, but you forget—I tasted your blood once. I know what you are and how much power you hold. You're not strong enough for this, little witch. It will take the caster herself to break these chains, but I can promise you she won't."

Black magic oozed like rot around the metal cuffs. I

recognized it. It was distinctive from any other magic I'd encountered. If I didn't have the ability to see magic, I wouldn't have known or had any idea in how to untangle it, but Lucifer was in luck—even though he didn't know it. "Who was the caster? Can you tell?" I asked out of curiosity, to see if he actually knew or just thought he did. He had no idea that I could see the grotesque black strands that clung to him like tar. At least I was fairly sure he didn't know. The ability to see magic was usually only a demon capability.

Only one other person I knew could do the same.

If I believed in coincidence, I'd say that was why the only other witch in existence that could see magic was the very person that created these chains.

My ancestor. The original black witch that started this whole fucked-up family.

"Morgan Le Fay."

TEN MONTHS AGO...

For centuries, that name had caused near as much terror among supernaturals as my own. She was almost as infamous. Twice as bloodthirsty. Madder than a hatter, and more possessive than even a demon could be.

Morgan Le Fay was a witch, but she'd stripped herself of all humanity in order to become *more*. She cast off her human beginnings, and all but killed that part of herself to become immortal.

Most witches would have turned and run at her very name, even those related to her. Especially if the rumors of what she did to them were true. But not this one. And that intrigue I felt—that pull toward Nathalie—strengthened and took form.

For the second time, the little witch surprised me.

Because she smiled.

"My family must really think so little of me. It would be insulting under different circumstances."

"And it's not insulting because . . .?" I trailed off, partly because words were becoming harder to form the more the iron burned. Fire seared my flesh and perfumed the air.

"Because I don't look a gift horse in the mouth," she said, pulling up her sleeve and extending her wrist. She placed it on my lips, warm and inviting. "Bite me."

The scent of jasmine and lilac made my mouth water.

"You don't know what you're asking for," I murmured, lips skimming her heated skin. My tongue darted out, the tip trailing over her pulse. I felt it skip, and her skin pebbled.

"Bite me, but don't take too much. I need blood to smear over the chains. It should be enough to release you."

My heart jolted.

"Are you sure?"

"No," she replied in an honest, shaky laugh. "But I think it will work. I'm related to Morgan Le Fay. She's my great-grandmother twenty-six generations back. Weak witch or not, her blood runs in my veins. There's a chance the magic will take."

No, there wasn't. I might not have studied witch magic, but I did create the first witch, and another dozen or so since then. I knew enough to know that what she wanted to try . . . it was a long shot. An impossible shot.

Even for her.

A chaos witch that shouldn't exist.

But with her skin pressed to mine and fire burning through me, for the first time in a long time I felt want and desire beyond a passing fancy. I wanted to kiss every inch of her skin and feel her writhe beneath me. I wanted to see what made her jump and learn what made her moan.

That wasn't an option, though. I knew that.

So I took the next best thing she offered: her blood.

My fangs pressed down, and she held her wrist firm as I pushed them into her skin. Copper blossomed. Sweet ichor touched my tongue.

The initial taste was sweet and crisp, like a breath of fresh air. What lived beneath that first taste was infinitely better. The very magic in her veins lurked like a secret hidden in the night. I pressed my lips to her wrist and took a hard pull. Her magic, while weak, still pulled at me. It wasn't the fire that my atmas had boasted. It wasn't boisterous or loud.

It was a gentle breeze. The sun on my skin. Snow melting to make way for new life, and a lullaby that gently guided you into sleep.

"Lucifer," Nathalie said in a rough cry. "Lucifer, you need to stop. I need to get your chains off."

I didn't want to stop.

In fact, stopping was the last thing I wanted to do.

But if I took more, it could actually kill her.

My jaw opened on its own, and my lips parted, releasing her. Blood ran freely for a few seconds, dripping onto my lips. I ran my tongue over them, feeling more clear-headed than I had in days. I opened my eyes to stare at her, almost entranced by what I'd just experienced.

But she wasn't even looking at me.

Hunched over, she swiped her wrist over each of my chains and muttered words in languages I'd learned and forgotten ten times over. Determination pushed her brows together and sweat dotted her temple. The heat coming from the chains was reaching an all-time high. That bitch Morgan really knew how to get to me, but I didn't let it.

Instead, I focused on Nathalie Le Fay with everything I had left.

It was easier than it sounded since I was hard as a rock from drinking her blood.

"Motherfucker," she grunted. "Son of a bitch. Piece of sh—"

"I told Mother we should have tied you up," another voice said. "You never knew when to leave well enough alone."

I didn't look because it didn't matter. I'd never let myself truly hope there was a way out, so I continued to focus on the witch even as her whole body went taut. The muscle in her cheek twitched, and I wondered if she bit it.

"Katherine," she said through gritted teeth. Blood touched her tongue, so she must have. "I'm going to assume you're not just here to gloat."

"Unfortunately not." She sounded like Nathalie, but the voice was all wrong. The tone. The inflection. I didn't find her twin sister even half as agreeable. "I've been told I get the *honor* of preparing you."

"Preparing me?" she asked, and to some it might have seemed innocent. Stupid, even. But there was intelligence in her eyes and a lilt to her voice. She was fishing. Despite being caught, she still looked for a way out.

It was no wonder I couldn't hold on to her and Piper. The two of them together . . . I really had no chance, as much as I hated to admit it.

"Yes, dear sister. You wanted to claim your birthright so badly. It looks like you'll get your wish," the other sneered.

"My wish?" Nathalie lifted an eyebrow defiantly.

"To lead the coven," Katherine said, pausing for dramatic effect. "You're going to perform the sacrifice and open the portal."

"Open the . . ." Her voice trailed off. Her eyes took on a faraway stare. "Where are they trying to open a portal to?" She spoke softly, then. Quiet. Like she knew, but hoped she was wrong.

"Hell, of course. We're going to find the source of magic."

I might have jerked if I weren't so weak already. The source of magic was in the Otherworld. Humans knew it as Hell, thanks to my own made-up stories about my home world.

If the entirety of the universe was a deck of cards, the Otherworld was at the top and the earth was the bottom. To create a portal that traversed all of them, from the origin to the world furthest from magic . . . it was suicide. Or in my case, homicide.

Something told me they didn't care.

"The source of magic—do you hear yourself?" Nathalie questioned her sister. "We don't even know if it exists" —it did— "and even if it does, why on earth would we want to play with that sort of power? If it's real and it did create all magic, then that thing also created demons. It takes a whole coven to summon and contain even *one*. How do you possibly think we're going to use the source of all magic?"

She shook her head in disgust. Meanwhile, my own interest in her simply continued to grow. I'd known the witches wanted to harness the power of all creation. I'd even known the lengths they'd go to. I just never thought *I* would be the one sacrificed for it.

Nathalie was a different kind of witch.

She didn't crave power . . . she respected it like the sentient being it was.

The other one moved into the circle. I recognized Nathalie's twin—a mirror image of her, except for the scar on her face.

"I don't make the decisions. I just do what I'm told." Great logic. Truly. Many Nazis said the same thing while apprehending people and sending them to their deaths.

"Of course," Nathalie said with a sneer. "You're nothing but a lemming. Parroting what your mommy and daddy tell you—even when the consequences will be so much bigger than us—"

"Save the monologue where you try to inspire me to turn against them and free you," Katherine responded sharply. "It's not going to happen. Besides, you should be happy. After the ritual you'll be a full-fledged member again. Mommy and Daddy will be *so* proud. They might even make you Marcel's whore if you're lucky."

I didn't know who Marcel was, but the expression that crossed Nathalie's face made me wonder if I'd underestimated her.

Maybe she did have fire.

"I don't want your sloppy seconds."

Katherine laughed. It was raspy and amused, but somehow hollow. "Darling sister, I'd still have him. Marriage is until death as far as the Pleiades Coven is concerned—and you know that well, don't you? You'd just be the side piece used to breed *our* witch children." Tension wound through every fiber of Nathalie's being, but despite the rage written all over her face, she didn't act. Her sister pouted. "You're no fun."

"Being told your family wants to whore you out and breed you will do that."

Katherine rolled her eyes at the emotionless words and reached into her pocket. "They said I had to ready you. Not that you needed to be awake for it."

She blew a handful of yellow dust in Nathalie's face, and the little witch collapsed forward. Katherine caught her carefully. Her lips pressed together, like she wasn't as okay with this whole thing as she seemed. I watched silently as she laid her down. As if she'd noticed my attention on her, the scarred witch stomped over. Grabbing another handful of dust, she blew it in my face.

"Nighty night, demon."

Darkness settled around me instantly. I welcomed the relief.

My life was ending tonight whether or not I was awake to ponder it.

I was a hedonist, not a masochist—and would take the bliss of unconsciousness over pain any day.

Unfortunately, it seemed like only a blink of an eye before awareness tugged at me. Fire burned my skin, hotter than the irons on my wrists and ankles. It licked at my arms and scorched my chest.

I moaned.

Dark chanting washed over me. The words hard to make out. I recognized the language as Hebrew, but I'd lost fluency in the last thousand years.

Still, I could pick out a few.

They were . . . daunting.

Blood. Channel. Magic. Power. Source.

Yep. Daunting was right.

If not for the scent of jasmine and lilac, I would have simply closed my eyes and surrendered to eternity.

I pried them open.

Sitting on my lap, athame in hand, was the little witch.

She carved my skin with a rapt expression, as though she were possessed. Her light brown eyes had morphed to a pure, brilliant gold. Her magic was everywhere.

In the air.

In my skin.

In the blood that ran in rivulets down my form, smudging her naked body.

Around us, what I could only presume to be the Pleiades Coven chanted. Cloaks covered their bodies, but in true black witch fashion, their sacrifices were naked.

I didn't focus on them, instead watching the witch that was killing me with . . . contentment.

Sure, the pain was terrible, but it made it easier to focus on her. Just her.

She wielded the athame like an extension of herself. My blood touched her bare thighs and arms. It smeared over her breasts and covered her hands. A sick sort of satisfaction filled me.

Her light brown hair floated on a nonexistent wind as she harnessed power beyond this world.

My power.

She cut my name from my skin by tracing the brands of my flesh from wrist to neck, to chest and stomach. The stinging in my back told me that was completed before I'd woken up.

Above her, a swirling abyss of white and gold and black was forming. The beginnings of not just a portal, but a channel to the Otherworld.

Despite her sure movements, her eyes screamed an apology.

Terrified and unsure, they betrayed what I'd already suspected.

Her actions were not her own.

I swallowed, but there was so little moisture left in me. My blood was being stolen and pretty soon they'd blow through the last of my magic.

"It's okay," I rasped, unsure if she heard me over the chanting. Her eyebrows drew together as she continued carving.

Her hair fell on either side of my face, creating a curtain between us and the prying eyes of the black witch coven.

"It's okay," I said again. "It'll never work. I'll die before any channel can reach the Otherworld . . ."

I coughed weakly. Blood splattered her face.

Suddenly, she stopped carving.

The room went silent, the coven's final note echoing on the high ceilings.

I began to slip away, my eyes closing for the final time.

Then she licked her lip.

It was only a drop of my blood.

Hardly anything.

My eyes closed. Everything faded away. Sound. Scent. Sensation.

I fully gave myself over to the end, ready to embrace death after ten thousand years of crippling loneliness.

But I didn't fade.

I didn't cease existing.

In the darkness of death, the world slowly started to take form once more.

Glass ceilings. Screaming people. Blood-soaked tiles. I stood in the center of the ritual, staring down at Nathalie Le Fay.

Except she was still sitting on me. *My body.*

The world practically burned around her as members of her family collapsed on the spot, dying or writhing in pain as the power they'd tried to contain fought back with a vengeance. She didn't look. She didn't twitch.

In a world of chaos, her eyes were focused on my unmoving face.

She was muttering. I stepped closer to hear her. In barely more than a whisper, she said, "*Live.*"

Over and over again, she repeated it.

I shook my head. This shouldn't have been possible. I shouldn't be here, in the veil. Yet . . . she'd tethered me.

She'd bound us in death.

Nathalie didn't realize it yet, but in her efforts to save me—she'd done the impossible.

"Clever little chaos witch," I murmured.

She jerked. Her head dropped to my naked chest to listen to my dead, unbeating heart, then she frowned. Her golden eyes scanned the dying cloaked members, looking for something—someone—that wasn't there.

Because somehow, even from the veil, the witch that hardly had any power *heard* me.

NATHALIE

LATEX WAS OVERRATED.

Sure, it clung to all the *right* places, but it clung to all the *wrong* ones too. The dress felt like a glove suffocating my body for the sake of sex appeal, and the boob sweat was real.

I wasn't sure if it was a blessing or a curse that it had large cutouts along my hips, waist, and thighs. While it gave those parts of me a tiny bit of relief from the sweltering, nonbreathable fabric, I couldn't help feeling like a busted can of biscuits.

I hid my snort behind the martini glass pressed to my lips.

My legs were crossed, appearing long and sleek despite my actual petite stature, thanks to a magically enhanced body oil infused with succubus pheromones. It would make me irresistible to my date for the evening.

Hopefully enough so his lips would come loose and let slip the location of an incredibly powerful magical artifact I was searching for.

Throughout the dungeon of Bliss, no clock ticked, but I sensed the passing of time. Keeping up with the seconds in the back of my mind as I waited.

An incubus approached, no doubt caught in the lure I'd cast out.

On another night, I might have sidestepped his attention. But with this particular target, having his interest would suit my needs.

I smiled demurely but with unmistakable interest, teetering on that line between being a flirt and too forward. His own smile widened. "Hello, beautiful," he purred. The incubus bent at the waist, extending his hand toward me. "May I?"

He was blonde—ashy, not golden. Once upon a time I might have taken him to my bed. Now I avoided blondes. Even if his blue eyes were pretty. High cheekbones. Full lips. He had a face I could sit on.

The subtle scent of my arousal hit him, and those eyes darkened a shade. "You may." I dropped my hand in his, letting him pull me from my barstool. The moment our skin touched, I got the feeling of yearning. A raw, unbridled ache longing to be soothed or forgotten entirely. He was so lonely, lost in a darkness that left him *empty*.

My heart sighed, deflating a fraction, even though he'd never see. I related to the poor man and the way he sought to fill the void that grief and resentment left in his soul.

The *tink* of my martini glass touching the counter was the last I knew of it as he pulled me through a crowd and away from the main room. Deeper in the dungeon, play chairs, crosses, and sex swings waited.

"Does anything pique your interest?" he asked me, a glint of sexual excitement in his gaze.

My lips parted and I leaned forward a fraction to point when a presence appeared behind me. I knew he was there despite being unable to see or touch him. He had no body, but his entire presence filled the space.

"What are you doing, little witch?" Lucifer rumbled; his voice dark. Gruff. The hairs along my nape stood on end in answer, but I refused to acknowledge his presence. Not anymore.

In an effort to keep him at bay, I severely limited my magic use. It seemed to work. But the small touch of skin led to my premonition about the incubus and gave Lucifer just enough of a crack to open the door and make his presence known.

Should have worn gloves, I thought, making a mental note to not make that mistake again.

I swallowed, then pointed at the cuffs hanging from the ceiling.

The incubus in front of me shifted his attention to them, completely unaware of the ghost in our midst or my unease due to it.

A sly smile spread across his face. He licked his lips, looking back at me with hunger. "You or me?" he asked.

The target whose attention I wanted liked pretty things. Submissive things. Seeing me bound and on display for another? He wouldn't be able to resist.

"Me," I answered with a wink.

The incubus smirked. "Hands up, beautiful," he murmured as he guided me closer. At my back, that presence grew. Silent, but not indifferent. If anything, his lack of speech said a great deal. I ignored it. Ignored him.

The ghost was dead. Gone.

Sure, I could hear him, but he wasn't *here*.

I offered my wrists, raising them high above my head. The incubus's fingers were cold to the touch, but soft. They weren't working hands, that was for sure.

The leather cuffs wrapped around my wrists, restricting my movement. If not for the heels of my boots, I would have struggled to stand.

"What's your name?" my partner for the evening asked, checking the grip. Months ago, I would have appreciated the care he took to respect my boundaries. Seeking permission. We would have had lots of fun together, a creature that fed on sex and a witch that liked to have it. It really was a shame so much had changed.

"Ophelia," I lied smoothly. I may not be the strongest witch by a mile, but I was a fantastic liar. "And yours?"

"August," he answered as he rolled up the cuffs of his button-down shirt. "Tell me what you like, Ophelia."

I opened my mouth to answer, right as my gaze slid past him. Nothing came out as golden eyes, bright as the sun itself, focused on me. Lucifer's white hair seemed to reflect the lights of the dungeon, but that was impossible. My mouth went dry at the look on his face. The sheer intensity with which he stared was startling.

"Two weeks," Lucifer said, not revealing a hint of emotion. "You've refused to use magic for two weeks just to shut me out, and when you finally slip, it's to fuck one of my children."

Stomach acid climbed up my throat, but I kept it down.

"Ophelia?" the incubus asked, drawing my attention back to him. I blinked, remembering myself. Lucifer was being dramatic. The incubus wasn't his child. He couldn't be. At least by blood. Magic was another story.

"Sorry," I murmured. "I thought I recognized someone."

The incubus glanced behind him, then turned back, brows pinched together. "Would you prefer—"

"Choking," I said, interrupting him. His mouth snapped shut, that dark hunger coming back. "Spanking. Biting. I like some pain, but not so much it leaves more than a mild bruise. My hair being pulled turns me on." I focused on him, refusing to look elsewhere, even if it meant I wouldn't see when my actual target approached.

"How do you feel about toys?" August wondered, studying a rack of options.

"Impact toys are okay. No canes. No clamps. I can't do pinching at all, but I'm all right with restraints. Hard no on any kind of hook."

The incubus glanced over his shoulder and lifted an eyebrow as his fingers hovered over a velvety eye mask. I shook my head. "Not here."

While a sliver of disappointment went through him, he acknowledged it. It wasn't uncommon for people to be uncomfortable with masks when taking a partner for the first time to play. My reasoning had more to do with needing to see the door, but there was no need to elaborate.

When he selected a single black feather, I tried to cock my head but couldn't, and settled for a lift of my eyebrows.

"Interesting choice."

"I'd rather start slow and find your limits than accidentally overstep," he said thoughtfully.

A ghostly tingle ran from one shoulder blade to the other as Lucifer stepped around him, circling me. "I wouldn't need to ask," Lucifer whispered in my ear. "I already know all your likes. Your dislikes. Your limits. Your boundaries."

My heartbeat intensified, filling my ears with the sound.

"May I feed from you?" August asked. The question grounded me.

He wasn't talking about blood. He wanted my pleasure. Normally I said no. While I wasn't inherently opposed, that was something I preferred only with partners.

Just as I was about to answer, Lucifer snapped, "No." The word was a growl. Possessive, though he had no right or reason to be.

Just to spite him, I said, "Yes."

Lucifer's golden eyes burned like solar flares. August dipped his head in thanks. "I'll be gentle," he murmured.

"I'm sure he will," Lucifer scoffed. "You guard your blood and magic carefully. You won't even give him your name, but you'll let him feed from you?" Lucifer asked me. I didn't answer. I refused. "What happened to not wanting to taunt the devil?"

So much. Yet so little.

Was it cruel? If I owed him anything, yes. But I didn't.

He was simply a ghost, and I was just the very unfortunate witch who'd been tied to him. While annoying, he couldn't do a thing to stop me.

August leaned forward, letting the tip of the feather touch me. A sheen of silvery blue magic covered him, letting me know he was disguising his actual appearance with a glamour. It didn't bother me. Half the people in the club opted for one. I didn't like the feel of glamours, the way they rubbed against my skin, stifling me. I preferred to use a fake alias when possible.

Under other circumstances, he would have asked me for a safe word before getting started, but that wasn't needed in this establishment. Not when they used the universal colors of red for stop and yellow for slow down. It was simplistic and easy to remember.

It also meant that magic enforced the rules.

"You have beautiful eyes," August said, letting the feather trail over my collarbone. "I've never seen eyes such a light shade of brown." The feather drifted over my abdomen, skimming the edges of where the dress cutouts let it touch my skin. Another kind of itch erupted in me.

My breathing slowed.

He leaned in and licked a trail up the column of my neck.

I gasped at the contact, and he groaned.

"You taste delicious. You shouldn't use the succubus pheromones. You don't need it."

My lips parted. How did he know that?

August lifted his eyes to me once more. "I have a *very* good sense of smell. I can scent magic and other things . . ." I heard the truth in his voice and let it lie. While uncommon outside of demons, I'd heard of some creatures inheriting a demon's ability to scent magic—since all magic came from them. I was an oddity myself for being able to see it.

He leaned in again, inhaling around my neck. He kissed a spot and despite it being nothing more than his lips, it felt tender, with a bite of lust entwined that I wasn't used to. It had been a while since I'd been with an incubus. The feather trailed across my abdomen and my stomach twitched.

Lips falling open, I lowered my guard a little, letting my eyelids flutter closed as I let the pleasure wrap around me.

"Nathalie."

I bit the inside of my cheek.

My eyes flew open to see a person on the other side of August, just over his shoulder. I couldn't say the newcomer was the very last person I wanted to see, but he was certainly near the top of that list.

The incubus touching me froze, stepping back a fraction. He glanced over his shoulder, expression neutral to the point of distaste. "We're in the middle of a scene." A polite dismissal if I ever heard one.

"Consider this production canceled." The not-welcomed guest unbound my wrists with a flick of his hand. "Scene over. Move along."

The incubus worked his jaw instead of dropping the topic and deciding it wasn't worth his trouble. He looked at me. "What would you prefer, beautiful?"

I gazed at him. He had to have known I lied about my name, but he was still interested, and unwilling to walk away unless I wanted it.

Regret tasted like ash on my tongue.

"Unfortunately, I can't ignore this."

He dipped his head. "Perhaps we'll meet again, then." He stepped away, walking backward to keep eye contact with me.

"Maybe," I repeated, knowing the odds of that were incredibly unlikely now that my cover was blown and that meant I couldn't return to this club without a glamour—which pissed me off even more. They were worse than the latex dress by a mile.

Turning to the man who'd interrupted me, I shook off all desire, letting a familiar mask drop into place. He grabbed my wrist without permission, making me instantly wish for my incubus companion. We disappeared, rematerializing in a graveyard outside none other than the Wicked Haunt, a church turned summoning center owned by the only existing coven of black witches in New Chicago.

"Marcel," I said curtly, yanking my wrist back. "I was in the middle of something important. I hope you have a good reason for interrupting."

I doubted he did. Severely doubted.

The heated look he practically branded me with solidified that thought.

But his words made everything evaporate.

"Your twin is missing."

two

NATHALIE

"MISSING?" I repeated.

Marcel took a step back but didn't drop my wrist. His touch was a burn I didn't want to feel. A brand I wasn't willing to wear.

I moved away, my shoes digging into the soft earth of the graveyard. One of the heels sunk and my ankle twisted to try to compensate for the uneven distribution of weight. I buckled, nearly hitting the ground.

Marcel tugged sharply on my wrist, pulling my back into him, wrapping his other hand around my bare hip. I tensed, swallowing hard as the scent of fresh parchment, ink, and oleander settled over me. The first two were so familiar yet bittersweet. Stolen pleasure in the aisles of my parents' library, black ink smudges against skin, my face pressed into ancient texts as he bent me—

I cut the memory off sharply. I could recall every scent and thing I saw, every touch, every feeling. It was the blessing and curse of my eidetic memory, and all too easy to lose myself in. So I focused on the third scent.

Oleander. Nerium. Poison.

I frowned for a moment, wondering why my ex smelled faintly of the deadly flower.

"Missing," he repeated after me, his cool breath fanning my face, entirely unaware of where my mind had gone.

"Care to tell me who this tool is?" Lucifer interrupted. His presence appeared at my side, and I couldn't help my eyes flicking up toward the ghost. Marcel noticed, his lips twitching in response.

"Please let me go, Marcel," I said, speaking softly but still firm.

"You need to be more careful, sunbeam."

The childhood nickname was nothing more than a whisper from his lips, but it felt like a sledgehammer after those memories. I jerked back. "I wasn't asking."

His dark eyes flashed. I recognized it all too well. The fire. The indignation.

"Neither was I." His words were soft despite the way he tried to brand me with his possessive gaze.

"Sunbeam?" Lucifer repeated. It sounded less like a term of endearment and more like a growled curse when he said it. The devil tsked. "I cannot *wait* to hear where that name came from." He'd be waiting a while because I had no intention of going into the messy, complicated details of my life involving the man that stood before me. The boy I'd grown up with . . .

Marcel appraised me, twisting his lips into a frown. "You don't look like yourself anymore."

I narrowed my eyes, clenching my jaw in frustration. "I don't look miserable and trapped anymore, you mean?" I shrugged. "Good."

"No . . . that's not exactly what I meant. You look beautiful, if unhappy."

"I'm actually quite happy, Marcel. I took the trash out.

All of it," I said, looking him up and down before continuing. "I love my work, and living without drama, as much as one can in this city."

Lucifer huffed. "You're busy, little witch. But that's not the same thing as happy."

I ground my teeth. Whose side was he on, anyway?

"Is that so?"

"Yes."

Marcel exhaled, a little sound of disbelief coming from his lips as he shook his head slightly. "You never could lie to me, Nathalie. I always saw through you."

I wasn't having this conversation with him. Looking away, I carefully stepped to the side and onto the hard, compacted dirt that formed the trail through the graveyard. "You said *your fiancé* is missing. Elaborate."

Marcel studied my face a moment longer before walking to my side, fingers brushing against mine before I crossed my arms. "She disappeared three and a half weeks ago. Went out to get supplies from the city one night and never came back."

"Supply runs?" I asked, more thinking out loud than anything. "That doesn't sound like Katherine. I'm surprised she didn't send one of the lower members of your coven to do it."

"She hasn't in almost a year," Marcel said, hesitating. "Ever since the fall of . . . well, you know. None of the Le Fays survived, save you, Kat, and Carissa. Rumor is the Morrigan perished in the fire that broke out across New Chicago. Kat has had to step up after that. Witches aren't exactly popular these days, so she's one of the few that can do the job . . ."

My mouth formed a grimace. I knew exactly what he was referencing.

"Since they killed me," Lucifer deadpanned, addressing the unspoken elephant in the graveyard. My jaw tightened. I wished I could tell him to shut up, but I supposed I'd be salty too if someone killed me. I'd rather him be bitter over that than poke into my private life any day. "Ungrateful children. They didn't like my rules? Now they're all dead or weak thanks to their own stupidity. Say it, boy. *That's* why Katherine goes on supply runs. The rest of your pathetic coven aren't strong enough if they run into trouble."

I turned, glancing over at Lucifer. He smiled, taunting me with knowledge about her he shouldn't possess. While I wouldn't address it with him in front of Marcel, I did plan on asking him about it later.

"Have you tried to contact her? Called her cell?"

"Of course," Marcel said, straddling that line between haughty, arrogant, and charming. "But the number was disconnected shortly after she disappeared."

I nodded. "Have you scryed for her?"

Marcel lifted an eyebrow in my direction. "A dozen times, if not more. There's no trace of her anywhere."

I sighed. There were a few things that could mean. "What makes you think she's in trouble?"

He paused, looking over the rows of gravestones. Broken. Crumbling. They covered the field in every direction, save for the edge of the woods and the small chapel that stood in the middle. What was once holy ground for a false god was now prime necromancy real estate—or it would be, if Piper hadn't banned the Ouroboros Coven from all necromancy together. "Kat is a lot of things, most of them not very good or nice—but she'd *never* turn her back on her coven."

I didn't disagree. Not about that.

Like a true black witch, she valued power and legacy above all else.

Even me, her twin.

"Fair. So assuming that, she's most likely hiding or in trouble with someone that can keep her magic signature hidden. Unless she was somehow killed without any of us knowing."

That narrowed it down, but not by much. Our world was full of powerful beings, and my sister wasn't exactly one of them. Not anymore.

A massive portion of people had received their power from Lucifer, my family included. They hadn't realized the complexity of how it tied them all together. Bound them to him in life *and* death. When he died, those with his desire magic coursing through their veins also suffered terribly. Their bodies didn't know how to cope with the loss of magic when it was ingrained so deeply.

That sort of loss did more than just weaken them.

It killed. It crippled. The more reliant they had been on that magic, the worse off they were. Katherine included.

"I don't think she's dead," Marcel said. "I can't say for sure, but I have this feeling she's alive and out there somewhere."

Dead. The word was hard to swallow, and yet not. There had been a time when I'd thought she was. I'd grieved in my own way. Then I'd learned she wasn't, and that she didn't give enough shits to tell me.

It left me with conflicted feelings even now.

Inside me, I felt a twinge of that loss and shut it down instantly.

"Why is this the first I'm hearing about it if it's been weeks?"

"I couldn't hunt you down because you have some sort cf block on you. I tried."

Obviously a good choice, too. An amulet I wore that prevented others from scrying for me, with very few exceptions. When you had a family like mine, you tended to want privacy. Tonight, courtesy of my latex dress, I had to leave it at home before I went to the dungeon so that it didn't tip off my target as to who I was.

"You unfortunately know where I live," I pointed out. "It's not like you couldn't have swung by."

"I tried that too," Marcel responded, his voice dropping in volume. "The old cat lady witch that lives in the shop below has a ward around the entire building that I can't get past."

I blinked. "Señora Rosara?"

He grunted in agreement. "She's evil, that one."

"I would love to know how he's aware that it goes around the entire building," Lucifer interjected. I didn't respond to the ghost, but I repeated the question to Marcel.

He looked away. "I tried to teleport onto the roof." My eyebrows lifted. "And into different rooms."

Different rooms.

"I'll be sure to thank the dear señora, then," I replied, keeping my voice even. "Why didn't you send a letter? I know for a fact you're capable of that. Katherine did it months ago . . ."

"Couldn't risk it getting back to Carissa," Marcel said. "I told her we should involve you weeks ago, but she'd refused because you're not part of the coven. She wanted us to search on our own. I had to speak to you in person."

That sounds like my eldest and most brainwashed sister's logic, all right.

We never did get along, even when I was a part of her

coven. She tried to kill me on more than one occasion. That kind of put a damper on sibling bonding. Not to mention the whole stealing my body for their spell because they needed my magic.

We were all living life just fine in this city—out of each other's lives and out of each other's business.

Until they kidnapped me and used me. They crossed every boundary known in our world and used me to commit a crime when even they couldn't fathom the reper-cussions.

I wasn't a vengeful person by nature, but in this, I agreed with the ghost that haunted me.

They were dead or weak thanks to their own stupidity. Especially Carissa. Of all the consequences suffered and lives it affected, she deserved it the most.

"If that's the case, why am I here?" I asked, not enjoying the moonlit stroll when my dress had me both sweating and freezing at the same time.

"Because Carissa might be the matriarch, but Kat is the one making all the sacrifices and leading the coven. I'm her second, and the strongest black witch we have. Carissa may not like it, but she can't do anything about it."

I laughed hard, and without restraint. "First, if you truly believe that about Carissa, then you're an idiot. Magicless or not, she'll find a way to punish you if she finds out about this." I knew better than anyone what my eldest sister was capable of. Even though she was barely in her thirties and looked like an old crone after having her magic stripped, it was her spite alone that kept her alive when Lucifer's death killed millions.

"And second?" he prompted.

"Don't refer to Carissa as my sister. Katherine either. We're not family just because we share blood."

I could feel both his and Lucifer's gazes on me, as if they might be able to burrow inside my head and learn my secrets.

"You're still her family even if you hate each other," Marcel said softly.

"That sort of toxic belief system is why I left to begin with."

Amongst other things, a voice entirely my own whispered inside me. I knew that, but I wasn't willing to say it.

Marcel sighed in disappointment then looked away. "Will you help me find her or not?"

He didn't like reminders of that time any more than I did, it seemed. Odd, since it was his choices that put us here.

"What does Piper think about all of this?" I asked, simultaneously surprised and also not that she hadn't said anything to me. She was my best friend and the Demon Queen of New Chicago. A badass boss bitch. She ran this city when it came to visible leadership, making all political decisions and otherwise that affected the millions of people that resided here. I didn't envy her position in the slightest. While she handled the outward-facing issues and protection, it allowed me to focus on my own ventures in a much safer way. Like hunting down rare artifacts and the occasional magical nuclear weapon.

Marcel didn't answer right away, making me groan.

"You haven't told her."

"It's not that simple," he protested. "Kat's missing, but we don't know why—"

"So the logical solution is to tell the all-powerful demon who can find her," I countered. "I can't believe you right now. You pulled me out of a very important thing—"

"You were at a BDSM club looking to get fucked."

My eyebrows lifted, lips parting. I could correct him, but I didn't. "*As I said*, a very important thing."

Screw him for asking me for favors and then acting like a prick when I owed him *nothing*.

His eyes narrowed. "Your twin sister is missing and right now you're worried about *getting off*?" He shook his head in disgust. "I can finger you here and now if that's what you *so desperately* need to help me. Or would you prefer I take you back to the Le Fay mansion and fuck you bent over my desk just like old times' sake?"

Only my caution and careful composure kept my mouth from dropping open at the audacity. Him. Of all people.

"What Katherine does isn't my problem," I said quietly instead. "I'm not my sister's keeper. I don't know where she is. If you're truly worried about her, then ask Piper, but I'm not getting involved." I lifted my hands in a show of washing them of him and this situation. I'd wasted enough time on this to know it was a mistake. I should have called Sasha in as soon as he grabbed me from Bliss.

Turning on my heel, I marched toward the other side of the graveyard.

"So that's it?" he yelled. "You're just turning your back on *us*? On Kat?"

I wanted to snap that Kat turned her back on me years ago. Long before now. Before I thought she died. Before she disappeared. Her and the rest of my family. My coven.

Even him.

There was no *us*.

It wasn't worth the wasted breath.

"Yep," I called over my shoulder without turning.

"Where are you going?" he continued. "I know you can't teleport. You don't have the magic for it." Reminding me that my chaos magic was weak wasn't the way to get my help. It was, however, a great way to piss me off.

"To tell Piper to tell you to fuck off, because if she gives the command, you can't disobey."

Literally. The blood oath he'd taken when he chose to be the second-in--command of the Ouroboros Coven ensured it.

Piper rarely threw her weight around, but I knew if I asked her to do this, she wouldn't hesitate for a second.

The wind shifted around me, and a hand grabbed my elbow mid-step.

"Stop. Please. I'm sorry for being an asshole—"

"No, you're not." I tugged on my arm to make him let go but he didn't yield.

"I am because it won't fix things, even if—it doesn't matter. I shouldn't have lashed out at you. Our issues aren't the problem right now. Please, just hear me out." Some of the cockiness left. His thumb grazed over my forearm, not actually touching skin thanks to the long sleeves of my dress, but still sending skitters along my nerves.

I turned around, crossing my arms over my chest. "Fine. But you keep your hands to yourself and stop being an ass or I'm calling in backup." I was only kind of bluffing. Sort of.

Marcel nodded. "We both know Piper doesn't care for Katherine, whether she's your twin sister or not. No one—not her, not her second, not her atman—none of them care what happens to Kat. She's a black witch, part of the reason the world went to shit." Well, he wasn't wrong there. "I gave Carissa a shot at finding her. She can't. She doesn't have the magic. So now I'm going to the only other person who might actually give a shit about finding her—and you have enough resources to actually do it."

Kat may be my twin, but she'd also betrayed me. In

many ways, she was worse than Carissa because we were closer than friends, closer than just sisters—but she chose power over me. She didn't deserve my help. Neither did Marcel. They were both shitty people.

Too bad I wasn't.

AUGUST

I STRIPPED MY GLAMOUR. The fresh air hit my skin, cooling the desire that thrummed in my blood.

I hated the damn things. If not for my ability to scent with one on, I'd find it nearly impossible to do my job. They inhibited my other senses, essentially locking me in the thinnest bubble of magic possible. I couldn't truly touch. Taste. Even my vision was hindered, the glamour dulling the colors and shadows of the world as if it were a faded shirt that had been stripped by time.

A part of me wanted to go back to Bliss.

To sit and wait until the brown-haired beauty returned.

If she did.

That was blasphemous. I knew little about her beyond the scent of her skin and the way she liked to be fucked. Even the name she'd given me was false, although that was to be expected. She would've had to have been brave or stupid to tell me her real name by choice.

And yet, I'd learned it anyway.

"Nathalie," I whispered so softly not even the wind

could hear me. Soft. Feminine. But with a sharpness to it. It suited her.

I wanted to know the rest of what she'd kept hidden.

Just as badly as I wanted to taste her skin *without* a glamour. To see if it was as intoxicating as her scent.

I traced the bottom row of my teeth with my tongue. There was little I wouldn't have given to do so. If not for the job I was on and the witch that whisked her away, I would have tried to take her into a back room. Somewhere I could lower the disguise in privacy, thanks to the wards they used. It would have cost a pretty penny, but I knew without a doubt it would have been worth it.

Thoughts of her luminous skin and the splash of freckles across the bridge of her nose followed me from the streets to the opium bar tucked behind a convenience store front. I ignored the fluorescent lights and aisles of basic necessities as I went to the storeroom labeled for employ-ees. The tiny girl who played both cashier and bodyguard didn't even lift her eyes from the sudoku puzzle she was solving.

She knew who I was and that I belonged here.

My eyes needed no time to adjust to the darker atmosphere. Smoke drifted through the cramped space, carrying hints of things far stronger than opium. If I weren't so distracted by thoughts of a certain brunette, I might have been tempted to indulge and stave off the feeding another week.

Instead, a very dangerous thing called hope decided to slither its way into my mind.

I was aware of its presence . . . wanted to let it linger, but I knew too well the danger it caused.

Most magic smelled repulsive. Tainted. Rotten. I couldn't stand the scent of it long enough to feed. I had to, nonetheless. It didn't matter that nausea swirled in my gut, or that I'd spend hours retching afterwards, my body attempting to purge the food it so desperately needed and yet couldn't tolerate.

Fate was a cruel mistress indeed.

I moved through the odd layout of the bar, stepping around mismatched tables and patterned armchairs. The patrons didn't pay me much mind, all too absorbed in their own musings or quiet conversations. Jazz music drifted in the space from an old record player in the corner, faint compared to the level at which humans played their music.

The people who came here weren't looking for noise and bodies to drown themself in. They sought solace. I offered it to them.

Brushing aside a fraying tapestry, I entered the back room I'd reserved for my half-brother and onetime employer, now turned friend. The person who'd sent me to Bliss in the first place.

He knew from the look on my face that I wasn't successful.

Anders sighed. "Dammit. Tell me what happened."

I shrugged, undoing the top button of my dress shirt, following up with my sleeves. "He didn't show. Again. I'm starting to wonder if your intel is wrong here."

Anders shook his head, blue eyes drifting as he got lost staring out the small, fogged window. I knew he wasn't truly *looking* at the city. "Not possible."

I was dubious of that claim, but didn't say it as I rolled up my sleeves and reached for the three-hundred-year-old brandy. I might not take the things that would black me out for a week, but after my evening, a pick-me-up was needed.

A woman so delicious and enticing, who smelled like

the first time I walked this realm and gazed upon the sun . . . and she'd slipped away.

"The intel came from the top. Sasha Loren led the interrogation herself." Anders glanced at me, gauging my reaction.

I side-eyed him from the antique bar. "I didn't know you had her on this. Fuck. Why do you need me if you've got her?"

Everyone knew who Sasha Loren was. She and her sister were Lucifer's *personal* assistants when he was ruler of this city . . . before the witches killed him off and fucked us all over in the process. Ruthless and cunning, there was very little the shifter-succubus couldn't do.

This should have been a cake walk with her help.

And I wanted no more part in it.

Anders shook his head. "Sasha can't glamour, and even if she could, she's got her hands tied up with Piper's council."

I was well aware of the inner workings of the council. A table lined with certain chosen supernaturals who had enough authority and influence to be worthy of the infamous Demon Queen. Two members per faction bound by magical oaths, they answered directly to the top. In return for their loyalty and political backing, she gave them power. Unimaginable power.

No one knew how it had all been done, or at least if they did, they weren't saying. Any creature she'd taken under her wing turned into a fearsome, almost godly being.

I wasn't sure I believed the latter, but I'd seen the increase in my own liege's power after he fell in line. There was no denying that truth.

"Rumor has it the council isn't working out quite as

planned." It wasn't a question, so much as a prompting to see what he'd observed on his end. Anders smirked.

"According to Rafael?"

It was my turn to grin. I knew who Anders answered to, just as he knew to whom I did. Rafael was the incubus representative on the council and a very powerful player in the game.

He was also my brother.

Well, half-brother. He and I shared a mother, where Anders and I shared a sperm donor. The difference in how I viewed them was Rafael was my older brother, and the one that mostly raised me. I didn't know Anders until I was a hundred years old, give or take a few years.

"No," I answered. While technically I wasn't supposed to disclose Rafael's thoughts or opinions to anyone, in this he'd thank me. If Anders's demon king thought he wasn't loyal to the fullest, they'd have no problem ending him—and while Anders might be fond of my older brother—he wasn't in the business of sticking his neck out for anyone. "He's actually quite content with his position, but you already know that. *Your* master would have killed him if he weren't."

Anders scoffed. "I have no master, but my king certainly would without another thought."

I snickered. Master. King. Call them whatever you wish, it was still subservience. We answered to them. If gods existed, it wouldn't be the demons who ruled this city and several others. How Anders somehow managed to circumvent having to bow to them and maintained some level of autonomy while simultaneously serving was something I'd never understand. Perhaps one day he'd share his secret with me.

"Rafael is loyal. His mate is loyal, and frankly,

disgusting in how she gushes about them." Incubi and succubi were unique because we have both aurae bonds and mate bonds. Aurae bonds were those that we created ourselves in a mutual exchange of lust and power. We had choice about accepting or denying them to a large extent. Mates were fated. One, we had control over to some capacity, and the other, we were a slave to. Much like any other species.

Where most immortals usually only had one mate out there in the vast unknown, there were more than one option in aurae bonds. You couldn't just bond to anyone, but there was a group of people who fit on a biological level —meaning one of you wouldn't overpower the other and extinguish them. It wasn't abnormal for an incubus or succubus to form more than one aurae bond if they didn't have a mate . . . unless you were 'lucky', as Rafael would call himself. The lovesick, matestruck fool found both in one person. Rajvi, his aurae and his mate.

They'd been inseparable ever since.

Anders chuckled. "It's the pregnancy hormones," he said and waved it off.

I shot him an unamused look. "Believe me, I know all about the hormones. Rajvi feels so sorry for me that she's taken to having a dozen men and women she thinks have my 'sort of vibe' at their house when I'm there. It's a new group every time."

Anders laughed at my expense. A slight sadness tinged his gaze behind the laugh, but neither of us chose to comment on its presence. "She's always been a romantic at heart," he said. "Balances Rafael well."

I nodded. "He's no longer insufferable to be around. She managed to remove the stick from his ass, a feat that I didn't know anyone could accomplish."

Anders tilted his head in agreement. Comfortable silence fell and Anders wandered toward the window once more, his eyes searching, always searching these days.

"Why do you look for her if she doesn't want to be found?" I asked him.

Anders tensed then deflated. If he thought I didn't know about his secret obsession, he was severely mistaken. "I don't know."

The raw vulnerability that punctuated that statement filled me with frustration I'd never let him see. She was a truly terrifying woman, the demon he was obsessed with. She didn't deserve him. His worry. His time. The rent-free space she was taking up in his head. She didn't deserve even a second.

But he gave it, nonetheless.

"I've followed every lead," he continued. "Hunted down every rumor. Faryn Lightseeker has it, and he's the only one that knows its exact location."

I dipped my head.

"I'll go back tomorrow," I promised. "And every night after if I have to."

"Thank you," he said quietly. "I know it's not your favorite place to be."

Understatement if there ever was one. Anders knew about my past and the unusual ability it'd caused me to develop. While incredibly useful in some ways, it was also a nightmare to live with.

He understood that, and even as an employer, he rarely pushed me into situations like this because of it. That he was asking now told me a good deal about the importance of obtaining this item.

"Don't thank me too much," I murmured, scenting the

brandy. Its smell alone was usually intoxicating. Not tonight. "It's not an altruistic offer."

Anders turned, the lost expression dissipating as he stared quizzically. "You met someone?" A smirk formed on his lips, both amused and delighted. "Are they a—"

"Don't get too excited now," I said. "She gave me a fake name and left with another man."

A beat of silence stretched like a suspended note.

Then he bent at the waist, laughing himself hoarse.

I rolled my eyes. Prick.

"Only you would find someone and pursue them after being rejected." He grabbed a second glass and poured himself some brandy. "Well, only you and me," he added as an afterthought. "What a fucking pair we make."

This cynical pity party wasn't like him. The cynical part, yes, but I had to wonder if he'd smoke any of the *specialties* I kept under lock and key for certain clients. A glance at his bloodshot eyes revealed a little too much.

"I wasn't rejected," I explained, my thoughts going back to the tiny little thing wrapped in latex and scented with another person's magic. "Things were progressing beautifully. She was open and willing. I asked to feed from her, and she'd agreed . . . then someone interrupted us. I didn't catch his name, but he wasn't exactly being subtle that he was there for her specifically. She didn't want to go with him."

The mirth fell from his expression. "She didn't go by force, I'm assuming?" he questioned lightly.

I shook my head. "No. I didn't get the impression she was in danger, or I would have stayed. She was annoyed by his presence, though it seemed urgent on his part. They appeared to have history."

They'd have to, for the way he stormed up to us, power

crackling at his fingers. He didn't break the rules, so no one stopped him, but the implication was clear.

Anders shook his head, clapping me on the shoulder. "I'd tell you to watch yourself—history like that often isn't pretty—but I know how rare it is for you to find someone."

"One in a million these days," I murmured, wishing I was exaggerating. Perhaps Anders wasn't the only one throwing himself a pity party tonight after all.

My oldest friend clinked his glass to mine, blue eyes sympathetic as he said, "To one in a million?"

I drank, but found the flavor lacking.

Even my prized brandy tasted like ash.

NATHALIE

TINGLES TRAILED DOWN MY NECK, like a ghostly set of lips brushing over me. I squirmed, snuggling deeper into the down comforter.

"Little witch," the voice of sin itself crooned in my ear. "I know you hear me."

The tingles spread, like a finger running down my spine. The relief of sleep faded fast as I suppressed my response. "I know you can *feel* me."

I almost shuddered, but that was exactly what he wanted. Acknowledgment in any form. This game was one I'd become unwillingly familiar with over the past months. I just had to wait him out and he would disappear again, as long as I didn't use magic.

I pretended to sleep, and he let out a low growl of frustration. I sensed him moving away as I continued to be unresponsive.

Finally.

Or so I thought.

"'*His eyebrows shot up in surprise, but he met my impassioned kiss, flattening his palms against my back.*'" He recited the passage using a girlish voice that made me shake with silent laughter. "'*I need you closer,*' *I said, the words coming out mumbled between our lips. 'Inside me.' Reaching down, I rubbed against his erection, feeling it throb at my touch.*"

Lucifer scoffed. "Are you going to continue ignoring me or shall I read more?" I knew the question was aimed at me, but I opted not to answer, still clinging to the hope that the ghost of the devil himself would find someone else to haunt.

"*He growled in frustration, trying to stop me from stroking him. 'This isn't what you want, Danni,' he said against my mouth. 'It's—' I felt his presence shift closer as he spoke, making my heart beat wickedly. 'I want you . . .' Flashes of fire burned my skin, but there were no flames. My lips parted, and heavy breaths came in ragged bursts. I needed release. I needed more. I twisted my body, using my legs for momentum and a strength I didn't know I possessed, rolling us on the bed until I was on top of him. My nails dug into his chest, and he gripped my hips. 'To fuck me.'*" Lucifer punctuated the character's statement using a soft, seductive voice. "Tell me, little witch, is that how you like it? Because rest assured, given the opportunity, I wouldn't be as chivalrous as our dear Elias here—or as gentle as the incubus from the club. All you need do is ask, and I would part those pretty thighs—"

"I guess it's a good thing you're dead then, now isn't it?" I snapped back before he could finish, not wanting to hear more of his silken promises or wicked temptations.

Shit.

I was not supposed to do that.

"Finally," he said to the sound of pages flipping, and a book slamming shut followed. I rolled in bed, throwing the comforter off me now that the jig was up. "I was wondering how long you planned to keep this going." He used that disgustingly charming voice when speaking, but I felt the darkness beneath it. The anger. The resentment.

He truly hated it when I ignored him.

But he only had himself to blame.

Throwing my legs over the side of my bed, I padded out to my hallway, pausing only long enough to hear Mist in the kitchen making another attempt at cooking. Mist was my current stray, as my best friend would say. I hadn't adopted her so much as accepted that she'd sort of fallen into my lap. After Piper and I rescued her from a vampire den of sex slaves her parents had traded her to, we realized that Mist had too much trauma to live in any sort of group home or shelter. Since I lived alone in a two-bedroom apartment and was safe from her volatile magic, it seemed the best solution at the time. It still was, but the scent of burning food made my lips twist. It was going to be one of *those* days.

A day when I'd choke down the teenage siren's truly horrendous attempts at making us breakfast. I told her again and again that I didn't mind doing it, but she insisted that it should be her—since I was letting her stay with me while Señora Rosara gave her lessons on how to wield her death magic. The kid barely had her head on straight and was still learning about basic care like personal hygiene and how to communicate her needs. I didn't have the heart to tell her how bad her cooking was.

I turned for the bathroom, going to brush my teeth.

Lucifer appeared in the mirror behind me, his phantom hand reaching to wrap around my neck. Golden eyes bored into me with a startling intensity that made my toothbrush slip from my fingers.

I shouldn't have looked. I knew better.

"You can be unhappy with me. You can rage, if you'd

like. Scream. Even cry. I will take it all, but you *will not* continue the silent treatment." His words were hardly more than a whisper, and the scent of blood and sex touched me. Just a hint, but it was enough.

I set the toothpaste down, putting my hands on the edges of the sink to steady myself. "You don't get to decide that."

He leaned in, and that tickling sensation rippled as his ghostly lips skimmed the shell of my ear. "I won't let you," he breathed.

"You can't stop me," I responded, trying to ignore my sweaty palms.

"But I can, little witch," he said. "I have." Lucifer smiled like he knew every sinful thought I'd ever had, like he could see inside my mind and hear my thoughts. I knew he couldn't, but it still made me uneasy.

"And you've reminded me exactly why I stopped speaking with you to begin with."

His smile pressed into a hard line as I picked up my toothbrush and went through the motions of brushing my teeth and cleaning my face.

"You'll never be rid of me," he said, dropping some of the false charm. "Where you go, I go. And try as you might to shut me out, you can't do it forever."

"Watch me," I said before gargling mouthwash. He waited for me to finish before continuing to argue with me.

"I do," he replied. "Always."

For some reason it sounded like we were talking about something else entirely. "I've offered to leave the TV on for you. I have every season of *Friends*, *Supernatural*, even *Grey's Anatomy*—"

"TV is mind-numbingly dull."

I shrugged, grabbing my hairbrush from inside the

mirror cabinet. "I'd offer to enchant a book, but it seems you've gained some small telekinetic abilities since you're able to flip the pages of one yourself."

"I have no desire to read."

"Oh, you're *that kind*. A man that doesn't like to read, unless of course you're reading and ruining my choice of books?" I asked, hiding a smile.

"Ruining?" He sounded insulted, which made it all the better for me.

"Dannika doesn't speak like a five-year-old schoolgirl," I replied. "Especially not when asking the *vampire king* to fuck her because she's in heat. You couldn't even do Elias's voice right, and you're literally the devil. Shouldn't sexy-man-voice be your specialty?"

Lucifer stared like I'd grown a third head. "I am the definition of sex appeal."

I snorted. "If you have to say it, you most definitely are *not*." His eyes narrowed. "Let me guess, you fancy yourself an alpha too?"

He didn't respond right away, sensing a trap. "Hard to be anything when I'm dead," he scoffed after a pause.

I smirked at his non-answer. "I get that you're pissed. I probably would be too. But the least you could do if you're so insistent on getting my attention is put your 'charms' to good use and make my book boyfriends sound delicious instead of like dumbass meatheads. I get enough of that in real life."

Lucifer narrowed his eyes in a way that would have brought a blush to my features if I weren't so good at controlling my reactions to him.

"Does my little witch want me to tell her every dirty thing I'd do to her pretty pussy if given the chance?" he asked, leaning in, his breath tracing the shell of my ear again. I hid the shudder that threatened to show how much he affected me. "You want me to pretend to be this Elias, who would deny a woman—"

"Respect," I corrected. "She told him no sex, and he's respecting it."

Lucifer rolled his eyes. "Fucking is fucking. Whether I use my fingers, my tongue, my cock—it's a means to give pleasure. To *worship*."

I hummed. "Mmhmm. Well, as I said, you have performance issues. You should really work on that. Perfect your reading skills. You could build a career out of reading sexy romance books to necromancers if you try hard enough . . . probably."

"For fuck's sake," Lucifer growled, running a hand through his phantom hair. "Is work all you think about?"

I shrugged. "I mean, reading is my hobby since the internet doesn't exist in the same capacity anymore. I might have a thing for Pornhub or nature documentaries if it did. Baby furballs too. Who doesn't like a good kitten video?"

Lucifer leveled an unamused look at me. The feeling was mutual. I just chose a different way to deal with it.

"Back to you and finding you some hobbies," I continued. "If you tried hard enough, you may be able to crochet with those newfound abilities—"

"*Nathalie.*"

I paused, swallowing. What was it with the men in my life? Or rather, the men that used to be. Lucifer was dead, and my relationship with Marcel had been nonexistent for years. Yet they liked to act like they owned me. My time. My energy.

I wanted to find it funny. Not one of them questioned my standing in this city. Not one of them questioned how much of New Chicago I owned. How many people I managed. Piper was a boss bitch, but so was I, and I had been long before I'd met her. I was just a quieter version. The silent hand that moved the pieces on the board.

But for some reason, these twats didn't think I owned myself—of all things. Despite the mask of irreverence, I felt irritated and drained by it all.

"You're giving me a headache."

"The feeling is mutual, little witch."

I pinched my lips together. "You're dead. You can't get headaches."

"How do you know?" he countered, crossing his arms over his chest. "Have you been dead?"

I rolled my eyes. "Headaches are caused by constricting blood vessels. Last I checked, you have neither blood nor vessels—"

"That's not completely true."

I paused, frowning at him in the mirror.

"I have you," he said, giving me a smirk. "And you have a piece of me—so in a certain sense, I do have blood."

I released a harsh breath. "You have a scrap of magic that's unfortunately attached to me like a fungus. That's not the same."

Lucifer snorted. "Some organisms need fungi to survive. They coexist together. A mutual partnership where they both benefit."

Of course, he would find a way to spin it so that he was somehow benefitting me. Narcissistic didn't even begin to cover it.

"I misspoke. You're a leech."

Lucifer touched a hand to his chest. "You wound me, little witch."

I snorted. "I wish."

"Do you?" he asked, turning the easy conversation to something else. It was too deep in its simplicity. I gnawed on my bottom lip, knowing the answer but not wanting to say it. "I didn't think so."

"Not wanting to hurt you isn't the same as wanting you here," I said. "I feel bad for you. For your existence. You should be dead and at peace, but you aren't."

"Peace sounds terribly boring," he replied.

I squinted, my nose wrinkling. "How?"

The devil tilted his head. "Peace is stagnant. It lacks passion."

"There's no rage in peace," I said. "No anger. No grief—"

"No joy either," he countered. "Or love."

His eyes dropped to my lips.

"Have you ever felt love?" I asked, unable to help myself.

Lucifer didn't answer immediately. I rolled my eyes again, tired of his games.

"No."

"No," I repeated. "Well, I think you can hardly speak on the matter if you've never even felt it. At several thousand years—"

"Nine."

I blinked. "Nine thousand," I corrected, speaking more softly. "You've never felt love or peace. I pity you." It wasn't an insult. Just truth. "I can understand how you'd be this way if you've only ever experienced negative emotions."

"I never said that was all I experienced."

I set my brush back in the cabinet and pulled out a small jar with moisturizer. "I still pity you. I'm sorry you're stuck in such a sad existence."

My fingers worked their way over my skin, rubbing in the lotion.

"You shouldn't," he said. "I may not have felt love, but I've been loved, by hundreds. Thousands, even. I've been worshipped. I've known desire so hot it consumed every facet of my mind. I've known longing so strong that I went to war for it." He leaned close, and the faintest touch of magic against my skin mimicked breath against my cheek. Blood and sex. I smelled it again.

Him. His scent.

"To be loved without feeling love is tragic." I capped the moisturizer and placed it back in the cabinet. "Desire that strong . . ." I shook my head. "It sounds like madness."

"Wonderful madness."

"Madness all the same," I replied, turning around. "As for longing—I'm assuming it was a woman you longed for this way?"

"More than one," he answered. "Men too."

I shook my head. "You're right."

Lucifer leaned back. "About?"

I pivoted on my heel in the small bathroom, pressing myself into the bathroom sink to avoid going through him. "I shouldn't pity you." He lifted his eyebrows. "Now, move." I could walk through him, but it somehow felt wrong.

"Tell me why, and I will."

Telling him wouldn't change anything, but I knew from experience that he held up his side of the bargains he made. While it was the one thing that allowed the bargainer any modicum of control over a demon—because their magic had rules that enforced it—I wouldn't have thought Lucifer would have to stick to them, being dead. We were different. As it turned out, because there was a piece of him in me, he still had to hold up his end of an agreement. Even in death. Or whatever this fucked-up scenario was.

"The number of people you've indirectly killed for passing fancies must be staggering. You don't deserve peace."

He nodded, as if he expected my answer. "Maybe not, but if you don't know the kind of longing or desire I speak of—it's I who should be pitying you, little witch. You've one life, and a mortal one at that, but you waste it on mice for men because they're *safe*."

I hid my flinch. "You're wrong."

"I don't think I am."

"I answered your question," I replied, no longer playing nice. "Now move."

Gold flashed, glowing brighter for a brief moment. "You can lie to the world and to yourself, but you can't lie to *me*."

He disappeared from the bathroom, but I knew better than to think he was gone.

Nothing with him was ever that simple.

NATHALIE

I COULD ONLY TORTURE my tastebuds for so long.

Halfway through Mist's abysmal attempt at breakfast tacos, I had to lie about feeling under the weather. She didn't question it as she went to clear our plates, though her expression became guarded as she struggled with how to respond.

"Should I talk to the señora about making you a remedy?" she asked hesitantly.

I shook my head. "No. It's just some nausea. I'm sure it'll pass." Mist nodded along, her dark hair falling in her face in greasy clumps. The iridescent scales on her forearms were shedding unevenly. "Mist," I began gently, "when was the last time you showered?"

She stiffened. Her hands jerked as she dumped the last of the food in the compost pail on my counter. Burnt or not, she knew better than to waste food in my house. While I was *very* well off thanks to my multiple business ventures, much of New Chicago lived well below the poverty line. I wouldn't serve them this food, but I'd drop it off to one of my girls at the food banks who was responsible for making trips to and from the farms I funded just outside the city.

While inedible for a human being, I had no qualms giving it to the pigs.

"I don't know . . ." she muttered after a pause. "I think it's only been three or four days."

I sighed. "We've talked about this. You've gotta shower, Mist."

She nodded her head, refusing to meet my stare. "I know. I'm just struggling right now."

Empathy filled me when I looked at this broken girl. She had so many chips and cracks that all the glue in the world couldn't repair them, but she was trying. "I can have Piper come guard the bathroom door, if it would help."

Mist gnawed on her bottom lip. "She's busy running the city and raising the twins. I don't want to bother her—"

"She'll make time if you ask her," I said quietly.

"I know . . ." She set the dishes down in the sink and turned the water off. Her massive wings were tucked in tightly behind her, but the oddly angled feathers only reaffirmed what I'd said. She was molting and seriously needed to get clean. "I just hate being such a burden on everyone—"

"You're not a burden."

"I'm the definition of one."

I groaned, not wanting to have this conversation so early in the morning, but Mist's emotions weren't something that could be put off. "Burdens have to be borne with difficulty. I don't find having you here with me difficult."

She rolled her eyes in a very "I'm sixteen and know it all" fashion. I would have chuckled if it wouldn't have backfired. "No one else has to have a guard outside the bathroom to shower last I checked."

"No one else has been through the horrors you have," I replied just as easily. "If I lost a leg and needed assistance around the house, would you begrudge me?"

"No, but—"

"No buts," I interrupted in a firm voice. I was only seven years older than her, but you'd never know it given the semi-parental role I'd stepped into. "You need to give yourself some grace. When's the last time you visited Hallie?"

Mist gnawed her bottom lip again.

Too long. That was the short answer.

Mist looked away, guilt and other dark emotions drowning her. She'd birthed a child against her will—the product of being held captive for sex and breeding. She was too young and scarred to be a mother, so she'd made the choice to give her daughter to Sienna—who wanted more than anything to be a mom but had no desire for a baby daddy. Open adoptions could be a beautiful thing, and Mist was able to be a part of their life. Anyone could see the internal struggle she went through. Seeing Hallie gave her brief moments of peace, and anytime she went too long without seeing her, the conflict was evident. Mist wasn't a burden to me. What she carried? That was the burden, but that wasn't something I would say to her.

I picked up my cell and called my personal assistant and second. Sienna answered on the first ring.

"Where's Hallie today?"

"Staying at Piper and Ronan's with Morfayus and Ailaine," she answered. "They're watching her and the twins." Morfayus and Ailaine were the twins' sworn guardians. Since Honor and Orson were basically gods in three-year-old bodies with powers never seen before, they needed more than a run-of-the-mill babysitter. That extended to Hallie by proxy.

"Sasha head out already?"

"I'm not sure—" Her answer was broken off by a knock at my door. I went and checked through the peephole.

"Never mind, she's here. I'll give you a call back in half an hour. I'm dropping Mist off with them for the day."

"Sounds good," she said, the noise muffled in such a way I could tell she pressed the phone to her shoulder with her cheek. "I'm checking in with Antonella and the white witch covens right now. Talk to you in a bit."

The line disconnected as I flicked the locks on my door one by one. The amount was overkill, but they were one of the few remnants of when Piper lived with me, before she mated with Ronan and became a mother and queen. It was certainly simpler back then, albeit more chaotic. I couldn't say I missed having fireballs blowing holes in my walls.

The door swung open, revealing a mildly irritable Sasha Loren. She was Sienna's twin sister and Piper's second-in-command. As a shifter succubus with gray morals and a mean streak when you got on her bad side, she was a good second. Her sharp mind was what made her a great one.

"I was just coming to find you," I said, more chipper than I felt. "Think you can give Mist a ride to Piper and Ronan's?"

Sasha glanced up at the teenage siren. I could tell the minute she realized how poorly Mist was doing. Her green cat irises narrowed. Instead of commenting on the smell coming from her, she said in a slightly more strained voice, "Sure. Hallie's been asking for you." She nodded toward Mist. "She'll be very happy to see her Angel." Mist grimaced at the term of endearment Hallie had taken to calling her birth mom, though the little girl didn't really know what that meant. She just loved Mist's wings.

I huffed like I was annoyed. "Chopped liver as always, I see."

Sasha snorted and Mist cracked a smile. "Join the club. I change her diapers and take her to and from every day but it's *Orson this* or *Angel that*." She shook her head. Neither of us were actually annoyed, but Mist perked up. Whether she said it or not, she did love being one of Hallie's favorite people in the world. I imagined on those really tough days, it was that little girl that got her through it.

"At least you're Honor's favorite," I said. "I went from being everyone's to no one's."

Sasha laughed, and even though it was sweet by her standards, it came out dark and sensual. Her cat tail twitched, like it had a mind of its own.

"I'm only Honor's favorite because I don't punish her or enforce the rules. Unlike the rest of you, I know when I'm outclassed. The little demon turned me magenta the last time I told her 'no.'"

I smirked, recalling how *pissed* Sasha had been. Piper had to step in and persuade Honor to turn her back. Not the easiest thing to do with a child who had the power to change reality at her fingertips.

"I'd rather be magenta than invisible," Mist lied, playing along. When Hallie wouldn't play with Honor and was focused on Mist, she'd resorted to turning Mist invisible more than once. We were all thankful Mist didn't actually mind it too much. She even preferred to shower when that happened, but a toddler wasn't the most reliable when it came to these things, and we didn't like to encourage that behavior.

"I prefer being neither," I said, grabbing my mini-backpack. While small on the outside, it was basically Mary Poppins's bag on the inside. Sienna had gotten it for me as an early birthday present so that I could "mom-friend better." I loved it.

"And that's why you're no one's favorite," Sasha said with a dip of her chin. "Ready to go, kid?" she asked Mist.

Her shoulders were far more relaxed than they had been ten minutes prior, and there was even a little bit of light in her eyes as she nodded. Taking each other's hands, they disappeared as Sasha's power over the void let them travel in the shadows. I continued on my way downstairs, locking my door and resetting the explosive rigged to it, setting it to detonate if someone were to attempt to break in. My apartment building may have been warded as much as some prisons thanks to my superstitious landlord and demon best friend, but I wasn't taking chances.

I took the elevator, my fingers tapping my thigh as I worked through all the things I needed to do today. I stepped out on the ground floor and into the apothecary she ran. Most herbs and animal parts used for common spells were on display, as well as different kinds of bones, blood, and salts.

"Señora," I called out, not needing to speak very loudly when one of her many cats perked up. She came through the door behind her counter a moment later, not at all surprised to see me. While she'd never said so, I had a very strong suspicion she was bonded to all of these cats. They were her prisoners and spies. A shiver ran through me at the idea of being trapped like that. Of being used. I had been once, when my family took control of my body and made me kill Lucifer. That was enough.

I tried not to judge most things. It wasn't that difficult to reserve the judgment, especially when I knew how awful life had become for so many people. They did what they had to in order to survive. It had been almost twenty years since a witch killed the American president on live television, revealing magic to the world and thereby kicking off the Magic Wars. Widespread chaos and fighting as factions of supernaturals battled those born without magic. As expected, the humans suffered terrible losses. There was so much death and destruction.

We'd always existed on Earth, living amongst the magicless. Lucifer had been keeping our kind in line for centuries, but then our existence was revealed. His reign didn't end when the wars started, but he severely cut back restrictions on the supernaturals once the secret was out. What chance did a human have against power like that? None. They starved and were forced into slavery of one form or another. Those lucky enough to escape imprisonment weren't much better off. As a witch that came from a powerful family and one of the strongest covens in the world, I'd lived a life of privilege. Mostly.

I also got out and saw what the rest of New Chicago was like and couldn't stomach it. So I got to work. I changed it. Every day I poured myself into bettering the lives of the people here, both supernatural and human . . . but I remembered the face of every broken body, every dead child, every starving family, every tortured soul . . . I couldn't forget, even if I wanted to. So I didn't tend to judge them.

A small part of me side-eyed the señora, though, because I was fairly certain these cats weren't cats. Not really. The number of times I'd seen her threaten to turn someone into a cat had me convinced they were people that pissed her off somehow.

Don't get me wrong, she treated her animals amazingly. But a cage was a cage, no matter how nice it was.

"What can I do for you?" she asked in Spanish.

"Mist is spending the day with Hallie, so she won't be in for lessons," I replied in the same language. "If you needed her to run any errands, let me know and I'll do them."

She waved me off, one her many rings hitting the light. While I noticed everything, this particular one drew my attention because it was new. A void stone. Instead of shining, it consumed any light that touched it.

"Don't worry about it. They can all wait till she's back. I've been telling the girl to go see her for a week now."

I nodded, half expecting as much. She put on a tough front for others, but I knew she had a soft spot for me and the siren apprentice I'd brought to her months ago. She was completely aware of the situation between Mist and Hallie, seeing as she'd delivered the baby, but she was also good at not pushing. At least not with Mist present.

"Do you know what's up with her? We'd made a lot of progress, but she looks like she hasn't showered in over a week." I didn't try to delve into her private affairs too much, but in this case it helped to be aware.

Señora Rosara looked over an inventory list on the front counter before answering. "Flashbacks. It was around this time last year she was . . . impregnated."

I grimaced. I should have realized that.

"Can you try pushing her toward talking to someone? I've tried, but she refuses to even consider it."

She tsked. "I have been. While the girl listens to me about magic, she is headstrong when it comes to her emotions and what she needs. Not at all like someone else we know."

I covered my laugh with a cough. Piper wasn't present, but I still wouldn't talk shit about her. Even if it was true.

"She runs this city now, you know."

The look she gave me said she couldn't have had less

fucks to give. "She could run the universe. It would still be true. Mist idolizes her. Tell her to set a better example and maybe she'll agree."

I nodded along. Piper wasn't the only headstrong one here, but I wasn't going to voice that when it wouldn't get me anywhere. She did have a point about speaking to Piper about it, however. Maybe she could convince her when I couldn't.

"I'll talk to her."

I started toward the door when I saw that she was deeply engrossed by whatever she saw when she looked at the void stone on her hand. I was almost to the exit when she spoke again.

"Samhain is not far. The veil between our world and the dead will be thin."

My feet dragged on the floor as I stumbled, but I caught myself on the edge of the wood hutch.

Every witch knew about Samhain.

A night when death magic swelled in power, reaching its peak strength. A night that sent a shiver down my spine just thinking about what had called to me in years past. In a world of magic, not much should be surprising. To most, it probably wasn't, but for me, my existence in this realm felt different. Strained. *Seen*. As the sun set and signaled the beginning of Samhain, the shadows would seek me. Voices I shouldn't hear telling tales I shouldn't know. My surroundings moving and shifting when all should stand still, the way it did the other three hundred and sixty-four days of the year.

A night when I would do my damnedest to find serenity, chanting through the night until my voice was hoarse and my body was weakened, striving for a modicum of peace in the darkness that beckoned me for reasons unknown.

"I know about Samhain," I said softly, not wanting my voice to give away the direction my thoughts had taken me.

"You ask the wrong questions."

"I didn't ask a question." The hairs on the back of my neck stood straight up.

She laughed, the sound quiet but powerful. A croak that rang of death.

"For a child born *in* the veil, you should."

Señora was a seer, and a powerful one at that. But her words didn't sound like a vision predicting what would become. There was no hint of a warning or prophecy.

It was advice, which made her cryptic statement that much worse.

six

NATHALIE

WE SAT AROUND AN EBONY TABLE: me and five other versions of myself.

In the real world, real life, I was sitting in my greenhouse on the roof of my apartment building, tending to my plants. Pruning. Repotting. Watering.

If anyone approached, that's what they'd see.

But in my head, gardening was the furthest thing from my thoughts. In my memory loci, a Frankenstein construct of different houses and rooms from my life, all the versions of me existed.

They lived here, in my mind, as the gatekeepers of all my memories and knowledge. My eidetic memory wouldn't allow me to forget a single moment. The power and weight of that could lead to madness if I didn't organize the shit out of it. In my short lifetime, the memory loci was already a mansion, bordering on the size of a castle these days, and pieces of myself held it together, carefully locking information away where it belonged.

One might think I was crazy, were I to tell them that. I didn't have multiple personalities. I had one personality—

one me. The versions of myself were like the ingredients that made me whole.

The ebony roundtable was where we held meetings, if they could be called that. I suppose in reality I was having conversations in my head, as myself, with versions of . . . myself. So maybe I was crazy.

"Katherine is an unknown variable. Searching for her will take up resources that are better used for more important things, like the Eye," Analytical Nat said. She was one of the first to appear inside the loci and was the epitome of rational thought. Wearing glasses and sharp designer suits, she was almost always in the library. Knowledge was power, and she knew it well.

"We have more than enough resources," Caretaker Nat said softly. "Is it really a burden to inquire about her? She is our twin, and we do care deeply about her, even if she's been difficult." She pushed the plate of fruit and cheese she'd prepared toward us as she took a seat. Always thinking of everyone else first.

"Kat hurt us," Protector Nat countered. She spoke with authority and good intentions. With guarded eyes and a wariness I couldn't shake, she ran most things in the loci. "She was part of the coven that used us. She let it happen, didn't lift a finger to stop it. Love or not, I'm hesitant to get involved and open that door all over again."

Caretaker Nat sighed. "Searching for her doesn't mean being involved. We find her and tell Marcel. Leave it there."

Analytical Nat huffed. "We all know Marcel won't leave it there, assuming we find her. They'll drag us back into the circle and that's what we've been avoiding for *years*."

Protector Nat tilted her head, crossing her arms over her chest. "I'm inclined to agree with Ann here." Everyone had shortened versions of their names, and Ann—with two Ns

—was chosen for Analytical Nat. An was an indefinite article, so *Ann* wouldn't accept it.

"Peace?" Caretaker said, turning to the fourth version of me. She had a greenhouse bedroom with a hammock that she spent most of her time in. When she wasn't in search of smutty romance books or the electric kettle for tea, that is. She and Ann tended to butt heads, as one used facts and logic and one was guided by feelings, but they both had my tea obsession.

"Can I go back to gardening yet? I really don't care what we do about Kat—"

"Peace," Caretaker Nat sighed. "We can't just leave her. If she's in trouble, she needs us."

Analytical Nat rolled her eyes, then turned to me. I was Primary Nat, or Prime. "The Warden agrees with me, and you know we're right." The Warden—Protector Nat—was held up with a spine of steel. She dressed in the most casual clothes of the group, jeans and T-shirts. Her hair was always tied back in a ponytail that hung past her shoulders. Despite her unassuming looks, she carried a baseball bat with her, ready to throw down at a moment's notice if needed. "Mama Nat is Caretaker for a reason. The bleeding heart that can't help itself. And Peace would rather forget Katherine exists."

"No one asked what I thought," the fifth Nat at the table said.

Seated directly across from me, with her feet kicked up on the table and a bored expression in place, was our newest resident: Bad Nat.

"We already know your opinion, dear," Mama Nat said, flashing her a sympathetic smile. She was the only one that even tried to play nice with the cigarette-smoking, leather-laden, inconsiderate asshole that took up almost half the table.

I grimaced.

"We also don't care," Ann said, wrinkling her nose in distaste. "If anything, your mere existence is another point in favor of leaving Katherine to whatever trouble she's found herself in."

Bad Nat lifted an eyebrow, taking a long drag of her cigarette. "That's a lot of disgust for someone that shouldn't have emotion."

"That speaks to your sheer uselessness. We all play a role. The Warden protects us. Peace balances us. Mama Nat holds on to our humanity. What do you do except sit around smoking and drinking all day?" Ann scoffed in annoyance. "From an *unemotional* but rational standpoint, I'd lock you up in the attic with Rage—"

"Enough," I snapped.

They all went silent, five heads turning in my direction at once. Only Bad Nat stared in challenge, like she was waiting for me to do something worthy of the power I held as Primary. I didn't like it. The animalistic nature of her was too wild. Untamed.

Ann may be harsh, but she wasn't wrong in her assessment of things.

"Everyone has made good points. Peace, I know you're running a bit ragged right now. I'm going out tonight before I decide—"

Bad Nat huffed, snorting like I was just *so* amusing.

I took a steadying breath. "Do you have something to say?"

She grinned salaciously, blowing out a stream of smoke in the direction of Ann, who looked ready to leap over the table and pummel her into the ground. The Warden would stop her if it came to that, but it was never a good day when it was even a consideration. Peace really did need a break from everything. A release. Just enough to let me center myself so we were back in working order like a well-oiled machine instead of the spluttering contraption that we were devolving into.

"You're a liar," she told me. "A good one, and the other parts of you lap it up without complaint, but you're still a liar all the same."

"That's uncalled for," The Warden said. Her strong jaw tilted, the shadows from the candelabra making it stand out.

"And mean," Mama Nat added.

"It's true," Bad Nat replied, not caring in the slightest what any of the others thought. "The Prime has already made up her mind. She knows all the reasons in the world she shouldn't give a fuck what happens to Katherine, but she's going to ask around—and if that fails, you'll go looking for her yourself. Won't you?" She smirked, but it wasn't amused, and such a strange expression to see on my own face.

All the versions of me had brown eyes. *My eyes.*

Except her.

Bad Nat's were gold.

"I haven't decided," I repeated, my tone more brittle than a moment ago.

She chuckled. Her boots dropped from the table to the walnut floors with two loud thuds. "Sure you haven't," Bad Nat drawled. Then she stood from the table and walked away, retreating into one of the many rooms of the memory loci.

Ann cursed her existence while The Warden nodded along. Peace's leg was bouncing beneath the table, jittery and not at all peaceful. Even Mama Nat looked displeased about how the meeting went.

I sighed, missing the days when these things were so much smoother.

Standing up, I gave them one last look. "The sun's going down. I need to get back. We're going to find someone to have a little fun with. It'll settle things again."

"I hope so," Ann said. Her voice was disbelieving, but not argumentative. I knew she missed how things were before our newest me showed up.

"I promise." I blinked away the memory loci, letting the franken-mansion drop from my mind along with the faces of all my selves.

The greenhouse on my roof appeared, where I was finishing up packing the potting soil around the tomato plant I'd just repotted.

I stood up and dusted my dirt-covered hands off on my jeans. I owned a pair of gardening gloves, but the feel of soil against my skin was oddly grounding, if messy. Sometimes it helped to do mindless things and let my thoughts wander.

Driving. Gardening. Cleaning.

They weren't the most engaging of tasks, but the lack of demand on my attention was a reprieve. Especially when that meant I could retreat into my memory loci without anyone freaking out about me just staring off into space for way too long. I already had enough issues with Lucifer criticizing what I did with my time. I didn't want to open that door for further discussion.

As though he'd heard me think his name, Lucifer appeared.

"A night without the baby siren. Please tell me you're not going to stay home and garden all evening." I debated not answering him, but considering I hadn't touched my magic since the other night at the club—and he was still as present and pushy as if I had been using it—I was beginning to think my days of being truly alone were gone.

And honestly, after working nonstop through the weekend to put out one fire after another, I didn't have the mental fortitude to ignore him all night.

"I don't know. Have you learned to be a better narrator?"

I closed up the greenhouse and he stepped through the plastic barrier to follow me. "We both know I wasn't actually *trying*," he said, voice rumbling and deep in a way it had no business being.

I snorted. "That's what they all say." The metal handle was cool against my palm as I opened the door to the stairs.

"Who are *they*?"

"Alphaholes with an ego the size of Texas when they get called out for sucking at something."

Lucifer laughed unexpectedly. I didn't think he'd take the insult well, even if I was being a smartass. His mirth surprised me.

"Little witch, the only thing I'd like to suck is your—"

"Ah, ah," I chimed, cutting him off. "You're dead, and even if you weren't, I'm not interested." Lucifer scoffed, which was more the reaction I expected to my alphahole comment. Should have known it wasn't far off.

"Your lies taste like—"

"Nothing," I interrupted as we went through my front door. "I'm not ignoring you right now. Keep pushing me and I'll go back to it."

That silenced him quickly.

"I'll read those dreadful books for you if you don't ignore me again," he offered after a moment. Despite the nonchalant way he said it, I sensed a vulnerability beyond what he was willing to admit. Not for the first time, I wondered what it was like to be invisible. Unknowable. A phantom of a man and unable to be seen by almost anyone . . . except me.

I locked the door and looked over my shoulder. "Why would I make that bargain with you?" He didn't use the words, but I felt the slight prickle of magic in the air when he'd said it. Magic. Sex and blood. Passion. Devastation. "You can't even read them right when I don't want you to, let alone *do*."

Lucifer shrugged. "Believe me or not, little witch, but I think we both know how well my voice could bring certain fantasies alive."

Heat pooled in my core.

I really shouldn't have gotten him going on this.

"Meh." I shrugged, feigning disinterest. A small part of me was tempted by the offer. I did know damn well how nice his voice was. He could read a shampoo bottle to me.

But he was dead. And a ghost. Not to mention the devil.

His bargains were binding. I wasn't giving up my one weapon against the creature I'd found myself tethered to.

"Meh?" he repeated, confused by my answer.

I strolled down the hallway toward my bedroom.

"Not interested," I called. "I'm not really the friends with benefits sort, ya know?"

Lucifer was inside my room when I opened the door.

"I'm not your friend," he said, arms crossed and utterly serious.

I nodded, letting my gaze skip over him as I opened my closet and started going through it. "Fair enough. Parasite with benefits, then?" I offered, pulling out a shimmery black dress that changed color in the light.

Lucifer sighed. "What are you doing?"

"Going out."

He watched me closely. "Going out *where*?"

I met his eyes in my vanity mirror. "To have fun. Now turn around."

He narrowed his eyes, disbelieving. "Seriously? You love to remind me of what I am. Say how awful you believe me to be. How you pity me and my hedonistic ways. You know I've seen a pair of tits before—"

"Lucifer," I repeated in a firm tone. "Turn or leave. You want to not be ignored? Respect my boundaries."

He dipped his head in acknowledgment and turned. I was happy he couldn't see my cheeks heating as I stripped and dressed in no time flat.

Barefoot, I slipped out of my room and into the bathroom. He followed me a moment later. Silent but staring with a particular intensity that conveyed his thoughts as I washed my face and then applied a little bit of makeup. Nothing much. Just eyeliner, mascara, and tinted lip balm. While humans and witches didn't mind a painted face, I'd long since learned most supernaturals didn't care to make out with a flesh chalkboard. Natural and healthy were far more attractive than minerals and drugs smeared on skin to enhance certain features.

I swept my hair back and teased it into a ballerina bun. The world's easiest fuck-me hairstyle for days like today when it was just a bit too stiff and approaching needing to be washed.

Tonight was about me, so I wasn't wearing a glamour. That didn't mean I was going to be stupid and just walk about without any sort of barrier. I opened my dry shampoo and dumped a smidge of the succubus pheromones in.

You shouldn't use the succubus pheromones. You don't need it.

The words echoed through my mind, unbidden, but not unwanted. It was a strange feeling. The incubus from Bliss had made enough of an impression for me to think about it now.

My finger waffled on the cap of the dry shampoo, debating spraying my roots with it.

"Don't be stupid," Lucifer said, jarring me from my debate. "If you won't use a glamour going out dressed like that, you need to cover your scent."

I bit the inside of my cheek. The urge to be defiant and reckless because he told me not to fought against my logical nature. Analytical Nat and Bad Nat were going at each other in my head, The Warden standing watch but not interfering. She was too split in her opinion. Her strong instincts said to leave it, but not wanting to leave myself open to the unsavory sort stalking me . . .

I set the dry shampoo down on the counter.

My eyes met Lucifer's in the mirror.

His jaw was tense, teeth grinding hard enough he might have cracked a tooth if he had an actual body. I tilted my head, silently making a point.

No one commands me.

Not my family. Not my friends. Not even a demon.

And especially not the devil.

seven

NATHALIE

I CUT THE LINE.

Felix leered at me, a little too eager in the way his eyes roamed my body as he lifted the rope. A meaty hand touched my back, just above my ass, as he "helped" me through. I flashed him a tight smile, making a note to tell Diego that they needed a different bouncer out front. If he was eye-fucking me, knowing who I am, then I didn't like to think of how inappropriate he was with people that didn't know his boss personally.

"You're more than just lax with your safety tonight; you're acting reckless. Being here without a glamour or masking your scent is incredibly stupid," Lucifer insisted, pouting as he walked beside me. He passed through very real, corporeal bodies as he kept stride.

I laughed under my breath.

"Is it the safest I've ever been?" I asked rhetorically. "No. Can't say it is. But the scent masking is more of an added precaution than necessity. I'll be fine."

"You're not exactly a powerhouse, little witch."

Indignation flared in me, but I bit the ire back. "You're right, but I'm not defenseless either."

My magic wasn't exactly strong or reliable, but it had done a pretty bang-up job at keeping me safe so far. Besides, Bliss had extra security measures in place. Ones I had a hand in designing. I wouldn't die inside the club even if something did happen.

"I'm dead because your family took control of your magic, in case you needed a reminder." The snarky attitude dimmed my anticipation, and I stopped walking. Trapped in a sea of people, I faced him.

"I'm sorry," I said, completely and utterly sincere. "Truly. I would take it back if I could, but I can't. As you said, my family did it. I was just their weapon of choice, but if we're going to go there, what a great way to show how unreasonable you're being and how you can miss such a fine detail in your accusation." I stepped forward, coming chest to chest with the phantom entity. "I killed you. *You.* The unkillable."

Gold flashed in his gaze. "You're not invincible, Nathalie."

I nodded in agreement. "I'm not, but I'm alive and I'm going to live a little—regardless of you trying to guilt trip or manipulate me. I don't know what unfathomable reason you have that makes you feel possessive of me."

Music drowned out my words, but I still whispered them. We never knew who was listening. Bodies brushed against me. Sweat and sex filled the air.

Lucifer leaned forward. My heart stuttered as his lips came within an inch of my own.

"*You* gave me your blood. *You* tried to save me. *You* cut my body to pieces and pulled my still-beating heart out."

My lips parted, blood rushing to my head. "Your choices led us here. I'm simply biding my time."

I frowned. "For what?"

His lips ghosted over mine. I shouldn't have felt anything, but the tingle that went through me was like being kissed by chaos itself.

Lucifer pulled away, and I hated the way my breath seemed to go with him.

"My second chance."

I reeled back, my eyes blinking rapidly. "Your second chance at what?"

The smile he gave me was cold but charming, edged with darkness. "Enjoy your night, little witch. I'll be watching."

He disappeared, leaving me flustered and frustrated. His ghost wasn't here and tormenting me with his silver tongue and wicked words. I should be happy that he backed off, especially here—the place I least wanted his presence.

For some reason, it felt like he won that conversation.

Which was dumb. Idiotic. It wasn't a competition, but it still felt like a sparring of wills.

I took a deep breath and let it go, releasing the unwanted emotions from me. Tonight wasn't about Lucifer. It was about me.

eight

LUCIFER

JUNIPER. Raspberries. Jasmine. Lilac.

I couldn't smell a thing beyond it. Her scent pervaded every part of my being. It intoxicated me. Drugged me with a perfume I couldn't escape.

I'd wanted many pretty things in my time. Queens. Emperors. Artists. Musicians. Beautiful and terrible humans that I bestowed gifts upon, whether it was my blood to give them immortality, or lavish presents to purchase their affection.

Nathalie was unlike any other creature I'd found myself yearning for. She was beautiful, but far from the exquisite men and women that typically drew my interest. She had power, but she wasn't a ruler. She was a queenmaker. An advisor. The invisible hand that moved pieces on a board, without the fame or political standing that being a leader came with. She didn't have passion bursting at her fingertips like Khutulun of the Mongol Empire, Joan of Arc, Catherine the Great, or Policarpa Salvarrieta.

I was drawn to greatness. To *more*.

Exceptional called to me like the moon did the waves.

My little witch wasn't any of those things, yet I found her to be the most fascinating of all. Her quiet strength. Her brilliant mind. Her breathy moans while she slept, twisting in her bedsheets. The way her back bent, spine arching for the ceiling as she gasped out single, almost intelligible words. Her slick skin and fingers aching to sneak between her thighs told me all I needed to know about what lay in her dreams.

Nathalie was the sun masked by mediocrity, pretending that she didn't burn brighter than all the underlings she associated with.

If only she weren't so fucking stubborn.

I lingered in the sex dungeon, out of sight, but never far.

In her deep violet dress, she would have blended into the shadows of the club if not for the glow of her skin. Short in stature but leggy, the Burberry heels that encased her tiny feet sharpened her calf muscles and showed the lean muscle in her thighs.

My mouth would have watered if it could.

Not for the first time, I cursed my undead existence.

Soon.

I'd been watching the chaos witch for ten months now. In the beginning, she couldn't see me. Not clearly. She'd heard me, though she'd adamantly denied it.

All the while, I was growing stronger.

Every time she used her magic, my body took shape faster. My voice grew louder. Provided enough time, I might be able to possess a body. That might have been my aspiration once, since she'd refused to even entertain the idea of bringing me back.

It was that very conversation that caused her to shut me out again. For months.

Then she came to Bliss and let an incubus stoke the flame of her desire.

I hated watching it.

In my almost fathomless existence, I'd rarely felt possessive over things. People. Places. I'd become possessive of New Chicago when I'd ruled it. Death stripped that away. I'd been possessive of the soulmate I felt owed. Reality broke that.

Now I was no one. Nothing but a phantom, and yet I found myself *longing* for the last person I should.

The woman who killed me.

The chaos witch that ignored me.

While she may have thrashed and moaned in her sleep, she never finished the deal. Never surrendered to the pleasure her body so desperately craved. But that night in Bliss, when she lowered her walls enough to let another touch her, it was a blessing and a curse.

I wanted to stroke her skin. To lick. To taste. To worship.

Instead, she was letting a lesser version of me do that very thing.

The witch boy interrupting her with the incubus was a welcome cockblock. Then I realized something.

I had grown stronger in the wake of her desire.

Her soul now housed a tiny piece of mine, and it was somehow feeding my desire magic with every caress.

She didn't know it. I was certain she wouldn't have returned here if she did.

So as much as I truly loathed watching another give her pleasure when that was *my* job, I silenced my objections and lurked in the places she wasn't looking. I might have been tempted to stay and see if I could join in the fun by whispering promises in her ear that no one else would ever hear, but her threat of ignoring me held more power than I liked to admit.

She may deny any feeling toward me because of her socially constructed barriers. I could handle that. But silence wasn't acceptable.

The months I spent as an invisible prisoner, drawn to her but unseen—*unheard*—were longer than they had any right to be for a creature my age.

Nathalie moved through the club with a sort of languid ease. Far too at home in this place, wearing a dress that wreaked havoc on my self-control.

I'd have said something if I hadn't thought she'd defy me and show up naked instead, just to spite me.

The stubborn little witch deplored commands.

At least mine.

Thinking on it further, it was possible that wasn't entirely the case. I wondered if she held a deep-seated resistance to any command given, no matter the person who spoke it. Her family commanded many, including their own children, and they had no boundaries. She'd suffered at the hands of their power. I wondered if I got the brunt of her ire because I was the safest target. It wasn't as if I could do anything in return, save read her shitty romance books mockingly, or tempt her with deeds I couldn't commit.

Soon, I reminded myself.

She took a seat at the bar, crossing her lean legs at her ankles. The open back of her dress showed the planes of muscle beneath her imperfect skin.

Nicks and cuts marred her back in the form of tiny white scars. They weren't large or even enough to guess that someone had done it to her intentionally. Simply faded white lines against an otherwise blank canvas.

She didn't have tattoos, as many witches did. Ground

stones, blood, and other minerals that could hold power mixed with ink, then injected into their bodies was common among her people. That she'd opted to not tattoo herself or wear anything beside a simple pendant that prevented other beings from tracking her was strange.

I may have called her reckless, but I'd learned she was anything but. Neither cocky nor arrogant, she was self-assured of what power she did hold, but not hungry enough to reach for more.

I didn't understand it.

I couldn't stop myself from being fascinated.

The way her mind worked was unlike anyone I'd met, and the compulsion to break her open and figure out what made her tick was undeniable.

Like other times she'd visited, Nathalie started at the bar. This time she ordered a Jasmine Blossom with two raspberries and no ice. A tiny hum of appreciation resonated as she took a sip. The bartender knew her, just like the handsy bodyguard. It was how she got away without carrying her wallet or any form of identification and just having a permanently open tab.

A few minutes passed while she enjoyed her drink, tension physically draining from her shoulders. That was before a man in a glamour started cutting his way through the crowd in a line straight for her.

I moved closer.

She lifted her head as he stopped beside her stool.

He took a deep breath others might mistake as him working up the courage to speak, but I recognized the action for what it was.

He was scenting her.

"You listened."

I narrowed my eyes. Nathalie turned her cheek. "Excuse me?"

"About the pheromones." His heavy gaze fell on her like she held the world in the palm of her hand. Within a second, a ripple washed over him, and his glamour changed to the blond incubus she'd met days ago.

"August," she breathed. Something foreign and nasty curled around my heart at the way she spoke his name, so very different from how mine sounded as it left her lips.

Where I was her curse, he had her adoration.

"Ophelia," he murmured, dipping his head toward hers a fraction. "Or should I say Nathalie?"

nine

NATHALIE

"I'M surprised to see you here again." *So soon*.

I wasn't sure if I should have warning bells going off or accept the subtle warmth that touched me when I realized who it was.

August was a stranger. I didn't know him. I didn't even know if August was his real name, or if his hair was actually blond, or if his eyes were blue. I knew almost nothing about him. Yet, part of me was happy he'd found me again.

"Are you?" he asked, eyes equally amused as they were serious. "You came back."

I lifted a shoulder in a shrug. "I didn't know you'd be here."

"I'd hoped you would be." My breath caught when I heard the truth in his words, not joking at all. I took a nervous sip of my drink.

"That's very . . ."

"Forward?" he supplied, lips turning up in the corners. I found myself wanting to run my finger over them, to see if they were as smooth as they looked. Was his glamour strong enough to make me feel them? Or would I feel beneath it?

His forthright approach turned me on more than the games I was used to people playing.

"Yes."

"I like you," August said. "It seems silly to pretend otherwise, given where we are." There was definitely mirth twinkling in his eyes as he glanced around the club before settling his baby blues back on me.

"How do you like me? You don't know me." It was an admonishment, but I couldn't help smiling as I said it. "You wouldn't even know my name if not for the interruption last time."

"No," he agreed. "But I'd like to." Tentatively, he extended his hand toward my drink but stopped short of touching it.

"You don't have to pretend, you know." I lifted an eyebrow at him. "I'm okay picking up where we left off. Hot sex with no strings attached."

I set my glass in his palm. August, if that was truly his name, tipped back the contents and drained the rest of my drink in one go. When he lowered it once more, his tongue darted out to sweep the remainder off his bottom lip. "I'd rather we didn't, if I'm being honest."

He set the glass back on the counter and extended his hand once more.

"Get to know each other in the biblical sense or . . ." I trailed off, waiting for him to answer. He let out a gruff laugh, warm and rich, like a fine whiskey.

"Fuck and go our separate ways." The way he stayed so wholly focused on me was unnerving, but incredibly sexy. "Something tells me I'm not going to get my fill of you."

"And if I don't want to pursue," I motioned between our chests, "this?"

"Then we don't," he answered simply. "And you'll mourn all the ways we could have had fun, or at least I will." He winked, not cocky but secure. It was such a strange combination and so unlike the partners I'd found myself with in the past.

Growing up, everything was a game. My heart. My soul. My relationships. I'd been tied to a boy before either of us even understood sex, all because my parents deemed it an *appropriate match*. Still, I'd fallen in love with that boy. Grew with him as I became a woman. I gave the man my everything.

And he'd ripped my heart out.

He'd betrayed me in the worst possible way, just like my family and friends. Again and again, I took chances. Most of them backfired, but not all. Now I had friends who were my family. I had unshakable bonds with people that I would do anything for.

It was because of those bonds that I found myself questioning. Doubting.

That realization made me sad, because when had I become so godsdamn jaded?

I momentarily asked myself what I would tell Piper, or Sasha, or even Sienna in this situation. It didn't take much thinking to determine the "what would Nat do?".

I'd tell them to live. The world was filled with shitty, terrible things, but not everything had to be. While there was darkness, there was also joy. Denying ourselves that because it could be dangerous to get close to people was insanity.

Living in fear meant letting the bad win. It was letting

my mother, my old coven, my sister Carissa, and all the others who tried to take a piece of me, win.

I was too strong to succumb to that.

Besides, getting to know someone and having my brains thoroughly fucked out in the meantime wouldn't hurt. If it went sideways, I could always just walk away.

Even if it hurt.

I dropped my hand in his, not letting Analytical Nat talk me out of it. The Warden was hesitant but not opposed. Peace looked forward to the orgasms to come.

The most surprising to note was that our newest resident was quiet.

Bad Nat seemed to be watching but had no desire to make her opinions known.

It was strange. Silence wasn't her thing.

"You know, I might be a terrible lay. You shouldn't write a check for a car you haven't driven," I said. "Think how much you would regret it if I was a total bore in bed, or we got there and had no chemistry."

He chuckled. "Consider me warned."

August tugged my body from my seat, pulling me flush against him. Sheer heat radiated from beneath his button-down shirt. I wanted to lean in and feel if his body was as hard as it looked.

A flash over his shoulder caught my attention.

Lucifer.

I should have known better than to hope he wouldn't be here right now. That he would afford me some semblance of privacy. It was a crazy notion since I was prepared to fuck August in front of strangers. But there was something incredibly intimate in the way Lucifer watched me. To be with someone else while he was hovering . . . I didn't want to think about that.

Last time I was here, I planned to catch a target. Meeting August and actually enjoying what he was doing hadn't been part of the plan.

This time, it was what I came for.

"Are you all right?"

My gaze slid sideways, seeing August's concern. "Yes. Just saw someone I'd rather avoid," I lied smoothly.

"We could get a private room." I think his words were meant to be reassuring, but I sensed longing in them. He wanted one, regardless of what spooked me. I couldn't help my curiosity as to why, but I'd save it for behind closed doors.

"We should," I agreed.

August led me hand-in-hand toward the back of the club where a section was roped off and guarded. "Dolores," I greeted in a friendly tone. The vampire glanced between August and me, an inquisitive expression on her face. Unlike many of the vampires who'd been turned in their prime, Dolores was turned in her fifties. The wrinkles of age and gray hairs frozen in place. Most people underestimated her because of her appearance, which made her a fantastic guard. They didn't understand that regardless of the age her body had been, she was just as strong and twice as viscous when it came to putting people in their place.

"Private room?"

"Yes, please. Put it on my tab."

She nodded, removing the rope to escort us back. August shot me a quizzical glance. "I'm not sure whether I should comment on how she clearly knows you well enough that you have a tab, or that you opted to pay for it without asking."

"Feeling emasculated?" I snorted, only half joking. This was part of the reason I rarely got past a decent fuck with men. I was the wealthiest woman in New Chicago, and not because I was some hoity-toity heiress. I was a self-made woman. A successful business owner and entrepreneur who had her fingers in more cookie jars than two hands could allow.

It was archaic to view the man as the provider, but particularly with long-lived species, that misogynistic idea managed to stick around. I had no idea how old August was. The quality of his suit and shoes did little beyond revealing he had money.

My little test would be enlightening to whether this could go beyond scratching an itch.

"Not in the slightest," he answered quietly. A secretive smirk pulled at me.

Dolores paused at a door and turned the handle, opening it for us. August guided me in first before turning to hold his hand out for the key.

She set it in his palm with one last look between the two of us. Then she was gone. August shut the door. The lock clicked into place.

We were alone.

I breathed easier knowing the room was warded from all things, Marcel and ghosts included. It was why I agreed.

Partially.

"Have you fed?" I asked, stepping into the dimly lit room. A king-sized poster bed took up one side, a rack and cross the other. Toys decorated the back wall. I drifted to it, reaching up to stroke my fingers over the leather.

"No," he said after a pregnant pause. "I was hoping you would still be up for that."

I inhaled the scent of leather and oil. It calmed my inner turmoil with the promise of dirty deeds.

My fingers slid over silk.

A mask.

I paused.

"How old are you?"

I sensed his curiosity about the change of subject. "Old," he answered eventually. My lips tugged up in a smile he couldn't see.

"Feeling insecure about your age?" I asked lightly. "I can guarantee anything you say won't shock me." Not when I knew Lucifer's age.

I mentally cursed myself for thinking of him.

"Apprehensive is a better word," August corrected. Fingers caressed the small of my back. Such a slight touch, but the scoop of the dress put him in direct contact with my skin. "Experience has taught me that those who are mortal don't like to be reminded of it."

I snorted. "We're all mortal. No matter how long we live, there are only two things promised to us in life. It's the same now as it was thousands of years ago: death and taxes."

August chuckled, his lips ghosting over my shoulder. A shudder I couldn't suppress ran through me. "I'm old enough to know how to feed properly," he said, answering my unspoken question. Young incubi and succubi sometimes had control issues. They took too much. Left too little. It was a delicate balancing act when letting another creature feed off your energy. It was the reason I didn't tend to do it outside of relationships, and even then, I was cautious.

Something about August made me want to trust him. To let him touch me and bring me to new heights.

His teeth ran over the length of my neck, stopping at the base where it met my shoulder to bite gently. The breath hissed between my teeth.

"Go slow. If I say stop, you won't want to push it. My

magic tends to respond poorly when it thinks I'm in danger." The last part slipped out, a threat for sure, but one I didn't know if I could even follow through on. When their kind fed, it was supposed to be the most excruciating pleasure one could experience. There were decent odds my magic wouldn't react because it wouldn't sense the danger.

"I won't hurt you," he swore softly. "Not unless you want me to."

The promise of a good time made bumps rise along my arms.

"Remove your glamour."

My hand on the wall fisted around the eye mask, crumpling the fabric in my palm as I used it to steady me. Firm hands grabbed my hips, pulling me back into him.

"Done," he breathed, voice husky.

I turned.

My breath caught in my chest.

He was beautiful. Breathtaking. Easily a head and a half taller than me, even with my heels on. His curly black hair was pulled back, preventing me from seeing how long it was. High cheekbones and sharp, prominent eyebrows complimented his features. The five o'clock shadow on his smooth, brown skin gave me wicked ideas about feeling it scrape against my thighs.

If not for my ability to see magic, I would have wondered if this was another glamour. He was easily hotter than any man had a right to be.

There was just one thing.

He didn't drop the glamour from his eyes. While they'd transformed into a deep steel-blue gaze, the haze of magic over them was still distinctly there.

I debated saying something but decided to let it go.

We were just getting to know one another, after all. It wasn't as if I didn't have secrets of my own.

"Tell me what you want, beautiful."

I ran a hand down his chest, stopping just short of his slacks. My lips parted.

"I can't decide whether I want to ride your face or your cock," I answered honestly. My own voice was thick and heady.

I enjoyed the rules and practices places like Bliss allowed me to revel in, but tonight I didn't want careful or methodical. I didn't want slow and tempered.

I wanted to lose myself in the moment and not think about it.

My hand pressed against his chest and August took a step back, releasing my hips. Confusion colored his glam-oured gaze, before I kept pushing.

Fisting both hands in his shirt, I used all of my strength —insignificant though it may have been—to throw him on the bed. August let me, not protesting in the slightest.

I sauntered up to him, stepping between his spread legs. My hands captured his face in an intimate hold. Then our lips met.

Gods.

The taste of him exploded on my tongue, sending me into a near frenzy. I knotted my fingers in his hair, needing to feel in control, especially when I very much wasn't.

His hands grasped me as well, pulling our bodies flush together so I could feel the very hard length of his erection against my center.

I kicked off one heeled shoe to lift my leg over his lap, then the other. Our bodies brushed right where I wanted him, making heat pool in my belly.

My back arched, pushing my chest into him as I broke

our kiss to breathe. August did no such thing. His lips caressed my jaw as he guided my hips into him, rocking me so that our bodies connected just right.

"Cock," I murmured. He chuckled, breath fanning the sensitive skin just below my ear.

"Do you always like to skip to the main course?" August mused, smiling against my skin before nipping my earlobe. I practically convulsed on his lap.

"Sometimes," I admitted. "Sometimes I want dessert before dinner. Other times I want a full seven-course meal with all the trimmings. More than anything, I just like variety."

I pulled my fingers from hair that had no business being as soft as it was, resting them on his strong shoulders. My nails bit into the fabric when he sucked on a spot that made me gush.

"So do I," he muttered against my skin. One of his large hands moved to cup my breast through the thin dress. He squeezed, then rolled my nipple between deft fingers. With the lack of a bra, I felt everything, and it made me moan.

We'd barely started, and I couldn't recall the last time I was with someone *this* good.

Actually, that was a lie. I could recall, but he'd had years to watch my every reaction and learn my likes and dislikes —August just *got it*.

He knew what to stroke, to roll, to pinch, to twist.

I was a sweating bundle of desire by the time I exposed the wide expanse of his chest as I moved his shirt. "God, you're ripped. If you're one of those workout addicts, I don't think we'll get very far, but I could be tempted to stay friends with benefits."

He laughed, pressing his face into my bare shoulder.

"Far from it," he said, lips skimming the edge where my

dress cut across my skin. "My line of work requires a certain . . . physique, and I despise running. Thankfully there are more pleasurable ways to maintain it."

I hummed in acknowledgment, running my fingernails down his chest. He groaned. The hand on my hip tightened. Our bodies were too close together to get to his pants. Putting some distance between us, I rocked back.

He reached for the clasp of my dress at the back of my neck the same second I leaned forward to unbutton his slacks. The shimmery material dropped away, revealing my small breasts as I freed his erection.

My hand wrapped around him, firm and sure.

The breath hissed between his teeth as I pumped it twice.

My fingers couldn't touch, and that didn't bode well for my cobwebs downstairs. I'd be feeling it tomorrow, but I didn't care one bit. I wanted the reminder.

With one hand between us and the other braced on his shoulder, I brought our bodies together.

August grabbed my hips once more to guide me, pulling me down at the same moment he thrust up. My mouth dropped open in pure ecstasy.

If not for his hands moving me, I would have stalled right there. Instead, August worked me over his cock, letting me feel every ridge of him.

My head fell back to let out a low moan.

This. This was what I needed.

He reached between us to tweak my nipple, setting me off instantly. My pussy clenched, gripping him tightly as it spasmed.

"Fuck," August cursed, rolling his hips harder to take me through it. My vision went black, but I heard him murmur, "You're so responsive."

"It's been a while for me," I rasped.

Sure. That was why I was putty in his hands.

Instead of calling me on my lie, August took in my trembling thighs and tsked. "What was it you said? Maybe you were a bore in bed?" Grabbing my ass in an unyielding squeeze, he nipped at my neck, and I ground into him. He flipped our positions without another word, pushing me further back on the black sheets. I expected him to keep fucking me, but he pulled out—leaving me too empty. Instead of protesting, I watched as he shuffled back and grasped both my thighs.

"Does this feel like no chemistry?" His steel-blue gaze locked with mine as he threw each leg over his broad shoulders and then flattened his tongue against my clit.

I jerked from the stimulation after having just coming down from an incredible high.

"Fuck," I groaned when he didn't let up. Instead, he licked and plucked and sucked my clit while finger fucking me with a deftness that would put the most skilled pianist to shame.

Then he blew on my clit.

Like a tower of cards facing one strong wind, I broke.

Literally. The first orgasm I saw black, but this time I saw nothing. The world narrowed down to a single suspended moment where I simply *existed*.

It was incredible.

Addictive.

I instantly knew he'd started feeding. Sex had never felt this good. It wasn't possible without magic.

"Nathalie."

The way he said my name made me think he'd been calling to me. Voice hoarse from the scream I no doubt let loose, I nodded. "Hm?"

He chuckled, breath blowing over my most sensitive parts. "I asked if you were taking birth control. I don't want to . . ."

Oh, shit. Right.

I waved him off, scrubbing a hand down my face. "I'm on a monthly potion. We're good."

He kissed my hip before crawling up my body.

"Still thinking you want no strings attached?" he asked, amusement and a tiny bit of arrogance entering his tone.

I couldn't fault him. August had a reason to feel arrogant if he could fuck like this.

"I never said that."

He loomed over me, resting his forearms above my head as he supported his weight. His cock brushed against my entrance as he grinned. "You heavily implied it."

In one stroke, he entered me again.

I gasped, grabbing on to his shoulders. My nails bit into the hard muscle of his traps. "I still don't know you," I said, mostly just clinging to my tenuous resolve out of stubbornness.

He rolled his hips, and holy shit, did I pant.

"While true, you know a few things." He repeated the motion and my eyes practically rolled back in my head. "You know what I look like." *Thrust.* "What I feel like." *Thrust.* "That I'm not emasculated by a woman who sometimes likes to lead." *Thrust.* "Or insecure enough to be bothered that you're clearly successful in whatever you do if you can pay for this room." *Thrust.*

Jesus. Fucking. Christ.

I didn't believe in gods, but his cock might just be one.

"So you meet the bare minimum to be a decent person," I said, hiding my smile. He chuckled again, the dark, brooding sound winding me up all over again.

"How about this?" he started, his voice lowering into a sexy rumble. "You know I can make you come."

My lips parted as our eyes locked and he rested his forehead against mine. He seemed to breathe me in like a fine wine.

I balanced on the edge of another orgasm as he slid in and out of me, only seconds from reaching another blissful crescendo.

Two thumps knocked on the door, breaking my concentration.

August let out a growl of frustration. "Ignore it."

"*Make me.*" I wrapped my legs around him, digging my heels into his back as I met him thrust for thrust.

The pounding started again. I reached for that release, fucking him as hard as I could.

August pulled back so he was kneeling on the bed and grabbed my hips. With a strength I couldn't possess, he pounded into me savagely. The pace brutal and inhuman.

It was exactly what I needed.

My climax swept through me, pulling all my muscles taut. My mouth opened in a silent scream. My eyes started to close.

"Look at me, sunling," August insisted.

It took more effort than I wanted to admit keeping my eyes open and on him as my release pulled me under.

The incubus I'd found myself in bed with thrust twice more before stilling.

Intensity burned in the depths of his gaze as he emptied inside of me.

Whatever words we would have exchanged in the aftermath were ruined by the very sharp return to reality.

"Fucking hell, Nat. It's kind of an emergency!" Piper called through the door, her voice tense with impatience.

My head hit the bed in frustration. I ran a sweaty hand over my face, pinching the bridge of my nose between my index finger and thumb. I blew out a tight breath.

"It can't be that much of one or you'd have broken the door down already," I mumbled.

August released my hips, letting me shuffle back on the bed so I could swing my legs off the side.

"I can send them away," he suggested while handing me a towel to clean myself up with. He was completely and utterly serious. I snorted.

"No, you can't."

"I can compel—"

"Don't even finish that sentence." I sighed. "If you tried to compel the woman at that door, she would kill you without a second thought, and that's the better outcome." I grimaced, pulling my dress up over my naked chest. It clung uncomfortably now.

August turned to sit on the edge of the bed, watching me get ready to leave. Again. "Better outcome?" he questioned with amusement despite the disappointment I saw behind his guarded eyes.

"Her mate is an alphahole bastard and won't hesitate to bang his chest a bit by torturing you." That was putting it mildly.

"Somehow, I doubt it's that bad," August said, smirking.

If only he knew.

This moment was a prime example as to why I didn't have time for anything beyond no strings attached. Between my friends-turned-family, my business, my ghost problem, and a city that couldn't seem to stay safe for two seconds, there wasn't much left at the end of the day.

"You've got sixty seconds before I have my second pick

the lock with her claw," Piper threatened. Now she was throwing around titles? Fucking hell was right. How many people did she bring with her?

I slipped my feet into my heels, lips pressed together.

"Sorry to have to leave so abruptly . . . again." I winced. That sounded just as bad out loud as it did in my head. "This was . . ." I struggled to find the right word without sounding either dismissive or like a blushing virgin who'd just seen her first cock. In the end I settled for, "I really needed that."

August watched me with an unreadable expression. "Are you sure I can't convince you to give me a chance?"

"August, I . . ."

Part of me wanted to say yes. There was no denying how attracted I was to him, and holy hell did he know how to fuck.

You've already got a ghost that won't leave you alone, Analytical Nat seemed to point out. *A traumatized siren lives with you. Your best friend runs the city. Your ex is sniffing around you, and Katherine is missing. That's enough to keep you busy without even considering the dozens of businesses you own and run.*

I sighed. Ann was right. Much as I might want to, I really didn't have time for this. The Warden agreed with her, as did Bad Nat. It was never a good sign when the three of them were on the same page.

I should really listen.

"I'm not asking for marriage or mating," August said softly with a smile. It was slight and sad. "Just a date. Dinner. My place. I'll—"

"I'm sorry," I cut him off, mentally counting down my remaining seconds.

Only seventeen left.

He sighed, releasing a frustrated breath but nodded. "All right. I can take no for an answer. If you change your mind, though—"

"I won't," I insisted, not wanting to give him false hope.

"If you do," he continued, getting to his feet, and closing the distance between us. "Go to the convenience store on 7th and Pike Place. Tell the girl at the counter you're there to see me."

Six seconds.

Half of my mouth dragged up in a sad kind of smile. "Goodbye, August."

A hand wrapped around the nape of my neck. He kissed me hard, like he was trying to imprint himself on my soul. I was kissing him back when time ran out.

With one last nip at my bottom lip, he released me.

"Nathalie," he murmured, hand sweeping toward the door. I knew he was refusing to say goodbye. As if that insistence would stop it from happening.

I shook my head, turning to the door as it jiggled.

Piper wasn't kidding.

My footsteps were quiet as I hurried to the door before they could break it open. The lock clicked open as I got there and I pulled the handle, slipping out before they could come in after me.

When it shut behind me, I crossed my arms over my chest and stared up at Sasha and Piper. While the former was slender with warm brown skin, sleek black hair, and fluffy cat ears on her head, she was anything but soft. Her tail twitched in agitation and her glacial green cat eyes narrowed in impatience. Piper was her opposite in looks. From her golden-blonde hair to her violet-colored eyes, to the glowing brands that covered her body from head to toe. They lit up the dark hallway, a miniature sun contained beneath her skin. I noticed her lack of flaming wings, but knew they were only out of sight.

Then there was me. Brown hair. Brown eyes. Unremarkable olive-toned skin. Weak magic. Covenless. Titleless.

Without a doubt, they both trumped me in basically every aspect of our lives.

Power. Control. Prestige. Even height—compared to me, they were both Amazons, but the heels I wore leveled out the difference some tonight.

Despite all that, they were here *for me*.

Because what I lacked in everything else, I made up for with my mind, great personality, and emotional maturity.

"What on earth is so important that you had to interrupt me?" I laid into them, half convinced it wasn't actually an emergency and just one of those times they *thought* it was. The fun thing about powerful friends with unchecked emotional damage was they saw crises where there were none.

"Murder," Sasha cut in, her hand wrapped around my wrist.

I'll be damned. Maybe it was important for once.

ten

NATHALIE

MURDER WAS AN UNDERSTATEMENT.

This was a massacre.

Five bodies littered the empty alleyway. I struggled to call them that, considering I was staring at five dried-out husks. They were the only thing left. I wouldn't have been able to identify them as humanoid in the slightest if not for their white bones, still fully intact. Surrounding each skeleton was black char. It had collapsed inward on most of them, thanks to the elements.

Between the wind and the rain, half of their remains were splattered on the ground and walls. The brittle black coal-like substance mixed with the water on the cracked pavement to form a thin black ooze.

I squatted down, running my finger through it.

No blood or skin remained.

Whatever happened here, they'd been changed on a chemical level.

If not for the teeth, they would be impossible to identify.

"I've never seen a murder like this before," I said. Standing, I wiped my finger on the dress—accepting that my dry cleaner would have one hell of a job.

"They're not the first," Piper said.

I pivoted sharply and lifted an eyebrow. "There are more?"

She scrubbed a hand over her face as she nodded. Exhaustion lined her features, accentuating the bags beneath her eyes, but it was easy to attribute that to caring for her twins, who had been born only months ago. If not for them growing at an unprecedented speed and basically being three-year-olds now, she'd probably have a more difficult time adjusting to the odd hours she worked. Like now, for example.

Honor went to sleep easily, but her son Orson was a bit more of a mama's boy. It was only recently he started accepting bedtime stories from her mate, Ronan, instead.

"We've been finding a new one every week. I wasn't sure what to make of it, but this many . . ." She shook her head. "At first, I thought someone just pissed off the wrong person. Then when they kept happening, I thought serial killer. But this doesn't align with that either." She waved a hand at the alley and sighed.

Part of me was jealous. Why hadn't she told me this before now?

Because you're not her second, The Warden piped up.

She wasn't wrong. I'd been offered the position and turned her down. I had reasons. Good reasons. That didn't change the flicker of jealousy. It was irrational, but most emotions were.

"How long ago did the murders start?" I asked, walking from one corpse to the next.

Piper looked up at the cloudy sky. "Ummm—"

"Three and a half weeks ago," Sasha inserted.

"That sounds about right, but we know how I've been with time."

I snorted. Also an understatement. Ever since the twins had been born, she struggled to keep track of it. That was normal. Sienna was similar. Her daughter was born the same day. However, Sienna only had one baby, and Hallie couldn't control time itself.

Piper's son could.

"So, three weeks. Three deaths, until today?" I asked, just to make sure I had it straight.

"Yep," Sasha said, crossing her arms over her chest.

"Have any of the victims been identified?" I looked from one skeleton to the next.

"Unfortunately, no," Piper said, running a hand over her hair to smooth her frizzy flyaways back. "All of them were in the same condition when we found them, and the lab hasn't been able to identify a positive match to their teeth."

Unsurprising. "These five are male," I said after a moment. "Do you know the gender of the previous three?"

Both of them shook their heads. "How can you tell?" Sasha asked.

"Hip bones," I muttered, glancing up and down the alley from every angle. Every second it rained, the scene became more contaminated. Less preserved. I needed to see as much of it as possible so I could analyze it later.

"You can just tell without measuring?"

"Eidetic memory." I tapped a finger against my temple without looking at her. That was mostly true. I'd never heard of someone having a memory quite like mine. I'd wondered if my ability to compartmentalize somehow made it better, or if I was just born with an even greater capacity compared to others with eidetic memories. In the end, I'd never know.

"We don't know the gender," Piper said, answering my original question. "One of them was a lot smaller, though. I'd guess either a woman or child." She hesitated at that last word. There were some lines you didn't cross without becoming something truly evil. Killing, hurting, abusing children? That was one of them.

"That makes it unlikely it's a serial killer, then. They typically have an age range they work within, as well as a gender, and one of those doesn't line up. Which begs the question, why kill them?"

I squinted my eyes, looking up and down the alley, but no magic apart from my friends was evident. If anything, it was remarkably clean.

Hm.

"What kind of magic do you think did this?" Piper asked. "I've never seen anything exactly like it. If we can narrow that down, or even the species, we stand a better chance of catching the person responsible."

"I've only seen something similar to this once," Sasha murmured. "It's not exact, but I can follow up with him. He may be able to shed some light on what we're looking at."

I grimaced. Either way, it was a needle in a haystack. There were millions of supernaturals that lived in New Chicago alone. More people had magic than didn't. Even if they knew the type or what caused it, it was unlikely to find the murderer unless we caught them in the act.

Saying that wouldn't help, so I opted to keep it to myself.

"I think it's impossible to tell what kind of magic was used here. You're a shifter and a succubus, but your magic is spirit based, not desire or rage. I've seen ghouls with desire magic and healers with death magic. If I had to guess, I'd assume this was death, but I'm not willing to rule anything out. Magic never does what's expected—and even if we do find out, I'm not sure how that's going to help us."

Sasha sighed, not liking my answer. Piper just inclined her head, begrudgingly agreeing.

"So, we have nothing to go on. Not a commonality or a motivation or even a kind of magic that does this." Piper nudged the skeleton closest to her with the toe of her boot. The charred-looking remains collapsed, making her scowl. We may not have much, but tampering with what we did have wouldn't help anyone.

"Were the other bodies all found in public places?" I asked.

"Yes," they both answered at once. I nodded slowly.

"My guess is that whoever our murderer or murderess is, they didn't know their victims. That's uncommon. Not if you want to get away with it, at least. But if they wanted to murder someone they knew, they'd have the means to do it someplace more private where it would be less likely to be discovered."

"Unless they also had that train of thought and did it publicly to throw us off," Piper said.

I inclined my head. "That's a good point. Have you talked to the neighbors? Workers?"

"No one saw anything," Sasha sighed. "I interviewed every person myself and got nothing. It doesn't help that we can't identify when any of these people died since there's not much left . . ."

Yeah, that was a problem.

"Hm," I hummed. There was an alternative, but it wasn't one I was a big fan of exploring.

"You're thinking," Piper stated.

"I'm always thinking."

"Fine," she groaned. "You have an idea. Care to share with the class?"

I rolled my eyes. "I do, but I'd rather explore other options first."

"We're running out of options," Sasha replied, a bit terser than I liked. I gave her a hard look, not appreciating the snappy tone she used. "What?" she demanded, looking between me and Piper. "We've interviewed everyone that works or lives within a mile radius from each of the places we found the bodies. For three weeks, it was one victim a week. Now it's five bodies and we're not even at the end of the week."

Piper rubbed her palm against her right temple. "She has a point. Time is of the essence right now."

I bit the inside of my cheek. They were right. I knew they were right, but the alternative path . . . it wasn't one I wanted to take.

Unfortunately, I wasn't selfish or heartless enough to refuse them.

"Necromancy," I said, letting it settle in. "All I need is a bone and some remains. If there are any parts of them still on this plane, they'd have to answer our questions. They could tell us what happened."

Piper's lips pressed together. "I see why you wanted to explore other options."

I gave her a brittle smile. "I can't do it myself. That's death magic, and we'd need a black witch—which I'm not."

She read between the lines, understanding what I didn't want to mention in front of Sasha.

"Why didn't you say so? We have a whole coven of black witches," Sasha said. "Piper can just make them do it."

"Because necromancy is dangerous," I answered in a

tone sharper than I usually took with her. "It's why Piper banned them from using the Wicked Haunt to do it. To speak to the dead, you have to give the veil one of the living in return, and they balance in limbo between life and death. I've seen people die from this sort of work, Sasha."

Usually, I didn't chastise her. While friends, we didn't have that sort of relationship. Not like me and Piper. Her blatant disregard for side effects didn't sit well with me. She wouldn't be so casual about it if it were a succubus who had to sit in the veil and chance not returning.

"People are already dying," she said. "And it's not like the Ouroboros Coven wouldn't be doing it anyway if Piper didn't ban them from it. At least they can do it for our benefit."

I pressed my lips together. It was a hard situation. Neither option was great.

"And if the coven is behind it?" I challenged, looking between them both.

I could tell Sasha hadn't considered that, but Piper had. Her violet eyes were contemplative. "They're bound by a blood oath. They'd have to be truthful if I questioned them."

"Katherine and Marcel have to be truthful," I corrected. "The rest of them didn't take an oath."

"They could," Sasha said. Always the hammer. Her solution to everything was to make it a nail.

"No." Piper shook her head. "We've discussed this. I'm not taking chances and giving blood. Odds are that none of them would survive it, but if they did . . . they may obtain magic they shouldn't. I can't risk it."

Once, she'd been a simple rage demon.

Powerful, yeah. But still a fairly normal demon.

That was before Hell. Before she'd nearly died and been

forced to do the unthinkable. I didn't disagree with her decision here. The kind of power she wielded now . . . no one should have that. Least of all anyone in the Ouroboros Coven.

"How many people do you need to do the spell?" Sasha asked.

"Two."

"Then Katherine and Marcel can do it," she said. "Problem solved."

"I'm not risking Katherine's life. She's Nat's twin," Piper said.

While relevant, we both knew the real reason she wasn't willing to use my sister. Kat was my psychic bondmate, and Piper would do anything she could to protect that, even if the bond hadn't been completed. I think she still held onto the hope that despite all the family drama and bullshit, one day we would finalize that connection so that I'd be grounded and less likely to go crazy like so many witches before me. I was pretty sure Sasha knew that too, but she didn't view it the same, which is why she closed her eyes and shook her head.

"What better options do we have right now?" she argued.

"A psychic," Piper offered. "Talking with the dead isn't that uncommon—" She stopped as I started shaking my head.

"Psychics can speak with the dead, sometimes. They can't make them tell the truth or find ghosts that aren't already around them. People who transition to ghosts have to have something that grounds them to this plane. People. Places. Something meaningful. We don't even know who we're looking for. We won't be able to find their ghosts, not without necromancy."

We all let out a collective sigh. No one was unhappier about it than I, but it was the truth.

"Is Katherine a death witch?" Piper asked.

"She is."

My best friend looked away, an unnatural stillness settling over her body as she contemplated something.

"Could she cast the spell while Marcel goes into the veil?"

My teeth clanked as my mouth snapped shut. Marcel and I had a complicated past. There was a time that I was pissed enough I might have gone for that.

Now? I didn't like it any more than the idea of Kat going in.

He hurt me. They both did. But some stupid part of me didn't like the idea of his life hanging in the balance, wavering in the veil.

"Yes . . . but there is one little problem there . . ."

"What now?" Sasha griped. Her cat tail swayed back and forth, impatient and frustrated. That made two of us.

"Katherine's missing," I said, getting the words out in a rush. "I found out from Marcel because he wanted my help looking for her. I hadn't decided whether I was going to or not, but without her, we don't have a black witch with death magic to cast it—not one that's truthful, anyway."

"When you say missing—" Piper started.

"Weeks," I replied. "Marcel said she disappeared on a supply run and hasn't been seen since."

"They don't know why?" Sasha asked. I shook my head.

"No, at least not that he's told me." Which could be a load of bull as far as I knew.

"Why haven't they come to me about this?" Piper demanded. Lightning flashed behind her, giving away her annoyance at the perceived slight.

Marcel's words came back to me. As much as I hated to admit it, maybe he had a point about no one wanting Katherine alive.

"It's witch business," I said, shrugging. "He didn't think you'd care—and Carissa doesn't want anyone involved."

They shared a look.

My skin prickled.

"Nat . . . how many weeks did you say Katherine's been missing?" Piper asked quietly.

"Three and a—"

I choked.

Piper's eyes turned sympathetic. Her expression softened.

"I guess we didn't need necromancy, after all," Sasha said.

As if the tension couldn't have been worse, Lucifer picked that exact moment to appear. He took a sweeping glance at the scene and lifted a brow.

"Oh dear. What did I miss?"

eleven

I SCRUBBED a hand over my face.

Whiskey burned a path down my throat, but I barely felt it. The warmth in my gut was little more than a numbing agent.

She walked away.

I knew there were good odds she would. Nathalie seemed like a woman who knew what she wanted. A woman with purpose. It only served to increase my attraction to her. Hell, her walking away increased my attraction to her.

No one ever turned me down, but instead of the bitterness I expected from it, I simply felt desire.

The only thing that cooled my longing was knowing there was nothing I could do, but even then, it was just barely dampened.

I told her I wouldn't pursue her if she didn't want it.

I may have been a liar in many other ways, but considering what I wanted with her . . . from her . . . I wouldn't break that promise to her. Not over this, at least.

But the sex . . .

I shuddered to think about it. About the way she came for me, and the *O* of her lips when she found release. About her intoxicating scent and the way it drove me fucking crazy.

There was very little I wouldn't give to taste her again.

That part I despised, because despite my best efforts to not get my hopes up, I had.

My sunling was more than one in a million.

She was the impossible.

My salvation wrapped in a sinful package of mortality.

Under different circumstances, I might have had an easier time shouldering her rejection because forever was a long time. I could wait. I'd waited this long.

But she was a witch.

She would age and die in another fifty years or so, if she were lucky.

Fifty years . . . it was nothing. Hardly any time at all to casually maneuver my way into her life. To bump into her just infrequently enough that she could write it off as coincidence.

My magic writhed within my veins, as if it were a living, breathing entity.

It was as though it could tell the debate I was having between being the man I wanted to be—the one who respected her choice to walk away—and the weak monster my insidious magic made me. The kind of monster that would stalk the city until I found her, then watch from the shadows, learning every piece of her life until I knew how best to insert myself in it so that she didn't turn me away.

It was tempting.

More tempting than I'd ever admit to anyone, except maybe Anders. He wouldn't judge me. Or maybe he would, but considering his own situation, he would know better than to cast stones. Glass houses and all that.

I swirled the amber liquid in my cup, staring into its depths for answers the alcohol couldn't give me.

To make matters worse, I'd only fed a very small amount. Enough to take the edge off, but not sate the hunger. I'd thought I would have hours with her. Time to *savor* her. To go so slowly she'd never question if she were safe in my arms.

But once again, reality tore her away.

Except this time, I'd had a taste of her and now my magic was craving it.

Craving her purity. Her untainted soul.

It was the first time in longer than I wanted to remember that I didn't get sick after feeding.

I groaned, draining the rest of my drink in one gulp. The heavy glass thumped against the tabletop. I ran a hand through my hair.

The door opened and closed. Heels clicked against the worn hardwood floors. I looked up, unable to strangle the hope that filled me.

It turned to ash.

"What are you doing here?" I nearly growled. Of all the people to walk into my bar, Sasha Loren was quite possibly the last one I wanted to see.

"I need your help."

I snorted derisively. "That's unlikely."

"And yet, still true," she said with a hard edge to her tone. It cracked like a whip, acting as a reminder as to who I was speaking to. How could I have forgotten the second to the Demon Queen of New Chicago, and my *mate*.

Not that I wanted her.

I'd sooner let an octopus fuck me.

I sighed, pushing away from the table to enter the private room I kept covered from prying eyes. I didn't hold the tapestry for her as I moved to take a seat on the small loveseat—purposely sitting in the middle and letting my arm drape across the back. I used every part of my body to exude an attitude of "don't fucking touch me."

The disapproving quirk of her lips told me she got the message, but didn't like it.

Too bad. I didn't care.

"What do you want?"

Her gaze heated, dropping to my lips for a second. The blood in my veins ran cold. My magic roiled at the very insinuation.

Mates were supposed to be our equals. Our other halves. The only being that could balance your magic—at least for most species. Our situation was no exception. But where she wanted the mate bond, both me and my magic couldn't stand her.

If fate were a person, she'd chosen wrong.

Sasha Loren was never meant for me, and I sure as fuck would never be hers.

"Well," I grunted. "What do you want? I have a bar to run." Her green eyes flicked back to mine, mouth twisting in disappointment. While my mate wore a tough exterior, she struggled to maintain it around me. It didn't help that I cut her down every chance I could get, but it was for her own good. I didn't love her. I didn't care for her. My magic wanted to rip her apart.

The mate bond alone made me protective enough to never touch her.

If I did, I'd end her.

And no matter how much I didn't like her, that wasn't a death I could stomach.

So I used cruel words and actions to force the distance, because if she ever acted on the desire I saw in her eyes, I wouldn't be able to stop myself.

"Tell me about your magic."

Her command was quite possibly the thing I least expected. I frowned. "No."

"August."

"Sasha," I responded mockingly. "You can't just come in here, tell me to jump, and expect me to ask how high." I lifted a brow, not amused by her tactics. She was used to getting her way. She was Sasha Loren, once the personal assistant to the devil, now the second-in-command to the ruler of the city. She had ambition in spades, rivaled only by her mean streak. The one I'd find myself at the business end of, rightly so, if she kept this up.

"There's been a murder," she started. "Well. Eight of them. The remains look suspiciously similar to . . ." She motioned to me, making her point known. My face blanched.

"You think I killed them?" I couldn't stop the disbelief from leaking out.

"I didn't say that—"

"You insinuated it," I snapped. "Let's see it. Show me the bodies."

I waved at her in frustration, and she dug her cell phone out of her back pocket. After a few taps, she turned it around to show me a dark alley with poor lighting. There was no mistaking the skeletons in black remains.

"This wasn't me."

"I know," she said, a hint of anger entering her tone. "I'm not here to interrogate you. I told you, I need your help. This isn't an exact match to what you can do, but it's the closest I've ever seen. I was hoping you might be able to shed some light on what I'm looking at."

My brows drew together.

"How would I know?"

She groaned in frustration, pinching the bridge of her nose. "Have you fed recently? You're being an asshole."

"You showed up here hoping I could tell you what killed these people because it looks vaguely similar to when I kill—something I don't enjoy doing—and you think I'm the asshole here?" I totally was, but the very insinuation irked me. "But yes, I have fed recently. Just this evening." Hurt crossed her face, but she buried it quickly. There was only one way an incubus fed.

Sex.

Never mind that I was toeing the line between sanity and going feral thanks to a brown-eyed witch whose magic and body made mine sing.

I might be cruel, but I wasn't that bad. Sasha knew to keep her distance, and I wanted to keep my little witch to myself.

"I get it. You don't want me here. The thing is, you answer my questions—or I'm going to have to let the Demon Queen know about this, and you'll be answering to her. I don't think I have to tell you how bad a spot that would put your brother in."

"Keep Rafael out of this."

"I can't," she snapped back. "He's on the council. He's bloodsworn to her. The queen never has to know about this, though. Tell me what I need to know so I can go about my business and find the one who did murder those people —before anyone else gets hurt."

My jaw clenched so hard it spasmed. Sasha may want me and our mate bond, but her ambition always came first.

It was a good thing. Except now when she used it to back me into a corner, as she rarely did unless it was because of her work.

"Fine, but you need to ask *exactly* what you *need* to know. I'm not playing guessing games here."

She dipped her chin in understanding. "What kind of magic do you have?"

"Spirit."

Her lips pressed together. "Don't lie to me," she breathed.

"I'm not," I growled.

"Spirit?" she questioned. "Really? Because I've never heard of someone with spirit magic leaving a husk of a person behind that resembles Groot more than it does a person—"

"Believe me or not, I don't care." My eyes flashed in fury, silver wisps of magic drifting up from my skin at the anger permeating inside me. "But ask your questions and then *get out.*"

Sasha's eyes narrowed, her black tail flicking behind her in annoyance.

"Fine. Spirit magic. How exactly does it work? What is it you do that kills them?" She crossed her arms over her chest, not expecting me to answer.

Little did she know, I wanted her out of here more than I wanted my secret kept. And maybe a small part of me hoped she'd be disgusted enough she'd stop looking for excuses to see me.

"I start to feed, but their magic is tainted. It's disgusting. I can't help the revulsion. My own magic lashes out, draining them of their magic and life force—which is why they look like *Groot*, as you said." I shrugged, like I was unaffected by the heinous act. "Taking someone's magic is akin to ripping their soul out. Their body fights it, which is why I end up pulling their life force along with it. Essentially draining them of every bit of life they have."

Sasha kept her response behind a closed mask of indifference, but the hesitance in her eyes when she saw the silver tendrils rising from my skin gave her pause.

"What do you do with it once you have it?" she asked quietly.

"Eat," I answered simply, choosing not to mention what followed. The hours of sickness. The retching. The purge.

I may be able to devour someone's soul, but I couldn't stand the corrupted magic.

Which made my little witch's purity that much more enticing.

"Okay, you have to be feeding to do this kind of damage. What would a witch need to do?"

I narrowed my eyes. A witch? "I don't know that a witch could do this," I answered. "I suppose anything is possible, but magic doesn't simply disappear. It has to be repurposed."

There were certain laws that governed the universe.

Magic could not be created.

Magic could not be destroyed.

But it could change form. Become something else.

"So a witch could use it to power spells?"

"Maybe," I mused. "There have been instances of it throughout history. It's common for them to trade for someone's life, but their magic? They would have to touch it somehow. Control it."

"A death witch couldn't?"

"Not any death witch I've ever met." Sure, they could kill someone to resurrect someone else, but the body and the soul were not the same. One was limited. The other, endless. "Then again, I've never known an incubus to be able to eat one."

She hummed, deep in thought. "What are the odds I could convince you to take a job from me?"

"Slim to none."

She frowned, not thrilled. "I don't want you to kill her. I just need someone that can get close enough to capture her. If she really can do what you can, there's not a bounty hunter out there I can hire who isn't signing his or her own death warrant."

I lifted my shoulders again. "Not my problem, Sasha."

"And when it's the Demon Queen who has to go after her and has her magic taken? When her mate ends the world over it?" she demanded.

"You're catastrophizing," I said. "Furthermore, this being your crisis doesn't make it mine. If she's smart enough to stay in power, I'd think she'd know better than to put herself at the mercy of a black witch after what happened to Lucifer."

Her cat irises thinned to almost invisible slits. "*Don't say his name,*" she hissed.

I swallowed, remembering that while Sasha Loren might be my mate and therefore weak when it came to me, she was also vicious as fuck.

Particularly when talking about her dead lover.

I nodded, accepting the warning for what it was. "My stance isn't changing."

"That's unfortunate," she said, hands clenched into fists. "I'll have to bring this to my queen, then, and she'll likely warn the council—because the last thing we need is another war breaking out. When she shows them the bodies, I have no doubt that Rafael will feel compelled to tell her about you, assuming she hasn't come looking for you yet. At which point, several *other* factions are going to have some very uncomfortable questions about some supernaturals that have gone missing over the years—only to be found later bearing a remarkable resemblance to the ones in the pictures, all of whom were conveniently enemies of Rafael." She lifted both brows, point made. I cursed under my breath.

"You wouldn't let them kill me," I responded.

She laughed. "I may not have a choice, August. With how you've treated our bond, I can't say it hasn't crossed my mind I might be better off without you."

The words would have stung if I didn't wholeheartedly agree.

She would be.

"It may not be you they want retribution against, though," she continued. "After all, it's Rafael who's in charge. I was forgiven my past because I wasn't the one calling the shots. I wouldn't put it past my queen to excuse you, and instead burn your brother alive."

My lips thinned.

I could handle a lot of threats. Her hatred was all I desired.

But to bring Rafael into this was unacceptable.

"Understand this, Sasha. I'm not a good man. I'm not a good mate. If you hurt Rafael, I will hunt you down. No one —not your queen, not your sister, not all the money in the world—could hide you from me, because I'm your mate. If he's murdered, I will end you. I'm fucked up enough I might even complete the bond before killing you, just to make your pain that much sweeter."

I smiled, showing my teeth. She couldn't hide her shudder.

"You're a bastard," she whispered. "A sick fucking bastard."

I nodded once. "When called for, yes."

She stood there, silent, our stare down nothing more than a battle of wills at that point. Minutes passed before she finally spoke again. "You have three days." Sasha pulled a bent piece of paper from her back pocket. "That's how long I'm keeping this a secret. At which point, history says she's going to kill again. I'll have to tell the queen, and whatever happens from there . . ." Her eyes went hard. Mean. I'd hit a nerve. Several, if I had to guess. "It's on you. The ball is in your court. Text me to let me know your decision."

"I don't have your number," I said, because anything else would just make the situation worse. She had me, and despite my threat, she knew it.

Sasha smiled, beautiful and cold. "I wrote it on the back," she said, waving the bent paper. "This is the witch I'm looking for, on the off chance you run into her . . ." She took a strangled breath and set the paper on the bar. "You don't deserve it. But I'd rather you didn't die. Not like that."

I didn't say anything, and she didn't wait for me to.

Sasha turned on her heel and left the opium bar.

I waited a few minutes before getting up and making my way to the minibar. I poured myself two fingers of brandy, picking up the picture she'd left behind.

Ten digits were scrawled in black ink.

I shook my head, peeling the paper back.

Shock rippled through me.

The glass slipped from my fingers, sending a good thousand dollars of liquor across the thin wood bar top and antique rug.

I didn't care. I barely even noticed as I stared down at

the face of the woman I was obsessed with. She couldn't have been more than twelve or thirteen, more a girl than a woman in the photo. Her hair was longer, and her left canine was slightly crooked. The dusting of freckles on her face was more pronounced.

But there was no mistaking the light brown eyes that stared back at me.

Nathalie. My sunling.

NATHALIE

THE PAGES FLUTTERED, a false wind blowing them. I held the book loosely in my hands. It was a physical manifestation of the alleyway, like all the tomes in the library of my memory loci.

Analytical Nat was busy scouring over every inch of the alley. She began to catalog things I saw in my initial pass but didn't register. Meanwhile, The Warden stood at the other end, watching us with a guarded expression. She didn't want me to get involved, not if there was even a chance Katherine had committed these crimes.

Surprising everyone, it was Caretaker who'd put her foot down, pushing the rest of them to take another look around the alley. She provided snacks, of course, bustling back and forth between each of my entities and fretting about us taking care of ourselves.

"The bodies are all facing this way. The spacing and angle implies they were trying to leave when they were killed."

"It makes no sense they'd run from Katherine," The Warden said.

"Unless she killed that one first and they got scared," Ann said, motioning to the one closest to me.

I sighed. "Kat doesn't have that kind of power."

Once upon a time they'd called her a prodigy.

Those days were long gone.

"She made a blood oath with a demon," Ann said. "Anything is possible after that."

I ran a hand over the book, the parchment so real against my fingers it was hard to remember that this was all in my head. "Let's say she did. Why? Kat may not be a good person, but she's not a murderer."

"Ugh," Bad Nat groaned. She reclined on the concrete steps that led up to a rusted door in a vacant building. "We know she did it. The Prime may not want to admit it, but if it looks like a duck and quacks like a duck, it's a fucking duck."

I sighed, tired of her antics as much as anyone else.

"I'm inclined to agree," Ann murmured, kneeling beside the body farthest away from me. "But without genuine evidence, it's not irrefutable."

Bad Nat rolled her eyes. "The timelines match up. The motive for her to run is there. She's disappeared and no one can find her. Why else would she do that if not to avoid being caught?"

"Why indeed," Ann said, eyes narrowed.

"Maybe she's in trouble," Caretaker said. "If they were running, maybe they cornered her, and Kat fought back. She might not have had a choice."

"And the other three bodies?" Bad Nat threw out.

Caretaker didn't have anything to say to that, instead offering Bad Nat a blueberry scone and tea. My poor-mannered personality shot a look of disgust at the tray.

"I asked for whiskey."

"I don't have whiskey."

Bad Nat threw her hands in the air and let out a curse. "We live inside her head, in a house that's akin to the Room of Requirement. You can conjure a greenhouse with exotic plants for Peace, and every kind of bullshit tea that Ann wants, but it's too much to ask for fucking whiskey?"

Caretaker's lips pressed together, and she walked away with a humph. Her long shawl dropped down to the backs of her knees, making her form frumpier and more shapeless despite the tense set of her shoulders as she exited toward the mouth of the alley.

"I'm going to the kitchen. Does anyone need anything?"

"A servant not from the Prohibition Era," Bad Nat muttered.

A chorus of "no thank you" sounded and she stepped out of the illusion, disappearing from view. "Has anyone seen Peace?" I asked, pacing the alley. "She hasn't checked in once since I heard about Katherine and the murders." The shadowed end was an abrupt brick wall, giving it only one entry and one exit.

"Greenhouse," The Warden said. "She's been up there, basking in her hammock, ever since you fucked the incubus."

"More like putting her head in the sand," Ann muttered. "She doesn't want to deal with Katherine or any of this." She waved a cleanly manicured hand toward the crime scene. "It's hard enough on her when you don't take time for you. She liked the incubus. She liked how he made you feel. It's easier for her to focus on that than deal with any of your family."

I nodded, more than familiar with the feeling than I wanted to admit.

"You know," Bad Nat purred, getting up from the stairs

to stretch in a particularly feline way. "You could just ask Lucifer."

"No," both The Warden and I snapped.

Bad Nat lifted her perfectly shaped eyebrows.

"If it is Kat—which, let's be honest with ourselves and admit it is—Lucifer could confirm one way or the other. He could tell you everything—"

"I said *no*." My tone was sharper than I typically used, even with her. "I'm not asking him. Not now. Not ever."

Bad Nat tsked, condescension written all over her face. "You're being obstinate for the sake of it."

I glared at her. "I'm being smart. His help is never free. There are always strings attached."

Bad Nat made a dramatic show of looking around. "Do you see the Prime anywhere? The one that knows how to make decisions? It seems that Stubborn Nat has taken her place."

I gaped at her. "That was uncalled for."

"It's honesty. Unlike the others, the purpose of my existence isn't to placate you. You're being an immovable ass because you're into him and don't want to admit it." She pressed her plum-painted lips together and tilted her head. Long straight hair fell over one shoulder like a waterfall, and she flicked it back with a shake of her head.

"Placate me?" I demanded. "No one placates me, they help me. But you are right about one thing. You are *not* like the rest of them. You're bitchy and mean."

She smiled like I'd given her the greatest compliment, spreading her arms wide.

"If that's what it takes to make you listen." She smirked, turning to Ann and The Warden. "Ann. You're logic. The most rational of all of us, correct?"

My very fact-based, emotion-lacking self looked up at her and narrowed her eyes. "Yes . . ."

Bad Nat looked back at me. "You in agreement?"

I bit the inside of my cheek, but nodded.

"Good. Ann, if we are questioning what happened here and how, is it not prudent to gather all evidence—especially a potential eyewitness account?"

I laughed, and it sounded just a little bit vicious and not like me. "Lucifer is hardly an eyewitness."

"He asked you months ago what you would do to know Kat's secrets. You didn't like what that knowledge would cost you, so you blocked him out and did your damnedest to ignore him. Look how well that worked out for you. Lucifer could be our greatest asset if you weren't being a damn hypocrite," Bad Nat said.

"He's a liar."

"He's a demon," she shot back, something like fire burning in her gaze. "Even dead, he's still bound by the laws of magic. If you made a bargain, he'd have no choice but to tell the truth."

I let out an anxious breath, glaring at her. "You know why I won't do that—"

"*Morals*," she said, using her fingers to make quotation marks. "That's a load of bull—"

"I won't become a murderer," I said, voice quiet with anger.

"But you'll let one walk the streets?" Bad Nat responded. "You'll wade through this blind while Katherine slaughters people left and right, all so you don't have to kill one measly soul—"

"It's playing god," I snapped. "I refuse to do that. Not only is it unnatural, but it's also illegal. Resurrection is a dangerous magic that can have horrifying consequences."

"You would know, wouldn't you?"

We all stilled. You could have heard a pin drop. Even the false wind seemed to quiet, sensing the storm brewing when Bad Nat pulled at the threads of something she had no business touching.

"To answer your question from before you two started arguing," Ann announced, breaking the silence. She stood up, brushing off her slacks. "Yes, it's prudent to collect all evidence. If she agrees to Lucifer's bargain, the results are more far-reaching and potentially could become an even bigger problem than the one we're facing—at least from the Prime's emotional standpoint. On the other hand, this isn't about morals. That part is a lie. While the Prime abhors killing, she would find a way to make it bearable."

"That's an assumption," I argued weakly.

Ann pinned me with a stern gaze as if to say, *you sure about that?*

"There's logic in killing one—a soul of your choosing—to get the answers needed. If it is Katherine, you'd find her before she can kill more. Is it more immoral to end the life of one for the better of all?" She posed it as a rhetorical question, but I answered anyway.

"It's an assumption that it's for the better of all."

"You'd gamble with a child's life when you could just as easily kill someone who engaged in the skin trade, or child trafficking, or pimping out unwilling blood donors?" Ann had me there, and she knew it. Unlike Bad Nat, she didn't gloat. She just shrugged. "It's not a moral dilemma. It's a matter of consequences."

Bad Nat shot me a look that said, *you see what I mean?*

"And you?" I rasped to The Warden, mouth dry and voice weak. "What do you think?"

Her expression was deeply troubled as she took the

three of us in. We were so vastly different. Me, Ann, and Bad Nat.

Ann wore her suit like armor, freshly pressed and free of wrinkles. Her heels were black and simple. Walkable, but still giving her height enough to convey an unspoken threat. *Boss bitch: do not mess with me.*

Bad Nat had donned platform Doc Martens today with her black skinny jeans and leather jacket. The black sports bra underneath showed off her toned stomach.

Then there was me. Somewhere in between.

Blue washed jeggings and a loose maroon sweater made of cashmere. I wore the same Doc Martens, but paired it with the blazer from Ann's suit.

Caretaker dressed so plainly in comparison, but it wasn't her clothes that mattered here. The rest of us used them to make subtle statements and intimidate in one form or another. The Warden wore yoga pants and sneakers, not a trace of makeup on her face. It was her eyes that showed her true nature. Always watching. Always guarded. She was fierce without a mask, and perhaps the truest form of any of us. Except maybe Peace.

"They're right," she said, her brown eyes pleading with me to not dismiss her. To understand. "I am your strength. Your protection. Your sheer will—which is why I won't lie to you even though it galls me to agree with *that one* on anything." She thrust her chin toward Bad Nat, who shrugged. "Kat is the biggest suspect, and rightfully so. She's cutthroat. Cruel. We all know this. That was before you left, and she had years in a black coven that will have shaped her. We don't know what she's truly capable of—but murder is most likely the least of it. I think we need to find out once and for all if she did it—they are right about that—but Lucifer isn't the only way. There is another option that doesn't require you to make a deal with the devil to resurrect him in return for answers." She paused, giving me a chance to get angry with her. To act defensive over her truth. Out of all my entities, though, it was The Warden I trusted the most.

Ann lacked emotion in making choices. Peace lacked logic. Caretaker was too kind for her own good sometimes. Bad Nat . . . well, it went without saying.

The Warden defied that all because she was my strength.

I closed the text that held this memory and the alley faded back to the immense library where every moment of my life was stored.

"I'm listening."

MARCEL

I STOOD OUTSIDE THE WINDOW, watching her without being seen.

Her brown hair was braided back and then spun up in a bun my fingers itched to unravel. Her slight frame was so still. Unnaturally so, but not for her. She liked to play at being "normal," clinging to the ordinary as she pretended to be just a weak witch. I knew better. I'd always known better, even when no one else saw it.

Her gaze was focused forward, but unseeing. The tea in her cup had gone cold minutes ago. Around her a waitress bustled between tables, checking on customers who wanted refills for coffee, tea, and cake. She didn't stop at Nat's, though. Not once since she sat down and ordered.

I suspected my sunbeam was a regular here, for the waitstaff to not grow concerned or uneasy during the prolonged periods of inaction.

It spoke to how comfortable she'd grown that she did it out in the open. Years had passed, and while she was still the same at heart, parts of her had certainly changed.

I chose that moment to go to the door. Bells chimed as

it swung open. Nat blinked, clearing the vacant gaze from her face that she no doubt wanted to hide. Little did she know I'd been watching for a good twenty minutes before deciding to make my presence known.

Her lips flattened together but the corners of her mouth tugged up. Barely. Not quite a smile, but I'd take it.

"Marcel," she greeted, motioning to the chair across from her. A two-foot wood table was all that sat between us. I disliked it, but I wasn't going to voice that. Not yet. She'd called this meeting, no doubt to tell me she'd decided to help.

Nat was many things, a bleeding heart included. She may have hated me, even hated her sister, but she wouldn't be able to stop herself from joining me in the search for Katherine. Bad blood or not, Katherine was her twin. Not to mention her psychic bondmate, even if the bond wasn't completed.

"Nathalie," I responded, lowering my voice.

She froze when reaching for the tea bag, clearly recalling the way I used to say her name while we hid between the stacks of her parents' library, and I fucked her like a man possessed.

I took my seat and rested my elbows on the table, hands loosely extended out. Her own were only inches away. Once, she would have grabbed mine and kissed them. Now she looked at me like dirt she couldn't quite get out from under her nails.

I hid my wince.

She resumed lifting her tea to her lips, drinking it despite the tepid water. I lifted a brow when she tried to suppress the shudder that went through her.

She hated cold tea. I wondered why she was forcing herself to drink it now. It irked me I couldn't ask, not without showing my hand. Nat would go on the defensive if I did, and possibly change her mind about working with me altogether.

I wasn't willing to risk that.

Not for Katherine, which I was fine admitting to myself, but for Nathalie.

"We need to talk," she said, setting her tea back down with a clank.

"I gathered. Unless you were inviting me here for other reasons?" I lifted an eyebrow again, and she flushed.

"No," she said with a little too much force. I believed she meant it. For now. "There have been . . . developments. I have some questions for you, regarding Katherine."

I nodded slowly, grabbing the fork off her plate of untouched German chocolate cake. I cut off a mouthful and brought it to my lips, trying and failing to hide my smirk at the way her eyes tracked the movement. I chewed slowly and finished it off by draining the rest of her tea.

"See something you like, sunbeam?" I took her napkin and dabbed my mouth, clearing any crumbs away. She blinked and jerked back as if she'd been slapped.

"No. I was just appalled by your lack of manners. Who eats another person's cake—before they've even taken a bite—then drinks the rest of their tea?"

The kind of person who knows she's too stubborn to order hot tea and will swallow that swill down, simply to not say it in front of me.

"I worked later than I realized today and missed lunch. I'm hungry. After having me come all the way into town, the least you could do is feed me."

Lie, and a lousy one at that, but she didn't call me out. Instead she nudged the tiny tray toward me and continued on. I was disappointed by her lack of reaction. She was even harder to rile than before. I had my work cut out for me.

"Tell me about Katherine's magic."

I blinked, tilting my head. I'd expected questions, but this wasn't one of them. "I'm not sure what you're looking for. You already know everything about her magic."

She didn't respond immediately, seeming to contemplate my response.

"When Lucifer died, she lost a great deal of it."

"I'm not hearing a question."

Her eyes flicked between me and the cake I wasn't eating despite insisting I was hungry, annoyance coloring her light brown eyes. "How much did she lose?"

My brows drew together. "Fuck if I know."

Nat huffed in exasperation. "Guess."

"I don't know. Really." I scrubbed a hand over my jaw, leaning back in the chair. My leg brushed hers as I extended it to stretch. Her expression remained unflappable. I hated it. "She wasn't afflicted like Carissa. No aging or new health problems like most of the population. I wouldn't have thought she was affected at all if I hadn't walked in on her attempting a summoning . . ." I probably could've stopped before mentioning that.

"Attempting a summoning," Nat repeated, pushing me to continue.

I sighed. "She wanted to speak to the Morrigan. She never told me why. She just lost her shit that I saw the attempt . . . and her subsequent failure."

She looked away, her eyes turning guarded.

"Failure," she murmured softly, but the word was filled with menace. "Such a delicate way to say murder."

"The girl didn't die," I corrected. "Katherine wasn't even strong enough to get her to the veil."

Nathalie's gaze snapped to mine. "So she suffered significant magic loss—and yet she was able to wield spells I've never seen when she all but demanded the blood oath from Piper in return for loyalty."

I shook my head, opening my mouth to answer just as the waitress popped up. "More tea?" she asked Nathalie.

"Please, and another slice of cake."

She bobbed her head, fire engine red curls bouncing with her. "Anything for you, sir?"

"He'll have a cup of oolong with a teaspoon of honey. No milk or cream," Nathalie answered for me. She didn't mean to; I could tell as soon as her cheeks darkened a fraction. Our waitress didn't notice, remaining oblivious to the growing tension between us.

"Anything else?"

"No, thank you," we both answered.

"Perfect. I'll be right back." She walked back to the kitchen with a bit of skip in her step, leaving us with our memories and the consequences of our past choices.

"Back to Kat—"

"You remembered my order," I said at the same time. The way her lips thinned again told me she'd rather drop it.

"I remember *everything*," she said flippantly. I knew she was referring to her eidetic memory, but the tone used was a tad too bitter for it to ring true.

"Me too," I said softly. She blinked, staring at me with distrust.

"That's not what I meant."

"I don't care."

Nathalie laughed in exasperation, without joy or amusement. "It seems we're in agreement there." It took a second for her words to settle. When understanding crossed my face, she continued. "Now. Katherine. I saw her use magic to try to pressure Piper into completing the blood oath with her. Where did that come from?"

I shrugged, dropping it for the moment. "I have no idea what you're talking about. Until she did the blood oath with Bree, Katherine was nearly powerless. She was desperate for a way to change her circumstances, which is why she hastily agreed to Piper's sister instead."

Nathalie groaned in frustration. "Fine. Tell me what you know about this."

She pulled out her cell phone and hit a few buttons, then turned it around for me to see.

Skeletons surrounded by some sort of black substance like coal lined the alley. The lighting was crap, making it impossible to pinpoint where this was, only that the picture was taken at night.

"Never seen this," I said, flipping through the pictures. Up close I could tell the black outlines were actually remains. Whatever happened to these people had incinerated everything, but left their bones untouched.

"So you know nothing about those bodies?"

"Other than what's in these pictures, no." I kept scrolling through the phone until the photos ran out. Part of me hoped she'd kept some of her, but I should have known she wouldn't. Nat hated having her photo taken. Always had.

"Any idea how they ended up that way?"

"An idea? Maybe. I can guess, but that's the best I've got for you." She nodded, waving for me to continue. "At first glance, the most logical thing would be fire. Except the close-ups you took showed a lack of cracking or scarring. Whoever they were, fire didn't do this. No other elemental magic likely could. While lightning is possible, if it were strong enough, the results are too consistent for that to be the case. Not even the greatest magic used would replicate that."

She nodded along, like I was saying things she already knew. "Whatever caused it essentially left the bones untouched but decayed the rest of the body so thoroughly it's practically coal."

"Right," I agreed. "Which leads me to believe that whatever did this drained all life from them."

She narrowed her eyes, a look I'd come to know meant she was putting together two and two. I just didn't know what that equation meant for her.

"Not many things can do that to the point of fossilizing someone," she said.

She nodded slowly, waiting to speak again as our waitress came out bringing our teas and another slice of cake. Nat pulled out her wallet and typed in the amount owed before extending it. Our server pressed the tip of her device to Nat's, the ends turning red. When they both pressed their thumbs down to signal the approval, the ends turned green, completing the transfer. I ate another bite of cake while Nathalie handled payment.

"I don't know of a supe that could do this," I said honestly. "My guess would be a demon."

She predictably rolled her eyes. There weren't many of them, and the ones that were around, she was well acquainted with. "Neither Piper nor Ronan would do this."

"Bree?" I questioned. While I was inclined to agree from what I knew about the former two, Bree was another matter entirely. As Katherine's second, I may have sworn a blood oath to Bree, but that didn't make me blind to her ways.

"Hasn't been seen in months. Unless you know something I don't?" She lifted an eyebrow, eating her cake. I shook my head.

"I haven't seen her since that day."

She nodded, expecting as much. "I could be wrong, but I would bet a large fraction of my fortune this isn't her. Bree doesn't hide her brutality. If she murdered them, we would know it's her. She'd be walking on their graves in designer heels."

I snorted. "Yeah. I don't know her well, but that sounds about right."

"That does bring up an interesting point, though . . ." She chewed for a minute, lost in thought, then swallowed. Her eyes cleared and I pretended not to notice she disappeared there again, albeit briefly. "Is it possible for a witch to use someone's life force and magic to fuel their own?"

I considered her, wishing I could see inside that mind of hers. There was more here than she was saying.

"Theoretically? Yes. Practically? Doubtful. Not even the sacrifices the Pleiades Coven used to do rendered results like this. They killed their victims, but the body remained untouched unless it required a blood sacrifice, in which case they slit the throat."

"They were using lives as payment for the magic. I'm talking *life force*. The very energy that separates us from a rock. Cells that are living in our blood and muscles and tendons—"

"Bones are living," I pointed out.

"The remains were hard, but brittle. Perhaps the bones had maintained shape, but are also brittle," she murmured.

"They weren't blackened, though."

"No," she agreed. "But I didn't think to break one open at the time and see what the inside looked like—that's a theory for later. The point is, it's possible. What do you think the odds are that Katherine did it?"

My fork slipped. "Kat? She wouldn't hurt—"

"We both know she's hurt people for less," she said, eyes heavy. Her peach-colored lips tilted into a frown.

"Hurt, yes. But kill? She doesn't do that without a purpose. What purpose would this . . ." I trailed off. Nat nodded once. "She took the blood oath with Bree. Even if she could do this, and was killing for that purpose, she doesn't desperately need it anymore. She's strong again."

Her fingernails drummed against the tabletop, distracting me. "These deaths started three and a half weeks ago."

Fuck . . .

Did Kat do it?

Now I wasn't sure. The timing was damning, and given we couldn't find her by scrying . . . "I still can't help asking why? Let's pretend she did—which I'm not sure I buy, but I can see why she's a suspect—why kill for power when it means she has to run? No matter how much she might get, the Demon Queen could end her with a thought, and she couldn't even fight back because of Bree's blood oath. She may not always think things through, but that would be irrational, even for her."

Nathalie nodded as if every point I presented she'd already worked through. The possibility made me sit back in my chair and level her with a look.

"You don't think she did it."

She didn't even pause in her drumming. "No, I don't, and neither do you."

"Then why all the questions?"

"Two reasons." She gesticulated with her fork as she

took another bite of cake. "I had to figure out how much you knew—"

"Again, you could have been direct and asked."

She laughed, then took a sip of her tea. "I'm sorry, but you seem to think I trust you. That can't be right. You already know I will *never* trust you again when it comes to telling me the truth."

"Never is a long time—"

"I'm not finished," she said sharply. I blew out a frustrated breath. "I had to read your reaction. I may not think Kat did this, but not for a second do I believe she isn't somehow involved. There are no coincidences. Her disappearance lining up with the timing for these murders is . . . Let's just say, we aren't the only ones looking for her anymore."

Shit. "Piper's involved?"

She nodded. "And Sasha. And pretty soon the entire council if she or the person who actually did this hasn't been caught."

If that was the case, it wouldn't be long before the entire coven was dragged into this.

"Will they kill her?"

Nat shook her head. "Unless they have no other choice —like if they find out it's her using magic that does this. In which case, Sasha won't hesitate to slit her throat. And for the record, I wouldn't blame her."

Gone was the soft, sensitive girl my sunbeam used to be. In her place sat a woman with too many shadows in her eyes. I had myself to blame, partly. Some were Katherine's fault. Some belonged to their family.

"So what's your plan? How are we going to beat them to her?"

She set her fork down and took a long sip of her tea. She

released a happy little "mmm" before placing the cup back on the saucer.

The serene expression on her face and neutral tone didn't match her answer.

"We aren't. Well, not directly. We're going to do a summoning." She slowly opened her eyes, and I could have sworn that a hint of the gold I knew she had in her peeked out. "Where there's smoke, there's fire. Katherine is good at not being found, but somehow, she's connected to these murders. We're going to summon each and every one of the dead souls to find the *actual* murderer. Katherine will follow."

She was utterly brilliant, but also insane.

"While I admire your forethought, you missed one minor detail: Piper *banned* necromancy and I'm bound by that."

She waved her hand like the Demon Queen's law didn't matter. "You can do it. I'll have her retract that command on you. Leave Piper to me."

While the calm confidence turned me on, there was still another matter that posed a problem. One I suspected would be a challenge for me.

"I don't have another witch with death magic, let alone a coven to do this. Carissa forbade me from getting help, and despite her lack of power, the rest of the Ouroboros Coven does listen to her."

Nat looked at me like I'd gone crazy. "That's not a problem because I'm going to do it with you."

My lips parted.

The very idea of me sending her into the veil to speak to the victims' ghosts . . .

No. *No.* It didn't matter that I'd done dozens of summonings. It didn't matter that necromancy was my specialty. It didn't matter that I'd never once lost a soul in the process.

"Absolutely fucking not."

She blinked, seeming shocked at my refusal. "I wasn't asking."

"Doesn't matter. Unless you find another witch or warlock, I'm not doing it—and you can't hold a summoning without me. You have to have a black witch with death magic for that."

"Why?" she demanded. "You're being completely irrational about this, so please tell me why you're refusing on the basis that I'm the one to enter the veil."

I narrowed my eyes at her. "You know why."

She laughed once, sarcastic and cold. "That's not a reason."

"It's all the reason you'll get."

"Don't get overly emotional about this," she argued. "I know what you're capable of. I'll be fine—"

"I won't risk it," I said. "I don't care about the odds. They're too high. I'm all but daring death to snatch you from me—"

"You don't have me," she snapped. Gold flashed in her gaze. I'd missed seeing it more than I would ever admit to anyone except myself, but now the sight made me feel bitter. Whatever progress I might have made would go up in flames with my refusal. "Dead or alive, we are *nothing*. Not now. Not ever. You blew your chance and now you're being a hypocrite because I know for a fact you've put Katherine in the veil before."

Multiple times. Kat had also done the same with me. Before Lucifer's death and her loss of power, Katherine and I were the strongest death witches of the age.

I resented that now and wished I could've seen it three years ago for the curse it was.

Back then I'd thought I could have everything. That I *deserved* everything.

Just to have the only thing that truly mattered ripped away from me.

But I couldn't change time.

"You're right." I scooted back in my chair, standing up. "I am a hypocrite. I'll own it. I've done it a dozen times with Katherine—but *she's not you*." Losing Katherine, however unlikely, wasn't something I'd relished the idea of, but I could live with it. I could breathe through that grief. Losing Nathalie . . .

"Find me another witch, or find another way."

fourteen

NATHALIE

"THAT ARROGANT, NARCISSISTIC—" I ranted, my fists hitting the handheld punching mitts Sienna sported.

"Watch your form," she instructed, ignoring my diatribe. "Make sure to pull the power from your hips, not your arm. You'll mess up your shoulder swinging like that."

"—piece of shit!" I grunted, following through on her correction as I slammed my fist into her right mitt. The force made her hand recoil a couple of inches. While that wasn't something to write home about for most people, it was a massive improvement for me.

Sienna was supernaturally faster and stronger than I could ever hope to be because of her dual cat shifter and succubus nature. Most supes were, witches being the primary exception. That I made her hands move at all was a good sign my hours of training weren't for nothing.

"Good," she praised. "You're really improving." A timer went off, signaling the end of our session. I dropped my hands to my sides, tired to the bone but still fuming over Marcel's refusal.

"It's too bad punching him in his stupid, smug face wouldn't make him do it," I griped. Usually I considered myself above those kinds of things, but desperate times called for desperate measures. Two days had passed, gone in the blink of an eye as I stewed over his response.

To add to my frustration, not even a whisper of Katherine was found. I had dozens of people combing the streets for her, and so far, the only thing they'd been able to report was a whole lot of nada.

"His face is too pretty to punch," Sienna said, tossing the mitts aside for one of the trainers to clean up when we were done. As part of my stipulations for funding the creation of a gym that supernaturals could train at in a safe, non-life-threatening environment, I had one of the rooms to myself for Sienna to train me whenever our schedules permitted. "I'm sure there are other things you could do to his face that might make him agreeable—"

"Nope," I popped the *p*, shaking my head vehemently. "Not happening. That ship has sailed."

Three years ago. It had been a one-way voyage to disaster.

Sienna sighed. "One day you'll tell me what happened there."

"There's not much to tell." I shrugged. "Boy meets girl. Boy befriends girl. Boy gets betrothed to girl. Despite hating the tradition, girl falls in love with boy. Would you like to guess the ending?" My wraps fell away as I unwound them slowly.

Sienna planted herself on the mat across from me and started stretching. "He fucked up somehow."

I snorted. "That's putting it mildly."

"I believe it," she nodded, her black hair falling into her face as she grabbed her sneaker and leaned over her leg, touching her nose to her knee. I plonked down where I stood, copying her actions. "You still have feelings for him. You're not the type to shove things down for the sake of being difficult, like some other people we know."

I chuckled despite myself. "I loved him a lot. More than anyone. And he betrayed me so badly . . ." My voice trailed. "I wish I could hate him. It would be easier. I think the only person I really hate is myself for falling for him to begin with."

"Ew," Sienna said, sitting up sharply. "Don't start that self-pitying stuff now. I already get enough of it from Sasha."

I doubled over in mirth, gripping my stomach. Gods. She shouldn't make me laugh after putting my ass through the wringer for two hours. Everything *hurt*.

"Fine. Maybe hate isn't the right word, but I am frustrated by my bullshit radar and how it let him past my defenses. He said all the right things and I ate them up, then asked for seconds. I was just so stupidly in love with him that I ignored all the warning signs." I shook my head, as if that could clear it.

"Ah, young love." Sienna smiled kindly. "If it makes you feel better, everyone has to fall stupid in love at least once. It's a rite of passage growing up."

I smiled back, but it didn't reach my eyes. "What about you? How did you fall stupid in love?"

"Which time?" she mused with a grin.

I blanched. "How many times were there?" Sienna stretched her long brown arms over her head, using her hand to grab her opposite elbow and pull it back. The muscle beneath her lithe frame glinted with light perspiration beneath the fluorescent lights. Something about being a succubus just made her sexy all the time, even after a sweaty workout that left me closely resembling a tomato.

"Seven," she admitted after a long pause. The slightest blush touched her cheeks. "What can I say? When I fall, I fall hard."

I scratched my head. "I'm both surprised and not."

Sienna dropped her arms and bent a knee, resting her elbow on it so she could prop her head with her hand. "What do you mean?"

"You wanted a kid without wanting to find a baby daddy. That's how you got Hallie. That doesn't scream hopeless romantic. It shows how practical and independent you are." She nodded along, silently waiting for me to continue. "But you also had a rough childhood. You were sold in the skin trade and got lucky that Lucifer purchased you. He raised you, and you ended up falling for him, but he wasn't as . . . enthralled by you," I hesitated with the last part, not wanting to hurt her feelings.

"You think my childhood trauma and desire for love made me this way?"

"I do, but I think our trauma shapes all of us, no matter what it is," I said, making sure she understood it wasn't only a Sienna thing. "But to counter that, your childhood also built you into a smart and capable woman. Everyone's gotta have a flaw, you know?"

She laughed, the sound like tinkling bells. "Thanks for trying to ease that one. I suppose it's only fair after I pressed about Marc—"

"Ah," I said, cutting her off.

She laughed and thinly disguised it as a cough. "He-who-shall-not-be-named."

The corner of my mouth tugged up despite my better judgment.

"He doesn't deserve that nickname. Voldemort was awful, but he didn't betray anyone he claimed to love. He just betrayed his peons—and they were fuckwits for the most part."

Sienna huffed a laugh. "Fair enough. Missed opportunity for the author if you ask me. Could you imagine the toxically amazing relationship he could have had with Bellatrix? He totally could have been my daddy—"

"Nope, nope, nope." I scrunched my nose up at her and shook my head. "Not my kink."

Sienna shrugged, her plum lips curving into a grin. "Pity."

We got to our feet and went to the ladies changing room to shower and change. The sun was below the horizon by the time we made it back out to my car. One of the streetlights flickered, and I made a mental note to call a guy about that in the morning.

"You good if I swing by the Lucky Dragon on the way home? I don't think I can stomach Mist's cooking after that workout."

"Go for it. I'll run in and grab food for us too. Hallie was asking for the skinny noodles the other night, but I was too tired to go get it and Sasha was out late."

"The night of the murders?" I asked quietly. She nodded.

"I didn't want to leave the apartment after hearing about it . . ."

"I don't blame you," I answered honestly. "I'd be lying if I said I wasn't looking over my shoulder a lot more right now. I know Sasha thinks it's Katherine, but I'm not convinced. I wish Marcel wasn't being so stupidly hard-headed about this because I'd breathe easier knowing who and what I was dealing with."

"You and me both," Sienna murmured. "I wouldn't be as concerned if this were six months ago, but I have Hallie now. If something happened to me . . ." She shook her head. I got it. She was everything to her little girl. Mist may be her Angel, but Sienna was her mama—and no one came close to that status in her life.

I parallel parked next to the Lucky Dragon. Instead of getting out of the car right away, I grabbed Sienna's hand and squeezed her fingers. "If anything ever happened to you, she would be loved and taken care of. Know that."

Her eyes watered and she flashed me a sad smile. "I know. Thank you."

We hugged, saying nothing more before we got our takeout. Loaded down with steamed vegetables, rice noodles, orange chicken, and egg rolls, we headed back to our building in a comfortable quiet.

Where her twin, Sasha, was a great compliment to my best friend, Sienna was one for me. She led with her head, but her heart was there too. She practiced kindness where she could, and she loved fiercely. She was practical as my assistant, but also the friend I needed at times when I didn't know how to say it.

When we got to the building, she hesitated to go inside. I stalled, waiting for her. "Everything okay?"

"Yeah, I just . . . hear me out. Marcel won't do the spell with you and he's probably not going to change his mind; not with his reasoning being based on emotion. Have you considered asking Lucifer if he can find those victims?"

I balked. "You know about him?"

Well, shit. I told Piper about my ghost problem but hadn't brought it up to anyone else. Especially Sienna, for obvious reasons. Like her once being stupid in love with him.

"Yeah. It wasn't exactly hard to guess when Hallie asked me about the guy with glowing eyes that was always talking to you." She pressed her lips together in an apologetic smile. "If it makes you feel better, she didn't know she was being a narc. She can't tell the difference between ghosts and the rest of us from what I've figured out." That didn't bode well for a number of reasons for the toddler siren, but that was a later conversation.

I sighed. "Have you told Sasha?" My teeth nibbled the inside of my bottom lip, aggravating the tiny sore I perpetually had from the bad habit I turned to when anxious.

"No," she shook her head. "And I told Hallie not to worry about him. Just ignore it. I knew if I told her not to say anything to Sasha, she would have run her mouth right away."

I nodded. "Yeah, that sounds about right."

"So," Sienna drawled. "Lucifer is haunting you. He's in the in-between. Piper and Sasha can't see the dead. A psychic may not be able to find the victims, but another ghost? I bet he could hunt them down and ask them about it."

She wasn't wrong, but it was also the very thing I was trying to avoid.

"He'll ask for something in return that I can't give him."

She lifted both eyebrows. "He wants to be brought back?"

I jerked like she slapped me. "How'd you know?"

"He's dead," she said. "Not much else a ghost could want from a witch."

That was a fair point. I groaned.

"To bring him back, I'd have to kill someone, which I'm not exactly pumped about. And even if I could get on board with that aspect, he's a large part of the reason our planet is fucked up. He spread magic all over the place, and as a result of that shared magic, a bunch of people died when he died. Not to mention the crap job he did at ruling New Chicago before Piper—no offense." I grimaced, realizing that may have come across as an insult to her since she had been more than just a lover. She was also his assistant at the time.

"None taken." She shrugged. "Like I said, we all have to fall stupid in love at least once. I just didn't learn my lesson. It's not my place to tell you whether you think he deserves to be brought back or not—"

"I don't want to play god," I said, needing her to understand my reasoning. "It's not that he doesn't deserve it. It's also not that he does. It's that I shouldn't be the one making that decision. It was wrong that he died as he did, but that wrong doesn't cancel out the wrong of killing someone else for him."

Sienna lifted both hands. "You don't have to explain yourself to me. I do get it. All I'll do is pose a question. If you're not the one making that decision, who is? I really doubt he'll give up. Given my toddler can see ghosts, I'd guess there's a significant portion of the city that can, even if it's not a lot in terms of actual numbers. He'd only need to find *one* with shitty scruples who'd be willing to make a deal—and they may not be as choosy with who they sacrifice."

I hadn't considered that, and it cast the whole situation in another, albeit unpleasant, light where taking the moral high road was becoming more an excuse and less a legitimate reason.

"But," Sienna continued, "when it comes to bargaining with the devil, I might know a thing or two that could help you if you're trying to get around that."

I sat back, considering her offer. She had a good point. She had been his assistant, after all.

If I couldn't convince Marcel, I wasn't willing to enter the veil with anyone else in control. I may be insistent on getting to the bottom of this, but I wasn't suicidal. He was the best and the only one I'd let take me there. Without that possibility, Lucifer was my only other option. At least as far as the ghosts were concerned.

"Tell me everything you know."

Sienna smiled. "The first rule of making a bargain with Lucifer is to make him think he won." All right. I could see that; very typical alpha male bullshit.

"That doesn't surprise me. He's got a powerful personality, and it's a rather acquired taste."

Like tequila. Or jet fuel.

"The second rule is that you have to accept that he will take more than you bargained for. No matter how many parameters you put down, he will find a loophole. He was alive a *long* time, and he was making deals through all of it. He's very good at getting what he wants. You have to accept that, or you shouldn't be making bargains to begin with."

I frowned. "That seems to be at odds with the first rule."

"Only if you choose poorly, which brings us to the third and most important rule." The way she paused told me everything I needed to know. If I didn't care for that second one listed, I really wasn't going to like the final.

"The devil may be *the* demon of desire, but desire doesn't always mean sex. Lucifer loves making people part with their true desire, whatever that is. He wants their secrets. Their truths they bury. You have to convince him that whatever you give is a sacrifice worth your soul."

 fifteen

AUGUST

HER PICTURE BURNED a hole in the pocket of my jeans. I walked the dark streets, clinging to the shadows. While I could focus on my surroundings and listen for whispers in the alleys, it didn't stop my thoughts from racing.

Nathalie.

The scent of her arousal and the feel of silky skin beneath my hands . . . the taste of her.

I shook my head in an effort to clear it from my mind.

The picture I'd been given was her face, but every part of my magic fought against the very notion that she could have been the cause of those murders. The way her magic lingered on my tongue . . . it wasn't tainted. It wasn't evil. There was a purity to it that I hadn't ever experienced. Black magic didn't taste like that.

I knew better than anyone.

Sasha claimed to need my help. It was one more desperate attempt to be in my life, and she had me by the balls when she threatened to pull my brother into it. A part of me questioned if she'd do it. She held on to a glimmer of hope that I would accept her one day. If she followed through and my brother suffered the consequences of my actions, deep down she knew that hope would die, and I don't know if she'd be willing to let it go. She was ambitious and ruthless. She was also hardheaded and refused to accept my rejection.

Still, here I was, tracking in the dark streets of New Chicago in an effort to keep her the fuck away from me and mine. It was one of my specialties. Tracking. Remaining anonymous. Invisible. Those I stalked and interrogated were so distracted by sex and pheromones, they'd forget my face by the end of the night, never realizing the predator in their midst.

I didn't worry about the dangers lurking in the shadows.

I was one.

When you could charm people into talking, they had no problem spilling everything they knew. Even with that, it took longer than I expected to get what I needed. Interview after interview, showing off the picture Sasha had given me, and I could only glean bits of information about her. Nothing settled me until I finally gained the knowledge that allowed me to breathe: Nathalie had a twin.

I hadn't expected that.

That dangerous little thing called hope resurfaced, daring me to think about her as mine.

So I scoured the streets in search of her, but also looking for the scent of decay laced with dark magic.

I would never tell Sasha, but the times I had pulled a life from someone, what remained of them had a distinct smell. A scent that could only be described as empty. Lacking. Hollow.

The bodies in those pictures were the same. No meat or

substance. No flesh. Just husks. There would be a scent to it, if you knew what to look for.

And I was right.

I'd caught the faint aroma on the wind, heeding it but still keeping my distance.

The scent of char and emptiness strengthened, pulling at my senses.

A building stood before me, and I questioned if I was right. If my tracking had led me to the correct place.

Of course this building would have those dead and dying. It was a hospital. I cocked an eyebrow, glancing around to gauge my surroundings. Nothing seemed out of place as I entered the building and headed to the elevator bay.

A woman passed me, looking up from her clipboard while she headed to the front desk. Her eyes roamed the length of my body and a flush crept up her cheeks. She pressed her thighs together subtly, no doubt feeling the effects of the magic I pulsed around me.

Remember sex.

Remember what you felt around me.

Forget my face.

The scent of her magic was weak, and it begged to soak up mine.

"Could you help me?" I asked, using a honeyed voice as I strode toward her, pulling the picture from my pocket.

"Yes," the woman responded, her breathy one-word answer coming out in a slight shudder. If I didn't tone it down, the weak vampire was going to come on the spot. I reined in my magic so she could concentrate and be of use to me.

"I'm looking for someone. It's an old picture, I'm afraid, but I was wondering if you've seen her here. Maybe in the last few hours?" Unfolding the picture, I held it up. Her face gave away her disappointment upon hearing my inquiry.

She pouted slightly, but still smiled. "Sure did, lovely."

"Are you certain?" My chest constricted.

She nodded. "Hard to forget a pretty face like that, you know?"

"That I do," I murmured. "Can you point me in her direction?"

"She left an hour ago, but I'm happy to give you whatever it is you want from her," she said, her tone changing with her offer as she cocked a suggestive eyebrow. Her body leaned into mine, sending me the clear signals that she'd be happy to take me into a closet and let me fuck her until she forgot what day it was.

"Another time, perhaps," I whispered, pushing my power around her form. Her eyes fluttered closed, and her mouth parted on a tiny gasp.

I took the opportunity to slip by while she had a brief moment of fantasy, and when she'd open them, she'd wonder what had just happened.

I took the stairs, following the unmistakable scent as it permeated the air, completely undetected by anyone else, until I came to a patient room.

And the source of the smell.

Two charred husks lay on the floor next to the hospital beds. If they had souls, they were long gone from this world. There was no doubt it was eerily similar to what my own power could do if I took it too far.

Turning around, I inhaled deeply, searching for the one thing I didn't want to find. Relief flooded me. The woman downstairs had said one of the twins was here, but there wasn't a trace of Nathalie in this room. I would know my sunling's scent across the realms.

While I surveyed the crime scene, I flipped through the possibilities in my head. There were only two supernaturals that would be capable of this, and it wasn't an incubus. It was still a scent of emptiness, but it was all wrong. This was new to me. There was a desperation to it. An evil. A muted odor deeply hidden behind the blackened dust that filled the room. It was . . . familiar. So similar yet still distinctly different. Like it pulled at a memory that was just out of reach.

"Katherine," I guessed quietly, scrunching my nose when I saw the torn curtain around the window. A struggle. But these two souls didn't have a chance.

My stomach churned, tasting the poisoned magic in the air, and I turned to leave. Now that I had the scent, I could follow it.

The problem was, the moment I hit the street, there was no trace of it left. I scanned the sidewalks, searching for another hit of the sickly aroma, but I came up empty.

Pulling out my phone, I hovered over messages, considering if I should call it in. Changing my mind, I tucked the phone away, and put my hands in my pockets as I walked against the wind that cut through the buildings downtown. I'd give it some time to see if I could find the scent again.

Ultimately, I didn't care about investigating. It wasn't Nathalie they were looking for, and that was what mattered to me. Sasha could fuck off. The bodies weren't going anywhere.

sixteen

NATHALIE

THE DOOR CREAKED. *My purple paisley blanket flew to the side, pulling my hair over my face in the process. I sputtered, snapping the book closed between my knees.*

"Oh god, are you seriously reading with a flashlight under your covers?" Prudence said derisively. Her platinum blonde hair was straight as an arrow and fried at the ends, even though she swore it was all-natural. She wore a short-sleeved dress and patterned tights. Cute. Chic. Basic. Prudence dressed in what her mother gave her. The perfect barbie doll—much like Carissa in that sense. The similarities stopped there. Carissa was cruel and actively tried to hurt me. Prudence was just thoughtless and didn't care. She was used to the way our parents' coven treated me, but she bullied me less because of Kat. It was a weird rela-tionship, but if someone was going to find me, I was better off with it being her or my twin. Anyone else would be awful, except maybe Marcel.

"Where's Kat?" I grumbled, holding my flashlight canted at an angle so that I could see both Prudence's face and the door. I wasn't too worried about the girl in front of me, but if others followed, as they sometimes did, I'd pay for it. Prudence may not

usually treat me like shit, but she wouldn't stick her neck out for me either. Her mom would snatch her up so fast if she got caught defending me. No, the only person she ever stepped in for now was Kat.

I had no one in my corner except my twin, and I tried to ignore that stinging reality. It wasn't Prudence's fault her mom sucked any more than it was my fault for being born weak, but it still hurt when I let myself think about it for too long.

Ann said there was no point in being upset about it. It was the way of the world, and the sooner I accepted that, the better. Rage didn't agree with her. They fought a lot.

"Worried about you, as usual," Prudence said, smacking her lips as she chewed bubble gum. It was incredibly annoying, and reminded me of a cow chewing cud, but I kept that to myself. "She insisted we look for you since 'mommy and daddy' have guests visiting for Yule. Wouldn't want anyone to wander off and find our little black sheep all alone, would we?" Her annoyance was typical but it still grated. I hid for this very reason. I didn't want anyone's pity any more than their ire. I just wanted to be left alone. "Kat's been freaking out for the last thirty minutes while you're holed up in here like a loser reading."

I rolled my eyes, making the choice to not take her ribbing personal, even though Rage very much did. "Well, you found me. Tell her I'm fine so you can go back to the party, and I can get back to my book—" I went to open the pages and the worn paper slid from my fingers. Prudence dangled it over me, out of reach. I didn't bother trying to reach it. She was nearly six feet tall at fourteen. I had six months on her and ten inches less. The difference might not seem that big, but when you added arm length, I was tiny in comparison.

I think she hated it. Her height. Mine.

When we were kids, she complained none of the things Kat and I wore were in her size because she was too tall. Then the boys made fun of her, since they were all runts until this year. They ignored me for the most part because of my name, and Kat's terrifying abilities. She took it personal when anyone went after me. That didn't stop Carissa or the older kids of coven members, but most of our peers left me be.

Prudence didn't like that. She was jealous of our relationship. She couldn't understand how a 'norm' like me got off easy. The comments became fewer and further between as we got older, and I stepped back into the shadows while Kat thrived under the spotlight with Prudence at her side. I thought she'd gotten over it because I 'let' her win.

I guess not.

"What are you reading that's so important . . ." Her words trailed off as she started to skim the page. Her pasty white cheeks turned pink as a red flush crept up her neck. "This is basically porn."

"Give it back."

"Where'd you get it?"

I chewed the inside of my cheek. She might not be the worst person to find me, but she was still a narc. I couldn't let her find out about the girl I met downtown. Claudia was human. Her mom worked at the library part-time. She switched out my book every Tuesday when I went with my dad to the auctions. He thought when I disappeared for a while that I was off learning about the different kinds of supernaturals and humans you could buy—not that humans were worth much, according to him. In reality, I was meeting with Claudia behind the building where her dad worked as a blood donor. She switched out the romance book for another and I gave her seeds I collected from the greenhouse. To me, they were nothing, but to her, they were the difference between starving and providing for her family. If Prudence learned about her, I wouldn't get to go to the auctions anymore.

"Doesn't matter. It's mine," I asserted, mostly for Claudia. I worried if my mom found out, she'd be able to trace it back to her. My spine tingled to think of what she'd do. The fear made me bold. "Give it to me—" I tried to grab it and she lifted her hand with ease, putting it out of reach.

"Tell me where," Prudence insisted, then licked her bottom lip. It was a reaction she had when excitement filled her. It told me this would get carried away very quickly if I kept pushing for her to give it back. Ann told me to back away. That a book wasn't worth it.

But Rage . . .

She was getting tired of backing away. Turning the cheek. Letting it go. She reminded me of what happened to humans that displeased my family. What would come of Claudia if my parents found out about our little arrangement.

Little, the tiny five-year-old version of myself that existed with me since I was a kid, took in the situation with a slight frown on her face. She didn't like confrontation because confrontation hurt. She was a coward. A child.

I told her to go away.

It was mean, but she made things worse. It was hard enough handling Rage and Ann . . .

There was another one now. She had showed up in the last few weeks. They called her The Warden.

I liked her.

She was nicer than Ann or Rage, but wasn't such a baby like Little. She was strong. Confident. The Warden encouraged me to trade the seeds and read what I wanted. She told me I was worth more than my magic or name. That all I had to do to not be like them was choose to be different.

I was pretty sure I loved her. I definitely wanted to be her.

"Come on, thing two," Prudence whined. "Tell me where you got it, and I'll be on my way." She liked to call us that. Thing one and thing two. Kat was one, because she was first.

First in Prudence's eyes. Born first. Stronger. The best at everything.

I didn't mind because it kept the spotlight off of me.

"I found it in the library," I lied.

Prudence laughed in my face. "Nice try. Dolores would never let us read something like this. The only books in that place are stuffy, old journals from dead people and grimoires."

She wasn't wrong. They were interesting enough reads too, but since I'd already read and therefore memorized them all, I broadened my horizons.

With romance.

The first time I went to the auction I saw Claudia reading a book with a man's chest on it. I went back a week later, and she had another one. I approached her and asked about it.

That was eight months ago. We've been trading books for seeds since then.

"Well, that's where I found it," I shrugged.

"If you don't tell me, I'm going to tell your mom that I caught you reading this during lecture."

Fear made me slow down, every person in my mind taking notice. I worked through over eighty scenarios in seven seconds.

"You do that, and I'll tell Kat."

Prudence flushed red with anger. Her pale skin turned splotchy. "She won't believe you."

I tilted my head, lifting a brow. "She won't?"

The uneasy expression that crossed her face made me feel like I was on cloud nine. I felt powerful, for once. Sure that power was only because I relied on my twin to back me up, but it was something.

Using her distraction to my advantage, I arched back and launched up, using the little bit of spring in the mattress to grab the edge of the paperback. It slipped from her hands, back into mine. I held it against my chest, then crossed my arms over it as

I backed away. There wasn't enough space and Prudence knew it.

"Just let it go, Prudence. Kat never has to know."

Prudence laughed. It was loud and mean. Like her. "You know, actually, I think you might need to learn a lesson, thing two. Kat's always here to shield you, but she isn't now, is she?"

A damp sweat broke out along my skin. The clammy cold made me shiver. "Even if it feels good now, I will tell her, and she won't forgive you. Walk away while you still can."

Prudence continued to laugh, letting me now just how much danger I was actually in.

"Unbelievable." She shook her head. "I haven't even done anything, and you're threatening to what? Ruin my relationship with Kat? You two may have been close when she was younger, but all you are now is a burden." She shook her head at me in disgust. "For years she's been putting herself between you and your mom. Playing the perfect daughter so they won't look too closely at the biggest failure the Le Fay house has ever put out."

I swallowed hard, moving to the side. She sidestepped easily, blocking me.

Rage and Ann were having an all-out brawl in my head. Tables flipped, food thrown, windows smashed kind of brawl. The Warden was trying, and failing, to break it up.

"Please, Prudence . . ."

One corner of her mouth tugged up. "That's better, but I need to know the lesson sticks. You've got a horrible habit of forgetting things once Kat's around to be your guard dog. She deserves more than that. We both do."

The door behind her opened.

Another figure stepped into the room.

I frowned. My heart raced in all-out panic.

"Me and Broderick here had a little chat. He's going to stop pursuing Kat because I'm going to put a silencing ward

on this room and let you two get to know each other." She smiled, her crooked front tooth giving her an even more malicious look.

I shook my head slowly. Ann was silent, working through our options as she went limp and stopped fighting. Rage was flying off the handle on the verge of burning the loci to the ground. Little sat in the chaos crying. Wailing. I wanted to slam my head against a wall and silence them all.

The Warden took my hands. She grounded me. Gave me strength.

"This is wrong. You know it. Broderick is a creep and a bully. Also like three years older. If he does anything to me, it's rape. Do you really want that on your conscience?"

She made a gagging noise. "You're so overly dramatic. Broderick promised me he wouldn't do anything down there." She waved to my lower half. "He just wants to have a little taste of that Le Fay blood. See what makes you, a norm, feel so superior. Just close your eyes and hold out your hand. It'll be like seven minutes in heaven . . . just not."

I frowned. "You can't be serious? Teach me a lesson with sexual assault? You're a fricken idiot if you think I won't just tell Kat but also my mom. You know my virginity is being saved for whoever I end up betrothed to. I may be weak, but you're a Glen. You're nothing." I lifted my head, trying to pretend I was stronger and braver than I was. Originally, this was about keeping Claudia out of my mom's hands. I wasn't sure when it had escalated so much. "She'll kill you for getting in the way of tradition."

"Nothing?"

She blinked, taken aback. Shock and rage filled her expression. Broderick stepped up beside her. "Hey, Prudence, look, I want to tap that but it ain't worth the Le Fays coming down on us if she won't go along with it—"

"Quiet!" she snapped at him. Her brow furrowed as a scowl took shape. Her blue eyes turned to chips of ice.

My strong façade fumbled.

Prudence took a step toward me, and I took a step back. "You just can't stop, can you? Nathalie Le Fay, the girl born with everything but magic. They handed you a silver spoon and you didn't even have to earn it. All because of your name. All because your sister will protect you." She shook her head. "I won't kill you. I'm just going to silence you and ruin that pretty face. Then no one will want you, even with your name. Kat will stop protecting you and focus on me. Everything will be just as it should be."

Her eyes began to glow as she chanted softly. I recognized the spell for what it was.

A binding.

She was going to take my voice, and I didn't just mean for whatever seven minutes in messed-up-bullcrap game she wanted to play. She was going to Ursula my ass, just like in The Little Mermaid.

I opened my mouth to scream for help. The consequences for what I'd been doing weren't as bad as what she was going to put me through.

Then the strangest thing happened. The room began to glow.

At first it was a soft, golden light, but then it grew. Brighter. Harsher. No longer soft, but instead blinding.

Prudence kept chanting, but her voice quieted. Her brows puckered as she took in the same strange phenomena that I was, and a roaring of blood running through my veins drowned out her casting.

I couldn't understand what was happening. My brain didn't process it at the same speed of reality. All I knew was that I was terrified, and that fear was all-consuming.

Prudence's magic was a noxious Pepto-Bismol pink, and

that magic dropped from her like sweat, as much her essence as anything. For most of our lives, it trailed off her skin in ribbons or floated like glitter, highlighting the difference between us.

Because even though I could see magic, I could never see my own.

If anyone asked me what color it was, I wouldn't be able to answer. I didn't know.

But now that horrible pink magic was pushing against her skin, pressing into her flesh, and trying to claw its way back inside like a cornered animal. It wanted to get away. I could only assume it wanted to escape the golden particles that were encroaching on it.

Prudence's magic slid beneath her skin, disappearing from view entirely before gathering in her chest and slowly rising back up her throat. The ball of pink was no greater than that of a golf ball. It was small but compact. Completely opaque, whereas magic usually looked like a colored smoke I could see through.

I didn't understand why it was rising from within her, traveling up her throat and forcing her mouth open to escape as if pulled by an invisible string. I couldn't grasp why it was floating toward me like a divine offering that I had no idea what to do with.

So I stared at it, dumbstruck.

The door to the attic opened again.

"What's going on?"

The gold light blinked out. The pink sphere hovering inches in front of me drifted back to Prudence. The roaring quieted, and silence reigned.

My twin, Katherine, was here.

She looked around the room at Broderick, Prudence, and me. "Nathalie? Prudence . . ." Her voice trailed as her best friend began to shake, then collapsed to her knees.

"I'm out of here," Broderick said, ducking around her and

out the door. She didn't stop him, instead bolting for Prudence who was devolving into a blubbering mess. Tears streaked down her face as she gasped wildly, voice hoarse.

"What did you do?" Kat looked at me just long enough to glower before turning back to Prudence. She got down on her knees beside her and put her hands on her shoulders. "Hey, hey, it's okay—" She broke off abruptly as Prudence threw her arms around her, squeezing tight.

Over my twin's shoulder, she looked up at me.

Eyes dry despite her wet cheeks.

Hate exuded off her instead of fear.

She was faking.

Rage riled further and I tried to retreat from the attic and get away before I said—and did—something I would regret.

The door slammed shut, only feet from me.

The lock clicked despite no one standing there.

I turned slowly, keeping my book close to my chest as I faced my sister and her lying butt nugget friend.

Kat pulled back from Prudence, eyes darting between us and narrowed with distrust.

"She tried to bind and take my voice," I said, motioning in her direction. "Then she was going to let Broderick use me for 'seven minutes in heaven' so I'd learn a lesson. She's fricken crazy, Kat."

I grunted, gritting my teeth in frustration when she didn't say anything. The doubt was right there, front and center.

"Then how did she end up like this?" Kat asked after a suspended moment.

"She's faking it."

Prudence sniffled louder and I rolled my eyes, hands clenched so tight my knuckles were white. "Really? She doesn't sound like she's faking it. What's gotten into you? Why are you being like this?"

Hurt slashed through me, cutting any confidence that my twin would believe me. "She found me. I was reading, minding my own business. She was the one that took my book and tried to blackmail me—"

"I'm sorry, Kat," Prudence said, leaning her head against my sister's shoulder. "I asked thing two for help with Broderick since he was all over you at the party tonight. I didn't think she'd be this upset. It's my fault. I wasn't trying to cause issues between you two . . ."

Kat turned her light brown eyes from me to her. The tension drained away from her shoulders and her face softened. "I told you I'd handle him."

"You're already under so much pressure with your mom. I just wanted to get him off your back for a little bit."

Kat sighed in contemplation.

Fury tore through me, swift and sudden. It sparked like embers catching fire and the flames rose in seconds. "Stop lying!" I snapped.

Kat's expression hardened. "It was a misunderstanding—"

"No, it wasn't," I insisted. "She's a liar. A two-faced, manip- ulative, bitchy—"

"Cut it out."

"I can't lie to you!" I shouted. My heart was breaking over far more than this single moment. It was trust. It was respect. It was everything. "I literally can't lie to you, but you're believing her when I'm telling you she was going to have me assaulted. What the hell, Kat?"

Indecision warred in her expression. A trickle of doubt formed when she looked at Prudence and then me. We may not have been as close as we once were, but there was one irrefutable truth between us.

We couldn't lie to each other.

No one knew if it was because of our unnatural birth—that

we were stillborn and had to be resuscitated—or because we were both twins and psychic bondmates.

But there was no denying Kat and I had a unique connection. Which was probably why Prudence wanted to take my voice away. Except something went wrong, or right, depending on your point of view.

Ann urged me not to speak about what happened, but Rage was out of control. Fueled by the tears of Little, who'd run upstairs to the attic in my memory loci, she spat at Ann and slammed her against a wall. The Warden grabbed her around the waist, but Rage threw her head back, breaking my favorite personality's nose.

"Please don't be angry with her," Prudence said to me. She turned, the picture of authenticity. If we hadn't all grown up in the viper's den, I might have wondered how she could be so two-faced. We were all liars because our parents. They taught us to lie to each other, to other families, other covens. How to tell a falsity but have it technically be the truth. I hated it. This life I was born into. I knew I should be thankful because I had food on the table and shelter and didn't have to be a blood donor or worse. But sometimes all the lying and scheming was too much.

The only one I could trust was Kat.

Or so I'd thought.

"I'm the one that messed up. I'm so sorry if it came across like that, thing two. You know I love you like the sister I never got, and it pains me to think you thought I would ever do something like that."

I didn't realize I was walking until I stood in front of her.

My hand stung, and a red mark appeared on her cheek.

The faint echoes of a crack became thunderous.

But did she show her true colors?

No. She didn't.

Prudence let her eyes water and stepped back, lifting her hand in surrender like I was the aggressor. The liar. The bully.

"Nathalie!" Kat yelled.

I couldn't control myself.

Ten minutes ago, I would have run, but now it was like a demon had possessed me, and all I could do was try to show Kat that Prudence was the fraud.

Not me.

I launched at her, hands clawing, teeth snapping, trying to take a piece of her for the irreplaceable one she'd stolen from me.

Glass shattered.

A cold wind rattled the floorboards.

Kat stepped between us, power lifting her hair on end. Dark blue magic flooded her pores. Her eyes glowed with a dark light as she commanded, "Enough!"

In my anger, my rage, my fury—I couldn't control the golden light that flooded the room. But I knew without a doubt when it happened again, it wasn't my eyes playing a trick on me. It wasn't some kind of coincidence.

Once had been a strange but fortunate thing.

Twice meant I had magic.

It meant that the gold light now encroaching on Kat, that was overpowering her dark blue witchcraft, and was taking control of those deadly glass shards that whirled in the air—it was mine.

I stopped in my tracks, hyperventilating as panic took over.

Sure, I knew I had magic. But it was barely anything. Certainly not enough that I'd ever seen its color.

But this . . . I squeezed my eyes shut and tried to will it away.

To force away the screeching wind and bitter cold and the treacherous glass shards.

To push the fury as far from me as I could.

To stop it all.

I cracked an eye open, and what I saw broke something inside me.

Cuts lined Kat's skin. Her face and arms were sliced in dozens of places. Her throat was crimson, and it spilled down her white Yuletide dress, bathing her in blood.

So much blood.

A new kind of panic took form.

A wet gurgle slid from her lips. She choked, clutching at her own throat.

I watched, like a living statue, unable to make myself move as horror overtook me. My twin collapsed on the attic floor and bled to death.

I stared and stared and stared—

"DO SOMETHING!" Prudence screamed, breaking the bubble of shock that had frozen me in place. I jerked, slipping on the blood.

Prudence had her hands pressed to Kat's throat and blood poured from the wound beneath her fingers. Kat had already gone still. I crawled on my hands and knees to her other side, and put my face to her chest.

Silence.

No pulse.

No movement.

Kat was dead.

I understood that intellectually, but emotionally I was so far gone I didn't stand a chance at processing. In the moments between seeing the blood and her dying, something clicked on my head. Or off, depending on how you looked at it.

A sort of numb, calm settled over me where emotion didn't have a place.

Ann and The Warden took over.

My logic and my protector.

They did the job I couldn't do.

So I did the one they couldn't.

They controlled me while I retreated into the loci and wrestled with Rage. I went head-to-head with her, letting her have it because this was her fault. Kat died because of her. We lost control because of her.

Logic couldn't stop her.

Protection couldn't hold her back.

But I could cage her.

So I did.

In the attic, where Little was curled in a ball, I dragged her forcibly by the hair, kicking the door open when I reached my destination. Glass floated around the room, golden light lit every corner with its insidious and chaotic intent.

I pushed her inside with a single look of disgust and slammed the door.

A lock formed where there wasn't one, with a key that only I had.

All it took was a click and turn of metal gears for that part of me to be closed off. Permanently.

Outwardly, no one would ever know the difference. Prudence didn't. Then again, she was so lost in her shock and panic that I was the last thing she paid attention to. It was a mistake on her part. They always say not to trust the quiet ones.

There's a reason for that.

I moved around her, forming the circle while she cried. I didn't need salt or a candle for this spell. I just needed a living, breathing person.

My book lay in the puddle of blood, crimson soaking its pages while I used my twin's life source to contain her best friend.

It never occurred to me that Kat wouldn't forgive me.

Even if it had, I still would have done it.

It was the only way.

My sister. My twin. My everything—for her lying, backstabbing best friend?

It wasn't even a question.

I'd never thought of myself as a sociopath, and I still didn't. I just learned that when I completely snapped, my others were capable of taking control. Of doing what I knew logically needed to be done, without feeling a thing.

I didn't wince when I stabbed Prudence in the throat with a piece of broken glass. It cut my fingers, which worked just fine since resurrecting my twin would require my blood too.

I didn't flinch when her blood spurted, and body jerked

I didn't care when she collapsed on top of Kat and died in the same messy way my sister had.

I just couldn't. There was no room for that sort of emotion, even if deep down, becoming a murderer stained my soul.

I didn't cry as I sat alone in the dark and chanted so quietly, not even a supernatural would be able to hear me over the screeching wind. I didn't move when the single digit temperatures made my fingers stiffen and then freeze entirely.

I didn't stop for a break—not for a single second of the longest night of the year. Not when Kat's life was at stake.

To resurrect the dead, you had to give the living.

All magic came with a price. Prudence paid mine.

So even with chapped, bleeding lips, frostbitten fingers, and a throat so hoarse I couldn't talk for two weeks after—I chanted. The ritual to bring the dead back to life was arduous because of the intensity it required from the summoners. The sheer stamina it demanded to not only kill another living being, but to then hold vigil throughout the night. To sit in the blood of your sacrifice, chanting the sacred words to some dark god in hopes he would return the spirit you seek.

My vigil was the longest seven hours of my life. But when the sun rose over the horizon, Kat breathed. She lived. And another piece of me died.

Prudence's life may have paid the price the spell demanded, but I paid the price for killing her best friend to save her.

Cold chilled me to the bone.

I blinked into the moonlight, noticing the cracked window that let a faint breeze through. It felt amazing on my sweat-slicked skin, but I knew with complete certainty I hadn't been the one to open it.

"You were having a nightmare," Lucifer said quietly, appearing out of the shadows. His white hair was combed and styled, not a strand out of place. His suit was missing its jacket, and the sleeves were rolled up to his forearms, white brands on display and glowing faintly.

"So you opened the window?" I pushed sweaty strands of hair off my forehead, pushing the past as far from right now as I could manage.

He shrugged, walking from the dark corner by my door and across the length of my bed, his eyes trailing over the things I left strewn across my long dresser. "I couldn't wake you, so I opened the window. The cold air did the job."

I swallowed thickly, hoping he couldn't see it.

That was an oddly thoughtful thing to do.

I didn't like it. No, that wasn't quite right. I did like it, but I didn't trust it. Lucifer was as much a manipulative twat in death as he had been in life. I had to remember that.

Even if the way he looked at me made my skin flush.

My cotton T-shirt clung uncomfortably, but I didn't want to strip out of it with him here.

And yet, I didn't tell him to go away.

"Your telekinesis got stronger."

He stopped at the end of my dresser, in the slim row between it and the end of my bed. Without lifting his hand, he made the window shut, flipping the lock. "That's a strange way to say thank you."

I bristled, but he wasn't wrong. "Thank you," I murmured. "For being a creep who watches me while I sleep. Next you're going to tell me you glitter in the sunlight."

He lifted a white eyebrow at me, and I couldn't tell if he was amused or not. "Unfortunately not. The best you'll get from me is my body turning into a reflector at night, I'm afraid."

I chuckled against my better judgment as I thought about our differences. I tanned a nice bronze shade in the summer when I could. Something told me that wasn't the case for Lucifer.

"That's a pretty lame superpower," I said, sitting up in bed and letting my sheets pool at my waist.

Lucifer gasped in mock outrage. "I can open windows and read shitty romance books too."

"Poorly," I scoffed.

"Oh no," he said, smiling just enough to hint at the savagery I sensed beneath his beautiful facade. "I've been practicing. I think you'll find my skills more than adequate in that department now."

"Prove it."

Crap. The words flew out of my mouth before I could think them through. Analytical Nat was throwing a book at me from the confines of her library, while Peace was poking her head out of her greenhouse, far too curious about the dangerous game I was playing. I blamed it on the shit sleep.

Clearly, I was out of spoons at the moment.

Lucifer cocked his head. Without even opening a book, he started to speak.

"He pushed me back, putting the bulk of his weight on his

hands that were still on the deck. My back hit the cool stone tiles, and I stared up into a dark and stormy sky while he worked his lips down my neck. Kissing. Sucking. Nibbling—but not biting. His fangs stayed clear of piercing my skin, true to his word. He moved down my chest, pausing at my bra."

Jesus. Christ. He wasn't joking. The hard stare he leveled at me as he spoke did nothing for my mask of control. Especially when his eyes tracked the same parts of my body in time with his words.

"Slowly, he dragged his teeth down the slope of my right breast, fangs catching on the lacy fabric. He tugged it down over my hard nipple and under the curve of my breast, pushing it up more. Then he turned to the other and did the same. 'Much better,' Ezra purred."

"You switched books," I commented, my voice coming out rougher than it had before.

Lucifer smirked. "I related to dear Ezra a tad better. Elias is disgustingly good," he scoffed. "But if you prefer, I've memorized a good portion of his book as well."

"Just the sexy parts, or the plot too?" I asked, trying to distract myself as much as I was him. It was criminal how attractive his voice was. A ghost should not be able to turn me on so easily.

"The plot?" he questioned. "That is the plot."

I pursed my lips. "So the answer is no, then—"

"I've memorized the entire book," Lucifer interrupted. "Even the *pretend* plot that's really just the bread masquerading as a carrier for the smut's butter."

I snorted. "So typical. Do you hold such disdain for all books or just romance, because the genre focuses on a happy ending for women and not just using them as a tool to aid some male savior with a hero complex?"

He squinted at me. "Most genres, to be fair. Science

fiction is just a shitty attempt at fantasy where the magic can be explained. Murder mysteries are boring when I don't consider murder a sin. Horror is a dramatized version of my reality and shit I had to deal with before I died."

"What about fantasy?" I mused. "There are a lot of different kinds. I like paranormal romances, but there's epic fantasy and urban—"

"Epic fantasy reminds me too much of the Otherworld," Lucifer said, speaking quietly. "I don't exactly miss it, but I don't like the reminders, either."

The Otherworld. Hell. The realm where all magic and demons originated. Lucifer was one of the first to come to Earth, but far from the last.

"I've heard it's beautiful," I said in a neutral tone, trying to feel him and this conversation out.

"Beauty is in the eye of the beholder, little witch."

A warm flush crept up my chest and heat pooled in my belly. I bit the inside of my cheek.

Back to safer ground. You know better than to stray with him. Give an inch and he'll take a mile.

"What about urban fantasy? It's a bastardized form of reality, but tends to stay away from romance. Think Jason Bourne meets *Supernatural*—"

"I know what urban fantasy is and it's *so blockbuster*. The male leads tend to be self-absorbed but portrayed as perfect. It's disgusting."

I snorted, and it devolved into a full laugh. That he didn't see the similarities between the "male leads" and himself had me rolling.

"So blockbuster," I repeated, choosing not to go the route of insults. I wasn't in the mood for that sort of verbal sparring tonight. "Okay, Mr. Book Critic. Is there a genre you *do* enjoy?"

He seemed to consider it. "Paranormal women's fiction."

"Bullshit."

He chuckled. "In all my long years, I've found it's women in their prime who are most capable. Make no mistake: a woman in her forties has no fucks left to give. There are always exceptions to the rule, but a woman wronged who then finds her own way? It's a tale as old as time, and yet never the one told until this century. The novelty of it amuses me."

I picked at nonexistent lint on my sheets. "That's a better answer than I expected."

"Why?" he questioned.

I shrugged, feeling the conversation slipping into less carefree territory once more. "You have strong opinions about books."

"That's not a reason."

"You're judgmental," I said.

He shrugged. "I've seen a lot. Let's just say that if I ever had faith in anything resembling humanity, it would be long gone. I spent most of my life in charge, where making those snap judgments was all that stood between me and some asshole trying to steal my throne."

I tilted my head, taking that in. "That sounds like a miserable existence."

"It was, and it wasn't," he admitted. "There were bright spots. I chased from one infatuation to the next and at the time, that was enough."

"But now?" I prompted, leaning forward and licking my bottom lip before biting it. It was an unconscious action.

"Now?" he asked, looking around like he must be seeing something I couldn't. "I can hardly classify what I'm living now as anything more than existence. If I had to define how

I felt about it, I suppose miserable is probably the closest word there is. I long for more; not for what I had, but for what I wish I *could* have."

I turned, looking away because it was too hard to continue staring at him. There was a question on the tip of my tongue. I wanted to know the answer more than I cared to admit.

I was still debating whether or not to ask when he spoke again. "What about you, little witch? Are you enjoying your existence?"

The casual answer of "I'm good" threatened to pass my lips, but I swallowed it back down. He'd been honest with me on several things where he didn't have to. While he hadn't answered the one question that plagued me, it was only because I hadn't yet asked the question. He'd given me his truths, so my own truth was something I could part with.

"I'm content."

Not happy. Not sad. I was satisfied.

That should be enough. Plenty of people would be thrilled to simply live a satisfied existence.

So why did I feel so empty sometimes?

"I have really amazing friends," I added after a moment. "Two adorable nieces and a nephew. My businesses are thriving. Mist is recovering. The house I'm building out by Piper's place is almost done, and—"

"Those are all great things, but they don't speak to the real question. Do you *enjoy* your existence?"

Yes. No.

Fuck.

I bit the inside of my bottom lip again. "Sometimes." Part of me cautioned against admitting truths to the devil. The rest of me . . . we understood what he claimed he felt far more than we led him to believe. "Sometimes I wish for . . . more."

I didn't look at him after that.

I couldn't.

Call me a pansy; I'd own it. But I feared what I'd see.

So instead, I laid back down in bed. I calmed my breathing.

"Thank you for waking me from my nightmare," I whispered.

"Always, little witch."

I pretended to sleep, but the real thing never came.

NATHALIE

THE FRYER LET OUT A HISS.

I ducked to the side, avoiding the inevitable oil spritz that came from making fried chicken. While tasty, it was a messy process, and I wouldn't have bothered with it if it were just Mist and me.

"Dinner's almost ready!" I called, not really yelling. It's not like I needed to go looking for anyone, despite the nearly six thousand square feet that was my best friend's mansion. Everyone except me had super hearing—even the kids.

Three toddlers rounded the doorway. Hallie's wings flapped, sending a few light brown feathers across the kitchen. Her black hair streamed behind her, longer than it had any right to be. Behind her, Orson wore a giant smile on his face while he chased her. His color-changing eyes went from pink to yellow as he stopped and sniffed the air.

"What's for dinner?" he asked, licking his lips.

His sister, Honor, disappeared and then reappeared, sitting on the counter beside me. She leaned over the fryer, inhaling deeply. "Mmmm, smells like—"

"Hey, not okay," I scolded. "You know you're not supposed to sit on the counter." *Or teleport*, but only one of these was worth arguing at this point. I grabbed her by the waist and set her on the ground, then dusted the breadcrumbs off the medieval Viking dress I bought for her a few weeks ago. She frowned up at me and stomped her foot. The demon brands that ran up and down her entire body changed from yellow to red.

All demons had brands, and most even changed colors. Not like Honor's, though. The kid was a walking mood ring from the seventies.

"Don't even think about it," I said, sticking my finger out at her. Red meant angry, which usually signaled the start of a temper tantrum of epic proportions.

Where Orson had a pretty calm and happy disposition, Honor's emotions tended to change with the wind. Her lips pressed together, a deep scowl forming between her eyebrows as colorful magic started to gather around her.

"What's going on in here?"

Piper's voice broke the tension and Honor deflated. "I was just trying to help Auntie Nat," she whined.

Little liar.

"Uh-huh," Piper said dubiously. I gave her a look to let her know Honor was full of shit. "Why don't you guys set the table?"

Dishes appeared on the walnut dining table along with napkins and utensils, each set themed after a different Disney princess.

Piper groaned.

I was starting to regret getting them a TV that had all the oldies downloaded.

"Honor," she sighed. "I said set the table, not conjure up dishes—"

"But I did set the table," she argued, making her way toward Belle, who was her favorite princess ever. At least this week.

She liked Belle because Belle liked books and then fell in love with a beast.

She thought that was *so romantic*.

Meanwhile, both Piper and I hoped that wasn't an indication of what her love life might look like one day. On the other side of it, we had Hallie and Orson, who were atma and atman—demon soulmates—even though Hallie wasn't a demon. Orson was attached to her side, and it was getting worse the older they got. While right now they were just the greatest of friends, at the rate the terrible three grew, it would only be a year before they were teenagers.

That was a scary thought.

I left Piper to deal with her reality-manipulating toddler while I pulled the chicken from the fryer and plated it. I loved them to pieces, but both my nieces and nephew were a handful. I didn't plan on having kids, but being around them had made me acutely aware of how much I enjoyed being able to do what I wanted, when I wanted.

Sasha appeared in the kitchen a moment later. "Need help with the food?"

"Please," I said, shoving plates across the long island so she could put them where they needed to be. Once the food was out, I started rounding up drinks, knowing what everyone was going to ask for by memory, save Sasha and Anders. They traded off bringing expensive wines from all over the world for the two of them to share.

One by one, the table filled up as Mist took a spot at one corner. She came to most Sunday dinners now but was still quiet and reserved during mealtime for the most part. It made Hallie's night when her Angel was here. Hallie took her seat, scooting it so close to Mist I thought she'd climb on her lap, and like the dutiful best friend he was, Orson sat on her other side. Piper and Honor took one end of the table, and Sienna took the opposite end, next to Mist and her daughter.

Figuring Ronan might like to sit next to his atma, I took the spot beside him. Sasha sat on my other side with Anders wedged between her and Sienna.

The table was loud, and porcelain clattered as we all loaded our plates. It didn't escape my notice that the dishes were still princess themed. I supposed when you had a child who could literally alter reality at their whim, picking your battles took on a whole new meaning.

"Have you heard from Bree at all?" Anders asked Piper lightly. Ronan sent him a narrow look, overly defensive about things that tended to upset Piper—especially when it came to her sister.

"No," Piper said softly. "You?"

He shook his head, and Piper's face became carefully neutral. Even among friends and family, she still hid her vulnerabilities.

"How about Katherine?" Anders asked, trying to steer the topic toward someone easier to discuss. He failed miserably.

I groaned. "You know the rules. No work."

He snorted. "That's not work, but all right."

I huffed, because it may as well have been.

"I haven't been able to find a trace of her," Sasha said after a sip of wine, not dropping the topic.

"Have you, Nat?" Piper asked, taking a bite out of a drumstick. I sighed. I should have known this was coming.

"Unfortunately, no."

"There's been some problems getting Marcel to help,"

Sienna added. I knew she meant to be helpful, but it was the wrong thing to say.

They were all doubling down on that tonight.

"Marcel?" Piper asked sharply. "From the Ouroboros Coven?"

I nodded, hiding behind my water glass and taking mouthfuls, but there wasn't enough water in the ocean to get me out of her questioning. While Sienna knew most of my plans, the rest of the people at our table did not.

"I reached out to him for . . . assistance." I kept my voice steady, not showing my hand. It wasn't that I kept secrets from Piper. Not really. I just omitted information in instances where she had a tendency to be a little overbearing. Particularly where black magic was concerned.

"With what?" Piper continued, lifting her violet eyes to mine.

"I wanted to do a summoning to talk to the ghosts of our victims," I murmured quickly, letting my words trail off into silence. The table went quiet.

I stared hard at my macaroni and cheese, pretending not to notice.

Anders started laughing, trying and failing to disguise it as a hoarse cough.

Sasha glared at him. "What the fuck, Nat?"

"Language," Sienna snapped at her twin sister.

Sasha rolled her eyes but dialed it back. "You literally just gave me a whole spiel about necromancy being dangerous—" she started, raising her voice.

"I know, I know." I pushed my potato salad around for a second. "But I wasn't having any luck with my informants, and Marcel is a specialist in necromancy. He's done dozens of summonings, and never lost a soul—"

"Why do you need to speak to the dead?" Ronan asked,

cutting into the conversation. "Piper said Katherine did it —" My best friend shot a glare at her atman, elbowing him in the ribs. Ronan didn't twitch, but his attention did sway to her as she started silently communicating with him. I couldn't tell what they were saying, only that they were using telepathy and all but cutting us out of the conversation.

"There's no proof of that," I said tersely, irritated that she was still operating on that assumption. I understood it; because of who my sister was, she couldn't afford not to. It still irked me, though.

"She disappeared at the same time the murders started," Sasha argued, pushing my patience a little more.

Fuck me. If it weren't for me being the one to establish a "no missing family dinners" rule, I'd have tried to get out of this one. I *knew* there was going to be a discussion about it. Sasha was worse than a dog with a bone.

"I'm not saying they're unrelated." I set my fork down, abandoning all pretenses of eating. "I'm saying she didn't do it. I'm not sure how they're related, but if I find the actual killer, I can figure it out."

"How's talking to a ghost supposed to—" Piper's mouth snapped shut as she realized the answer to her question. Her lips pressed together in a "yeah, I just did that" face.

"There are no witnesses. No magic signature. No clues at all." I leaned back in my chair as I explained my approach. "The only people that can tell us who actually did it are the victims. We talk to them. We'll at least get a much better idea of who our killer is, and if he's targeting them, why. Hopefully with that information I can get ahead of them before more people die *and* figure out what it has to do with Katherine."

"Well shit," Piper said. "That's actually kind of brilliant."

The corner of my mouth quirked up. "It would be, except Marcel refuses to do it if I'm the one who enters the veil."

"What's the veil?" Hallie asked, reminding all of us about the little ears listening to our not-very-appropriate conversation. I wasn't her parent, though, so that wasn't my call to make.

"It's where ghosts live," I answered.

Her dark eyes flashed with interest. "You mean like—"

"That's enough, Hal," Sienna said, interrupting her daughter before she could potentially give away Lucifer's existence. "Focus on eating your dinner. Mommy's got an early day tomorrow, and I don't want to be out any later than necessary."

Hallie grumbled, but returned to shoveling chicken in her mouth as fast as her sticky fingers would allow.

"He won't do it with you because of his . . . feelings?" Piper said after a moment of silence. I could tell she was trying to be diplomatic with her word usage. She didn't know the full story, but she knew enough of it and that I never forgave him.

"Something like that." I sipped my water, wishing I were at home where I had a lovely bottle of white waiting for me. Piper and Ronan didn't keep alcohol in the house after her spiral some months ago, when she turned to liquor for comfort. They didn't mind people bringing it, but I didn't think to, and the red Sasha brought this week was too dry for my tastes.

"I could make him," Piper offered.

Tempting as it was, taking someone's will away didn't sit right with me, especially not forcing them to do necromancy. That screamed all sorts of danger. "I appreciate it, but no. I'm just going to have to find another way. The problem is witches with death magic aren't exactly easy to come by. Let alone ones I can trust."

Piper nodded. "I bet you could get away without using a witch."

I frowned. "What makes you think that?"

She used her fork to gesticulate as she said, "The person that goes into the veil is the . . . offering," she said after a quick glance at the kids. "They're not controlling the spell; they just need to have magic capable of entering the veil and coming back."

I considered what she was saying. Her past as a bounty hunter came in handy at times when I least expected it. "It's possible. I'd have to ask Marcel if he's ever done it with a non-witch. My gut says no, but I could be wrong."

"If it's death magic you need," Sienna murmured, wiping Hallie down with a napkin, "I could do it easily."

I stiffened. "Absolutely not. I won't let you risk it."

Sienna froze. "Don't pull that." Her voice came across with quietly simmering anger.

"Piper may be right, but it's still—"

"Are you really going to say *exactly* what Marcel said to you?" Sienna said, her voice tight as she glanced up at me.

I shook my head, letting out a stiff breath. "You have Hallie to think about."

"You think I don't know that?" she said defensively. I deflated, hating the direction this dinner had taken. "If it's safe enough for you to do it, it's safe enough for me."

I pushed my lips together and bit the inside of my cheek to keep from responding. It would just make this situation worse.

"*If* he can do it with a supernatural that has strong

enough death magic, there's likely going to be increased challenges. I wasn't lying when I told Sasha that this kind of magic is dangerous. It is, but I was willing to take the chance because I know how to mitigate the risks."

Basically, I knew Marcel would rather die than let me die in the veil.

"I think we should try it," Sasha said.

"See," Sienna motioned to her twin. "Even Sasha agrees—"

"Yeah, no, I didn't say you should be the one to do it. I agree with Nat on that. I just think it should be done, and sooner rather than later," Sasha said. "Which is why *I'll* do it."

Sienna gaped, looking back and forth between us. Anders lifted his hands in surrender and scooted away from the table, not wanting to be stuck between them. "I'm not in the business of telling anyone what they can or can't do with their body, and seeing as I have spirit magic, I can't exactly help here either. Don't mind me while I start doing the dishes."

Anders started to clear the table and Ronan joined him, muttering something about hardheaded women that ended in Piper's foot hitting his shin.

"This is why I didn't want to discuss this here," I said, putting an edge to my own voice.

Sasha lifted a hand, pushing away from the table. "Hold that thought. I need to take this."

She stepped into the other room, but Sienna sent a worried glance at her sister's back. It surprised me since she was pissed at Sasha, and everyone knew it. Her cat ears twitched, and she frowned when I assumed she recognized the voice I couldn't hear coming through the speaker.

"There's been another murder," Sienna sighed, closing

her eyes. The crease between her brows deepened, and she pulled Hallie onto her lap, holding her close. The little girl wrinkled her nose at her mom in confusion.

"Fuck," Piper muttered, scrubbing a hand over her face. "I hate to be that person, Nat, but you're right. We need to figure this out. I'll release Marcel from the binding preventing him from doing any necromancy."

I nodded, knowing there wasn't much point in arguing with her. Not that I disagreed, but there was still the matter of *who* was doing it that we couldn't agree on.

Ann muttered about us all being martyrs from the confines of the library in my memory loci. I could see her point.

We were all being difficult about this, me more than the others.

Sasha came back into the room, face grim. "Double homicide at the hospital Isadora's coven owns."

"It just opened up last week," Piper grimaced. "Please tell me no one else was hurt."

"No injured, and no witnesses either," Sasha all but growled. "It's twenty-four hours old."

"And they only just discovered it?" Piper said incredulously.

"It seems there's been some spells in place, and potential memory tampering."

"I'm coming with you," I said, getting to my feet.

"Can you drop us at home on the way?" Sienna asked. Sasha nodded.

"Do you need me for this one?" Piper asked, glancing between her second and her atman, who was giving her and the kids a hard look.

Sasha shook her head. "I can fill you in tomorrow morning on the way to the meeting with the ghouls."

Piper nodded her head in thanks. "Mist? You staying here tonight?"

The young siren got up and ran a hand down her jaw. "Actually, I was hoping Sienna would be okay with me staying over with Hallie." She tried sounding sad, but hopeful. "With everything going on, I'd rather be with her if that's all right—"

Sienna wrapped an arm around her shoulders while carrying Hallie with the other. "Always," she said. "You are *always* welcome in our home."

Relief flashed across Mist's face. She mumbled her thanks as Sasha put a hand on Sienna's shoulder and held a hand out for me.

"Let me know when you're both home safe, please," Piper said as she picked Honor up.

"Will do," I responded. Sasha just nodded as she grabbed my wrist.

The void opened up, and we disappeared.

NATHALIE

THE FOYER WAS LIVELY when we got to the hospital.

Staff bustled all around us, most paying no mind as we started toward the elevators. I frowned. "That's not what I'd expect after a murder."

"They don't realize it," Sasha said. "My informant told me he was following a lead when he discovered the bodies."

"I'm not sure how you discover them inside a hospital without anyone else seeing, but all right." I couldn't help tapping my foot as the elevator took its sweet time climbing the six floors.

Sasha glared at my foot but didn't say anything.

I stilled my nervous energy, all but running from the elevator when the doors finally opened.

Only to freeze on the spot.

"What the hell?" I murmured, staring up and down the hallways. Magic laced with some sort of black rot wound its way down the empty hall and around each corner. I took a few careful steps, but it didn't respond.

"What?" Sasha asked, looking around. "What is it?"

"Magic," I said in a heavy breath. "A lot of it. Whoever cast this spell, they're stronger than any witch I've encountered before."

"It's not Katherine's?" she asked, her tone neutral. It annoyed me that she would even question whether I would hide that from her.

"No," I snapped back.

She exhaled. "Nat, I didn't mean—"

"You did," I said, stepping around her. "Don't make it worse by lying to me on top of it."

Her footsteps followed mine as I stalked down the hallway, searching for the source of it all. Thick ropes of black-tinged spirit and death magic tangled together like roots the closer we got to the room.

"I'm sorry," she said quietly. "That was shitty."

"It was," I agreed. "Thank you for the apology." My own irritation simmered down as we stopped in front of the door. I studied the structure, both perplexed and fascinated by what I saw.

"Is it safe to open the door?" she asked.

"Yeah."

She grabbed the handle and went in first, but I took my time. This was the first crime scene I'd seen magic at, and not just magic, but two different kinds.

There were five types of magic in total.

Death. Spirit. Rage. Desire.

Chaos was the fifth, and it contained all four in one.

But it was still *one.*

There was no such thing as possessing two kinds of magic. Everyone had one of the five and that was that, but whoever had done this . . . had two.

"I'm going to take a shot in the dark and say both our victims were staff," Sasha said.

I pulled my attention in from the spell that was slowly breaking down.

Inside the room, there were two hospital beds and a torn curtain. One of the bodies laid next to the bed, an abandoned clipboard beside it. The other had a stethoscope's circular end poking out of the charred remains. The metal glinted beneath the fluorescent lighting, making it easy to identify.

"If they're not, someone staged this very cleverly. How'd you say your informant found this?"

"He thought he found Katherine and followed her. She was gone when he got here."

"Convenient story. You believe him?"

Sasha worked her jaw, thinking about it. "Yeah. He's a bastard, but he wouldn't lie to me about this."

I knelt by the body closest to me and grabbed the femur, wrinkling my nose at the black smudges that clung to my skin.

"What are you doing?"

"Testing a theory," I muttered, before bringing the bone down on my lifted knee. It cracked, splitting apart.

Dread pooled in my stomach.

"The magic used to keep staff from entering this floor? It was taken from our victims." Black threads webbed throughout the brittle bone that broke far too easily. "Whoever did this has figured out how to use a life force to fuel their spells. They're controlling it somehow."

"That doesn't sound good," Sasha remarked, picking up the notepad.

"It's not." I dropped the bone fragments and stepped over them, toward the sink to wash my hands. "Any chances the security cameras might have caught what happened?"

"I've already requested they send the footage over to me and Sienna for review. I can have them send it to you too, if you'd like?" she offered, flipping through the intake papers.

"I'm good. If it shows anything, Sienna will let me know. I want the records pulled on the victims. I don't get the impression they were targeted, but I can't ignore the possibility."

She nodded, frowning at the clipboard. I took the chance to walk around the room, taking in the bodies from all angles. The ripped curtain. The slashes in the thin fabric. There were signs of a struggle but no blood or sign of injury, only—

My heart skipped.

Sasha heard it and her head whipped up. "What do you see?"

"There's just a wisp of it, hardly any at all," I murmured, approaching the bed. Unable to help myself, I reached out a hand to touch the dark blue strand.

The magic flared in familiarity and my own rose, turning the single strand gold. I released a harsh breath and dropped my hand.

"Katherine was here."

Her informant said he was following her. I just didn't believe it until now.

Sasha's mouth tightened. "I'm sorry," she said.

"We don't know she did it," I replied, but the words sounded hollow, even to me. Sasha didn't argue, but I could see it in her eyes. Kat's magic being on scene was not just damning. It was one step short of a guilty verdict.

"I don't recognize the name on the paperwork, but the person admitted was described as brunette, brown eyes, roughly five and a half feet tall, and underweight. I know a lot of people have brown hair and eyes, but that coupled with her magic being here—" she stopped, trying not to be an asshole in making her point. I appreciated the effort.

Silently I extended my hand for the clipboard.

One look at the name was all I needed. My fingers gripped it painfully. "Elena Gilbert," I said, smiling with something close to relief. "Katherine came here for this. It's a cry for help."

Sasha's eyebrows rose. "You're going to need to explain that one because I'm not seeing it."

I shook my head. "Elena Gilbert was the heroine in *The Vampire Diaries*. It's a TV show we watched growing up. She hated that she was named Katherine because it was the same name as Elena's evil doppelgänger. Not relevant, but the important bit is she *knew* I would see this. Which means she didn't do it. She wouldn't leave me a message at the scene of a crime if she was the one who committed it."

"Unless she knew you'd think that way," Sasha pointed out, still skeptical.

I pressed my lips together but didn't correct her. That was just manipulative enough I could see it as a minor possibility. "Fine, either she committed it, or she knew it was coming and gave that name so I'd know she's in trouble."

Sasha nodded, pushing her black hair out of her face. Her tail twitched in frustration.

"We need to do the summoning," she said. "That's the only way we'll know which we're dealing with—a victim on the run, or a sadistic serial killer."

"I know," I sighed, dropping the clipboard on the bed. "I'll pay a visit to the Ouroboros Coven tomorrow."

Sasha grimaced. "Do you want backup?" She was begrudgingly offering it, but I knew she would do it if I said yes.

I shook my head. "I need to talk to Carissa, and she won't play nice if you're there."

"She won't play nice, period," Sasha said dryly.

"Yeah," I agreed with another sigh. "But she won't be on her guard because she thinks she can walk all over me. It's possible I'll learn something. Maybe she knows more than Marcel thinks she does."

Sasha shrugged. "I wouldn't rule anything out at this point. You think fuckboy will be ready to do it tomorrow night?"

I choked on a laugh. "Fuckboy?"

Sasha pinned me with a knowing look. "Sienna mentioned some of what happened there."

I groaned. "I can't believe her. Next time I'm not saying anything."

Sasha laughed. "You can't blame her when we share a room. Besides, I already knew there was history, and that you were once engaged. Lucifer's PA, remember?"

I couldn't forget, even when I wanted to.

"I'll get him to do it, but it won't be at my place. Necromancy is bad juju, and I don't want those vibes in my apartment. We'll do it at the Wicked Haunt—don't bring Sienna."

Sasha nodded along like I wasn't saying anything she didn't know. "No shit. You may want to avoid her for a couple days, though. She's going to be bitchy when she finds out."

"I'm not hiding it from her," I said defensively. "But you offered, and you don't have a kid. I love you both, but on the very slim chance something happens, I'm not leaving another orphan in the world."

Sasha came around the bed. "I'm not arguing there. I get it, and I'd rather it be me over her any day. Am I good to call Isadora for cleanup here?" She nodded toward the room.

Isadora was the white witch coven leader who was also on Piper's council. No one liked her. She was more of a necessary evil. A pain in the ass to deal with, but ultimately harmless.

"She's going to bitch."

Sasha snorted. "I hope she does. Piper will put her back on volunteer duty. Not much brings me joy like watching that witch have to humble herself."

She cackled like a witch herself, and I couldn't help chuckling, but my heart wasn't in it. Too much weighed on me. "Yeah, she can deal with it. I've got everything I need. You mind dropping me at Bliss before going home?"

She hiked a perfect brow. "Again? Wearing that?"

I looked down at my skinny jeans and sweater. It wasn't exactly club attire, but I was out of fucks to give. "Yep."

"My, my. One might think you've found yourself a booty call."

I snorted. She wasn't wrong, but she wasn't right either. I shrugged with one shoulder, not feeling the need to explain. "I'm keyed up after this, and Mist is with you guys tonight. I'm going to enjoy being single and childless."

Sasha laughed. "A-fucking-men to that."

I wasn't sure which was more disappointing—that I barely had a buzz after three Manhattans or that I was still sitting at the bar instead of playing with someone after two hours of being here.

It wasn't that I hadn't been approached. Contrary to

Sasha's side-eye at my regular clothes, that didn't deter everyone here. Particularly when the idea was to take them off. The problem was that none of my potential partners interested me.

One was too shy in his approach. Another too forceful. The third made the mistake of touching my bare hand, and I instantly got bad vibes from him. The only person I was even half tempted to take up on their offer was the female succubus with dyed purple hair and dramatic makeup. Her sarcasm and dry wit made her feel safe in theory, but she was hoping to feed tonight, and I wasn't down for that.

Not here. Not with her.

From the greenhouse where she resided, Peace whispered, "Go find *him*."

Him. Yeah. I knew who she wanted.

We *all* knew who she wanted.

It didn't help when Caretaker agreed with her, thinking the incubus was worth the headache sure to follow. The future didn't concern either of them. They just wanted me to focus on me and my needs right now, in the moment.

Meanwhile, Ann and The Warden thought it was a questionable decision even being here. There were two more murders and Kat was implicated. Logic said I should go home and lock my door. Read a smutty romance book and have some alone time to take care of myself. Do what's *safe*.

If only there hadn't been an itch beneath my skin, driving me forward. It was crawling to get out, but after four failed passes my way, I had to finally admit defeat.

I'd come here hoping to run into a certain incubus. I didn't, which meant there were two choices. Go home, like half my inner personalities were insisting—or do the dangerous thing and go looking for him.

I gnawed on the inside of my bottom lip for a long moment, mulling it over.

Bad Nat kicked her feet up on the library table, dropping bits of dirt on the polished surface. She looked straight at me even though I wasn't completely in the memory loci right then. "You're not going to do the safe thing either way, you know," she remarked, putting her hands behind her head and leaning the chair back on two legs. "If you don't go look for the incubus, you'll end up crossing the line with Lucifer. Nothing wrong with that, but you need to pick your poison and drink up."

I stumbled getting to my feet. It had nothing to do with the Manhattans and everything to do with the insinuation that I would cross any sort of line with Lucifer.

One, he was dead. You couldn't fuck a ghost.

Two, I wasn't bringing him back tonight. Even if I did eventually—which I wasn't saying I would, but even if I did agree—it wouldn't be now, and it wouldn't be for sex.

She was full of shit.

There's more than one way to cross a line.

"Everything okay there, Miss Le Fay?" the new female bouncer called after me as I all but ran from the bar. I waved her off, taking a sobering breath of the chilly fall air.

My legs carried me through the dark night. I tucked my thumbs into my jean pockets, still debating internally as I walked toward the convenience store on 7th and Pike Place.

My pulse started to climb when the lights came into view.

Was I really doing this?

I told him I didn't want to see him anymore. This was me totally going back on that. Then again, it wasn't that I didn't want to see him, it was that I didn't have time for anything.

Make time.

Easier said than done.

A small, flickering sign above the door illuminated the name of the store: Fives. What kind of name was that? I stared through the glass windows to the tiny shop. A girl was sitting at the register, listening to something on headphones. There were only three aisles with junk snacks, basic toiletries, and a couple of drink options. Should have been named Threes.

It was clearly a front for something, I just didn't know what.

My hand lifted the push bar. Fingers trembling, I held my breath and took a leap of faith.

Nothing happened.

The girl at the counter didn't even look up.

I frowned. She really shouldn't be listening to music if she couldn't hear me. It wasn't safe at night in New Chicago. Even with the Demon Queen and her king, crime was still high, and with the murders recently . . . I shuddered, happy it was only me here with her.

Instead of approaching the counter to ask for August, I walked down each of the aisles, taking in the goods. It was stupid. I'd fully admit that.

I'd come all the way over here and was chickening out.

It wasn't like me to be half in and half out of something, but I also wasn't one to take risks like this.

"*Risks,*" Bad Nat seemed to snort. She thought I was funny, like a goody-two-shoes teenager who was sneaking out for the first time.

I rolled my eyes, wishing she hadn't shown up. The only saving grace was Lucifer didn't seem to be lurking around. He tended to give me Sunday nights off. At least until I went to bed. He didn't care for family dinners, which was both unsurprising and mildly amusing that they made him uncomfortable.

The kids in particular.

I stopped in front of a rack with mini-doughnuts. Mist would like doughnuts. What teenager didn't like processed garbage? Don't get me wrong, I could eat my way through some strawberry frosted Pop-Tarts, but that didn't change that it was still garbage. I could afford real, nutritious food, unlike nearly ninety percent of the city, so I didn't tend to buy anything processed.

But I needed a distraction before I started hyperventilating.

So processed crap it was.

Unable to make up my mind, I just grabbed one of each and dropped them on the counter unceremoniously. The girl lifted her gaze in a slow fashion, clearly not all that bothered. Silently she rang up each of the doughnut packs. "I hope you have a bag. We don't use plastic."

"The packaging is plastic," I pointed out. She shrugged.

"I don't make the rules, I just repeat them."

Guess it was a good thing I'd brought my mini-back-pack with me. I dropped it off one shoulder, letting it fall to the side so I could get my electronic wallet out of it.

"Will that be all?" she asked in the same bored tone. Her jaws smacked like a cow as she chewed a wad of gum, then she blew a bubble nearly the size of her face.

It popped, and she sucked it back in, waiting for my answer.

Was that all?

I opened and closed my mouth trying to find my willpower, but The Warden had decidedly fucked off where this plan was concerned.

Fuck them. All of them.

"Yeah, actually," I forced the words out. My mouth was drier than the desert. "I'm looking for—" I stalled, groaning internally. "Never mind."

She squinted at me, as if trying to decide what drug I was on.

Stupidity, I wanted to tell her.

She probably wouldn't find it as funny as I did.

The door opened behind me and I tensed, not trusting the teenager with no sense of self-preservation to alert me if I was going to be stabbed in the back.

I turned, only to wish I could evaporate on the spot.

August stood there, black curls wet, as if he'd just showered. His brown skin looked way too good in the shitty lighting, the same lighting I was pretty sure it turned me a sallow yellow.

"Nathalie." His lips wrapped around my name in a way that made my blood quicken. He smirked as if he knew it. His glamoured slate-blue eyes slid past me to the counter. "Out for a late-night snack?" he asked, quirking a brow.

"Something like that," I said, proud I managed not to sound like a breathless twit, fully aware I'd just been planning to walk out of here and he would've been none the wiser.

August stepped closer. He leaned around me, long fingers skimming my arm as he plucked one of the packages from the counter. His head inclined forward, putting me in his shadow as he locked eyes with me. "It must be quite the craving to bring you here," he murmured.

The innuendo scorched me. My cheeks heated.

"That is usually how one caves to bad decisions."

His lips twitched with amusement. "My place or yours?"

Heat filled my veins at his boldness. I wanted to call

him on it, but there wasn't much point. I came here with my own two feet. I licked my bottom lip, and his eyes tracked the movement with predatory interest. "Yours."

He flashed a smile, like I'd made the right choice somehow. "We'll take these to go," he murmured, putting the doughnuts in my mini-backpack. I turned to help him but all that did was brush more of me against him.

My heart pounded.

"I've got it," he whispered low. I was happy I couldn't see the cashier's face. Then again, her lack of fucks to give probably applied to me panting and all but spreading my legs on the counter for him.

He zipped my backpack closed with exaggerated slowness. At least, it seemed slow to me. I was eager to leave, which made me jumpy when he rested his hand on the small of my back and pulled me toward the back of the convenience store. "Please tell me you don't live in a supply closet," I said as we stopped before a door labeled Employees Only. "It's not your mother's basement, but this isn't what I had in mind when I said your place."

He chuckled, opening the door in answer.

A short stairwell led into another room with mismatched furniture. Jazz drifted through the space, coming from another room farther on. I crossed the threshold, my curiosity pulling me deeper. Paintings from different centuries adorned the walls. While I couldn't be certain they weren't prints, the textured surface and magical barrier over them suggested they were real.

The floor raised another foot with each room, small tables and cushioned chairs in each of them. Some had people smoking and deep in conversation. Others were empty. All of them paid us no mind. We stepped into a much larger space where the music originated. A couple of people milled around, and a barkeeper was polishing a small antique setup. A large tapestry hung down in front of another room to my right and a recorder sat in the back corner next to a small hallway. The windows were large, illuminating the dreary fall night.

"Where are we?" I asked quietly. August's presence was both a comfort and an agitation because of how tightly wound I was.

"The Poppy Garden," August said, lightly pushing me forward. "Come, this way." He led me up to the tapestry and pushed it aside. The room we found ourselves in was much smaller. I quietly took it in as he stepped around me, nudging a curtain out of the way to reveal a full-length mirror. He reached up, grasping what appeared to be a hanging planter strung up with wool, except there wasn't a plant in it.

He grabbed something out of it and only when he threw it at the mirror did I understand. The "something" had been dried and crushed sage.

"*Verum revelare,*" I said at the same time he did. The glass rippled then shifted, showing a completely different room on the other side.

"You're familiar with mystports," he noted.

I nodded. "My family used them." My answer was vague, but the look he gave me said he knew that and was letting it slide.

August held out his hand, motioning for me to go first. I should have paused to think about it. This doorway could lead to anywhere in the world, and I had no way of knowing how to leave or get help if I needed it. At another time when I was thinking more clearly, I might have felt the proper level of embarrassment that I didn't hesitate for a second.

Three steps into his home and I knew I loved it.

My brain quickly cataloged the leather sectional and marble coffee table. More art from the ages decorated his walls, like a live-in museum. My bag slipped from my shoulder as I let it drop to the floor beside me and turned back to August.

He stood in front of the mystport that was mounted on the back of a door, watching me with intense interest.

"It's a little better than a supply closet," he teased. Amusement danced across his features.

I dipped my head, smirking. "Part of me wants to ask why you have a mystport from a hidden opium bar to your house."

He took measured steps, closing the distance between us, too slow for my liking. "And the rest of you?" he asked.

"Isn't interested in talking," I said, voice thick, letting a sliver of my desire show.

His eyes darkened instantly. "Are you hungry?"

"Are you?" I replied, gripping the edge of my sweater. I pulled it over my head, then dropped it on top of my backpack.

August crossed the space between us with haste. Supernaturally strong hands gripped my waist, dragging me up his front. My nipples pebbled against my bra, tightening in anticipation. I ran my fingers through his hair, fisting it like I *owned* him. And for tonight, I would. My butt touched the wood island, jean-clad legs spreading to make room.

"Starving."

nineteen

AUGUST

SHE TASTED like jasmine tea and sunshine. It sounded cliche. Flowery even, unless you'd lived without the sun long enough to forget what it looked like. During that dark time when I couldn't see, I realized there was a taste to it. An exhilarating, freeing feeling associated with the burning star in the sky.

Nathalie tasted like that and so much more.

I pressed my lips to hers, more forceful than our last time together. Only a week or so had passed, but it felt so much longer after having fed from her. Sex was one thing, but feeding . . . I'd never enjoyed my food. Not like her.

Nathalie was a first for me in more ways than one, which made it all the more crushing when she'd walked away without a second glance.

Then I walked into the convenience store and the scent of juniper and raspberries hit me. My mouth watered, and it had to have been the work of some god she didn't see how hard I was. Jenny was eighteen and used to far worse things than my tented jeans, but the filthy things in my mind? The lust coating every breath?

She didn't need to feel that. It was part of why she worked for me, to escape the life that an empath like her might have led under different circumstances.

It took all my self-control to escort Nathalie through the Poppy Garden and not stop there to fuck her where they could all hear—and know—she was with me.

The word *mine* threatened to make an appearance, but I fought against the animalistic monster my magic and past had made me.

No person should belong to another.

Even if I desired to own her with every fiber of my being.

That wouldn't stop me from devouring every inch of her skin tonight. Here, in my apartment, where no one could interrupt us.

I pressed my tongue to the seam of her mouth and she opened readily. Using my grip on her waist I pulled her closer, forcing her legs wider to accommodate my size. She groaned when my hardness brushed against her. The hands fisting my hair pulled enough to give me a bite of pain, and I nipped her bottom lip in response.

The gasp she rewarded me with was gas on a bonfire.

I ran my lips up her jaw, breathing in her scent like the gift that it was.

"What are you in the mood for tonight, beautiful?" I whispered against her skin, sucking and nibbling small patches of flesh from her jaw to her collarbone.

Nathalie arched her back into me.

"Dominate me," she breathed. My heart skipped a beat. "I don't want to be in charge or in control. Throw me around. Punish me. Use me. Feed from me. I don't care, just don't *stop*."

I nearly unraveled.

I'd played many parts in the bedroom, and I got the feeling she had too. Dominating was the one I was most familiar with, simply because I wasn't generally comfortable enough with my bed partners to fully flip the coin.

For her, I would.

But that wasn't what she asked of me. She wanted to hurt. To be *used,* as she put it. I was already planning to feed from her. I didn't think I could help myself even if I tried. She was my ambrosia. My weakness.

Which made it all the sweeter that this would be the first time I would revel in my power over another person.

I released her hips and started to pull away. Her hands tightened in my hair. I gently but firmly grabbed her wrists, silently commanding her to let go.

I nearly regretted the loss of her skin on mine when she obeyed.

Her form trembled the farther I got from her. Raw desire turned those light brown eyes the color of honey. It didn't take a genius to figure out something had happened that sent her to my door, needing *this.*

I could guess what, but we wouldn't be getting into that tonight. No. She was caving to her own baser urges, and I was going to use that to my advantage, because while I wouldn't go against her wishes, I'd be damned if she walked away again without the promise of more.

"What's your safe word?" I asked, turning my back to her and undoing my cuffs as I methodically calculated how exactly I was going to go about this.

"Red," she answered instantly.

That made me smile. "Playing by the rules of Bliss?"

"I *made* the rules at Bliss."

I didn't respond by asking questions the way I wanted to. Not yet. I already knew she was well off, but that admission alluded to more. My sunling had friends in high places, but I was beginning to suspect that she may be even higher.

"Mercy for slow down?" I asked instead. There was a pause before she stammered, "Y-yes." I smirked at the emotion in her voice.

Needy.

I'd have her mewling in half an hour.

My fingers skimmed over the metal buckle of my belt. I undid it, sliding the leather free and laying it across the back of the couch.

"That's easy," I said, turning when I reached the sectional. I sat down, stretching my arms across the back. "Are there any rules I need to know? Anything at all that you haven't told me before?"

She was still sitting on the counter, exactly as I left her. Her lips, red and swollen from our kiss, cheeks and chest flushed. "Do you remember my limits?"

I'd thought about them more than I would ever admit to her.

"Yes."

She nodded once. "Then no."

"Good, then I'll state mine. They're simple." She nodded once, tongue darting out to swipe across her bottom lip. My cock strained against my jeans. "If you lick your lip one more time, I'm going to bend you over and spank your ass, then choke you with my cock." A jerk went through her as her eyes widened slightly, pupils blown. She was excited by the prospect. "No speaking, moving, or coming unless I give you permission. If I ask you a question, you'll answer it *honestly.*" Something flashed beneath the honey in her eyes, but she didn't voice it. "You'll only refer to me as Sir, unless you're coming. Then the only thing I want to hear on your lips is my name. Understood?"

Her chin dipped, and that damning tongue flicked out once more to lick her bottom lip. Not an ounce of fear shone in her eyes. Only undiluted lust.

"Stand up."

The command was simple. She moved without hesitation, her long legs sliding off my counter. Her boots hit the floor harder due to her lack of heightened senses. I didn't mind in the slightest.

Not when I savored being able to hear every step, every breath, every beat of her heart, completely unencumbered by other noises.

"Come here."

She turned on her heel and walked with her head high. Her brown hair was pulled back in a sloppy bun that I'd be undoing very soon.

"Stop," I said when she was only halfway across the room. I kicked my marble end table to the side, pushing it all the way up against the opposite side of the sectional so not even an inch of her skin was hidden from me.

Her feet jerked to a complete stop mid-step.

"Undress for me."

She didn't lower her eyes or pretend to feel shame about her needs or wants. She wasn't insecure, at least not with her body. I liked that about her. The blatant sexuality that she was unapologetic for in any way.

Nathalie kneeled down to undo one of her boots. She didn't fumble, but the process was taking longer than I wanted. My eagerness toyed with me. I wanted to pound into her and hear my name echo off the high ceilings.

I told that impatience to go fuck itself.

One by one she undid her boots and stepped out of them, then removed her socks. Next, she went to her jeans, only briefly looking down as she unsnapped the button.

Her eyes were back on mine when she lowered the zipper. She had to wiggle a little to get them down the curve of her hips and thighs.

Her tongue flicked out by force of habit, wetting her bottom lip as she stepped out of her jeans. My hands clenched with restraint. She noticed the action and seemed to realize what she'd done. Her teeth came down on that plump flesh as she bit into it, kneading it instead. It was worse than watching her lick it.

"Forget the clothes," I ordered as she reached back to undo her bra. Her hands dropped to her sides instantly. "Get on your knees."

The honey in her gaze shifted to something brighter. Like a flicker of candlelight. Fire was often called red, but the most common flame burned yellow with just a touch of orange. That was the color her eyes turned as she sank to her knees in nothing but her black lace-covered bra and panties, the material standing out against her heated skin.

"Crawl to me."

She bit the inside of her cheek, a tiny dimple forming there. This order gave her pause. I wanted to smirk. Instead I lifted an eyebrow.

"Every second you hesitate is another smack on that luscious ass. By all means, keep me waiting; I'm looking forward to it."

My words had the desired effect. She swallowed her inhibitions and crawled the remaining seven or eight feet to me. It was hardly any distance, but that didn't matter. She crawled. To me.

I'd never asked that of another, but something about her made me want it. Made me want everything that I'd been denied or denied myself. Every filthy dream and desire I hadn't been willing to even consider before this moment because it would have been with someone my very soul couldn't stand.

At my feet, she waited patiently, head raised and eyes on mine.

That was another first. I never looked into the eyes of my past partners. Her, I would never command to look anywhere else but me.

Her eyes were everything.

They were the sun itself. Or they would be.

"Bend over my lap," I said, putting two fingers under her chin. "You earned thirteen smacks."

She didn't hesitate. I didn't think she would. She'd okayed impact toys apart from canes. You didn't give that knowledge to a stranger without knowing yourself and your limits.

Nathalie climbed on the couch beside me, putting her knees against my thigh, she lowered herself over my lap. I let her rest on her elbows, ass in the air. "You asked me to punish you. Do you still want to be punished?"

We'd been together before, but not in this capacity. My desire to keep her made me go slower than usual, testing each and every limit with caution.

"Yes," she groaned. I hadn't even touched her yet.

Reaching underneath her, I dragged the cup of her bra down, letting it push her breast up. My fingers pulled on the nipple, twisting just enough to hurt but also making it stiffen. Nathalie gasped.

"Yes, what?"

"Yes, *Sir*."

"Good girl," I murmured. Using my other hand, I ran my palm down the length of her back, over her panty-clad ass. "Count with me."

The first smack was always the most jarring.

Her reaction was an expected jolt, followed by a breathy, "One."

I popped the opposite cheek. The action itself didn't do it for me. I wasn't a sadist. It was the surrender. That she let me do it to her. She let me have this power over her.

That was a heady thing.

Power given freely was a drug of its own.

"Two," she said, speaking low. I kept going, alternating cheeks. The crack of my palm was definitely hard enough to sting, but it shouldn't bruise. She'd said she was okay with that, but I wasn't. I'd leave marks on her, but bruises were the last thing I wanted. Her mortality was at the forefront of my mind, making me hold back the majority of my strength. I'd used more power killing a mosquito.

Only the final smack she croaked, "Thirteen."

I smoothed my hand over her ass, rubbing her stinging flesh. She'd likely gone numb to it already. I liked the warmth of her blood rushing to the skin. It heated my palm and only took a couple seconds for her to start squirming.

Unable to deny myself, I rubbed my fingers over the slit of her panties.

They were soaked.

Nathalie rocked her hips back, and I smacked her pussy once.

The resulting moan nearly undid me.

"What did I say about moving?" I asked her, going back to rubbing her wet cunt with hard, seeking fingers. Her body trembled, but she didn't move.

"Not to do it without permission."

I hummed, pushing the thin fabric aside. I prodded her entrance, only going as deep as the first knuckle. It was a test.

She shook like a leaf in the wind, but her hips didn't move.

"Then why did you move?" I asked.

It was the beginning of my questions, testing how easily she'd give.

"Because I wanted more, Sir."

I smirked. She knew what she wanted, all right. I rewarded her by pushing one finger to the second knuckle and started rubbing her inner walls. The breath hissed between her teeth. "More of what, my sunling?"

"You, Sir," she whispered.

"Me?" I questioned, feeling her tighten. She was close. "Or my fingers?"

She lifted her head, turning to look over her shoulder at me.

There it was. The sun.

"Both, Sir."

I was tempted to keep finger fucking her just because I wanted to hear her come saying my name. I'd be a sad excuse for a Dom tonight if I let her off and lost my control that easily. She wanted me to take control from her, so that's what I'd do.

I dropped my hand, and she groaned in frustration. I didn't call her on it.

"On your knees," I told her. Of course, I'd denied giving her an orgasm, so she opted for teasing me. Her back arched as she bent backward, using her core muscles to lift her up, giving me an eyeful of her breasts while at it. The lace of her bra slipped back over her exposed nipple, and the tiny smile she wore as she slid off the couch and onto the floor said it all.

"I think you enjoyed your punishment a little too much," I said, forcing myself to lean back. "Unbuckle me."

"Unbuckle you where, Sir?" she asked, blinking with false innocence. I couldn't help the smirk that time.

"You have ten seconds to start sucking my cock."

She moved to unzip my pants, running the palm of her hand down my length in the process. Nathalie stroked me again before pulling me out entirely.

Her tongue traced along the edge of her teeth as she bent forward.

"Eyes on me," I said, a bit sharper than needed. The second her tongue touched me, those golden eyes flicked up. She took my cock between her pretty lips, licking my head before sucking it into the wet heat of her mouth.

Her hand wrapped around my base, pumping me while she did.

I buried one hand in her hair, tugging her forward. I hit the back of her throat and she gagged. The rush of lubricant only made me swell more.

Fuck. She was perfect.

Her mouth was perfect.

Her cunt was perfect.

"I asked myself why you insisted last time was goodbye when we have chemistry like this. I have to assume it's baggage." There was a flash of something behind her eyes. The sun dimmed. I didn't like that. Not one bit. "I don't know who hurt you, but I guarantee whatever dumb fuck left you still struggling from their damage, they aren't worth it."

Nathalie swallowed, and the action brought me painfully close to the edge.

"Let me in," I told her, talking about more than just her throat. She obeyed and relaxed, making it easier for me to slide deeper. I groaned.

I stroked her cheek with my other hand, catching the

teardrop that spilled over. "I'm not going to pretend or play petty games with you, Nathalie. I want you. I want to know you. I want to know who hurt you and I want to erase their touch from your skin. I want to know what you like to have for dinner, cook for you, and then eat you for dessert. I want to know what you do and why you do it. I want to share my world with you, but more than anything, I want to be part of yours. When you've lived as long as I have, you learn to recognize what you want pretty quickly. I'm a patient man. I'll wait for you." I punctuated my statement by rocking into her. I couldn't tell if it was a hum or a purr, but her throat vibrated around me, making my lips part and the hand in her hair tense. She groaned, definitely liking that. "But you're only frustrating us both when you tell me no and walk away. Whoever wronged you, they're not here. They're not the one you're coming to, trusting not to hurt you while giving you what you need. I am."

Her eyes narrowed as I pulled back, but she used the reprieve for what it was. A chance to catch her breath. Then she stole mine by sucking so hard her cheeks hollowed out. I had to stifle a groan.

Originally, I had planned to have her choke on me for a second and then fuck her, but seeing that sharp tongue wrapped around me changed my course.

I thrust up, forcing myself deeper. She gagged again but opened to me right away, bobbing her head as she tightened her hand.

"Think about it, sunling. Now, I'm going to come in this pretty mouth, and you're going to let me." Her cheeks turned red from my words. I liked the color on her. I liked it even more, knowing I put it there.

Nathalie unsheathed her teeth to run the edge of them

over me while licking my underside. I snapped, pulling back slightly to come in her mouth.

"Open up." She did as I told her. I ran a hand over her cheek, dipping my thumb in her mouth to smear it on her bottom lip. "Swallow."

As she did, I slipped it back in her mouth and she wrapped her tongue around my thumb, sucking softly. I went half-hard again instantly. Her eyes tracked the movement before lifting back to mine, awaiting my next command.

"Stand."

She rocked back on her heels, then stood straight. Flushed, heated cheeks and lips puffy from abuse, I'd never seen anything more beautiful.

"Should I make you crawl again? Just because I can?" I mused, keen to watch her reaction. The slight narrowing of her eyes amused me. "You were such a good girl. I think you've earned a reward."

She liked the sound of that. Her heart rate increased. I could see the slickness between her thighs if I looked. "Come here."

Her legs slid over mine as she straddled my lap. My erection lay flat against her panties, but the dampness of her thighs challenged my restraint. I cupped her ass as I stood and strode through my apartment. Nathalie let out a tiny squeak. Something told me she wasn't used to being carried. I took advantage of our power dynamic to indulge myself and made a mental note of how much I enjoyed holding her in my arms. She felt so slight despite the fullness of her thighs and ass. I smoothed one hand over those curves, relishing the feel of her soft skin.

Tiny pants escaped her, chest rising and falling rapidly.

As I turned to open my bedroom door, she focused on

something over my shoulder. "*The Lovers*," she murmured. The painting behind me depicted a couple kissing, but they both had a white sheet wrapped around their heads—preventing their lips from actually touching.

It took her a second to realize what she'd done, breaking the rules yet again.

"You're easily distracted," I commented as I carried her into my bedroom. Her lips pressed together as she tried to stifle her response. "Tell me what you're thinking."

She blinked, as if surprised by my command. "That you're right, and yet you have an uncanny ability to hold my attention." I placed her in the center of my bed. The warm glow of her skin contrasted against the black sheets. The wall behind her was painted a dark matte gray, covered in more art from my travels.

"And yet the painting in the hall caught your attention."

She gnawed on her lip, and I leaned in to bite it. Not hard enough to draw blood, just to sate my own desire to do so. "I told you to tell me what you're thinking."

"You wouldn't want to know," she hedged, avoiding my eyes.

I reached past her to the leather restraints on the bed. I'd bought them for a very different purpose, but this would be a more pleasant one. I pulled her right arm up and secured it around her wrist, then repeated the process with the left.

With her arms spread above her I settled back between her legs, one arm braced over her head to hold my weight. The other skated over her belly.

She jerked the second my fingers swept between her thighs, rubbing her through her panties. Lips parted, she let out a low moan, her head falling back.

I moved the flimsy material aside so I could circle her clit.

"So responsive," I murmured as she tried to rock her hips into me, all but thrashing against the restraints. "Do you want to come?"

"Yes, Sir," she gasped.

"Then tell me what it is you think I wouldn't want to know."

She stiffened, her whole body locking up.

"Please, Sir . . ."

"You know the words to use if you need them. Begging won't work."

I pushed two fingers into her, and she arched off the bed, her hands fisting the cuffs. "*The Lovers* represent that love is blind," she breathed, rushing through her explanation. I wasn't shocked by her interpretation. It was a common one. That she recognized the painting instantly intrigued me more. Once upon a time, that might not have been significant—but in an era where art was not shared as it once was, for her to know it meant she had an interest in it.

I wanted to know more.

"You're holding back." I stopped fingering her, and she gritted her teeth.

"It made me think of . . . my past. About how love is blind to the point of ignorance, yet we still choose it. It's madness, but we crave it too much to ever break free."

NATHALIE

WAY TO GO, *Nat.*

Really. Well done.

You're interrupting what will probably be the best sex of your life because a painting made you think about, well, not Marcel per se, but everything. What he said. What it meant. What Marcel did, and yet you're walking on the edge of that cliff right this second. Of all times. That's madness.

It wasn't love. Not yet.

But that was what complicated it further. Love was a choice. I firmly believed that. Somewhere along the way, you have to choose to fall or choose to leave. Here I was staring that in the face, and yet I was also contemplating saying fuck it to my reservations because it was so true. Whatever chemistry was between us was hard to ignore, and I'd denied myself this feeling for so long. All of this? The electricity between us? It was downright intoxicating.

I didn't tell him everything running through my head, but I'd said enough to make it awkward.

I started to regret not coming up with a lie because I was going to combust if he didn't let me come soon.

"Look at me." His voice was deep and dark with want.

I bit the inside of my cheek but found the will to turn my cheek. Slate-blue eyes bored into me, no less intense than before. "Some might say *The Lovers* represents the desire to love. Magritte thought genuine love was unattainable because of people's own inhibitions. If they took the sheet off, they would see—but instead they let themselves be isolated by their own fears of what they'd find."

My lips parted. "You knew him?"

August nodded. "For a time." He must have seen the curiosity that sparked because he continued, "He was horribly depressing. I'll tell you anything you want to know about Rene Magritte over dinner. We can happily discuss the meaning behind *The Lovers*, just not tonight."

I lifted an eyebrow at him. "You're persistent."

"You came here for me to fuck you, did you not?" His fingers pushed deeper as his thumb circled my clit.

All thoughts of *The Lovers* evaporated as I rocked my hips into him.

My lips parted as my legs started to stiffen. His fingers disappeared, taking my impending orgasm with them.

I yanked against the restraints, but they didn't budge an inch. "I asked you a question, Nathalie. I expect an answer."

I bit my lip in frustration. "Yes."

He slapped my pussy, sending a jolt of pleasure through me. I moaned. "Yes, what?"

"Yes, Sir," I murmured. His fingers slipped into my panties once more.

"You came here to get fucked and didn't want to be in control. Why is that?" His voice was a rumble in his chest that resonated in mine.

"I . . ." The words dried up on my tongue as I tried to

form a coherent answer while he had two fingers buried in me.

"Words," August said in a growl. "Use them or I'll change my mind about that reward."

"I can't forget," I whispered hoarsely.

"Forget what?"

"Anything." It was both less and more than I wanted to admit, but my body made me weak in his quest for answers. "But I can be distracted," I added.

Understanding crossed his expression. He didn't. Not really. No one understood what it was like to remember every moment of your life with perfect clarity. What it meant to exist without being able to truly forget. To be a literal library of information that was always growing because I sought out new experiences like a beggar did food.

But he understood enough.

"I'm your distraction."

"You have an uncanny ability to hold my attention, *Sir*," I repeated.

He snorted, the action so at odds with the way he worked me into a desperate, needy mess. "You could have gone to Bliss if you needed a distraction." I groaned but didn't respond. My face must have betrayed me because a wicked glint entered his eyes. "You did, didn't you?"

I wanted to deny it. To lie. To pretend that I didn't go back there or that it took being hit on to realize I didn't just want *any* distraction.

August withdrew his hand entirely, and I nearly cried out in protest. He moved back, kneeling between my legs. "Answer me," he demanded, running his nose over my slit and breathing me in.

"I did, Sir."

The sadistic satisfaction in his gaze shouldn't have turned me on more. August slipped his thumbs under opposite sides of my panties, then pulled. The material ripped at the seams. He flung it aside, then placed his hands on my bare thighs to spread me further. "Why didn't it distract you?"

"I couldn't find a partner, Sir."

He lifted both his brows, doubting that. "Did no one ask you?"

I bit the inside of my cheek. "They did . . ."

"They?" He repeated the word so softly, I might have wondered if I heard it right under different circumstances. "How many people asked you?"

I squirmed under his watchful eyes. "Four."

"And you couldn't find a partner?"

His tone was only a touch condescending, but it turned me on. "Not the right one."

"The right one?" he asked, lips brushing against my hip bone. "What were they lacking?"

I opened then closed my mouth. "We didn't connect. The vibes weren't good. The one I did like—" He licked me once, the rough scrape of his tongue on my clit making me jolt.

"You were saying?"

I swallowed hard and tried again. "The one I did like, she wanted something I wasn't down to give." He brushed lazy circles over my clit with his thumb.

"What was that?"

When I didn't immediately answer, he stopped. "If I have to repeat myself, you won't like the consequences when I fuck these." He leaned forward to lower the cups on both my breasts, pushing them up. I was a modest C, at best. If deep throating him took effort, my boobs would be covered in bruises from how hard he'd have to grip them for that.

"She wanted to feed," I admitted. Not because the idea of that punishment scared me, but because I knew he'd get it out of me, eventually.

"Was she a vampire—"

"Succubus," I said in a rush. "Sir."

My admission sat between us, like a storm brewing. His eyes were the clouds, heavy with rain. My body was the lightning rod, just waiting for the rain to start and electricity to strike.

"And yet you invited me to feed from you *again*," he said, his cheekbones appearing sharper between the low lights in his bedroom.

It wasn't a question, so I chose not to say anything at all.

To my surprise, he accepted that, and lowered his face between my thighs. Two fingers pushed into me in sharp, hard movements. He sucked on my clit, bringing me right to the edge.

I threw my head back against the midnight pillows. Any pleas I might have made, I swallowed down as he continued to toy with me. "I feel you tightening," he said. "Do you want to come, *my* sunling?"

"Yes, *please*, Sir."

"Then beg." He continued pumping his fingers into me, hitting a certain spot just right to keep me right there on the edge. "Show me how sweet you can be. That those pretty lips are good for more than sucking my cock."

He was filthy like this. It was exactly what I needed. Permission to be nothing and no one but this. The object of his desire.

Some people exercised to find relief. Others found peace

in nature or cooking. I found absolution from being Nathalie Le Fay in *this*.

"Please, let me come." I arched my back, trying to grind my hips into his hand for more friction. "I'll be good. I'll be so good. You can do anything you want to me, Sir, just please—I want to feel you feed from me."

He withdrew his fingers again, and I nearly screamed. "Nooooo, please," I groaned heavily. "I need to feel you. Let me please you. I'll do anything—"

His cock nudged my entrance and then slammed into me. I was so wet there was no resistance. Just gliding. "You say my name when you come," he grunted.

Then his hips rolled. The fullness overpowered me. I wrapped my legs around his waist, pressing my heels into the small of his back. The chains on my cuffs rattled against the metal headboard as my body pulled taut, stretched to its limit.

"Yes, Sir," I moaned.

His fingers bit into my thighs as he bent my legs further, pulling them around to hook on his shoulders. The results made my world narrow to focus on two things.

Him, and how deep he was fucking me.

Everything in me stiffened as I hovered on the precipice of bliss.

"Come on my cock," he commanded. "And keep those eyes on me." It was all I needed to fly over the edge.

La petite mort.

The little death.

A period of total blackout where one moment I was crying out his name and the next there was *nothing*.

All too soon, my body convulsed again, pulling me back to the surface as it clenched around him. Then again. And again.

I'd never had an orgasm last so long, the shudders racking my core, sending spasms down my legs. It was unlike anything I'd experienced. I knew without a doubt he was giving me what I wanted and feeding from me, because this orgasm didn't last seconds. It went on for minutes.

"Fuck," he cursed, pounding into me. "You taste so good. So perfect." He leaned in close, biting my neck roughly while his cock threatened to split me in two.

I'd be covered in more than a couple of light bruises tomorrow . . . and I didn't give a flying fuck. It was worth it.

The way he fit inside me and instinctively knew my body.

The way he looked at me like I was his world.

The way he held me like he never wanted to let go.

Everything I'd experienced this night.

It was all worth it.

twenty-one

I LAID IN BED, listening to her heartbeat as the early afternoon sun crept into the Parisian sky. It was still early in New Chicago, but in Paris, the day had already been underway for hours.

After the half-dozen times I'd fucked her through the night, Nathalie seemed to sleep like the dead. She was also a bed hog. I didn't mind; it forced her to sprawl over my chest, leg tossed over me with one arm wrapped around my neck and the other splayed across my sheets. My fingers trailed up her smooth calf to her bare thigh.

I was sincerely tempted to wake her with my mouth between her legs, but couldn't bring myself to. Not when I knew waking her would likely result in her leaving. I wasn't sure if she'd meant to spend the night, or had simply been too exhausted after the many ways I'd taken her and fed.

While experienced, I rarely took enough and kept it down sufficiently to actually be full. For the first time in centuries, I felt sated.

A light scratching at my bedroom door told me Estrid was awake and was demanding breakfast. I didn't want to move. Not when Nathalie's body was warm and naked, draped across mine. One leg arched up, curling around my waist. The black sheet had ended up on the floor during the night, giving me a glorious view of the golden curve of her ass. Every pore. Every freckle. Every scar.

I wanted to memorize them all.

Estrid meowed, growing impatient, as if she knew I was awake and ignoring her.

With a heavy sigh, I carefully slipped out from under her and stuffed a pillow where I'd been. She hummed in her sleep, curling her limbs around it, none the wiser.

My cock twitched, but I ignored it, walking silently around to my closet. I pulled out a pair of sweatpants and tugged them on before slipping out of the room. To make sure I heard when she woke, I kept the door cracked as I padded into my kitchen.

Cat food wasn't prepackaged like it had been in the old days. In terms of things that carried over, pets weren't really one of them. They were just another mouth to feed, when so many struggled to feed themselves. I purchased tuna fresh from the market twice a week for Estrid and sprinkled on the ground vitamin mixture my brother's mate, Rajvi, made for me. The mixture was prepared in a container I kept refrigerated, which meant every time I got anything out of the refrigerator, Estrid firmly believed it was her food and proceeded to yell at me.

Fortunately for her, I wanted to keep Nathalie asleep. So an early breakfast it was. I was so preoccupied with my thoughts, I didn't notice what should have been obvious.

"How long have you been fucking her?"

My entire body stiffened. The good mood I'd found myself in turned dark.

I turned to set Estrid's dish on the island and placed my

hands on the edge to keep from doing something I shouldn't.

"What the fuck are you doing in my apartment, Sasha?"

Sitting on the couch, exactly where I'd been not eight hours ago with my cock down Nathalie's throat, was my mate. She wore all black and her legs were crossed, body language stiff, as she no doubt smelled what we'd been up to.

Livid didn't describe my emotion. I would have yelled, had Nathalie not been sleeping right on the other side of the wall.

Sasha's green cat eyes narrowed. "You left the scene after taking your sweet time to report it to me. I couldn't find you anywhere. Not at the Poppy Garden or your brother's. You weren't answering your phone. Then it died. I wasn't sure if something had happened . . ." She looked away and took a deep breath, then closed her eyes.

"I'm not yours to worry about," I said quietly. She meant well; I knew that. I simply didn't care.

Sasha was the mate I didn't want, yet she struggled to accept that. Her refusal to try continually put us in these terrible situations.

"But you're hers?" she snapped.

Black edged my vision. My grip on the counter turned lethal and the wood beneath my fingers started to give under the pressure.

"It's none of your fucking business," I growled. "You know you aren't welcome here. Not now. Not ever."

A wounded expression crossed her face. A hurt so deep she couldn't keep it behind the mask she so desperately clung to. It vanished quickly, only to be replaced by cold fury.

This wasn't good.

"I'm the Demon Queen's second and you were first on the scene. With the way you just disappeared, I'm entitled to inquire about where you've been and with whom. Rather suspicious, don't you think?" She was stretching, and we both knew it.

"You were the one who ordered me to look for the woman in the picture. I did. I reported back. There's nothing suspicious about going home—"

"With her twin sister?" Sasha replied.

I clenched my teeth. "You're having me followed." It was the only possible explanation. There was no way she should have known that the woman I was pining after was Katherine's twin. It was both a relief and a complication when I started asking about the girl in the picture and got two different names.

I'd been wondering how many identities she could possibly have until I found someone that knew them both. Katherine and Nathalie Le Fay. Daughters to the nearly extinct black witch Le Fay family.

Except Nathalie wasn't a black witch and Katherine was.

A few years ago, Nathalie had disappeared, falling off the radar of many people after some great falling out between the sisters. Her family had all but disowned her.

If not for the few people that recognized her as someone that served soup at a food bank, or handed out clothes at a women's shelter, or sold seeds and plants in a largely human market every other Saturday, I might not have any idea where she'd been during those years. The information was conflicting, but after scenting Katherine when I was at the hospital, I was sure of at least one thing. They were not the same person.

I was relieved in more ways than one. At first, I'd

thought Sasha was playing me out of jealousy. Then I thought she truly didn't know about Nathalie. I'd wanted to keep it that way.

Sasha scoffed at my accusation. "I don't need to have you followed. I recognize her backpack and the sweater on your floor because she was wearing them last night at the *family dinner.*"

Family what? Sasha was an orphan. Nathalie was a witch. There was no possible way they were related. Sure, I'd briefly scented my mate on her, but Sasha met with a lot of people, and after learning Nathalie was volunteering all over the city, it wasn't farfetched to believe that was the reason. It was hardly anything to dwell on. At least that's what I'd convinced myself of when I made the choice to pursue her.

"You don't have a family," I replied tersely. "You're an orphan. Not even your beloved Lucifer could find them. I know, because he asked me to look."

She stared at me in shock with something close to hatred. "Not all family is blood, asshole." She wasn't wrong, but I was going to cling to every possible thread I had here. I couldn't just let Nathalie slip away. Not my sunling.

"Fine, so you're friends." I shrugged, but the action was jerky because the tension in my muscles wouldn't dissipate. Not while my fucking mate was in my house. "It doesn't matter. I don't have to like all her friends to be with her."

Sasha licked her bottom lip, something visceral entering her gaze. "Does she know?"

Estrid rubbed against me, purring as she tried to sucker me into giving her more food. I ignored her. "Does she know what?" I snapped, not wanting to answer her. I didn't know they were even friends, and I'd yet to mention that I had a mate, so that was going to be a resounding no.

"Does she know that I'm your mate?"

twenty-two

NATHALIE

I FROZE WHERE I STOOD.

Blood rushed to my head, making me dizzy. The room started to spin, and I put a hand on the wall to steady myself.

Surely, I'd heard wrong.

He couldn't have a mate.

It couldn't be Sasha.

I didn't see her, but I knew her voice better than most. There was no mistaking it. No mistaking her.

That was why Lucifer woke me. I thought he was being a jealous prick, hellbent on interrupting my sleep. Now I wanted to walk back into the room and pretend I'd never heard it, but that's not the kind of person I was. I may ignore some complicated shit in my life, but not at the expense of my friends.

My footsteps were quiet compared to the two beings in the living room, and my presence had remained unnoticed while they fought. August had yet to answer her. So she asked again.

"Does she know I'm your mate, August?"

"No."

Both heads snapped toward me. However impossible it seemed, they hadn't realized I was here listening to them until the damning words had left their mouths.

On the couch where I'd crawled to him, Sasha sat, dressed in black, as if in mourning. Her expression was so cold. So angry. I was familiar with her anger, but the emotion that caused this was hurt. That, I hadn't seen on her before.

"Nathalie—" August started. He walked around the counter and a fluffy, pure black cat followed him. His sweats hung low, leaving every possible delectable inch of his skin on display. I flamed red from checking him out, and from the preceding guilt from that action after what I'd just heard.

"You have a mate." I didn't know what else to say. How to act. What to do. This wasn't a situation I'd ever found myself in, but I was intimately acquainted with betrayal.

"It's not what you think," August started. He approached me rapidly, reaching out to touch me. I saw the pain and jealousy that flashed across Sasha's face and recoiled. He stopped, fists clenched and jaw rigid.

"You're not her mate?" I replied, my voice bitter but strong. I was thankful for that. Thankful that The Warden decided to make an appearance, even though she hadn't wanted me to go find him to begin with. Thankfully, Ann kept her mouth shut while Caretaker tried to console Peace, who was utterly distraught.

"I am, but—"

"Then it's exactly what I think." I bit the inside of my cheek and turned away, trying to stop the water from forming in my eyes. "You lied to me. You led me on. Gods.

You've been all but begging for a date, and you're mated to one of my closest friends?"

Disgust bubbled in my stomach. Disgust with him. Disgust with myself.

Inherently, I knew this wasn't my fault. I truly hadn't known about them.

"I'm not mated," he insisted. Sasha let out a haughty laugh. Mocking. He glared in her direction. "I'm not. Yes, Sasha is my mate, but I've refused the bond. I don't want her—"

"And that makes it better?"

The way she seemed to go totally still over his words broke me. Sasha may be rough around the edges, but she deserved love and happiness. I hadn't known she'd found her mate. Under different circumstances, I might have been irked. Right now, all I felt was sympathy because I could understand why she'd never said anything.

I'd neglected to tell people about my betrothed. That he cheated on me. I could only guess how deeply it cut to have a mate who didn't want you.

August growled. Turning to Sasha, he said, "This is your fault. You just can't help yourself, can you? You had to ruin my one chance because it's not with you, and then wonder why I want nothing to do with you."

Sasha regarded him coldly. "You're the one who chose one of my friends to shack up with."

"I didn't know," he roared back. I jolted, and an apologetic expression fell over him instantly. It made me feel worse somehow.

Sasha scoffed. "I had to touch her to drop her at Bliss last night. There's no fucking way you didn't scent me on her. You're a godsdamn liar."

I immediately recalled what he'd told me about his

sense of smell. She wasn't wrong. If it was strong enough to scent magic, it was strong enough to smell her on my skin.

I looked at him, waiting for an explanation. August sighed. "I was aware you'd met her or been in contact with her somehow," he said to me. "But not like this. I swear to you, Nathalie—"

"Your words mean nothing," I whispered. "You lied by omission. Even if you didn't know who Sasha was to me—or me to her—that doesn't negate that you have a mate. Her magic is literally the *only thing* in existence that will ever balance you. Even if you don't want it now, you'll cave. If my best friend, a woman who spent her entire life hunting and killing our kind, can fall in love with a demon, you're all but hers already."

I backed away. There was nothing he could say to change my mind. I only wished I wasn't drenched in his scent and standing in his living room wearing nothing but his shirt when it all came crashing down.

At least I'd found out before I dove too deep. Before I pulled the white sheet over my face and let myself be tempted by an ignorance that would only ruin everything. Especially my already fractured heart.

"I'm not," August said, stepping toward me. Desperation and anger had taken over his features, and it was clear he was struggling to keep himself under control. "I've known for years that she's my mate. We both have, and I've never even kissed her. I may not have asked how you knew her, but just because fate chose to fuck me over by tying us together, that doesn't mean anything will ever come of it."

I shook my head. "That you speak of her that way . . . It's only going to hurt you both when you do eventually give in. You'll regret this. All of it." I motioned to the couch and winced. I could only hope that Sasha thought I was motioning to her and not what we'd done there.

August growled. It made me freeze, against my better instincts.

"So that's it? We could have *everything* together, but because of a bond I did *not* and have not *ever* chosen, you're going to punish us both?"

I wasn't so stubborn I didn't see what he was saying. I just disagreed with the outcome. I'd seen the mate bond firsthand in so many situations. It always won. Always. Magic might be a gift, but it came with a price to the immortal species. Their futures were not their own.

Where witches had psychic bondmates, that kind of bond could be anyone. A child. A friend. A sister. Not just a lover.

Mates, brides, atmas—they were all the same. A single person destined for an individual that would prevent you from spiraling into insanity—in return for the insanity of infatuation.

I may have had issues with my own mortality, but I didn't envy their mate bonds.

"I'm sorry you see it as a punishment," I said honestly. "But I'm no one in the grand scheme of things. This fling," I motioned toward him, then shrugged. "It's *nothing*. She's your endgame, and you should really focus on fixing the issues between you two." I turned to Sasha, struggling with how to convey to her that I never meant to hurt her. "I'm so sorry. I didn't know."

Her expression softened. Green eyes sad, she nodded. "Get your things. I'll take you home. If that's what you want . . .?"

"Please."

I stepped around August to go for my bag, but his hand reached out to stop me.

Fingers tight and rough, he wrapped them around my forearm, pulling me to a complete stop. "If you're going to hold the mate bond up as some sort of eventuality, then you need to know that you're a bond potential."

My head whipped around as I looked at him. "Excuse me?"

"Our kind may have mates like almost everyone else, but we also have a different type of bond. It's—"

"I know what an aurae bond is."

Biologically, his magic had decided that *I* was not just acceptable, but rather that I was the absolute optimum for fucking, feeding, and impregnating. All succubi and incubi had them. While uncommon, they weren't the same as the mate bond because there was a hell of a lot more choice involved. But they were also easier to ignore.

"Then you know that I don't have to be with her, because my magic has accepted you."

I blanched. My breath came hard in anger. "I'm not sure if I'm more offended that you think you can just replace her with me, like we're some kind of one-size fits all—"

"That's not what I'm saying."

"Or," I continued, "that you knew I was a bond potential and were pursuing me for that reason, yet never mentioned it until now because for whatever reason, you're determined to throw away your mate." I flung my free hand toward Sasha. Meanwhile, his cat remained unperturbed by our argument as she wound her way between our legs.

"And when was I supposed to mention it, exactly?" he bit back. "When you were swearing up and down you just wanted a quick fuck at Bliss and nothing more? When you refused to give us a shot and repeatedly walked away?"

I shrank a little at the accuracy of the jab. Even angry, I could see his point. That was, until he turned cruel. "Or would you rather I mentioned it when I was spanking your ass and fucking your throat? What about when you were tied to my bed, begging for me to feed from you—saying you'd give me *anything* if I just let you come?"

"Fuck you," I snarled.

I wasn't an angry person by nature. In fact, I did almost everything in my power to prevent being angry. It demanded every bit of restraint I had to keep that door closed when he acted like this.

"Gladly," he growled. "Since the only time you're willing to give into this is when my cock is in you."

Shame and desire hit me hard. My own arousal spiked, making my face flame red. I was always into assholes. I knew that. It was like I had a dickface radar that just homed in on the men that would fuck me dirty but leave me broken. I'd started to think August would be different. What a rude awakening it was.

The potent combination sent my anger over the edge.

My free hand swung, slapping him with the full force of my hundred and forty pounds. Seeing as he was a supernatural creature, the hit didn't do anything except make me feel better. "You're being crude just to hurt me because you're pissed."

August leaned in, inhaling deeply.

"That's where you're wrong. I'm not crude to hurt you, I'm crude because I can smell your arousal and want nothing more than to fuck you on my kitchen counter and be done with the bullshit games." His voice was deeper. Gruff. It rumbled through him in the same tone he'd used when commanding me the night before. Which only made my own arousal worse because I could so easily picture what he said. "I'm pissed that you're refusing to acknowledge half of this argument. That you're choosing to be *ignorant* about my rejecting Sasha and actively pursuing you." His word choice didn't evade my notice, and I glowered. "You can't insist that we're a lost cause because of the fucking mate bond and then completely ignore that you're a bond match. Some unknown magic may have picked her, but *my magic* picked *you*. You're one in a fucking million for me, and you're being obstinate despite wanting me as much as I want you."

He left me speechless.

What did one say to that? I couldn't even wrap my head around learning I was a potential bond for him—one he wanted—despite having Sasha as a mate and rejecting her completely.

The logical part of me said there was more going on here. I didn't know the entire story, but it made absolutely zero sense for him to choose me when he couldn't seem to stand her.

"Nathalie, I'm leaving. You can either get your stuff and come with me or don't, but I'm not listening to any more of this."

Guilt slammed into me. I pulled away from him, and despite the rock-hard grip, he let me go. Tempted as I was to dress in my own clothes, I didn't think I could be in his apartment any longer. Grabbing my backpack, I threw it over my shoulder and tied my sweater around my waist. Thankfully, my boots were in the living room. I didn't want to have to buy and break in new ones.

"You know where to find me when you change your mind," he said, the picture of cool, calm control again.

I laughed once, but it was empty. "I'm a quick learner. I don't make bad choices twice."

He shook his head, but I refused to look him in the eye. I didn't want to see whatever was there.

"I'll be back for the debrief of the crime scene," Sasha said, standing to meet me partway across the room.

"You'll never step foot in my home again if you know what's good for you," he replied. "I'm done playing investigator. If you want my cooperation, your Demon Queen will have to make me."

Sasha tilted her head as she took my wrist. "So be it."

twenty-three

NATHALIE

WE STEPPED out of the void, directly into my apartment.

I dropped my bag on the kitchen counter and my boots by the door. "Do you want to talk about it?" I did and didn't, but was well aware what I wanted didn't matter much in this situation.

"Do you think I want to talk about *my* mate who has rejected every single advance from me, but wants to complete his bond with you?"

It was a fair response.

No, it wasn't cool she was taking it out on me—but I could give her a little grace. At least for today. That couldn't have been an easy thing to walk in on.

I nodded and started to walk away. I need to shower and get the smell of sex off me. The smell of *him*. Not to mention the dried remains of August's release chafing between my thighs.

Echoes of the things he said and the way he made me feel played through my mind.

I already knew better than to think I could forget, so I did the next best thing.

I told The Warden and Ann to pack it up. Put those memories away and deal with Peace. Caretaker wasn't enough for this, and Bad Nat . . . I didn't want to speak to her.

The mocking eyebrow she lifted in my direction was enough.

"Wait—" Sasha broke off, sighing. I paused, turning back to her. She seemed to be struggling with whatever it was she wanted to say. I made it easier for her.

"It's okay. I won't stand here to be your punching bag. I don't deserve that, but you don't owe me anything. Take whatever time you need."

She wrung her hands in a way that was very unlike her. A strange combination of frustration and guilt confused her expression. Sasha closed her eyes and blew out a breath. "It's not you," she said eventually. "You didn't—you're not who I'm angry with."

I nodded in complete understanding. "That doesn't change how hard it is."

Truly. I'd been in her shoes. I'd walked this path. I'd walked worse, because instead of a friend who didn't know, it was my sister, who did. I didn't wish that betrayal on her.

"Yeah," she sighed. "On one hand I feel like an awful bitch because he clearly has feelings for you . . . On the other hand, I wanted to slit your throat when I saw you wearing his shirt. He's never looked at me the way he looked at you. He won't touch me. He refuses to talk about it. There's never been anything, because he can't stand to be around me. Hates me . . . he always has, but the way he spoke to you—" Her mouth snapped shut as emotion clogged her throat. So many things were reflected in her eyes, most of them painfully reminiscent of my own past. "You're handling this better than I can. I really . . . appreciate it. Thank you."

I dipped my head in acknowledgment. "For what it's worth, I really am sorry."

Both for the reasons she knew and the reasons she didn't.

I wasn't just sorry I'd fucked her mate. I was sorry for how much I *liked* it, and how much I liked him. Sorry that I still did, even knowing what I did now.

Sorry that a small part of me was happy that they weren't together yet.

It wasn't cheating in the conventional sense. He really did want *me*, and I liked that. Too much.

I wouldn't say it, though. Just as she had her feelings, I had mine.

The good. The bad. The ugly.

She laughed bitterly. "I know. Don't take this the wrong way, but it just speaks to how good and kind and deserving you are that you're apologizing to me when you shouldn't have to. You didn't know. You're even an aurae bond potential . . . Of everyone I know, you deserve love and happiness more than almost any of them. The things you do for this city. What you've done for Sienna and me—I'll never be able to repay you for taking us in when she almost died. You gave us a home, jobs, a whole life. If it were anyone else but him . . ." Her voice trailed away, eyes begging me to understand. Sasha didn't beg. She didn't plead. But for him, she was.

I didn't like that any more than the insinuation that she owed me for being a decent person, or that she'd give up someone she liked to pay that imagined debt—were it anyone else but August. Anger turned my stomach.

Yet, there was a small part of me that was not just angry *for* her, but *at* her. He'd rejected her. They'd never been anything, they both said it. What gave her the right to him over me? A bond that he didn't want?

Gods, did I understand that.

Wasn't it I that said I didn't envy immortals their mates because they lacked the right to choose?

Was it truly lying by omission when I did keep walking away and never gave us the chance to be anything more than a fling?

Those were ugly thoughts. The ones I didn't like thinking, but acknowledged they were there. Thoughts by themselves weren't a problem.

Actions were.

She was his mate. No words could break that. Unless one of them was dead, no rejection would ever be absolute. At least when it came to mates and lovers.

He was hers, whether he saw it or not. Sasha would also always feel that. Except, unlike him, it was painfully obvious she would be his mate in every sense of the word if he let her. Those feelings wouldn't just go away overnight, if ever.

Above all of that, she was my friend. A good and true friend. What would that say about me if I continued to hook up with her mate, even if he didn't want her, knowing how much it hurt her?

There were too many variables. Too many feelings. Too much emotion.

That's why Ann and The Warden needed to handle this. Whatever I felt toward August, it wasn't worth the trouble it would cause.

"If you want to talk about it, we can talk about it. But

I'm happy to put this behind us if you are," I said eventually.

Sasha twisted her mouth, forming a dimple in her left cheek as she hesitated, then nodded. "This is going to complicate the case with your sister."

I hadn't forgotten. August was her spy that discovered the last crime scene, I'd learned.

"We'll deal. If we don't find the killer soon, I'll have to talk to him about what happened at the hospital. If you talk to him, you might as well kick a hornet's nest."

Sasha blew out a breath. "Yeah. We really need Marcel to agree to do the summoning tonight."

Her desperation to find Kat and our killer had reached new levels with the way this had gone. I wanted to ask *who* August was that she'd chosen to use him as an informant, but it would likely make her more suspicious or hurt. Now more than ever I needed to be able to trust her.

"I'll deal with Marcel. Has the hospital delivered records on our victims?"

Sasha shook her head. "Not yet. It seems this mess has highlighted their lack of record keeping—they don't know who was assigned to floor six that night."

I grimaced. "Is there proof of everyone who was on shift?"

Sasha nodded reluctantly. "There's a record, but we don't know if it's been tampered with."

"Send it over and all the footage of that night. I'll find them."

Sasha frowned. "We have a whole team on this. Isadora—"

"Is going to drag her feet and try to cover her own ass. Kat is involved in this somehow, and she's potentially in danger. I need to know who those people were on the off chance they weren't random targets so I can figure out the pattern." I tapped my fingers against my thigh impatiently. Things weren't moving fast enough for me on this front. I partly had myself to blame, and that would be rectified soon.

"I'll have everything sent over. Where would you like the remains taken?"

"The Wicked Haunt," I said. "They'll be needed for the summoning. Bring them with you. A bone from each person as well. I'll have him do them all at once."

A small dip formed between her brows. "There are ten victims. He won't be able to—"

"Marcel can do it," I interrupted, feeling a bit edgy myself after the morning I'd had. "He's not your average warlock—and it's safer than having to repeat the spell again and again. Entering the veil and returning . . ." I kept my face carefully neutral and devoid of emotion. "It will take a lot out of you. Be prepared for that."

"I'm immortal. If a witch can do it, I should be fine."

I didn't think she meant it to come across as crass, but I had to hide the way my body wanted to stiffen. I wasn't sure if it was the immortal comment or the condescending assumption. "I hope so," I responded. We weren't sure how things would end up using a succubus versus a witch. There was no way to know. Would it be better, because they had supernatural healing, or worse, because their magic wasn't like ours?

"Is there anything else?" she asked me. I lifted my eyebrows as she added, "That I need to know about tonight? Anything I need to bring?"

"Wear something you don't care about and bring a change of clothes. Things can get bloody."

That was putting it mildly. Sasha nodded, lifting a foot to step into the void.

"Oh, and Sasha?" I stopped her just before she left, disappearing into the world of shadow that allowed her to go anywhere in the world with a single step.

"Hm?"

"You should feed before tonight."

I purposely didn't look at her because I didn't want to see whatever expression played out on her face at the mention of feeding. I didn't want her to see the look on mine either. Not when August had been doing that to me only hours ago.

She didn't respond, yet I knew when she was gone.

The cold had lifted, but the numbness was just beginning to settle inside of me.

twenty-four

I FLIPPED the marble coffee table.

It went six inches through the far wall then cracked down the middle. The metal stand vibrated from hitting the floor too hard, chipping the wood.

I breathed hard, not feeling the slightest bit better.

Contrary to the careful control I maintained around my sunling, her leaving with Sasha smashed the door wide open for the other side of me to come barreling through. The side my magic created. The monster with a hair-trigger temper that had already grown far too attached to her in so little time.

I'd fed last night, thinking that would soothe the cravings.

It only worked till she left with my fucking "mate," still smelling of me and our coupling. Then all it did was use that energy I'd gained to fuel the anger. The wrath. At Sasha. At her. At myself for not handling this problem sooner, the way my magic wanted to. It whispered sweet and terrible things—telling me to kill Sasha. End her existence. That she was the barrier between us and the one we desired.

Logically, some part of me knew this wasn't completely true.

Nathalie had been reluctant *before* she knew about Sasha. After last night, I'd been fairly certain she would come around within the next six months.

Now, those hopes had been obliterated and replaced by a cold rage.

Estrid stood on the island counter, staring at me with resting bitch face, unamused by my behavior. Her fluffy black tail waved back and forth behind her, showing her irritation.

"Don't look at me like that," I snapped.

She let out an obnoxious meow, as if she could understand that I was dismissing her.

"No. You're not getting second breakfast. You let that cunt in here and didn't even tell me before she ruined everything." I motioned to my empty apartment.

Estrid cocked her head.

"*Meowwww.*"

For fuck's sake.

I was talking to my fucking cat.

Growling in frustration under my breath, I started for the mystport that would take me to New Chicago. Nothing good would come of me staying here right now, not when everything smelled of sex and anger. The scents of my bond and my mate mixed together, riling my magic. Pushing it to lash out and wipe Sasha from the face of the earth because just breathing the same air as my sunling *tainted* it. It was unwise to put myself closer to Sasha Loren, but even more so to stay in my apartment with the rageful side of me so close to the surface.

The Poppy Garden was all but empty.

I ignored the urge to dig through my opium stash for the tea mixture I preferred. Drugs would *not* help the situation. I needed to keep my head about me now more than ever, because I couldn't afford to spiral and fuck this up further.

Jenny was off duty when I entered the convenience store front, which was a very good thing. I would have struggled with my response had she been a smartass and asked about where Nathalie was.

Outside, the late October air brought a chill with it. Especially when I was dressed in nothing but sweatpants, but I was concerned about what would happen if I entered my bedroom again—where her tantalizing scent was most concentrated. Unwilling to risk it, I hastily threw a glamour over myself to avoid attention then hailed down a taxi.

There was only two people on this godsforsaken planet that knew about the urges I fought against my whole life, thanks to the cursed magic in my veins.

My brother—who I would rather step on nails than speak to about this—and Anders. It was an easy choice who would get my bright and scowling face for a wake-up call this morning.

Anders's apartment was in an okay part of town at best, where the streets always looked empty but never truly were. Muggings were common. Murders less so, not that he or I had to really worry about that. We were some of the worst sort that walked this city—and we had the reputation to back it up.

Mentally I reached out to him as I climbed the stairs of his building, nodding to Tina and Angie on their balcony— his next-door succubi neighbors. Unlike most women, I struggled less with them because they were mated lesbians who'd never made a pass at me. Tina nodded back, sensing I wasn't in the mood to chat. Angie waved with a slight smile on her face, friendly but never overly so.

I need your help.

His groggy response came a moment later. *With what? It's nine in the morning—*

Anders's bitching cut off when I thumped my closed fist against his door.

It took a minute, but he answered. His dark brown hair was loose and unkempt. Sleep still lined his eyes.

I dropped my glamour and his eyes widened a fraction.

"Fuck," he groaned, holding the door wide. "Get your ass in here."

I didn't need to be told twice.

His apartment was nice but humble. He didn't keep mementos of his years on this earth like I did. He preferred a minimalist approach that divulged little to nothing about the man if you didn't know him.

The wood from the ship he'd served on in the eighteen hundreds had been preserved, then used to lay his floors. The scent of sea water was still there if I paid attention to it, even after two hundred years. His armor from the Middle Ages had been melted down by his own hand. He fashioned hardware for this place and a dozen others he had around the world. The bones of his various steeds were carved into art that adorned his walls—those were the only things that truly resembled sentimentality to the untrained eye. Each piece told the story of what life he'd lived with that animal.

The last one he created was over a hundred years ago.

Before he'd worked for the devil. Before he'd fallen in love. Before he'd lost his wife and child.

I'd been the one to pick up the broken pieces of him back then.

"When was the last time you fed? You know you're not supposed to go so long—"

"Last night," I bit out. "You know the woman I told you about?" I took a seat on his couch, then got back up and paced.

"You found her again?"

I nodded. He scrunched his features, trying to figure out where this was going. "I thought she was a bond potential. Hell, you didn't accidentally kill her, did you?"

"I didn't kill her," I snapped, crossing the distance between us in a beat. Anders lifted his hands in surrender.

"How about this, you talk and tell me why you look like you're on the verge of going feral, and I'll listen and save my questions for after?"

I looked away, ashamed of my own reactions but unable to fully control them. I nodded, and he exhaled a taut breath, then went around the counter to brew his breakfast. "Coffee?"

"No."

"More for me."

My jaw muscles tensed, but I let it go. His nonchalance and unflappable demeanor were why I came to him in moments like this and not to Rafael. "I'd found her again at Bliss not long after our first encounter. She let me feed from her that night . . . before running off again."

I heard him choke on a laugh before trying to poorly disguise it as a cough. "Are you done yet?" I snapped.

"Sorry, mate," he said, not at all sounding apologetic. "Continue."

"Before she left, I told her where Fives was if she changed her mind. That was over a week ago. Last night on my way home, she was right there at the register buying doughnuts from Jenny." It was far too easy to recall the look on her face and the sound of her heartbeat when she saw me. The memory constricted within my chest.

"Okaaaay," Anders drawled.

"I took her home."

He froze. "To Paris?"

I nodded. "I couldn't help it. After I tried her once, I had to again but without the possibility of us being interrupted."

Anders seemed to consider that, turning to lean back against his counter and crossing his arms. "Smart, given how the previous times have gone. I take it she let you feed from her again?"

Like a fucking buffet.

"The entire night."

His eyebrows lifted dubiously. ". . . and you didn't kill her?" One look from me and he looked away and muttered, "Didn't kill her. Got it."

"That's the thing," I said, running a hand through my hair and pulling it hard in an attempt to relieve the building pressure of wanting to throw something. Again. "She's not just a positive match. She's *the* match. I've found aurae bonds before, and none of them come anywhere close to what I—"

"You talk about her like she's your mate."

At the mention of Sasha, my magic riled once more, pushing at my barriers and self-control.

"Sasha showed up at my place this morning, while she was still there."

Whatever amusement he might have had dropped away instantly.

"Shit. Did *she* kill her?"

"No! She's not fucking dead. No one is fucking dead," I

growled. "Sasha had blackmailed me into looking for someone—"

"Sounds like something she'd do," Anders snorted.

"—because the murders that have been happening look similar to what I can do. She gave me a picture, and it was my su . . . it was her twin, but I didn't know it was her twin until I did some searching. Then Sasha was pissed I didn't sit around and wait for her at the crime scene I called in. She showed up this morning *in Paris,* enraged I had someone there with me, claiming I'm now a suspect, and then drops a truth bomb that not only are they friends— they have a goddamn family dinner night." I stopped speaking when Anders's face cracked. He looked around his apartment as if avoiding my gaze and then ran a hand down his face.

"Of all the women in New Chicago, your aurae just *had* to be Nathalie Le Fay."

I tensed. "You know her." It wasn't an accusation, but it sure as shit wasn't a question either.

Anders nodded. "You know that I serve the demon, Ronan, now. His atma is the Demon Queen. I knew Piper before she was that, back when she was a bounty hunter masquerading as human. That's when I met Nat." He said her name with a familiarity that I didn't have, and the illogical part of my brain almost lost it. "She's Piper's best friend. I'm not sure how they met, but Sasha and Sienna used to live with them, all under Nat's roof. They're more like sisters than friends." Anders sighed. He looked mid-thirties in appearance. All fully mature fae did, but every now and then his true age showed when he just looked *tired.* This was one of those times. "What happened after she found out?"

I explained how the conversation went downhill from

there and ended with her leaving. A heavy pause sat between us when I finished.

"Fuck it," Anders muttered, grabbing the whiskey from the cupboard, and spiking his coffee with it. "Do you want advice, or just someone to keep you from doing something stupid?"

I sighed, taking a seat once more. The anger hadn't necessarily drained away as I spoke, but it changed. Became cooler and more calculated. I wasn't convinced that was a good thing. "I'm not sure. That depends on the advice."

Anders snorted and took a seat in the armchair across from me. I was older by a hundred years, give or take. That didn't mean much in the grand scheme of things.

"The good news is she's *not* dead and no matter how pissed Sasha was, she wouldn't hurt her," he said. I wasn't sure I believed that, and he shook his head. "I get it. One of them is your mate, and the other is your aurae, but in this, you don't know them like I do. Nathalie is one of the few people in this world Sasha actually gives a damn about. She won't hurt her, even if you guys did continue things . . ."

I laughed bitterly. "I don't see that happening when she is refusing to listen to me and is only considering Sasha's side."

"She doesn't know you," Anders said. "She's into you, but she doesn't know your history or why her being your aurae is such a big deal, or even why you won't accept Sasha. Correct me if I'm wrong, but other than the fact she's a match, she knows next to nothing about all this?" He motioned to me. I nodded. "She's got history with Sasha, and she's known you all of a couple of weeks. It's a clusterfuck, but you've got to give her time."

I shook my head. "I can't do that."

"Brother," Anders warned, but I lifted my hand to stop him.

"I physically can't," I breathed. I put an inch between my thumb and index finger. "I'm hanging on by this much. I don't give it three days before I flip, and the magic takes over if I don't see her. If that happens . . ." I looked at the ceiling. "When I fed from her, the bonding process was triggered. My magic has a single-minded focus right now that I can't curb indefinitely."

Anders cursed. "You're joking, right? Feeding from her twice shouldn't be enough to trigger it—"

"I'm aware."

If I'd known, I wouldn't have done it to begin with. As much as I wanted her, we had unknowingly started a bonding process that she hadn't agreed to.

Aurae bonds usually spent a great deal of time together and fed frequently. It was a chosen bond, not a forced one. We weren't sure when or why, but the actual process of bonding wasn't usually triggered for weeks. Sometimes months, or even years. By the time it did, both parties were fully on board, and unlike mate bonds where it was a one-and-done, aurae bonds wound tighter with time. They grew. They evolved. It was part of what made aurae bonds sacred to my kind.

"Does she know?"

"No." I shook my head. "Not yet. When the fervor hits . . ." I swallowed.

"Before you even ask, I'm not putting you down. Neither will Rafael. So don't even think about it."

He knew me well. Better than anyone.

"That's not what I want. I want *her*. The problem is, thanks to fucking Sasha, she may not want me now.

August-the-man knows how to respect that. My magic, however, does not." I ran a hand over my jaw.

"We'll figure it out," Anders said. "I won't let you hurt her if that's what you're worried about."

"You won't be able to stop me." My voice was gruff. We shared a look, and as much as either of us hated to admit the truth for different reasons, he wouldn't.

"No, I won't," he agreed. "But I know someone who can."

"Small comfort that is." I rested my head in my hands, staring at the floor. "I'm not the only one who will be affected when it happens. She will need me and go searching. I need to talk to her before we hit that point. Even if she doesn't want to complete it, she deserves to know what's coming and then make the choice."

Anders dipped his head. "I suggest if you want to stand a chance that you don't lead with that. Nat isn't one to cave to pressure. She doubles down and will tell you to go fuck yourself."

Somehow that didn't surprise me about my sunling. She'd already told me exactly that. "I need to remove Sasha from the picture."

"Easier said than done."

"No shit. Next you'll tell me the sky is blue."

Anders rolled his eyes and downed the rest of his coffee. "You're not going to like it, but the best way to deal with her is to be honest."

"I have been—"

"About *everything*," he said sharply. "Yes, you don't like her. You're going to need to dig a bit deeper than that if you want to drive the point home, and I don't mean to hurt her, *but to free her*. You want Nat to come around? Sasha has to be able to move on from you and not ruin their relationship."

My hands clenched into fists. "I've rejected her dozens of times."

"Right," he said, getting up to pour more coffee. "But she just thinks you hate her for no reason, or at least one she doesn't understand. Maybe if you explained—"

"Her inability to take no for an answer doesn't mean I need to show her my damage," I said firmly. "My past is my own, and I don't owe her any of it. That she's playing the victim here is ridiculous. I'm in this situation because of her blatant disrespect for boundaries."

Anders poured more whiskey than coffee into his mug this time. "You're right. You don't owe her anything. She doesn't owe you anything either, and since you're trying to pursue someone that gives a shit about her, you're going to have to give on some things. From what you said, it sounds like Nat thinks mate bonds are inevitable. It makes sense. She watched Ronan pursue Piper relentlessly and break down her barriers. If you want her to see that you won't change on this, you need to make sure they both under-stand *why*."

I was quiet for a moment.

"I'll think about it."

Anders shrugged. "I care about you, August, but I care about Sasha too. I understand why you will never be with her, but I also spent years as Lucifer's second and watched her grow up. She's like a sister to me." He thought for a second, then added, "A really hot sister." I rolled my eyes at him.

"This isn't Old Alabama."

Anders snickered. "You get the point. As for Nat, I'll see what I can do in terms of pressure. Piper isn't likely to give you much sympathy, but Ronan understands your situation to an extent. He came here from Hell for Piper and had to work for their bond."

I'd heard the rumors. While I wasn't sure how much truth there was to them, I didn't particularly care.

In general, I tried to stay far away from demons.

One bargain was enough for me. It was a debt I would forever owe.

Most things just weren't worth that cost.

"In the meantime, I suggest you talk to Rafael and create your own opportunity, so to speak. I'm not sure how much you know about her with your hatred for discussing politics, but Nat's the Rockefeller of New Chicago these days. Very little happens that she isn't involved in. Knowing your brother and Rajvi, I'm sure they'd be more than happy to find a reason for a one-on-one meeting and then be unable to attend." I lifted a brow at him, and he just smirked. "I'm sure you could find it within yourself to do him a solid and go in his stead."

Anders winked.

Clever bastard.

twenty-five

NATHALIE

"GO AWAY."

The engine flared to life at the press of a button. I pulled out of my parking spot and started heading for the place where my nightmares began.

"No," Lucifer said, reclining back in my passenger seat like he was really there instead of a ghostly apparition. "We need to talk, little witch."

"I have no desire to talk to you today." My hands gripped the steering wheel a tad more than necessary and I relaxed them instantly. "I have a negative desire. Bet you never thought you'd inspire that in someone."

"That's not a thing."

"It is if I say it is."

He chuckled. "Always so petulant. I find it cute, but I prefer your honesty over the diversion. It might work on your friends, but I'm not them."

I flipped my turn signal and waited patiently at the stop sign. "All right. I've had a trying morning, and I'm out of spoons for whatever it is you came to bother me about today. Kindly go haunt someone else."

"That might possibly be the nicest 'go fuck yourself' I've ever heard." He was grinning. I could hear it in his voice.

"You can't fuck yourself. You're dead. It seemed rude to rub it in."

"That's never stopped you before," he said a bit more testily. He wasn't a fan of being reminded about his current existence unless he was the one bitching about it. I was prodding an old wound in hopes he would actually do just that, before I really was a bitch.

I shrugged. "Consider it my thanks for waking me up this morning."

"Ahhh," he hummed. "Now we get to the real problem at hand."

I hit a button on my steering wheel and music filled the car. There were only two radio stations in New Chicago nowadays. One was human patrol reporting crimes to help humans avoid getting caught up in things that were better left alone. The other played every genre of music and ran on donations from the people of the city. I was one of their big supporters because I saw how much the women's shelter really benefited from it.

Music was a balm to the soul, and in a post-Magic Wars world, everyone needed something to help them get through the day.

Johnny Cash started singing "Folsom Prison Blues," drowning out Lucifer. A second later the radio turned off. I glared in his direction then turned back to the road, not wanting to go flying off the interstate and join him.

"You're upset I woke you."

"Never said that. Pretty sure the word out of my mouth was 'thanks.'"

"You didn't need to. Your actions tell me you're angry."

"Gee, I wonder why I'd be upset after learning the guy I

was with was actually Sasha's mate. Not everything is about you, Lucifer."

You're his aurae, Peace whispered.

I needed her to be quiet, or I was going to let Bad Nat do whatever she wanted.

"True," he acquiesced. "But you've been ignoring me since Sasha left."

"Because you won't go away."

"I disagree," he responded, still seeming unperturbed. "I think you're upset I woke you. I think you wanted to be in denial, because you found you liked the incubus a little too much—"

"I will salt you," I snapped.

He grinned like the frickin' cat that got the canary.

"For someone who spends so much time helping their friends overcome their damage and process their emotions, you have an uncanny ability to neglect the emotions you don't like."

A locked door within my memory loci rattled.

He'd hit a little too close to home.

"I'm pissed at you because I know the only reason you woke me is out of some stupid jealousy and ill-placed possessiveness. You didn't like that I was with him. Stop pretending you woke me up for selfless reasons when you did it to be an asshole because you couldn't stand me fucking someone else."

Lucifer went quiet.

If not for the sense of his presence, I would have wondered if he left. I refused to look at the passenger side of my car and give him any satisfaction.

"Interesting," he murmured eventually.

I nearly hit the brakes, surprised by his reaction.

It really wasn't safe to talk and drive. Not with the devil.

"You got your honesty. Happy?"

"Yes," he said. "We've made progress. I wasn't sure. You try to keep so much hidden from me."

I felt his eyes focusing on my body like the sun heating the desert sand.

"Only you would be pleased by me insulting you."

"You use deflection to cope. Insulting me is just another form of that. It means that some part of you has actually deemed me safe."

I bit the inside of my cheek. Where the hell had that come from?

While I constantly griped at him for never leaving, I also didn't want to examine how familiar he had actually become with me, that he'd not only read the situation, but he'd read it correctly.

I'd bought into the illusion he was just a narcissistic ass.

He was, but he was a narcissistic ass that had been toying with me for months. The devil liked to bargain, and he was determined to get me to bring him back. Watching me was just how he stored ammunition until he learned the right place to fire.

"I wouldn't say safe, so much as harmless." It was a partial truth. The best lies were.

"Harmless?" he scoffed. Lucifer didn't like the implication of being weak.

"You want to talk about shitty feelings? You can't tell anyone what I say to you. You can't hurt me. You can't do anything to me. I'm petulant with you, and sometimes rude, because I don't have to care. That's the hard truth."

If I thought I might have gotten to him before, I was wrong.

He didn't make a sound as he leaned forward, running his phantom lips over the shell of my ear.

Instead of the faint feeling I'd grown used to, there was something nearly tangible in that touch. It was nothing but a brush against the smallest patch of skin, yet it felt *almost* real.

Far more than ever before.

I hit the brake, harder this time. My tires screeched and rubber burned.

"Shit," I muttered, easing off of them.

Lucifer chuckled, and I felt it against my skin. "I think I do far more to you than you want to admit. The incubus was safe until he wasn't. The witch boy lost his shot. But I'm bound to you. Tethered for as long as you shall live. Till death do us part—"

"We're not married." I rolled my eyes.

"No, because a marriage can be dissolved. Contracts can be broken. This is forever. So while you act petulant and unbothered, know that I see through it, little witch." His lips touched my neck, and I swallowed hard. My mouth had gone dry. "I can handle your mean side. I can take your worst. Be as cruel as you like, because those are the pieces you hide, and *I want them.*"

Bad Nat seemed to stall in her pacing and look up. Her keen golden eyes focused on him and our conversation.

I didn't like that. Not one bit.

I shook my head slowly. "You're insane. No wonder I thought I was going crazy."

Lucifer laughed. "Insane? Hardly. I've been there, and this isn't it."

I wanted to ask what he meant, but I'm sure he'd only take that as me being interested and encouraging him. Then again, he thought my insults were practically heart doodles on a notebook. I wasn't sure why I cared.

"Tell me about it."

Lucifer tilted his head. "No."

"Why not?"

He considered his answer. "You won't like the story."

"Let me be the judge of that."

"Those memories are not enjoyable. If I tell you about it, I want a story in return."

I lifted a brow while I focused on the road. Of course he'd bargain for something as harmless as a story. "I'm not sure it's worth bargaining with you. Watch it be about some woman cheating on you and your fragile ego just couldn't handle it—"

"I've never been cheated on, so I'm afraid your imagination would be incorrect."

Bullshit.

"You're so full of it."

"Cheating means we were in a committed relationship. I've never been in one."

I spluttered a laugh that spiraled into a deep, utterly dangerous cackle that left me with tears forming at the corners of my eyes while driving.

"Okay, so you didn't care if your partners were with other people when they were with you?" I said once I recovered. "Somehow I find that hard to believe."

"My 'partners,' as you call them, rarely strayed because they were enamored. Most beings couldn't resist the pull from the demon of desire. I grew bored easily. If that hadn't been the case, then you'd be correct. I didn't particularly care."

I licked my bottom lip then bit it, recalling the hunger on August's face when I'd done that in his apartment. His filthy and erotic words whispered in my mind, calling to me. The way he'd made me crawl . . . *Gods.* Dismissing those thoughts proved harder than I wanted it to be. "I think you're lying."

"I swear that I am not."

The tether between us flared briefly, a thin gold strand that ran from my wrist to his like a glorified pair of handcuffs. Lucifer was a demon and couldn't deceive me if he swore on it. He was telling the truth. "That's surprising."

"How so?"

I narrowed my eyes at him for a brief second before looking back at the road. "You were jealous of August and you're a ghost. When you were a flesh and blood man? A demon of desire?" I shook my head. "I have a hard time believing you were fine with your playthings moving on."

"Do you want me to admit that I woke you hoping you'd hear them, hoping you'd break it off? Because the answer is yes. I did, and I am not ashamed to admit it. You didn't even know him, and you let him feed from you."

"See? That's utterly ridiculous—"

"I didn't say I've never been *possessive*, Nathalie. I said I've never been in a committed relationship. I can count on one hand the number of people I've desired that way. It's a short list, little witch."

I took a deep breath and let it out. He was baiting me, as always.

"Well, I hope you're happy with the outcome, Lucifer. That in your shitty existence, your attempts to ruin mine are noticed but inconsequential. I would have found out eventually, but thanks for saving me the trouble."

He didn't say anything more for the rest of the drive, but he also didn't leave. I wasn't sure what to make of it. Only when we began to approach my childhood home did he deign to respond.

"You have opinions and beliefs as to what you think I

want, or why I do something, but has it ever occurred to you to ask?" He only paused for a second before continuing. "I *am* jealous of him. I *am* happy you ended it. I'm *not* happy that it pains you. I don't like seeing you torn up over someone that doesn't deserve it. You're right, though, you would've found out eventually, which is why I did it today. You feel hurt now. How would you have felt in two months if I'd done nothing only for you to find out later?"

I rolled to a stop outside the imposing manor. The huge circular driveway only had a few cars. It was practically a ghost town for the Le Fay residence.

I cut the engine but didn't get out immediately.

"I have a question for you." Despite the fact I was willing to say it, I still had a hard time asking. "You want me to bring you back. I know that. You haven't brought it up for months, but I'm not stupid. All of this," I motioned toward him without looking, "why do you do it, if that's your end goal?"

"All of this?" he asked softly.

"This," I repeated harder, a hint of a growl in my tone. "You annoy me and then you're thoughtful. You act like a jealous ass, but then you give me space. I don't understand this whiplash with you. Are you trying to act like you care in the hopes I'll be fooled? If so, I don't understand why you act so intolerable half the time. I just —" I threw my hands up in frustration. "I don't understand your angle."

A slight amused smile lined his lips. The five o'clock shadow he'd died with did wicked things to my already tangled thoughts. "My angle?"

"Yes." I nodded. "I don't understand what your logic is. Explain it to me."

A wide smile broke across his face. He laughed, the sound musical and sensual, but layered. I stared at him, waiting for some sort of answer. When it became clear I wasn't going to get one, I got out of my car and slammed the door behind me.

It took me twelve seconds to get my cool back, and I severely needed it before facing Carissa. Just as I pivoted, Lucifer appeared in front of me. His chest pressed into mine. It should have been impossible. He had no physical form—but I *moved*.

And not by my choice.

My back pressed into the Audi behind me. A very present, masculine form pressed into my front. He boxed me in, putting a hand on either side of me.

"I'd bargain with you for that truth, but you wouldn't believe me, anyway."

I started to protest when his lips pressed against mine. Seconds.

Logically, I knew the chaste kiss only lasted seconds. But that was it. It was a *true kiss*. Smooth skin slid against my lips, coaxing them apart. In my shock, I went with it.

A groan ran through him, making my core heat.

My lips parted, and I breathed him in, just as he did the same.

Blood and sex. He always smelled the same. Except now, there was another scent layered under it. Subtle. More like a hidden note than a true scent at all.

Almost like . . . lilac.

His scent was fusing with my own. Taking on properties from my magic that didn't belong to him before.

Our kiss deepened.

He pulled back, sucking my bottom lip with him. His teeth nipped me, aggressive rather than playful.

"I don't just want to be brought back, little witch. I

want to *live*. Flesh or no flesh, I have zero desire to continue a lonely, meaningless existence. Not anymore."

His arms dropped from the Audi.

Lucifer backed away, taking my breath with him.

"There's no angle, Nathalie. I just want you. All of you."

He disappeared on the spot, leaving me stunned.

I pressed my fingers to my lips and found the most shocking thing of all.

Blood.

twenty-six

MARCEL

I RUBBED MY EYES. Frustration leaked through me as I slammed the leatherbound tome shut. Magic pulsed at my fingers. Deadly and destructive.

Exhaustion ate at me, but I couldn't sleep. Not when my body turned against me, filling me with adrenaline. The chair scraped against the hardwood as I scooted back, digging the grooves even deeper. I stalked away from my desk, from the piles of books I'd been searching. Scouring.

From the opposite corner of the room, my rumpled bed called to me. I ignored its pull and paced. For the better part of fourteen years, these four walls had been my home, sanctuary and prison that it was.

My mother had been taken to the witch camps shortly after becoming pregnant with me. That single action led to the most significant event in history. The one that changed our world.

Upon my birth, the now-extinct Sirius Coven managed to extract me from the camps. They couldn't save my mother. My grandmother appealed to the ruling demon, Lucifer. He did nothing.

When my mother, impregnated by a guard, finally died from the torture sustained—my *mère* snapped.

I could still remember that day in crystalline clarity.

It was the last time I saw my grandmother.

Her brown hair had only just started turning gray. The light highlighted it when she'd knelt in front of me and took my hands. She smelled both sweet and spicy, like cinnamon and chili flakes and sugar cookies. It was an odd scent, but it smelled like home. Mère had been the closest thing I had to a parent.

"The world will hate me for this. They're going to tell you so many awful things about me. Your mother . . ." She swallowed hard. Mère shook her head. "They will try to make you feel guilt for something you had nothing to do with—and they will hate you by extension because you're an Abernathy." My eyes welled with tears. I was only five, after all.

"I don't want to be hated."

She smiled sadly at me. "*Mon chéri*, they would hate you either way. Maybe not now, while you're just a boy. But one day you will be a man, and our world has never had an issue holding innocent young men responsible for the sins of their ancestors. You're a strong warlock. Your mother was strong too, but that didn't stop them from taking her. These humans . . . they have to be stopped. The devil won't do it. The Le Fays don't want to get involved." Mère sighed, releasing one of my hands to cup my cheek and brush the tears away with her thumb. "Don't cry, Marcellus."

I didn't fully understand at the time that she had been saying goodbye. The general ominous feel to the conversation was enough to get to me.

I hadn't known what to say, so I did what any child would. I threw my arms around her and held her as hard as

I could manage. My grandmother's cold embrace warmed me. "I love you, Mère."

"I love you too, *mon chéri*. You're my everything. You and your mother both. I couldn't save her, but it's not too late to save you."

I frowned, not understanding. Not until she tried to pull away, and when I wouldn't let go, Aunt Renata grabbed me from behind. Between the two of them, my five-year-old strength never stood a chance.

Ren wrapped her arms around me from behind, trying to comfort me while she whispered to my grandmother. "I have him, Dryanda. Go . . ."

The last thing I saw, through watery eyes, was my mère walking away.

She wore a plaid jacket with her hair tied back. Her shoulders shook as she cried, but that didn't stop her from going through with it.

The next time I saw Mère was on TV.

She murdered the president, the vice president, the entire Cabinet, and the White House staff on a live broadcast.

All because secret government-sanctioned witch camps had killed her daughter, and she feared one day they might kill me too.

She was right about what would come after.

People hated my kind, but even more than that, they hated me.

The warlock whose family brought about the Magic Wars.

The Sirius Coven raised me for as long as they could, until the Le Fays aligned with several other prominent houses to have them disbanded. I was taken in as a ward at twelve years old. The four walls of my bedroom were bare of possessions beyond my books. For a room that had been mine more of my life than not, I had nothing of sentiment there. Shelves covered as much space as possible. They weren't even, and many hung at a slight angle since I'd installed them myself at different points over the years. Books covered as much of the walls as those shelves would allow. Some I'd written. Most I'd read. They weren't mine, as the family that took me in *loved* to point out, but the Le Fay's library was so large, they rarely noticed when something went missing.

With the exception of Nathalie.

Somehow, she always knew.

Books had been my escape for as long as I could remember. The knowledge in them became my power. I didn't have friends, save for Katherine. After Nat left three years ago, I wouldn't let anyone close again. I spent all my time reading, learning—and what had that gotten me?

For all the knowledge in the world, I couldn't find Katherine.

I'd scryed every possible way. I'd tried every version of a summoning I could think of that didn't require necromancy or another death witch.

Nothing worked.

Nathalie's proposal to use her came to mind, and I shuddered. Anyone, literally any other person, I would be willing to try it with—*except her.*

I may have been the strongest death witch in living memory, but I wasn't infallible. The possibility of losing her to the veil . . . it was the only risk I wouldn't take to find Katherine.

I loved them both, in radically different ways.

Katherine was my friend. My confidante. The sister I

should have had, if my own hadn't died in the witch camps with my mother.

When my world all but ended, Katherine was the one that pulled me back. When I nearly died time and time again, she was the one that waited out the fever and held my hand through the night, unsure if I'd see the morning.

She was the sister of my soul.

There were no secrets between Kat and me.

She was my ride or die.

But Nathalie . . .

I shook my head, pulling my hair hard. I swept a hand across my desk, scattering the books. Spines cracked as they landed haphazardly on the ground.

My jaw ached from clenching it.

A quiet knock pulled my attention to the door. I strode across the rickety wood floors. The hinges squeaked as it swung open.

"What do you want, Estefania?"

She recoiled at my tone, expression turning guarded. "Never mind." She turned to leave.

I had to tamp down the frustration that was quickly turning to anger. It wasn't her fault I was wound tight. She wasn't the reason Katherine was missing. She didn't hold power over me, standing with an executioner's blade, just waiting to swing the moment I made one wrong move. "I'm sorry," I bit out.

She paused at the stairs. Her dark eyes narrowed in mistrust. We weren't friends, but we were more than acquaintances. Estefania had become a ward of the Le Fays two years ago. While neither of us ever made a point of spending any length of time together, she was probably one of the few people I could usually consider an ally in this godsforsaken mansion.

"Nathalie's here. She's talking to Carissa about Katherine."

She didn't mince words or stick around to chat. Her footsteps were quiet as she hurried down to the second floor to hide in her bedroom.

I cursed under my breath and closed my door behind me, spelling the lock before I left.

The stairs creaked under my weight. I didn't bother trying to be stealthy as I hurried down.

Carissa's voice echoed through the halls.

"Unless you're here to swear your loyalty to the Ouroboros Coven, get out."

The pitch she reached made me wince. Carissa had lost her voice after the failed attempt to use Lucifer's magic. It never fully came back, and the damaged vocal cords made her sound like a violin in the hands of a child for the first time.

Nathalie hummed, sounding unbothered. "You're doing a bang-up job taking care of the family home." I rounded the stairwell to see her run a finger along the dusty shelf over the fireplace. Her nose wrinkled in distaste. "I'm loving the new look."

Carissa's eyes flashed. Her jaw tightened, the withered skin pulling taut. "I may not have power like I used to, but I'm still the Le Fay matriarch, and you will show me the respect I deserve."

Nathalie nodded along as her eyes swept over the family room. She wore body-hugging black pants and a shimmery top that cinched at the waist and flared at the hips. The neckline was modest, but the fit was sensational. My mouth went dry.

"Of course." She continued walking, taking in each painting and artifact on the walls like she hadn't seen them a thousand times before. "Per the laws of hospitality, you should be offering me a drink, as well as your time—and in a more appropriate demeanor—since I'm not here as a Le Fay, but as a representative from the Demon Queen." Carissa's spine went straight. "Also, because I'm a witch of greater power and status than you, it is technically *you* who should have bowed in respect." Nat paused in her slow gait to look at Carissa, her gaze sharp and expression blank. "If we're going to use formalities, that is. Personally, I find them a waste of time and would rather ask my questions and leave."

She'd grown substantially from the humble girl who'd sought her family's praise. I'd told her a hundred times they didn't deserve it, but now I believed she finally understood it on an emotional level. That, or her mask had become so good, not even I could see through it.

I didn't like that thought. Not at all.

"I'm in a meeting, Marcel," Carissa said in an attempt to dismiss me. Neither of them had given any indication they knew I had arrived.

I stepped into the room, making a point to meet her eye. "I'm on the Demon Queen's council as Katherine's second. Nathalie is here as a representative. This is my responsibility to handle."

It was the nicest way I could tell her that she was the one who was interrupting and didn't belong. Not that it made her leave.

The dark glint in her eye told me I'd pay for that.

Before Carissa could snap back with whatever caustic remark she'd planned to make, Nat intervened. "Stay. Perhaps you'll be useful to this conversation."

Her voice was as cold and apathetic as the one she'd used with her bitch sister. I didn't flinch the way I once would have, instead smiling back like she'd invited me to dinner. Ignoring my politeness, she glanced down at her phone briefly. Whatever had just come in caused her to blink twice, but she kept her face neutral. She tucked her phone away, looking back up again with indifference. I hated the distance between us, despite being the one to have put it there.

"What can we do for you, Nat?"

Her eyes narrowed at the use of her shortened name. It wasn't professional in the slightest, but I would never pass up an excuse to try to get beneath her skin. Not even in Carissa's presence.

"I'm here about Katherine." Her gaze slid from me to the Le Fay matriarch. "I'm aware she's missing. The Demon Queen would like to know why she wasn't immediately notified when you could not find her."

Carissa sneered. "And who told you she was missing?"

I didn't react, but I waited for her to throw me under the bus. Her face didn't twitch as she said, "I employ almost half the city. I have my sources."

Unfortunately, her elder sister didn't take the bait.

"You employ so many that they told you she's missing, yet they haven't found her?"

Nathalie didn't respond; she simply stared, waiting for an answer.

Her silence was a power move, and a good one.

"Katherine's whereabouts are witch business," Carissa said after a minute had passed.

"So she's not missing?" Nat asked, cocking her head. Carissa didn't answer, and Nat laughed once under her breath. "She entered a blood oath with a demon and swore fealty to any of Bree Fallon's line. That includes the Demon Queen. Need I remind you, it's in your best interest to answer me truthfully? The next person she sends won't be so patient."

I was hard as a rock watching her put Carissa in her place. Sixteen-year-old Nathalie would be weeping with joy if she could see herself now.

"Katherine disappeared from a supply run," Carissa said begrudgingly. "Five weeks ago now. Maybe six? She hasn't come home, and we haven't seen her. If you want more than that, you'll have to ask her."

Nathalie nodded like this was information she didn't already have. "Was she acting different in any way before the supply run?"

"No."

"Did she maintain regular contact with anyone outside the Ouroboros Coven?"

"No."

"And in the coven?" Nathalie hedged. "Who was she close to?"

Carissa smiled like the bitter bitch she was. I already knew what she was going to say, but it didn't stop the dread I felt.

"Her husband."

twenty-seven

NATHALIE

MY EXPRESSION SHUDDERED. The mask I held on to so desperately threatened to fall. I could barely hear past the roaring in my ears when I turned to Marcel and repeated, "Husband?"

"We never signed any papers." His words were hard and angry, aimed at my eldest sister. But his eyes—those dark, damning eyes—they tried to plead with me. To understand something I never would.

"You're married by witch tradition and laws," Carissa replied in a not-so-subtle purr.

I hated her.

Hate was such a potent emotion. It hurt the person who felt it more than the person at whom it was aimed. Like a poison, it ate at you, letting them occupy a space in your mind rent-free.

I hated that I hated her, and yet I couldn't help it.

Ever since I was a child, Carissa had made my life miserable.

It took a turn on my eighth winter solstice. We'd played a game; Carissa, Katherine, and me. That was before Kat and I had our issues, and it was quite possibly the only reason I had survived.

That year we'd been vacationing in Canada so our parents could rub shoulders with other black witches. A frozen lake was next to the place we were staying. We played truth or dare with a broken beer bottle we'd found on the shore.

Carissa dared me to walk on the ice. All the way to the middle.

Like the sensible person I was even then, I refused.

So she made me.

With magic.

That was her excuse when I fell through the ice. If I hadn't been such a baby, she wouldn't have had to do it. If I hadn't *forced* her to do it, I wouldn't have fallen in.

Even at fourteen, her logic skills were lacking.

Still, my mother went easy on her punishment. Whereas I suffered nerve damage and still couldn't feel the tips of my fingers to this day. She deserved more than writing sentences, but Dolores Le Fay wasn't big on punishing her eldest child.

If not for Katherine losing control and melting the ice by setting fire to the lake, I would have died. There was no doubt in my mind.

Before then, I knew she didn't like me, but the depth of Carissa's cruelty wasn't something I really understood until that day. That's when I made a point of avoiding being alone with her at all costs.

This wasn't much different. She couldn't physically cause me pain anymore, so she hit the only thing she could. My emotional trauma.

A door within my memory loci rattled against its frame.

Wind stirred my hair despite not a single window being opened.

Inside me, Bad Nat was prodding at a door she had no business being near. Ann and The Warden knew better than to leave that room unattended. If not for Peace appearing at the end of the hall, I was certain she would have unlocked it and released havoc.

My softer, kinder personality stared at Bad Nat with a somber expression.

It made her hesitate long enough that Ann could intervene. She dragged her away from the room of nightmares.

I blew out a harsh breath and my hair settled once more.

Acting like nothing happened, despite the side stares they were both giving me, I said, "I wasn't aware you married. Congratulations." The words were clipped. Cold. So cold. I had to tamp down all emotions in this situation because otherwise I'd show how much that revelation affected me.

He didn't deserve my pain.

Neither of them did.

"They had a lovely wedding last Samhain," Carissa continued, rubbing salt in the wound. "We would have sent you an invitation, but, well, Dolores was concerned you'd turn it into 'The Nathalie Show' and ruin Katherine's big day. We all know Katherine was her favorite."

My palms sweat. It was taking more than a little effort to keep my head about me. I remembered last Samhain vividly, for one reason and only one.

Against my will, my eyes locked on Marcel. A glamour covered his body, for reasons unknown. Even now he stood next to me drenched with lies. But that wasn't what caused the rising emotions within; it just added to the truth of who he was.

Anger built inside me, born from betrayal—from pain.

He'd come to me in the middle of a coffee shop I'd never set foot in again. His dark eyes were beseeching as he spun sweet lies, asking me to come back to him. Marcel swore he wanted me and only me. That he made a mistake those years before, regarding Katherine and my family. All I had to do was say yes and return to the fold and he'd handle the rest.

I didn't.

I refused.

It tore me up to do it, but I refused to go back to the man who left me for my twin sister. I hadn't trusted him, and I'd never been so pissed off to be proven right.

Instead of ripping into him like I wanted, I turned to my sister. "Shame she didn't survive Lucifer's death. I may have been the black sheep of the family, but Mother would be rolling in her grave—if she had one—knowing that the matriarch who leads now is powerless."

Carissa laughed. It surprised me. I expected ire, but her unhinged cackle? Not so much. She valued status and power over all else. That should have been the gravest insult for a Le Fay, but somehow it didn't hit the mark I was aiming for.

"You're right," Carissa said. "But if she had known what we know now, she wouldn't have sacrificed Lucifer. She would have used the Demon Queen before she became a queen and completed the channel to the Otherworld. Then we would have dealt with her *and* had a demon to breed."

The nonchalant way she said it made my entire body stiffen.

"For someone whose coven swore loyalty to the Demon Queen, you've put a lot of thought into that plan."

"I can be loyal and still have hindsight," Carissa said.

"Mmm," I murmured, not agreeing but needing to steer the conversation back to what I was here for. It wasn't exactly a surprise that she didn't like the power Piper had over her. My family had never enjoyed being governed by a demon, regardless of the fact they very much needed it to keep them in line. "So, the only person Katherine talked with regularly before disappearing was Marcel?"

Carissa shrugged. "I'm hardly her keeper. Your guess is as good as mine. I told them to work on repopulating the Le Fay line, so I hope they did a bit more than talk."

"*Enough!*" Marcel snapped. Raw power snapped through the air, and it wasn't my own.

I turned my face to hide my flinch at her words. Little did she know, her needling was only aiding in cementing the walls I'd built against Marcel. With the exception of his wedded status, there was very little she could say at this point that would surprise me regarding him.

"Excuse me?" Carissa lifted her brows, eyes wide as if she couldn't believe he spoke out of turn. Marcel had always been a good little warlock, obeying my parents and our family at every turn.

"I said enough. I will not stand by while you spew these lies—"

"Lies?" she asked. Another laugh bubbled up out of her raspy throat. "It's nothing but the truth, *boy*. You did marry Katherine, and I did tell you to work on getting her pregnant. That's your purpose." Turning to me, she said, "You want to know what we talked about before she disappeared?"

I stared at her silently, hoping it came across as aloof instead of speechless.

"I'd been giving her a fertility drug for months. She should have been pregnant. I was going to step it up with a lust potion and lock them in the basement for a month if she wasn't with child come Samhain."

My lips parted. "That's—"

"The only thing men are good for," Carissa interjected with a sneer. "Why else do you think we kept him around? To look pretty?" She rolled her eyes. "Marcel has power. His seed is ripe. Dolores knew it. That's why she tolerated you two fucking like rabbits when you thought no one knew. Nothing encourages teenagers like letting them think they're doing something wrong."

To my credit, my cheeks didn't heat. She was trying to shame me for being with him and make me feel small. I wouldn't let her. Not when her own actions made my stomach turn.

"You disgust me."

She laughed like I'd told her something hilarious. "Le Fays have been carefully cultivating our line since the very beginning. You, yourself, are the result of it. You could have been the strongest witch seen in five hundred years. Heir to the Morrigan. But where your blood is impeccable, your temperament is a disappointment. She took the boy from you, hoping you'd be incentivized to prove your worth beyond being a womb. What did you do instead? You ran away." Carissa rolled her eyes. "Such a waste of potential. All of you. Katherine included."

I shook my head when she was finished with her little monologue. The depth of her own insanity regarding our lineage was staggering. My sister had always been awful, but this bordered on psychosis. "Thank you for your cooperation." The words were clipped. Unemotional, as I put distance between us but didn't immediately leave, even if my skin crawled with every moment spent here. "Now I know why Katherine left. All I have to figure out is why someone is trying to kill her."

"Kill her?" Carissa snorted. "As if. You want to know why the Demon Queen wasn't notified? Because Katherine went off the rails after her blood oath. She couldn't control her magic any more than I can control the wind. She killed Diana McMahon during one of her outbursts. I told her to get with child or get out. I wasn't protecting her from your queen unless she held up her end of the deal. So she left."

Whatever I might have said was lost in a dull roar.

Magic pulsed heavily. Red strands wove through the air.

"You said Diana left the Ouroboros Coven to see if she still had family in New Eidyn—"

"I lied," Carissa said, shrugging him off. "Katherine and I had a deal. She would give me heirs, and no one would learn the consequences of her lack of control."

Holy. Shit.

"You had no right," he said, speaking deathly quiet.

"No right?" she repeated in a mocking tone. "Katherine had become a liability. If she killed the wrong person, the Demon Queen would come down on us all. I made a decision—"

"You blackmailed her," Marcel interrupted. "You manipulated her. You're the reason she's out there in trouble!"

"Please. The girl can take care of herself. If she were truly in trouble, she would have returned and done what she should have from the beginning. Katherine is doing as all spoiled children do: throwing a temper tantrum. She'll learn soon enough I'm not her mother and won't handle her with kid gloves like Dolores did." Carissa scoffed, rolling her eyes once more. She may not be able to see magic like I could, but she had to feel it. The cold touch of death magic as it began to wind around her like wicked tendrils.

I rolled on the balls of my feet, letting the vines wrap around her throat and cut off her air circulation before stepping in. I wouldn't let Marcel kill her, but it never hurt to put the fear of death in someone that clearly needed that hard knock of reality.

"You don't know the first thing about being handled with kid gloves," Marcel said quietly. Almost all witches and warlocks needed to speak to give birth to spells. Not him. Marcel didn't use words to slowly choke Carissa. He simply twisted his fingers, and the noose tightened.

A shiver ran down my spine.

I knew Marcel had power. It was not why I had been with him. Sure, it was why my parents betrothed us, but it wasn't why *I* had chosen him.

As I watched him now, I wondered if this was there before. Could he always control crimson strands of death? Had his powers grown? Or had he hidden it, like everything else?

I'd never know.

"Stop."

"No," he growled. "She deserves it."

I reached out a hand, tugging on my own magic. Where Marcel's poured off him as if his body couldn't contain it, mine was hardly anything. Just a dusting of gold that coated my fingers. I lifted one hand, running my fingertip over one of the angry red coils. The gold spread like a plague, consuming everything it touched.

My family had always claimed I was a weak witch.

For a long time, I believed them.

Chaos magic, while rare, wasn't dependable for many things. Spells rarely did what they were supposed to. Hexes backfired. Sure, I managed the simplest things through sheer force of will—but I'd never be able to cast on the same scale as Katherine did, let alone Marcel. Even after I'd killed Prudence and brought Kat back. I took my lack of self-control for weakness and only used my magic in secret. I thought I was broken because it didn't work like theirs.

I just couldn't create enough of my magic to do those things.

But I could steal *their* magic.

Turn it into my own.

Take control of any spell. Release any binding. Undo any ward.

Judging by the look on Marcel's face, Katherine never told him. I certainly didn't. For a long time, it was my most closely guarded secret; my weird magic.

Now it was a tool like any other, one I wouldn't hesitate to use if needed.

"She does deserve it," I agreed. "But she may prove useful in the future. It would be stupid to kill her before Katherine is found."

My eldest sister clutched at the magic around her throat. It wasn't as desperate as I would have thought based on the shade of maroon her face turned. Her dead eyes stared me down, as if challenging me to do it.

To end her.

She'd probably like that. In her twisted mind, it would somehow prove that I wasn't useless after all.

I commanded the magic to release her.

She hit the floor with a thud.

The tendrils dissipated into nothing as gold fell like glitter and disappeared entirely.

"Besides," I said to him over my shoulder. "I need you to conserve your magic. You'll be doing a summoning tonight. I found a volunteer to go into the veil to talk to the ghosts of the murder victims." I sighed like I was bored. That was probably the furthest thing from the truth, but neither of them was safe for me. Neither of them was trustworthy. But just as Carissa had a purpose, so did Marcel.

Carissa gasped, a wheezing inhale that turned to a hoarse cough. She sounded like she smoked a pack a day for twenty years. Still on the ground, she turned her face to the side, letting her bare cheek press against the wood so she could glare at us.

"You told her already," she rasped, focusing on Marcel. "You brought her into this!" She pointed at him accusingly, her finger gnarled, a broken nail hanging off the end.

"Yeah," he said in a hard voice. "And I'm happy I did. I can't believe Katherine didn't just kill you for what you did, but don't worry. Next time Nat won't be here to save you *from me.*"

"Get out of my fucking house," she screeched, pulling herself up into a kneeling position.

"Gladly." He spat on the floor toward her and turned to me. I ignored him entirely. Just because I wasn't screaming in his face like she was didn't mean we were good. Far from it.

"LEAVE! You're no longer welcome in the Le Fay household. You can wither and rot for all I care!"

My brows nearly touched my hairline. Maybe Katherine wasn't the only one losing it. Carissa may be awful, but she was usually more calculated than this. Having her magic stripped had really fucked with her head.

My heels clicked as I walked forward and squatted down to her level.

She narrowed her eyes in distrust.

"This is the last time we will see each other. I won't return if I need more information from you. Sasha Loren has her methods and can handle you well enough. Goodbye, Carissa."

I moved to stand and a cold, clammy hand grabbed my own. Broken nails dug into my skin.

"You may hate me now, but one day you will wish you listened to me. All you and Katherine had to do was carry a child to further our line and instead you chose *this*. I won't forget your disrespect—"

"I hope you don't," I said, speaking down to her. "I hope you never forget this moment. I certainly won't." I pulled my arm away, and she relinquished my hand with a deep frown.

"Why not let him kill me? You've proven you have the means and could summon my ghost if you needed more answers. Why stop him?" She baited me to kill her, not realizing her words mattered very little. I wasn't sure why she would do that, knowing that in death she was as good as gone with how little magic she had.

Was it desperation? Or something more nefarious?

I didn't know or care enough to find out.

"I wish you a long and miserable life of insignificance," I said, cutting her off. Carissa got to her feet and dusted off her powder blue dress. It hung loose and limp, two sizes too big on her now-bony frame. Her cheekbones jutted out, giving her a lifeless look that reminded me of a skeleton. "When the Ouroboros Coven disbands, and you no longer have followers, and you're left alone and disregarded, and everyone that ever knew of you is dead, you'll be nothing. A sad, pathetic disappointment who had no one by their side and left no legacy—a path you paved by your own hateful actions. You'll be nothing more than a faded memory that turns to ash, forgotten."

Her lips parted in shock and rage.

I didn't stick around to hear any more. Whatever she might have to say, it wasn't worth the time I'd spend listening. We'd passed the point of usefulness. So I turned on my heel and walked right out of my childhood home. Out of a mansion filled with deceit and secrets and lies. This house was built on a foundation of brutality, led by the same detestable parents that created Carissa and encouraged her vile behavior. The toxicity of their beliefs and traditions perpetuated generational trauma and fostered abuse.

Not anymore.

That shit ended with me.

twenty-eight

NATHALIE

MY HEELS TAPPED against the cobblestone driveway. Heavy footsteps ate up the space behind me faster than my legs could carry me.

"Nathalie—"

"Save it, Marcel."

I didn't slow my pace. I needed to leave. I had other things to deal with now, but I also didn't want to be here for one more second. The dead grass and trees surrounding the Le Fay property cast an ominous vibe despite the clear skies. Fitting.

A rough hand wrapped around my wrist.

My body jerked to a stop.

I placed my free hand on my hip, cocking it as I pivoted. I bit the inside of my cheek, tasting copper. "You wanted my help finding Kat, and I'm going to. Unless it has to do with her, we have nothing to discuss."

He blew out a harsh breath, dark eyes hardening. A muscle twitched in his cheek. "It's not what you think. I never slept with Katherine. Carissa is trying to get under your skin."

279

A cold chuckle slid from my lips. "What you do with your *wife* is none of my concern."

He closed his eyes as if pained by my words. Good. "Stop. Don't do that."

"What? Tell you the truth?" I lifted a brow. "Yeah, I could see you struggling with that. Lies come so much easier, don't they?"

His jaw clenched. A spark of fire kindled behind his eyes. An ember in the endless night. I used to love his eyes. Their depths.

Now I knew to be cautious of the secrets that hid in them.

"I never wanted to marry Katherine."

Like that made this any better? "That's unfortunate for you both. You should really work on your marriage."

"Nathalie," he repeated my name in desperation. As if he were a dying man begging for one last look. He reached for me with his other hand then stopped himself, closing it into a fist as his control was pushed to the edge. "Please. Just stop, okay? Give me five fucking minutes to explain—"

He stopped speaking when one corner of my mouth tugged up in a half smile. Another chuckle swelled, this one shaking my chest.

"You really don't get it, do you?" I took a step toward him, the heels closing some of the difference in height between us. I still wasn't eye level, but it beat staring at his chest.

"You're wrong. I do get it. Gods, do I get it." He sighed, shaking his head while ghosts danced in the depths of his gaze. "I made a bad decision agreeing to marry Kat, and I've been paying for it every single day that I don't wake up next to you—where I should be."

"You're too late." I tilted my head, the look I gave him a

mocking expression of sympathy. "You burned that bridge and then pissed on the ashes. You've lied to me so many times now—"

"I never lied," Marcel growled, and I snorted, my eyes roaming the shimmer of glamour magic around him. I wanted to call him on it. To ask why he was wearing a glamour now if he wasn't a liar. I couldn't even guess a reason. Witches aged, but he was too young to need enhancements. He was older now, sure. More filled out than he had been in his early twenties, but not to the point that I thought using a glamour could be a vanity thing. There was no way I could ask without giving away my hand and revealing my ability to see magic. For a long time I'd thought it was a worthless gift, but then I learned how powerful knowledge could be—and I wasn't giving Marcel *anything*. Certainly not pieces of myself. "That's what I'm trying to fucking say if you would just *listen*. I never wanted to marry Katherine, and she never wanted to marry me either. Your parents forced the issue when your magic wasn't progressing fast enough—"

"I'm well aware why my own family deemed me unworthy of *you*." My, my, Carissa and Katherine weren't the only ones drinking the crazy juice. I should ask Piper to have the water checked up here. Just to make sure it wasn't causing psychosis by idiocy. "That you think that makes this any better is baffling to me. Like sure, point out the reasons why I was treated like shit by all of them. Surely that will make me forgive you for still going along with it when you had a fucking choice in who you married, *unlike me*."

Marcel groaned in frustration, raking a hand through his unkempt hair. The wavy black strands were longer than he used to wear it. The stubble at his jaw, a few days more than his usual five o'clock shadow. Dark circles lined his eyes.

"I thought I was doing the right thing by you at the time. I knew you'd be pissed but I didn't realize how badly I'd fucked up until the damage was done."

"Obviously." The look he gave me reminded me of the one I often gave to Lucifer during our little disagreements. The difference being Marcel had zero reason to wear it. "What? You said it. I just agreed."

He shook his head, blowing out a tight breath. "I thought I could have it all—you, our life together, but also the name and privileges being a Le Fay could offer—I thought I could protect you both. Your parents were so insistent about Katherine and I marrying, and I tried to get out of it. It wasn't what I wanted. Please try to understand that, Nat. When they came to me about her, my choices were limited and nothing short of horrible. I was stuck between a rock and a hard place. I wanted to explain it to you, but your mother refused. She held the cards. She had the control, and I couldn't speak about it. Then of course she delivered it in the worst way possible because she wanted to hurt you. I may have agreed to marry your sister, but that didn't mean I loved her. Not like that, at least. Kat's like a sister to me—"

"This isn't an episode of *Game of Thrones*, Marcel."

"Fucking hell," he snapped, stepping away from me to run a hand roughly through his hair before fisting it in anger. He was older than me. More experienced. He had always been so controlled when we were younger. Always maintained his cool. It's part of what had attracted me to him in the first place. Where this impassioned stranger came from, I didn't know. "I told you, I've never fucked her," he said quietly. "I'm happy to take a binding oath if that's what you need to know I *never* touched her."

I snorted. Part of me wanted to listen. Truly. But I couldn't go down that road again. It nearly destroyed me once and I wouldn't do that to myself. "No, you just married her."

"It was nothing more than a contract and means of survival," he insisted.

"Oh, go sit on a cactus." I'd had enough. I twisted my arm to pull away, but he didn't let go. "You've got some real goddamn nerve thinking you can just play the victim, like my parents 'made' you do it. We all have choices, Marcel. You admitted that you had choices. Yeah, you made the wrong ones. Just because you're admitting it now doesn't mean you get a do-over. Just because you say you're sorry doesn't mean I'll ever forgive you." I turned to leave and this time he grabbed my wrist, tight and firm, but not painful.

"I don't need your forgiveness. I just need *you*."

"Well, you can't have me!" I shouted in his face, breathing hard. "You had your chance. You blew it the day you decided to marry my twin and asked me to be your fucking side piece—"

"Never call yourself that again," he snapped, the rumble of his chest stirring the magic in his veins. "You were never a side piece. I may not have been able to marry you because Dolores changed the fucking deal, but Kat and I had an agreement. She understood that it was never her and that I would be excommunicated before I ever fucked her. Even if it killed me, you would be the mother of my children. The love of my life. The only one to *ever* share my bed."

I shook my head, swallowing hard. "I'm never going to give you another chance. You've destroyed any love I once held. Just let it go, Marcel. For Katherine's sake, for your own, for mine even—focus on finding my sister. The sooner we do, the sooner you never need to see me again."

The kernel of flame in his eyes seemed to grow. His muscles turned hard as stone. "No."

I threw my hands up. Or rather, I tried to. He still hadn't released my wrist. "This is insane. I've told you no in the simplest way possible. At this point it's starting to get pathetic." When all else failed, bitchy Nat was here to play. I'd tried every other tactic. Maybe he needed a little cruelty to get the message, because nothing else seemed to be working.

No matter what his truth was, I'd lived through the pain once and I wouldn't subject myself to that misery.

The only way to keep myself safe from that and him was to close myself off to it entirely. Just like I did with Little and Rage when they went too far.

Marcel leaned in.

I tried to lean back, but he wrapped his second hand around me, gripping the nape of my neck so I couldn't pull away.

"You're mine, sunbeam. I've been in love with you for over half my life, and that's not changing." He leaned his forehead against mine, eyelashes mere centimeters from brushing my own. "I'm sorry I hurt you. You will never truly know how fucking sorry I am, but letting you go isn't an option for me, Nathalie. You gave me your heart once, and I'm never giving it back. You can try all you want, but you'll have to pry it from my cold, *dead* hands, because only then will I stop loving you. You're mine, and I have *always* been yours."

His lips loomed so close that if I breathed too hard, I might brush them.

My body shuddered as indecision warred in me. I wanted to lean forward. I wanted to push him away. Unable to decide, I stayed frozen in his embrace and tried to find words.

"If that's what you choose to think, I can't stop you. But no matter how much you want to believe it, that doesn't make it true." My words were hoarse with emotion. Desire and despair. Heartbreak and hope. I hated the dichotomy.

When I breathed out, he breathed me in. A faint groan ran through him, as if he were struggling to control himself.

Our lips brushed. A tingly of *something* I shouldn't feel shot through me, like an arrow to the heart from cupid himself.

Marcel's scent consumed me.

My body shook with the force of both want for him and the need to stop this. A memory of all the times he'd kissed me ran through my mind like the flipping of pages in a book. I remembered every forbidden taste as I'd found solace in him during the worst years of my life. My body knew his touch and missed it as if he were vital to my survival and not the cause of my broken heart. My mind screamed that I was an idiot.

Marcel licked my bottom lip, and I parted against my better judgment. A strangled sigh escaped me. The tension in me melted the harder he kissed me.

It was everything it *shouldn't* have been.

More than want. More than lust.

He wrapped a hand around my nape, licking the seam of my mouth. I parted for him, and it felt like coming home.

That alarming realization jarred me, pulling me back from the insanity that was threatening to consume me.

My knee shot up, nailing him in the balls.

Marcel exhaled into me as I leaned away. His fingers

slipped from my skin as he collapsed at my feet. His knees hit the cobblestone with a crack that sounded painful.

I was still burning even though he no longer touched me.

"I'm not the same girl you remember, Marcel." Unsure if I was reminding him or myself, I forced the words out even though I didn't know if I believed it. "You don't have my heart anymore. No one does."

I turned and strode toward my car like a boss bitch even though I felt like a scared girl running from big feelings.

"This isn't over, Nathalie."

His voice was quiet but deathly serious. I'd known Marcel long enough to know he meant it. Despite my refusal, he wasn't giving up.

"I'll see you at the Wicked Haunt. Eleven o'clock. Don't be late," I managed. I needed to get away from him, and I needed my wits about me for what was going to come next. Not only tonight, but with what I had to take care of now.

He was still watching me when I pulled out of the driveway. Our eyes met in the rearview mirror. The promise in his dark gaze sent tingles over my lips, a reminder of the softness of his mouth against mine.

I inhaled sharply and shivered.

He was right about one thing.

I had a feeling everything between us was far from over.

twenty-nine

THE SECOND I turned on the main road and was out of earshot of any potential listening spells, I opened the text I'd received while I'd been talking to Carissa. Talk about terrible timing. I inhaled deeply and prepared myself before hitting the call button.

The phone rang once, and a gravelly female voice answered. "Grac."

It was a strange name for a woman until you realized her given name was Grace. When she died and became a ghoul, the guy in charge of processing new supernaturals half-assed the name tags and wrote 'Grac'. Pretty sure he'd been a coffee shop barista in a former life. At any rate, the newer version stuck.

"Tell me about Faryn's body."

My cellphone connected to my car's Bluetooth speaker while I turned onto the highway and floored it. Before the Magic Wars, there was such a thing as speed limits. Nowadays, law enforcement didn't have enough people to enforce legitimate crimes, let alone traffic violations. So few people had cars now, with the cost of gas and upkeep being

"

astronomical. I was one of the few. Marcel had thought me having a car was pointless when we were younger. He'd said it was 'impractical' and a waste of resources when he could teleport me anywhere I needed to be. I shook my head, hands tightening around the wheel.

With how everything had turned out, it was a good thing I hadn't listened to him.

"I've been around a while. Seen a lot of things. This one is different, that's for sure," she said. "I showed up for my shift at eight, as usual, but the house was torn apart. Furniture was ripped, doors broken, beds flipped. I called his name, but no one answered. It only took me a minute or two to find the body. He was long dead. At least eight hours. No more than a dozen, though. He suffered but bled out fast. Whoever killed him made up for their lack of experience with . . . enthusiasm, shall we say?"

I frowned at her tone. "Did you taste him?"

"No," she grunted.

"Grac," I said her name once, and she blew out a sigh that whistled through the receiver.

"Fine. Just his blood. I knew you wouldn't like it if I took a piece of him before you've seen it."

"You would be correct. I'm on my way. Thirty minutes. Don't touch anything."

"Wasn't planning to," Grac said.

My stomach turned, but I didn't voice my disgust. It wasn't her fault she needed flesh to survive any more than a vampire needed blood or a siren needed male hearts.

Magic was flawed. Corrupt. Devastatingly so.

Ghouls paid for their immortality by eating the flesh of the living or newly deceased. The faction leader currently in charge of the ghouls within the city had been a devout, spiritual man when alive, and he steered his kind toward the latter, choosing not to take a life for sustenance. Not everyone agreed, and many didn't like his restrictions, or Piper's, for that matter.

The skin trade ran deep in our city because there were so many things a living, breathing person could be used for.

Vampires wanted their blood.

Succubi and incubi wanted sex.

The fae wanted servants.

Ghouls wanted organs.

Preferably, fresh. Straight from the body. And there were only so many ways to get them . . .

"It's interesting, though," she mused.

"What was?"

"His blood," she answered, oblivious to my unfair judgment. To be fair, in her culture, eating people was normal. A powerful person like him would be considered a delicacy that I was letting go to waste. I understood that. But I couldn't help the undercurrent of revulsion. "It tasted kinda sweet. Like vanilla."

"He was bound to the chair, yeah?"

"Yup."

"Truth serum," I muttered. "Whoever killed him wanted answers."

But what about?

Was it information they were truly after or something else?

"My hat's off to whoever did it. I've been working for this guy for six months, and he's careful. Wards his place good and tight. Doesn't bring people here. If I hadn't been digging through his trash every week, I wouldn't have known all the shady shit he was mixed up in."

He was smart with his business. His personal life? Not so much.

But I wouldn't say that out loud.

Grac was in my pocket, but that didn't mean I trusted her. While I preferred to see the good in all people, I also planned for the worst.

Especially where there was money to be made.

And Faryn Lightseeker's death? If that didn't bring out the worst, nothing would.

I was lost between my head and the road when noise filtered through the speaker. "I didn't know you were here already. I thought you said it would be half an hour—"

"I'm not," I answered. A thought occurred to me that made my palms sweat. "Hide. Whoever's there isn't someone I sent."

I pressed my foot harder on the gas pedal. The needle inched into the nineties. Under normal circumstances, I was a fairly safe driver. I always wore my seatbelt and used my blinkers. I might speed, but I wasn't the type to weave through traffic.

Grac grunted her acknowledgment before the phone sounded muffled. I heard shuffling. The click of a lock. I didn't know where she picked to hide, but she kept the call on so I could hear her.

I wanted to ask more about what she saw and heard, but didn't want to risk giving her away. Someone breaking into his apartment would harm anyone in their way.

If I was considered the finder and fixer of New Chicago, Faryn would have been my alter ego. He could find what you wanted alright, but he only dealt in the worst sort of trades, and it was all for personal profit. Weapons. Slaves. Human trafficking. I might stray the line in some of my pursuits, but I did my due diligence. I didn't want to hand off material that could kill someone if it were put in the wrong hands. Faryn had no such compunctions. If you had the money, he had the means.

Silence made the line turn staticky. I pushed the speedometer to the edge of a hundred miles per hour. When I got to my exit ramp, I had to hit the brakes hard enough that my tires squealed like a dying pig.

Internally, the Nats cursed and shook their heads.

Peace gripped Caretaker with white knuckles. She was the only version of me that would willingly be Peace's safety blanket. Meanwhile, Ann paced her library, hands locked behind her back, spine stiff. The Warden patrolled the hallways, her chin high but mouth turned down. There was a tightness behind her eyes that betrayed the tension.

Bad Nat stood in the entryway, head tilted, and eyes narrowed.

I pulled the wheel taut and the wheels skid across cold asphalt. Smoke burned my nostrils as my Audi drifted through a red light, narrowly missing a cab.

Lucifer appeared in the passenger seat, one hand on the safety bar, the other on the back of my seat. I tried to ignore his presence as I closed the gap between me and Faryn's apartment.

Grac's continued silence was a good sign.

Whoever was there hadn't found her yet.

"You won't be any good to the ghoul dead," Lucifer chastised quietly. "And unlike them, you will not survive a crash at these speeds, little witch. I know you hate commands, but for the love of all that's unholy, *slow* down." I would have rolled my eyes under different circumstances, but I wouldn't have been driving like a maniac then, either.

The church Faryn had converted appeared just ahead. Spiral towers, brick walls, and gothic wrought iron fencing betrayed what the building had been twenty years ago, before the fae thug renovated. All it was missing from the outside was a cross.

We pulled up to the already open gates and rolled right up the cobbled driveway to stop along the curb by the double front doors. I hit the brakes so abruptly, my chest pushed against the seatbelt. It rubbed uncomfortably against my collarbone.

I threw the car in park and flung the door open wide.

My seatbelt unclasped itself, courtesy of Lucifer, as I grabbed my cell phone and mashed the buttons to make it disconnect from my car.

I ran toward the doors.

They were cracked.

All the wards Faryn had in place were now gone. They must have been linked to his life, disappearing upon death. Unless someone managed to take them down . . .

On the other end of the phone, a male voice I recognized said, "Now I'm only going to ask you once before I break through your mental shields and pull the answers from your mind by force. Who are you?"

I stopped in my tracks, and frowned at my phone as Grac answered, "I'm the cleaning lady, you pointy-eared piece of shi—"

Lucifer's concern evaporated as he heard the same thing I did.

"Anders?"

It was quiet for a fraction of a second before the telltale signs of a phone shifting hands and Grac cursing up a storm filtered through. I followed the thumps I heard from upstairs, taking the steps two at a time.

"Nathalie?" Anders called down the hall incredulously.

I breathed a sigh of relief.

Of all the people to come across Grac when Faryn was dead, he wasn't one that had ever crossed my mind.

While I walked, I pulled my backpack purse around to my front and dug for a pair of spelled latex gloves. The sound of cursing led me straight to them.

"Has he touched anything?" I asked Grac.

"My last nerve."

I sighed, taking in every inch of the scene while it was still uncontaminated. As much as it could be since she admitted *she'd licked him*. And not in the sexy way. I shook my head; happy she'd sent me the picture so I at least had a heads-up about the gruesome scene.

"Nat, what the hell is going on here?"

"Well," I hummed, walking around the office chair where Faryn's corpse rested. Or what remained of it. "It looks to me like you broke into Faryn Lightseeker's house and came across his cleaning lady." My eyes raked over the serrated cuts along his arms with keen interest.

"No, I mean, what are *you* doing here? Why were you on the phone with the ghoul? And why are you here circling his dead body?" I took in every inch of the scene so I could go through it later, after I searched for the object that was supposed to be in his possession. The one I'd been after for *months*.

The ground beneath me squelched as I accidentally stepped into the still wet puddle of blood. I must have made a face because Grac laughed at me.

"Not one for the dirty work?"

"It's not my favorite part, no."

I bit the inside of my cheek and mentally said to hell with it as I walked right up to the chair. Generic rope tied his wrists and forearms to the chair. A noose hung loosely around his neck; the other end secured to a crude hook that didn't match the rest of the décor.

It was a safety measure more than anything. The lack of rope around his legs or chest meant they used it to coerce him into not struggling. If he knocked the chair over trying to get free, he'd hang himself.

But that's not how he died.

The rope left ligature marks, but nothing that would have caused asphyxiation. The cuts on the other hand? Those intrigued me. They were shallow but sloppy. Like the person wasn't trying to kill him but didn't have a good grasp of biology and where to avoid cutting.

His shirt was slashed open, leaving his chest on display. What I could only assume was the murder weapon protruded from it. The handle was thick and crude; the angle poor if the goal had been to end him.

I grabbed it and pulled with some effort. The blade was stuck in bone.

His rib snapped, and the metal came free, showing a wicked curved edge with serrated teeth.

"Expensive blade. Fancy. Not good for killing, though," Grac said, shaking her head. "You're not going to get through bone with that sucker."

"No, you won't," I murmured. A thin trail of magic surrounded the blade. Yellow-orange in color. It wasn't a binding of any sort. More like the opposite.

Whoever enchanted it did so to *unbind*.

I took in his wounds again, considering them in a new light.

There wasn't enough blood on his chest for this to have been the killing blow. He'd already bled out a good bit, and the killer just used his lower sternum to leave their calling card.

Which lent to the theory that whoever it was felt cocky. Arrogant.

They weren't worried about being caught.

Then again, there weren't many people that could see magic—or tell that their blade would have let them unbind any runes or enchantments he may have had for protection.

But they tipped their hand when they removed the eyes.

Two gaping fleshy, pulp sockets stared back at me.

There weren't many reasons to take eyes unless you didn't want them to be used. With the right spell and a spirit witch, they could be used to replay what the victim saw in their final minutes before death. Without them, or a ghost, there was no way to use magic to find our murderer.

"Are you planning on answering me, or should I just wait here while you swap notes with the ghoul over there while she salivates over the dead body?"

"What's with all the ghoul hate? *I* didn't kill him. I'd be charging Nathalie double if I did *and* asking for the liver. Fae liver is the best. So juicy."

"For fuck's sake," Anders muttered. "I'm calling Sasha—"

"Which order would you like your questions answered in?" I said, stepping away from the body momentarily. I needed to put up my hair for the part that came next.

"Avoiding Sasha, little witch?" Lucifer asked, leaning against the bookshelf with not a care in the world.

I paused to look up at him.

He stared right back, focused on me, but not revealing a damn thing.

Anders sighed with exasperation, completely unaware of the silent conversation the devil and I were having. "Don't really care what order as long as you start talking."

"I'm here because I've been keeping a close eye on Faryn

for the last two years. In the beginning, it was just that. Watching. Then I found out he brokered a deal that . . . I couldn't ignore." I glanced sideways at Lucifer. Faryn had been the one to tell the Morrigan where he was. That information led to my family capturing and killing him. Millions that had been tied to his magic died because of that action. "He needed to be taken care of, but I didn't have the means myself, so I started flipping his people. Bodyguards. Sex workers. Anyone I could. There was just one problem. None of them had access to his home. Six months ago, Grac here replaced his last housekeeper after his old one mysteriously disappeared. Rumor was, she had a case of sticky fingers and took something she shouldn't have. I approached Grac after she got hired and offered her a deal. Since then, she reports to me." I finished pulling the scrunchy taut around my bun one more time before picking up the knife off the desk where I set it.

"And this?" He motioned toward Faryn's mutilated and rotting body as I began cutting his clothes away. "Why the strip search when he's dead?"

"Faryn had something I want. Under normal circumstances, I'd assume whoever did this had it out for him, but *how* he died . . ."

"You think he was collateral?"

"I'm not sure what to think just yet," I responded, removing his shirt then methodically cutting his pants at the seams.

I really didn't want to have to conduct an autopsy. While crude, every inch of skin needed to be shown so I could see if there was any lingering magic around or in him —whether from his attacker, or anything that might have been left behind.

"I never thought I'd say this, but I could watch you

undress dead men every day of the week." Lucifer walked up behind me, lowering his palm to the curve of my ass. I froze and glared over my shoulder.

Grac squinted back in suspicion. "What are you looking at? I didn't say nothing."

Ugh. Crap. I was so going to give him a piece of my mind once we were in private.

"Nothing," I lied, scrambling for an excuse. "I just realized I left my car idling outside in the drive. This is going to take a while, though. Can you take it back to my place? I'll have Sienna meet you there for the keys and a chat. Just to make sure I didn't miss anything while it's still fresh on your mind."

Interest made her perk up. "You brought the Audi?"

She was going to make me regret this. "Don't I always?"

Resting bitch face morphed into a wide grin. "You got it, boss."

She whistled to herself as she started for the door, not paying any mind to the scene she was leaving. Most people would have been a mess after discovering this. The lack of concern might have made me pause under different circumstances, but Grac was a little different, even for a ghoul. You don't just take a job for Faryn Lightseeker and then accept another one spying on him unless you were some level of fearless or stupid. Grac had been special forces in her human life. My bet was on the former.

I finished stripping him down to nothing while we waited in silence as her steps faded. Disappointment rushed over me when not a single wisp of magic appeared near him, dashing the naïve hope that the Eye was still here.

The state of the house suggested it was unlikely, but I held onto the idea it could have been possible. Maybe, just maybe, he'd have hidden it on him, but there was no way I wouldn't see its magic signature.

Only when the front door closed did Anders cock a brow.

I stepped back and pulled off the latex gloves, relieved to be done, but frustrated by the lack of results.

"It's possible he just pissed off the wrong person," I said as I leaned over his desk to feel every inch and groove. Several magical enchantments protected parts of it, and I was glad I'd already dismissed Grac so I could unbind them without an audience. "I could be wrong. This could be personal. He had a lot of enemies, and with good reason."

"But you don't think that's why he died?"

"No." I started untangling the magical threads of the binding closest to me. "If it was a hit, there was no reason to ransack the house. Get in. Get out. Job done." I pulled the drawer loose, sea green magic turning to gold and falling away like glitter. "Whoever did this took great risk in sticking around. I think they were searching for something." In the otherwise empty space was a single manilla envelope.

"The murder itself was messy. Usually seasoned killers do better, I'll give you that. Maybe the murderer was the wronged party and did it themselves? Would explain some of this." He waved a hand toward the body.

"Maybe." I shrugged. "Could also be a thief that wanted something he had, and the inexperience is because they've never done it before."

He squinted at the scene, then shook his head. "If they were simply a thief, there was no need to make him suffer. They could have ended it faster and been in less danger of him escaping—whoever did this took precautions, but also took their time. A thief turned killer would be hurrying through. They'd be too scared of getting caught. My bet is this was either personal or a paid hit trying to look like a crime of passion."

"Unless the thief was arrogant," I pointed out.

It was all just speculation either way. Maybe whatever was in the envelope would illuminate something. I twisted the metal ties to open it then dumped the contents on the desk.

Pictures scattered.

Pictures of . . .

"Carissa?" Disbelief filled my voice.

"That looks an awful lot like you too," Anders said quietly, pointing at one picture, then another. He picked me out in a dozen or so photos. Some with Carissa. Some without. I'd have questioned if these were old, had Carissa not been gray-haired in each and every one. Her expression was cold as always. Lacking empathy or anything resembling true human emotion. "You sure there's nothing you don't want to tell me? You know who I used to work for. I'm not going to judge—"

I glanced between them, taking in my chocolate brown hair and bourbon-colored eyes. In most of the photos, my shoulders were tense and my skin was pink from the cold. There wasn't a single thing off or unusual.

Except I had no memory of these things, and I remembered *everything*.

"It's not me," I murmured. "It can't be." Anders frowned dubiously. "I'm not lying," I snapped at him.

Anders lifted both hands in surrender. "I wasn't saying you were. I'm just trying to understand—the same as you. If that's not you right there—" He touched the tip of his finger to one photo that was head on. I was looking almost directly at the camera. Or whoever was pretending to be me was. "It's a damn good glamour. They'd have to need a piece of you to get that exact. Even that expression, right there. You make it whenever you're pensive or plotting something."

He wasn't wrong. Whoever the impostor was clearly knew my mannerisms. This wasn't some rookie who didn't do their homework.

It hit me.

"Katherine." I interrupted, touching the glossy sheen where it cut off, only showing a fraction of the outfit I was wearing. "Marcel bought me that dress for my nineteenth birthday. I left it behind when I moved. There's no one else that would have it."

Worry danced across his light blue gaze.

"It's the only thing that makes sense. I can't be glamoured. Not this perfectly. I take a potion that makes using my hair, skin, or blood impossible. It renders it useless if I'm not the one doing the spell. They would have had to know me, my expressions, my aphorisms. Know my tastes. My brands." I shook my head, tracing where the outline of a scar should have been. A lot of them didn't show it, because you needed a direct face shot to see her scar and whoever had taken these managed mostly side profiles. "It has to be Katherine. We're exact matches. All she would need to do is glamour her scar and no one would know the difference. In passing, at least."

"But why pretend to be you?" he questioned.

The answer was so obvious it might as well have slapped us in the face.

"This is how she's hiding."

I thought about the lack of reports I'd been receiving. Despite how many people I employed, there wasn't a trace of Kat anywhere—apart from her connection to the deaths.

Fuck.

"That's why we can't find her. Why no one has had a lead in the weeks I've had people searching. They all think it's me. And if they think it's me, then Faryn likely did too."

"Okay, but back up," he nodded slowly. "Katherine has been missing for a while, according to Marcel, but Carissa is in these pictures. Nat . . . are you sure they've been telling you the truth? Could Marcel be lying?"

"No," I said quietly. He didn't know about this morning. That I'd come directly from saving her from certain death. "Marcel almost killed her this morning. He blames her for Kat's disappearance. Apparently she was blackmailing them for heirs. . . There's a whole mess where that's involved, but I'm sure Marcel isn't in on whatever lie might have been told. We also have to consider that these could have been taken before she disappeared. There's no time stamp on them."

Anders tilted his head in acknowledgment. "Something isn't adding up."

I sighed. "Welcome to my life. Where my family is concerned, that's the norm."

He shook his head, flashing me an empathetic look. "For what it's worth, I know what it's like. My father's wife held me prisoner for years to punish him for mating my mother."

"Isn't your father a demon?" I said slowly, lifting my eyes to his.

He smirked wryly despite the depressing topic of conversation. "You've done your research."

I lifted one shoulder in a half shrug. "I was curious about your past. You did serve Lucifer, after all. No such thing as too careful in our world."

He nodded, blowing out a breath. "No, I suppose there

isn't. A few decades ago, I fell in love with a human woman. We got married and had a son. They were the best years of my life. I went to my father and asked him to change her. Only demon blood can do it, and there are only a dozen or so demons in the world. I'd never asked him for anything, even after what happened with his crazy wife. I thought he'd do it, no questions asked . . ." Pain laced his features. It was there in the tightness of his jaw and the lines by his eyes.

"He didn't," I whispered.

"No," Anders said quietly. "He didn't. Instead, he broke her mind to show me how weak she was. We'd had a child, which meant if he turned her, she would have been my mate. I knew it before I brought her to Ireland, but I thought because of the problems my father had gone through with his own mate that he would understand." Anders looked away. I wanted to know what happened to her, his lost love, but I also didn't because this wasn't one of my romance books. This story didn't have a happy ending, that much was clear. "She killed herself three days later. Hung herself from the rafters. My father hugged me and said one day I'd understand. That he did it to save me from myself because a mate was a weakness. She wasn't a supernatural, so we couldn't bond, and because she had no magic, there was no ghost that I could have had a witch resurrect. She was just gone."

I touched his arm softly. Water welled in my eyes. My heart bled for him. For his loss. For his shitty family. For the love he should have known.

"He came into my employment to spite his father," Lucifer added, not that Anders could hear him. "I'd banned Dagda from entering the Americas when I took over in World War Two. He might have a strong hold in Europe, but he wouldn't set foot in my territory. Not with how many supernaturals I had."

I cleared my throat of the emotion clogging it. "Family is shitty because they can be. They think because we share blood that we owe them something. Our loyalty. Our time. Our peace." I squeezed his shoulder in an act of comfort and solidarity. "But we make our own family."

Anders nodded and released a taut breath. Haunted shadows still danced in his icy blue eyes, but I was beginning to think they always had. Now I just recognized them.

"We both deserved better," he said after a moment.

"We found it," I reminded him, bumping his shoulder with mine. A slight smile tugged at his lips.

"That we did."

I looked down at the pictures on Faryn's desk. There were a couple dozen photos, but no answers as to why he had them or what they meant. But there was one thing that struck me as odd.

"I wonder how Faryn knew that was Katherine," I mused after a comfortable silence.

"How do you know he did?"

"There's no way he should have known the difference, but I'm in none of these. With this many photos, surely he would have gotten a picture of me at least once if he were tracking *me*, right? I'm all over this city. But he didn't. Which means he knew this was my sister. How?"

I chewed my bottom lip, mulling over the possibilities.

"You think either of them could have had something to do with Faryn's murder?" Anders asked. "Whoever did it had to have a lot of money to purchase a blade like that."

I glanced back at the body that was starting to smell.

"Maybe? Seems unlikely. Carissa is too weak to overpower someone, and Kat has enough magic that she doesn't need to resort to this. I won't say it's impossible, but they're not my first bet."

"Fair enough," he said, sighing deeply. "I need to call this into Sasha. Maybe she'll see something we haven't. But Nat?" I lifted my chin, still half lost in thought.

"A drawer full of pictures doesn't look good for Katherine. Not when she's already connected to other murders. I'm not saying she killed anyone—but she's clearly gotten herself into something she shouldn't have."

He gave me an understanding if pitying look.

I swallowed around the lump in my throat.

"Make the call, Anders."

He nodded once, stepping right outside.

My phone buzzed, and a text from Sienna informed me that she was ten minutes away from Faryn's. I continued searching the desk while bits and pieces of Anders's conversation drifted toward me.

"No. It doesn't match the others, but we found pictures of Katherine and Carissa."

"She knows."

"No. So far no sign of it, but I just got here. I need to search the place before we bring anyone else in."

"Gimme five before you come over."

There was an extended pause. He walked back around the door, stowing his phone in his back pocket. "Sasha will be here soon. I heard about what happened this morning, so I'm giving you a heads-up."

Right. Of course. It seemed like more time had passed between her walking into August's apartment and ripping the floor out from under me, to now, standing in Faryn's crime scene.

How much could happen in one fucking day?

"Thanks for that. I need to take a quick look around

before getting back to work, but I'll have Sienna take over for me here. She's on her way."

He nodded, expecting as much. I can only guess what he'd heard from her by now. Hopefully she at least gave an honest portrayal.

I went to collect my backpack, pausing at the desk. "I want these when she's finished looking around. Have her make copies if she needs them as well."

He nodded along, watching me with a mixed expression as I gathered my stuff. "Oh, I meant to ask. Are you here on official business? Or personal? You beat me here, and I have the staff in my pocket . . ." I slung my bag over my shoulder and waited for an answer.

"Both." His vagueness was unexpected, especially after the incredibly personal things he'd just told me about his father. "Can't speak on Ronan's. That's his business. I'm just the one executing it. Faryn had something I want, so I figured I'd see if it was here while I was at it." Made sense. He was a finder, after all. Like me, he collected many rare and expensive things. Some more so than others.

I dipped my head. "Fair enough. Just seemed odd since you've not been at the other crime scenes."

He smiled ruefully. "Piper deals with the civilians, and Sasha by extension. Ronan's business is more . . . lucrative. You really should be hiring out more help to look into these things given how much you deal on both ends of the spectrum."

I snorted. "That an insult?"

"It's an observation. You look tired. Exhausted, actually. You should get some rest before tonight."

I chuckled. "I'll sleep when I'm dead."

His hand gently touched my forearm when I stepped around him to leave the office. "Sasha is hurt, but she's also irrational about this. It's not her fault. The bond does things to people . . ." He shook his head. "Give her time. She might come around, and I'd hate to see you miss out on happiness because she was so lost in her own emotions to see how unfair this morning was to you."

I jerked, mostly out of surprise. "It's not a big deal," I stammered. "We'd only been together a few times. I'll get over it. I just hope she does too."

Anders gave me a pitying smile. "Sometimes when you know, you just know. Sarah was a waitress when I met her. By the end of my dinner shift, I knew she was meant to be mine. I don't know what you're feeling, but if it was more than just a fling like I suspect—don't discount that. The real thing may come along more than once in a lifetime, but it's rare and fragile. Sasha has good reason to be upset, but she's never been with him, and she never will. She can move on, if only she'd look past what the bond is telling her. If she did, she'd see the truth."

My lips parted. "Why are you saying this? You're her best friend."

"Did you tell Piper what she wanted to hear, or did you tell her the truth?"

The sudden chill in the hallway told me we weren't alone. I pulled away and nodded a plaintive greeting to Sasha as I stumbled downstairs. I really needed to search for the Eye, but my head was all over the place. Carissa. Katharine. Sasha. August.

Hell, even Anders's wife was now occupying a space in my heart and head.

Screw it. Sienna could do the search.

"Where are you going, little witch?" Lucifer asked. My ever-present stalker couldn't just let me be.

"Work. Contrary to what everyone around here thinks, I do have shit to do outside family drama."

Lucifer tutted. "You're distracting, but who am I to tell you that you can't?" He spoke sarcastically, very much aware of how I'd respond if he attempted to command me. If I were in a better mood, I might have made a comment about old dogs learning new tricks.

A few minutes passed while I waited for Sienna. Agitation ate at me despite the arid chill of New Chicago in late autumn. My breath came out in white, frustrated puffs. "Do you think he's right?" I asked, chewing on my lip.

"About which part?" Lucifer mused.

"Sasha. August. All of it. They both worked for you. You raised her. What's your opinion?"

He cocked his head, considering his answer. "I *think* that what the rest of us think doesn't matter. Or at least it shouldn't. You work yourself to death and bend over backward to make everyone else happy when the only person you have to live with is yourself. Yet, you do the least for yourself. Regardless of what Sasha or anyone else does, you refuse to put yourself first. I wonder what life would look like if you did?"

I didn't.

I may not tell people everything, but I knew myself. My wants. My desires. My every horrible thought and feeling.

They all think I'm this good person that's selfless.

What they don't realize is that I'm not.

I'm simply too intelligent to let my own hedonistic urges take root because I know what life would look like if I did.

And it wasn't pretty.

NATHALIE

SILENCE SCREAMED THROUGH THE GRAVEYARD. Single-paned windows rattled in a phantom wind.

I glanced up at them, peering through the dirty glass to the clear night sky beyond.

"You look like a graverobber."

His quiet voice made me jump. I whirled around, narrowing my eyes at Marcel. "Blood is messy. It's wasteful to ruin clothes when the black will hide it."

Amusement tugged at his lips. Unlike me, he was still dressed in gray slacks and a stained white button-down. The collar sat oddly, and it was unbuttoned one more than typically appropriate. And there it was again . . . glamour. He wasn't showing his true self. A part of me wanted to know why. Another part of me reminded me I wasn't supposed to care.

"I already told you I won't let you be the sacrifice for the veil. I haven't changed my mind about that."

My teeth clenched. "And I told you I found someone else, not that you're in much of a position to argue now that you're covenless, houseless, and if I had to guess, broke."

He chuckled, strolling down the center aisle of the abandoned church. "You would be guessing correctly."

"I usually do."

Instead of laughing at me, he stopped a few feet away, raking his gaze over my face. "I like this newfound confidence you have. It suits you."

The compliment washed over me like acid burning through my skin. "Not newfound," I corrected.

He lifted his eyebrows. "You rarely used your voice to speak up for yourself when we were together. Now you're all sarcasm and cool arrogance."

I snorted once. "I didn't voice it at the time; that's not the same as lacking the quality. Being away from the black witch covens taught me a lot. Like to never silence myself for someone else's sake."

Not even if it cost me my twin.

It took a long time, but I eventually found peace with myself over that night. Different choices would have led to different outcomes, but that didn't change that Kat chose Prudence. She chose the bully that lied to her face over the sister that could only tell truth. The truth of it was, she chose her before that night. I was just so desperate to have someone that I accepted the scraps she gave me as if they were a feast.

Never again.

Marcel cocked his head. "I never wanted you to be silent."

Of course he took it as an insult aimed at him. Though he was right, and I couldn't deny it. Marcel never did want me to quell my thoughts. I did that all on my own to lift him up after he became my rock. I played the part of the dutiful daughter because my parents' praise reflected on Marcel, and I wouldn't have anything less for him. Not when he was all I had. I was silent because it was the only way I could portray the girl I was expected to be.

It took leaving them all to become the woman I was born to be.

"No, you just wanted me to not see my worth so I'd be your concubine."

Anger flashed through him, an echo of our earlier conversation.

The temperature dropped as Sasha walked in from the void. She appeared out of nowhere to the untrained eye, but the darkness that clung to her could only come from one place. The sub-dimension that existed between one shadow and the next that let her traverse space to be anywhere in the world with only a single step.

I'd never been so glad for an interruption.

"Marcel, I'm sure you remember Sasha Loren." I gestured to her as she dropped a bag of bones and ash at my feet.

"Charmed," Sasha said sarcastically.

"She's a succubus shifter."

We both looked at him. "Yes, and?"

"I need a black witch with death magic. I told you—"

"I have death magic," Sasha cut him off. She lifted her chin to level him with a stare. "That's all you really need to send someone into the veil with a hope of them coming back, yes?"

"Well, in theory, yes, but—"

"Then we're good. When do we start?"

Marcel sighed. Ignoring Sasha's presence entirely, he shot me a pointed glare. "You told me you found a witch." The accusation in his voice was amusing at best.

"I said I'd found *a volunteer,* and I have." I motioned toward her with a wave of my hand. "We need answers, now more than ever after Carissa's admissions. You either do it with her or you do it with me, but it needs to happen tonight."

The muscle in his jaw strained. His knuckles turned white where he grasped the back of one pew. "And if I refuse?"

I stepped forward, my hands settling behind my back as I did so. "Then we're done here and you will never see me again." His brows furrowed. "We're working together under a common interest," I explained. "You want to find Katherine. So do I. If you refuse, then you're actively impeding that goal. Which means I have no reason to speak to you again, especially since you're no longer a member of the Ouroboros Coven and therefore not a representative on the Demon Queen's council."

Sasha's emerald eyes bounced back and forth between us, taking in the interaction. We'd already spoken briefly about what went down at the Le Fay household when she'd called to tell me that the hospital cameras had been wiped before we could get the footage. She'd at least found the identities of the dead staff. I'd spent the afternoon combing through their records and conducting my own interviews with their respective families. By all accounts, they seemed to be just innocent people caught in the line of fire. That didn't make me feel better; not with Carissa's insistence that Kat was the one killing people out of a lack of control.

Still, it only partly fit the scene of the crime.

I wasn't willing to let it go just yet.

"I'm homeless and covenless, as you pointed out. If I do this, I want something in return."

I tilted my chin, surprised he asked. I shouldn't have

been. The whole reason he'd wanted to latch on to my family was the perks that came with it. He'd said that himself not twelve hours before.

"I can pay you for your services."

"I need somewhere to stay. I want it to be with you, at least while we're hunting Katherine."

I laughed. The sound reverberated off the haunted walls. "Absolutely not."

He didn't look amused. "Why?"

My lips parted at the audacity. "Do you really need me to list all the reasons?"

He didn't speak for a moment. Right as I went to list them, he said, "No."

"Fifty thousand. I'll pay half now. Half when Sasha is brought back—regardless of the answers she finds." It was a modest offer at best. The spell I was asking for was easily worth five times that, but I was a businesswoman, after all. If they didn't roll their eyes at the amount, I'd offered too much. Contrary to what people believed, the best way to remain wealthy was not to spend it frivolously, but to hoard it.

Marcel shook his head, lip curling in disgust. "I don't want your money."

"You're not staying with me, so it's that or—"

"A date."

Sasha tried to cover a laugh behind a fake cough. I glowered at him, ignoring her. "I'm not a commodity to be bargained over. It's insulting you think that."

Wisps of death leaked from him. They didn't reach for me, instead writhing against his skin. "No, you're just so fucking stubborn and refuse to meet me in the middle."

"There is no middle. Not in this."

The vein in his neck seemed to throb.

"As much as I can appreciate the fuckboy's attempt at winning you back, we're on a bit of a schedule, are we not?"

"We are," I agreed with a jerky nod. "What's it going to be, Marcel?"

He wanted to argue. That much was obvious with one look at his face, but I wasn't going there. He either took the money or he didn't. I wasn't offering myself up in any form or fashion.

"Can you get me an audience with the Demon Queen?" he asked in a tight voice.

I blinked, exchanging a wary look with Sasha. "What do you want an audience for?" I asked.

"That's between her and I," he answered. I wanted to deny him on principle, but it wasn't the most unreasonable request. I knew Piper would never betray me in any way, so if he was hoping to gain some advantage over me, he'd be wasting his breath. If not, then he was right, it wasn't my business.

"I'll speak to her. That's the best I can promise."

"Fine," he said with forced calm. "I'll do the spell in return for you doing your best to get me an audience with her, but I'm not taking money from you." He seemed appalled, like the idea of accepting payment from me was repulsive. I didn't understand it, but I didn't need to.

"Suit yourself. If you enjoy being broke, that's on you."

Sasha snorted, but Marcel just stared. With a flick of his wrist, the pews moved to either side of the room, clearing the center of the chapel.

It was an impressive show of power not even my mother could have done.

"I'm going to need salt. A lot of it."

I smiled as I pulled my backpack around. He frowned, as I unzipped it and turned it upside down.

"Salt," I commanded the magic. It wasn't mine, but the enchantment answered all the same. The zipper stretched as not one ten-pound paper sack of salt fell onto the floor, but ten.

Marcel's eyes widened in surprise.

"How's a hundred pounds work?"

thirty-one

I SAT outside the ring of salt.

Three inches thick and seven feet in diameter, it took up most of the chapel floor. The outer edges strayed close to the pews shoved to either side of the room. I took a seat on the steps, watching the clock at the back of the room while Marcel explained to Sasha what was going to happen.

At five minutes to midnight, they both stepped into the circle.

The athame I'd cleansed the night before rested in Marcel's hand, like it was always meant to be there.

"To push you into the veil, I'll have to stop your supernatural healing abilities. It's a reversible process, but you'll have to sit on the edge of death for an extended period of time." He explained it to her quietly, his eyes glancing over at me every few seconds. Sasha nodded.

"I can handle it."

"I hope so," Marcel said. "You'll be under for one hour exactly. The candle will burn for precisely that long. It's your guide. When it gets to the end, you *have* to return to your body. I can't undo the binding on your magic until afterwards. If you panic, you'll bleed faster, and it'll be harder to keep you alive."

She let out a harsh breath, then said, "Let's do this."

Marcel motioned to the dusty floor. "Lie down."

Lucifer appeared beside me as Sasha sank to the ground in her yoga pants and a thin ribbed tank top. Marcel maneuvered her limbs where he needed them with sure fingers. Palms up. Arms spread.

He took the bowl of paste he'd prepared while I made the circle. Inside, half a dozen herbs had been ground into powder. He'd mixed them with his own blood, and dirt from a grave. The result was a dark maroon-colored substance.

"You shouldn't be here," I breathed, turning my head and running my hand over my lips as I did so to try to hide what I was doing.

Lucifer cocked a brow at me. "Do you really think I wouldn't be here when the *boy* attempts to summon ten ghosts?" He snorted derisively, then shook his head. "Besides, Sasha won't see me. Your secret is safe."

I pressed my lips together in a hard line, trying to pay attention to what Marcel was doing. The paste clung to two fingers as he used it to draw on Sasha's wrists. His movements were lithe and graceful as he maneuvered around the circle. Despite his impressive height and the muscle he'd packed on during the years I'd been gone, he moved like a jungle cat instead of a lumbering bear. Then again, I wasn't sure how much was truly him when he wore a glamour all the time.

"I have to ask," Lucifer started when I didn't respond to his earlier question. "What is it about him that drew you in?" His honey eyes flipped between me and the symbols Marcel was drawing on Sasha's chest. "He's pretty, but nothing I haven't seen before. He chose the other one over you, which means his intelligence is questionable at best. I can tell the boy has power, but it's still nothing compared to me." Lucifer continued to compare himself to my ex, seemingly oblivious to the way my chest constricted uncomfortably.

I recognized the nasty emotion that was trying to crawl its way into my heart, but I wouldn't allow it.

My lips pinched together as I slowly turned my head, needing to look away from the way Marcel's fingers skimmed Sasha's breast in the itty-bitty tank top as much as I needed to glare at the devil on my right.

I cocked my head as if to say, *I'm kinda busy.*

"We both know it's going to be a long night and I've never been one for the fanfare." He waved his hand toward them like the summoning was inconsequential, even though he'd already implied otherwise. "If I had to guess, I'd say you aren't either, given how infrequently you cast spells. I wonder . . ." He leaned in close, lips trailing up my jaw, brushing me with the slightest caress. "Do you avoid your magic because of me? Or because of him?"

I jerked like he shocked me.

Marcel looked up, his dark eyes seeing far too much for my liking.

"Everything okay?"

"Yep," I said louder than necessary. He narrowed his gaze, but went back to what he was doing. Lucifer chuckled, cool breath fanning my face.

I glared at him as an idea came to me. Reaching into my back pocket, I pulled out my cell phone and opened the notes app.

I can't talk to you while they're here. Fuck off. I typed in a rush. I went to close the app when Lucifer's pale fingers wrapped around my wrist.

"You're using that to talk just fine."

As he said it, Marcel sank to the floor and assumed a cross-legged position. The clock chimed midnight.

I need to pay attention.

Lucifer snorted again. "No, you don't. He's going to sit there and chant for an hour while Sasha leaves her body."

Which is precisely why I need to pay attention. If something goes wrong—

"If something goes wrong, there's nothing you will be able to do to stop it. Worrying about her is wasted effort."

I rolled my eyes as Marcel began the ritual. He spoke, the words low but authoritative in a tongue I knew but wished I didn't.

Magic was power, and a witch or warlock's power often needed a purpose to manifest. It needed words. We were molded by tradition and learned several ancient languages growing up, because it was in those tongues that spells were cast.

There was great power in words.

Especially repetition.

The first witches created our system of magic by giving it will. They told it what to do, and through enough trial and error, the magic yielded.

Like anything, it came easier the more it was done.

Generation after generation, we passed down those spells, each new group of witches having it just a little bit easier. The magic became just a little bit tamer.

Necromancy was a relatively new practice as far as witch kind were concerned. It started five hundred years ago with the first black witch, Morgan Le Fay.

My dead ancestor. It was an odd sort of cosmic intervention that she found a way to live forever as a mortal but still died the night Lucifer did with the rest of the Le Fays.

The Morrigan paved the way for the rituals that allowed us to speak to and summon and even raise the dead. The newness of it made the spells temperamental on a good day. They were volatile in the most skilled of hands and required more brute strength and control than any other study of witch magic.

It was why Marcel studied necromancy to begin with.

He wanted to conquer the hardest practice that existed and be the very best. Watching him single-handedly invoke the veil while speaking the dead language Akkadian made me think that he might have succeeded.

Marcel lifted a match, and it burst into flame. He used it to light the wax candle that sat on the ground in between them.

A chill ran down my spine as he lifted the athame. The next part was admittedly a little traumatic after the ritual my mother and sisters had forced on me that ended in Lucifer's death.

I'd had to carve his name from his very skin. The brands that were its only written form traced from hand to jaw, all the way down his chest and back. That was before taking his heart. It was a lengthy process. Bloody.

This particular ritual was a lot simpler. He didn't need to carve her like a piece of meat—he just had to slit her wrists.

I looked away when the knife pressed into Sasha's light brown skin, holding my breath.

"This is why I wanted to distract you," Lucifer said. He grabbed hold of my face, turning it back to his. "Let me."

My brows furrowed as I gave him an unamused stare. The devil chuckled, too close for comfort.

"I promise to be good if you do."

Despite my friend bleeding out on the floor not ten feet from me, heat pooled in my core. My jaw clenched, because how shameless could I be?

I liked sex, but lately I felt like I was lusting after everyone I shouldn't.

The dead demon bound to me included.

I tapped a slow message out on my phone, biting the inside of my cheek while I did.

What did you have in mind?

This was a horrible idea, but what was the worst that could happen? He had a point about me needing distraction. My palms were beginning to sweat horribly as my heart rate climbed.

"A game of sorts. I believe humans call it quid pro quo." He smirked at my dubious expression.

That's not a game. It's an information exchange.

Lucifer shrugged. "For every question you answer honestly, I'll answer one of yours." I lifted both my eyebrows at him. Did he think me stupid? Or just incredibly naïve?

Anything?

Surely he wouldn't—

"Anything," he repeated, speaking slowly. My breath hitched.

The chance to get answers from him for something as simple as the truth was incredibly appealing. I stalled for a second, debating what to type next.

Katherine?

He glanced down at my phone, then turned those amber eyes on me. He ran his thumb over my bottom lip. It felt so real despite the lack of warmth. His skin was smooth and supple yet hard and firm as it touched mine.

"If that's what you really want to know about, yes. I'll answer your questions about Katherine to the best of my ability."

I pulled the inside of my bottom lip between my teeth, kneading the already sore skin. A nervous tic I struggled to break even when it bled.

What's the catch?

"No catch," Lucifer replied. "If you answer my questions honestly, I'll do the same."

And if I don't?

I almost didn't type it, but I couldn't take the words back once they were there. Lucifer pressed his thumb into my bottom lip, staring at the spot where we touched.

"Every lie or non-answer is a kiss. I will choose when to collect."

Ahhh. I saw it for what it was then. Not just a trade of truths. This was a bargain.

What if you lie? What do I get?

Lucifer smiled, dropping his hand from my jaw without moving back to give me space. "If I were to lie, you'd never know the difference," he said, making me less inclined to play his game. "I'll give you a choice, though. You can either take a kiss for questions I choose not to answer, or I will promise complete honesty—even if you don't."

I debated my response. It was a compelling offer. Complete honesty in return for the same, and if he asked anything I wasn't willing to answer, I just had to give him a kiss. Since he seemed to have no issue taking them whether I wanted to or not, it seemed like a waste to turn down the opportunity to ask my questions.

Sienna's warning came to mind.

"He will take more than you bargained for."

Could I accept that? The loopholes? The game seemed

simple enough, but I wasn't so arrogant as to overlook her advice. Lucifer didn't bargain unless he wanted something, and somehow this was a way for him to get whatever that was out of me.

I didn't have to answer, my brain pointed out. I could accept the kiss. It's not like he was a terrible kisser. Besides, a kiss meant nothing. It wasn't marriage or anything so binding—and I'd already done that.

Shoving down the doubts, I typed a reply with my heart hammering in my chest.

You have to answer everything honestly.

Lucifer smiled at my response, unsurprised at my choice. I got the distinct impression he was pleased with himself. "You have my word."

Say it.

Lucifer chuckled. The scent of blood and sex drowned me in its hedonistic ways. "I swear to tell you the truth in return for your own truth, but for every lie or non-answer, I will claim a kiss."

I nodded my head slightly. Just a small dip.

The golden tether between us flared, winding around our bodies like a thread attempting to tie us together. It pulsed with energy under our bargain.

There was no going back.

If I thought he'd be a gentleman and let me go first, I was sorely mistaken.

"Now, tell me, what made you fall in love with him?" Lucifer thrust his chin toward Marcel. I'd known he wouldn't let it go, but I didn't think he'd waste his questions on my love life.

While not the most comfortable question to answer, it could have been worse. I considered my reply.

He saw me for me . . . and he still wanted me.

Lucifer's gaze narrowed. He was looking for the lie in my features and must have been miffed not to find one, if I were to guess by the exasperated sigh he let out. I wasted no time typing my question. Whatever his thoughts on my answer, they didn't matter. What happened between me and Marcel was in the past.

Did Katherine murder those people?

Lucifer huffed. "Waste of a question if you ask me, but the answer is, I don't know. I didn't see her kill any of them. I can't say either way."

Disappointment gnawed at me, but I did my best to push it away. I knew there was a chance of that. With any luck, Sasha would have the answer soon enough, but hearing it from two sources was better than one.

"The incubus," Lucifer whispered, leaning in close. I stilled. "What was it that you saw in him?"

I bit the inside of my cheek as I typed out, *Elaborate.*

A smirk flashed across his face and disappeared just as quickly. "You went back for him. Twice. Then you stayed the night with him. What convinced you to let your guard down?"

I swallowed, looking away. Sasha lay still in a pool of her own blood while Marcel continued chanting in the language of ancient Mesopotamia. Bits of bone stuck out of the pile of ash where Sasha had thrown pieces of all ten people in indiscriminately.

Weakness, I typed eventually.

Lucifer tsked. "Weakness didn't convince you. Answer the question, little witch. Unless you'd rather I take a kiss?"

If I couldn't answer his second question, I was sincerely going to regret the outcome of this bargain. I wasn't sure why I was holding back from him, though. He couldn't exactly tell anyone.

My breath turned white as the temperature in the Wicked Haunt dropped.

I liked him. I liked the way he treated me. I felt unburdened.

Lucifer considered this answer longer than the last. The word "unburdened" rolled around on his lips as I mashed the delete button until there were no words on the screen.

What do you know about Katherine?

Lucifer chuckled. "A great many things. You're going to need to be more specific."

I glowered, seeing the evasion for what it was. I rephrased my message.

What do you know about Katherine's magic?

The smile on his face almost seemed pleased. "Better. Still not what I would have asked or how I would have put it, but I'll tell you what you're looking for all the same." He put an arm around my back, resting it against the step behind me. The black T-shirt clinging to his body did little to hide the corded muscle of his phantom arms that I totally should not have been eyeing. "Your twin has death magic. Nothing has changed that to my knowledge. However, someone *has* been teaching her new tricks. She's been using spells in English that I haven't seen before, and while I will admit I haven't been the most observant in regard to black witches in the past, I have been around for a long time. Whoever taught her created a weapon with little regard as to when or why it might go off."

What do you mean?

"Ah, ah," Lucifer said, stretching his long legs out, as if we were just two people having a chat anywhere, rather than the devil and the witch bonded to him sitting in the most unholy chapel that had probably ever existed. "It's my turn. I want to know why you ignored me."

I frowned. I'd already told him, but if he wanted me to

waste a question on spelling it out, I wasn't going to stop him.

You push my boundaries. I don't like it.

"And before that? When you were pretending I don't exist?"

That's two questions.

He shook his head, grinning like a fool. "No, it's not. I didn't ask why you ignored me. I said, I want to know why—it wasn't a question."

"Semantics," I hissed. If not for the way Marcel's voice was echoing off the walls, I wouldn't have dared to speak it.

"The devil is in the details, little witch. Sienna warned you."

My lips parted. He knew about our conversation that day in the car.

Motherfucker.

Lucifer scoffed. "Of course I've fucked mothers. I'd hardly waste my attention on a blushing virgin who wouldn't know my cock from my balls, let alone what to do with them. I've never understood why humankind thought I wanted innocence. Now answer the question—or take the pass and acknowledge I'll collect on my own time."

I forced out a hard breath, teeth gritted as I typed painfully slow. It killed me a little to give him the answer when he'd manipulated me so easily. I'd need to be more careful.

I thought I was hearing voices.

He didn't laugh or smile at that response, instead waiting quietly for my question.

Now tell me what you meant before.

"Ask a question," Lucifer said, the corner of his mouth tipping up. "I'm hardly going to fall for the same tricks I use on you."

Contrary to what he'd thought, I wasn't actually trying to trick him. I was just overzealous in wanting to understand what he meant about Katherine.

What do you mean by someone has been teaching her new tricks?

Lucifer shrugged. "The spells in English are the main thing. She was casting them before she took the blood oath with Bree Fallon, yet she didn't have the power to do such things back then. Someone taught her a workaround."

A workaround.

As in, another way to fuel her spells?

I'd seen the magic he spoke of only once before. She'd commanded a room to break, and the floor cracked like a splintering star.

It was devastating.

My chest felt heavy, weighed down with suspicion.

"Voices," he said. "Plural. Have you heard voices other than mine?"

The hard shadow in his eyes made me shiver.

I wanted to deny it, but in doing so, I'd still answer the question at hand. I wasn't a bad liar, but something told me that the devil would indeed see right through it.

Instead of typing, I dipped my chin in the slightest nod.

His expression was utterly unreadable.

I didn't ponder on it when I had my own question to ask and answer to seek.

Do you believe Katherine is using living beings to fuel her spells?

The corner of his mouth twitched. "Clever phrasing this time. I can't say for certain, but yes, I do believe she's using the living to fuel them." My head dropped forward as I took that in. "Answer time. These voices, who are they?"

I nibbled on my bottom lip. There was no way he'd guess. Of that, I was completely certain.

Was that truth worth a kiss? A debt?

"I don't know," I answered, forgetting that I needed to be silent.

"Liar." He didn't look as happy about me owing him as I expected. I shrugged and pointedly typed, *Guess I owe you then.*

The glare he gave me would have made grown men piss themselves. It surprised me. I'd half expected this game to be a farce so he would have an excuse to kiss me.

I just ignored him.

Did you know she ran away before Marcel told me?

"No," he said. "You were still ignoring me. It's difficult for me to go far . . ." He trailed off, not finishing the sentence.

Curiosity made me want to know the rest of what he was going to say.

Common sense told me I should leave it.

They warred as he considered his next question. "You won't tell me about the voices, but you thought I was one. Why did you save me?"

You were Piper's atman. Even if it wasn't meant to be, she would feel pain if you died—and she did. I was trying to prevent that.

He waited expectantly. "That may be part of the truth, but it's not all of it. You're hiding something. I can *feel* it. You tried to undo the chains and save me when you could have run—"

I know what I did, I typed hastily.

"You licked my blood and chose to forge the familiar bond. Why?"

He saw that? I barely even remembered it. The act was

as much a compulsion as it was a last-ditch effort at the time. I'd known he was dead, but I thought I could change that somehow. That if I made the familiar bond, he'd be brought back.

I was wrong. I ended up with an immortal stalker instead.

Yay me.

The true answer wasn't something I could easily explain, but it also wasn't exactly a secret.

That one is hard to explain over text.

"We have time." The dismissive way he answered told me this was another question he wasn't going to let go. I sighed and began typing.

The first time you touched me I had a vision. It was because of that.

I tried to avoid looking at him, but it was easier said than done when he said, "That was remarkably simple for something that's hard to explain over text."

Asshole. He laughed. *Can you actually feel it when I'm hiding something?*

I shouldn't have asked it. My questions belonged to the things that mattered, but this felt important. Significant, even though nothing about my relationship with a ghost should have been.

"I can," Lucifer said, voice full of gravel. "What was the vision?"

Images flashed through my mind.

The first time we touched. It was long before Piper became queen, before I killed Lucifer, before the Underworld burned in her explosive fire—I was just a witch, in over my head. Similar to him, I'd had a premonition when I met Piper and I knew she was my future. If I wanted to stay alive, I needed to stay with her. Not an easy task when she'd pissed off the devil and he was hunting her. When he finally caught up, I was apprehended and then put into the fighting pits; a gladiator-style spectacle for supernaturals to fight to the death. The devil ran the Underworld—basically the seediest place in New Chicago—and I was that night's entertainment.

Everyone thought I was no one. Including me.

Then I defeated one of his most lethal fighters and I claimed the attention of the devil himself.

Everything changed.

It was there that Lucifer bit me and learned the truth of what I was.

While he was stealing my secrets in blood, I'd had a series of visions that rattled me.

His death was the first. I saw myself straddling him with a knife to his flesh and the light leaving his eyes. That one had already come to pass, but the others . . .

I sighed. I already owed him a kiss. The things in my visions always happened. I knew—whether I liked it or not—the rest of it would too, eventually. Maybe that's why I found myself weak at resisting my attraction to him. Some things were inevitable.

I saw many things. Your death. Us fucking. You taking several bullets for me. Killing several people too.

I tried to be as vague as possible while answering. Lucifer froze as he read my response. His white eyebrows inched upward, lips parted. It seemed I'd managed to do the impossible.

I'd shocked the devil speechless.

You said you can feel when I'm hiding something. What else can you do?

Lucifer turned his cheek, grinning at me. "Curious little

witch. I wonder if your vision did me justice when we were fucking—"

Answer the question.

He chuckled. "I can tell when you're lying. Your words taste sweet, like syrup. When you're omitting information, it's like cinnamon. You already know about telekinesis, but so long as I'm dead, that seems to be the extent of my abilities right now."

So, he couldn't compel. That was good to know. I didn't think he could, but I needed to be more careful where he was concerned.

"Have you had other visions like this that also came true?" The hand behind my back pressed into me, feeling far too solid.

I nodded as I typed. *Every time I touch someone skin-to-skin for the first time, I have a premonition. Sometimes it's a vision. Others it's a feeling, like a sixth sense. They've never been wrong.*

"That explains a great deal about the way you sometimes respond to strangers. I'm curious what you saw about the incubus that made you so willing to let him feed from you without knowing him."

At the spiteful tone he'd used, I said, "What I felt had nothing to do with it. That was all because of you."

To piss him off.

It had worked at the time. A little too well, if he was still pissed about it.

How do you know Sasha won't be able to see you in the veil?

Lucifer flicked his eyes over that question and then over to where the ritual was still happening. "I'm in the veil, but not. You can see me because we're tethered—but necromancers can't. I don't believe I'm as dead as we both originally thought."

I blinked in shock.

Hallie can see you.

"She's basically a god due to her unique creation and now fueled by Orson's interference." I wasn't sure why, but I was surprised to hear him speak of Orson. We rarely talked about Piper's children, even if she, herself, came up often.

And Bree.

Before she'd disappeared, Piper's sister had revealed that she could see the ghost following me. So far, she and Hallie were the only ones.

"She's a demon. Our magic is never as straightforward. I could be wrong . . ."

"But you don't think you are," I whispered.

"No, I don't. Especially not with your vision." He paused, as if considering something. "If you've known this since the beginning, why have you been so resistant to bringing me back? I don't understand why it bothers you when you know my return is inevitable."

Why indeed?

I'd asked myself the same thing and every time my answer was the same.

To bring you back, I'd have to pick someone to die. To choose someone who I deem bad enough to take your place. It's not my job to decide who's good and isn't. I won't play God.

I was still typing when he nodded. "You've mentioned this before, but it's not even a half-truth. It's a lie."

I released a hard breath. He was right, but . . . "It's a good reason. An honorable one," I whispered.

He lifted his hand from my back to push a stray lock of hair away from where it had fallen into my eyes. How he could be so gentle, yet so ruthless, was mystifying. It would give me whiplash if I let myself think about it too much, so I tried not to.

"But it's not yours."

I wished it was. Gods, how I wished that simply choosing something could make it so. Unfortunately, I wasn't just Caretaker, who would always do what was best for others. Morals were easy for her. She didn't have to contend with logic like Ann, who would have already done the resurrection and moved on. The Warden would have accepted the consequences with a grimace and a stiff lip, because dead or alive, we were stuck with him. By her rationale, it was better the devil you know than the one you don't. That's how she saw Kat and the murders. An unknown. She didn't like unknowns.

In this, the voice who had been the loudest in me was also the one who spoke the softest—Peace. She didn't want to do it, because doing so meant accepting change. It meant a disturbance to the blissful masquerade we'd been conducting in front of my friends and family. It meant the possibility that *everything* would fall apart.

Lucifer returning wouldn't go unnoticed.

Someone would have to answer for it, for him, for the havoc that would no doubt ensue.

Peace simply wanted . . . peace.

But there was one other Nat in the memory loci. One calling me on my bullshit loud and clear. Demanding that I acknowledge the truth, that it wasn't my morals that were stopping me, but something I didn't want to name.

I nodded slowly, debating my answer. My fingers stalled over the keys.

Resurrecting you . . . complicates things. I may have seen it, but that doesn't mean I want to make that decision. My life—

I paused, chewing on my bottom lip. Lies were easy. The

truth? That was brutal. It stung. When did I start caring that it would sting him?

My life is good. It may not be perfect, but it is mine. Your return will disrupt it.

"You're afraid," Lucifer murmured.

More than he would ever know.

Exhaustion weighed on me. Tension built behind my tired eyes. The hour was late, and the ghost summoning was coming to a close. My fingers lifted, stiff and cold in the drafty chapel. I pressed them to my lips.

I still had one more question.

You drew blood. This morning. How did you . . . Why can I feel you?

Blood and sex. Devastation. Salvation. He leaned in close, strong fingers touching my wrist to move my hand. My fingers dropped from my lips as he pressed my palm to his chest. His breath touched me.

"We're tethered." The smooth tips of his fingers skated over my jaw, light as a feather. "I'm dead, but not. Because you're not. At least that's my theory. Part of me lives in you, because you sacrificed a piece of your soul to save me." My breath stalled as he spoke. "You're my anchor."

"What does that make you?" I whispered, lifting a brow.

"Your ship," he answered with total seriousness. "I raise you up when your job gets too hard and remind you to live." His face was almost solid enough to no longer see the church on the other side. It made it harder to be distracted and dissipate the tension building between us.

"To live?" I mouthed and tilted my head. "Let me guess. With you?" I chuckled, shaking my head. How gullible did he think I was? I lowered one hand to the step to push up, when his index finger and thumb caught my chin in an iron grip.

Anger flashed behind his eyes.

"Would you ever choose me?"

I blinked, thrown off by the question. It probably shouldn't have, if I considered the line of thinking all of his questions followed. But there was something vulnerable about this one that gave me pause.

Lucifer was possessive and aggressive and a lot of other things ending in -ive. He lacked remorse, even though he had the hindsight to know when he should have done something differently. He was pushy and controlling. Thanks to his narcissism, it made it easier to see through his manipulations.

Despite his many, many flaws, however, he was still just a man.

One who'd lived nine thousand years only to realize in death he'd never actually lived. His words, not mine.

He'd never loved.

I didn't think this was that. But for the first time, I wondered if his interest wasn't entirely a diversion. If he wasn't faking it. If it was more than a manipulation.

He'd all but said it, not that I believed him any of the other times.

This question was different.

It left him exposed.

Showed a weakness that could be exploited.

Not just for him, but for me. Any answer I gave revealed too much. Even a lie he could taste would tell more than I was ready to admit.

In my silent debate, I didn't notice the silence of the chapel. Not until Marcel's concerned voice broke through.

"Nathalie . . . we have a problem."

thirty-two

MARCEL

SHE STARED INTENTLY at the space before her, eyes locked on something I couldn't see. The position she sat in was oddly strained. I wanted to keep watching to see what she did, but time was running out.

"Nathalie . . . we have a problem."

She jerked, a violent twitch that resulted in a sharp gasp, like I'd caught her in some illicit act. She blinked once, swallowing hard enough I could see the bob of her throat in the low candlelight.

My curiosity regarding anything and everything to do with her was piqued, but it was quickly muddied by the problem at hand.

"What is it?" Her voice was hoarse, but was it from disuse or something else? My suspicion rose.

"She's not waking up."

Nathalie flew to her feet, eyes wide. "What do you mean, she's not waking up? You've done this spell dozens of times—"

"I'm aware of how many times I've done the spell," I interrupted. Her blame wouldn't help right now. Neither would my anger. "I did the spell correctly, but I've never done it with a succubus or a shifter. Maybe it changed something . . ." I glanced down at the woman lying on the cold stone floor in front of me.

Dark bruising surrounded the cuts on her wrists. Blood leaked from the open wounds, slowing more every minute. The edges had turned hard and crusted. Her brown skin became unnatural with death's pallor. A thin sheen of sweat covered her body.

"She has death magic," Nathalie said, arguing more for herself than anything else. "It shouldn't have changed anything. She was just the sacrifice. She wasn't casting."

The shallow rise and fall of the woman's chest acted as the ticking clock. Nat could spit out facts all she wanted, but she knew what was happening whether she wanted to admit it or not.

"The candle should have guided her back." I stared at the still-burning flame that was incredibly close to the end of the wick. "It should have been extinguished with the closing of the spell."

She approached the edge of the circle, and I held up a hand.

"If you enter it, the flame will go out and the chances of her waking up drop dramatically."

The fire was her guide. Without that, if she was still in the veil, she may become lost to it forever. Wandering as a ghost that didn't belong.

"If her body dies because she bleeds out on the floor, she won't wake up either," Nathalie hissed through gritted teeth. Her boots clicked against the tile as she paced with agitation. "I knew I shouldn't have let her do it. This wouldn't have happened if you'd just let me be the sacrifice—"

"That was never going to happen," I said slowly, trying to temper my frustration with her. "So get it out of your head. Blame me, if you must, but this is exactly why I wouldn't let you do it." She was trying to gain a measure of control in an uncontrollable situation.

"Has this happened before?" she asked, gold flickers firing to life within her eyes. I loved to watch it. The way her eyes changed under extreme emotion. She went from Nathalie Le Fay to otherworldly. It was stunning, under other circumstances.

"Not for me."

The strain in her jaw made the muscle twitch. "Exactly." She turned away from me, showing me her back as she approached the steps. "Can you see her?" she demanded, staring at nothing but the empty altar.

Concern for someone other than Sasha filled me. All witches had to be bound to their psychic bondmate, or they'd contend with the madness caused by the imbalance. Most didn't feel the effects until their forties. It just depended on how much they used their magic. While Nat had shown signs of something, it wasn't psychosis.

"Nathalie," I called her name gently, trying to coax her attention back to me.

"I don't give a damn about your question!" she snapped. "She's my priority. Maybe I would have seen what went wrong if I hadn't been playing stupid games with you."

The cutting edge in her tone made my blood chill. It pushed my anger down in favor of a growing worry. "Nathalie," I barked, hoping to startle her into answering me. She continued like I wasn't in the same room.

"So you can't find her?" Her face flushed in fury as she tracked something or someone with her eyes narrowed. Her attention focused three feet to my right. "Can you see anything else? Any other ghosts? Anything that could help."

Whoever it was, she didn't like the answer she received.

"Useless," she muttered, looking away. "Everyone is fucking *useless.*" She shook her head, as if trying to clear whatever dark thoughts were running through her mind. Another concern took form, seeing her one-sided conversation. If it wasn't a hallucination, then she was speaking to a ghost.

It was an extremely rare ability among our kind.

Rarer still that she'd never shown signs of it before.

A crazed look entered her eyes as she stared at Sasha's body. Unblinking. Unmoving.

"You want the truth?" I hardly recognized her voice, soft, but filled with so much rage. "I will *never* choose you because nothing good could ever come from bringing you back. You ruin everything you touch. You're a damned *monster.* Why would I ever choose that?"

"Who are you talking to?" I asked slowly.

I wasn't sure if she'd heard me or if she'd retreated to that place in her mind I could never reach. The one she seemed hellbent on pretending didn't exist, even if I saw the way all signs of awareness faded away.

"No one," she said, without looking at me. "Just a ghost."

My chest tightened. "Whose ghost?"

Whoever it was, they clearly had history. An intimate history, if her half of the conversation was a response to anything close to what it sounded like.

There weren't many ways to interpret what she would be choosing this person for. My fists balled, and under different circumstances, it might have been laughable. I was jealous of a ghost.

But that ghost, whether they realized it or not, had gotten under her skin in a way no one but me ever should.

I didn't like it.

She took another step toward the circle. Her body moved as if compelled. Face strained and head tilted, she stopped at the edge of the circle, not even an inch from the salt line.

For a second, I thought she'd tell me who she'd been speaking to. Who had stolen a piece of her from me.

The candle flickered, and Nat's stuttering inhale was the only sound I heard as the light went out.

A thin trail of smoke whispered through the chapel.

Dread filled me. I didn't know Sasha well. I'd met her a couple dozen times in passing. She was no one to me, but that clearly wasn't the case for Nat. Tears filled her eyes, giving them a glassy sheen as she locked on the ash remains of the candle.

"It doesn't matter," she whispered as she dragged the tip of her boot through the salt, breaking the circle. "You need to undo the binding on her healing."

"If she's not in there, there's no magic that can heal her," I said slowly. "Magic is the soul. The soul is magic. Every ancient text I've studied states that. If she's not in her body, removing the binding won't do anything—and healing her will only make it more difficult for her to re-enter it."

Gold flashed as Nathalie turned that hard stare on me and raised her voice as she spoke. "And if we do nothing, she fucking dies."

I sighed, not liking the corner this put me in. "If she's not in there, it doesn't matter. The only thing that can bring her back is . . . a resurrection ritual."

"No." Nat shook her head. The golden light of the sun

winked out in her gaze, and her eyes turned to their usual light brown. Tears spilled over her cheeks. I reached out to comfort her, and she slapped my hand away. "I refuse to let this be it. If you won't do anything, I'll take her to someone who will."

Her knees bent, banging against the tile as she dropped down into the pool of blood. She carefully maneuvered Sasha's arm to her chest, then the other. The angry side of me, the one that was furious for her dismissals and repeated rejections, wanted to watch her struggle to save her friend as I'd struggled for years to save her.

But she'd never forgive me.

So instead of standing back and letting her attempt to move Sasha without making it worse, likely killing her in the process, I squatted next to her.

"I don't know *how* to fix her. That's not the same as choosing to do nothing." I tried to be gentle in my explanation, but she glowered at me, mouth stiff with fury. Fingers trembling. "She's in a precarious position, and the wrong move will kill her."

"Doing nothing is the wrong move." Despite the tears on her face and shaking hands, she spoke with a surety in her voice. "I won't let her die. I will not allow it, Marcel."

"Then tell me what to do," I said, frustration filtering through my poor attempt to keep it in check. "This isn't my magic, but if I can, I will help her. Whatever it is."

Her brow furrowed. She didn't trust me. Fair enough. We had a history of distrust, and to add insult to injury, she'd just found out I got married last year . . . on the same day I'd asked her to return home and be my wife. Not my best or brightest move, in hindsight, but I'd been desperate. Now that trust was thinning even more.

"Tell me how to fix it, Nathalie." My jaw clenched.

"I don't know how!" she yelled, sucking in a harsh breath. Tugging her fingers through her hair, she choked back a sob. She brushed her friend's hair back in a gentle sweep. "Hold on, Sasha," she whispered, then looked up at me.

Reaching down, I placed two fingers on Sasha's wrist, feeling her faint pulse. My lips pressed in a thin line, and I glanced at Nat. "She's dying, Nat. What do you want me to do?"

Nat's wide eyes glistened with unshed tears as she held my gaze. "I don't know how to fix this, but I think I know someone who can." I dipped my chin, waiting for instructions. She grabbed my arm, holding Sasha with her other. "Teleport us over to Señora Rosara's."

I exhaled loudly, tilting my head to the side. Of all the places for us to go. That witch hated me, and I didn't trust her for shit. Those cats were unnerving.

My momentary hesitation set Nathalie off. "NOW, Marcel!"

"Fucking hell," I muttered, grabbing hold of Sasha while I held Nat, pushing us through space and time.

thirty-three

NATHALIE

WE APPEARED HAPHAZARDLY in the middle of the shop. My elbow struck something hard, and I stumbled trying to catch myself. My feet found purchase, but then my hip knocked into a table. Glass shattered, sending shards all over the floor. A bookcase tipped sideways, knocking into the one beside it, causing glass jars of body parts and who knew what else to rattle and threaten to fall.

Marcel grunted after the impact and cursed up a storm about our rough landing. He held my arm protectively, checking his hold on Sasha to make sure she was okay. She didn't stir as havoc ensued around us.

Several of Señora Rosara's cats approached and let out a low hiss. They were either pissed I'd brought Marcel through the wards or that I'd brought a part-cat shifter, and they wanted to be territorial.

I didn't care. I didn't have the time to talk them down.

"Where is the señora? Get her now!" I told the cats in Spanish. All but one darted away. The remaining loner narrowed its gaze and pinned its ears to the back of its head, keeping a watchful eye on us.

In a matter of moments, the beads that separated the store from the back room clacked.

"I need your help," I rushed to say, pointing at Sasha. "We did a ghost summoning ritual. She went into the veil—"

"I know what you did, child," she said, shuffling toward me in her nightgown. "Why do you think I am here at this hour? I saw your arrival as I was preparing for bed."

Marcel glanced at me cautiously, but stayed quiet. Señora Rosara was a short-sighted seer with impeccable accuracy, and the void stone ring on her finger amplified that ability. To what degree, I wasn't certain. I'd never asked, but her being in the shop and prepared for our arrival spoke volumes about her abilities.

"I didn't know what else to do," I said, emotion clogging my throat again.

"Bring her to me. Quickly," she said, then snapped her fingers and four cats appeared. They shifted rapidly from your standard domestic tabby cat to four naked, muscled, and *collared* men.

My mouth went dry, and my jaw fell open.

"Wha—"

"You will not like the answer," she said, waving her hand to the backroom as all four men crowded around us. Marcel grabbed my forearm and pulled me back as they carefully lifted Sasha, careful not to disturb her. "Better to not ask the question."

My chin bobbed as I opened and closed my lips several times, then slowly followed them around the corner. Señora Rosara extended her hand, blocking my path. I jerked, turning from the backroom where they'd carried Sasha, then back to my landlord. Her dark brown eyes were inscrutable.

"Can you fix this?" I asked, crossing my arms because I didn't know what else to do with my hands.

"I can't see that far into the future, but I'll do what I can to keep the vessel alive."

"And her soul?" I pressed, fear leaking into my voice. Every supernatural had a magical signature. I was the only one that could see it, as far as I knew, but Sasha's . . . it had disappeared when she went into the veil, and it never returned. Her body was just that now: a body. Nothing more. Nothing less.

"That's unknown. I can't control the souls of the dead," she said after a pregnant pause. "All I can do is create a lure. It will act as a beacon within the veil."

"And entice every malevolent entity within a hundred miles," Marcel argued, finally speaking up with a raised voice. She flicked her ice-cold gaze toward him. "What are you playing at, Renata?"

"It'll do what?" I asked, looking between them.

"If you think the magic I play with is bad, ask your dear señora what exactly she plans to do with Sasha's body— before it's too late to undo it," he said. "The risks are substantial, and the outcome is risky at best."

"Don't question my motives, *boy*." The señora's gaze narrowed on Marcel.

"Stop," I said to him, holding up a hand. "Tell me about the lure. Will it really call to . . . everything?" I pressed, ignoring his other accusations. They weren't irrelevant, but I didn't exactly have a better choice right now. Señora Rosara looked back at me, a slight and unusual softness in her eyes as she inclined her head. "What are the odds this doesn't work and harms her instead?"

"Greater than the possibility of success," she said. "You have to decide what's worse: trying and failing, or not trying at all. The longer her soul is away from her body, the more likely it is she'll die."

I bit my lip, tasting blood. This was a decision I couldn't make alone. Not when her sister needed to know. "Marcel, take the elevator to the third floor. Get Sienna. She needs to know what's happened."

"I hope you know what you're doing here," Marcel muttered. "The hag—"

I spun to face him. "Is an incredibly powerful and *experienced* death witch who won't hesitate to turn you into a cat if you keep insulting her in her own shop."

Señora Rosara let out a raspy chuckle. "This is why I've always liked you. You're smart and respectful; a rare combination for a Le Fay. *You,* on the other hand . . ." She lifted her chin to assess Marcel and his features hardened under her scrutiny. "Impulsive. Imprudent." She clicked her tongue. "An Abernathy, through and through. You could have been the greatest warlock of this age, and instead you've squandered it being a plaything to powerful and manipulative women. You didn't stop and think for yourself. Dryanda would be ashamed, but I don't see much point in you trying to change the pattern now."

The breath hissed between his lips. He took a step toward her, and amusement flickered across her expression.

"Stop," I repeated, and took a step forward, blocking him. "Go get Sienna. *Now.*"

He hesitated, lingering at my side and glancing at the cat-turned-men. Señora laughed. "I've been watching over this girl for years. Ever since you threw her away. She didn't need you then, and she doesn't now. But please, stick around and we'll see how long it takes me to collar you too."

"Marcel," I repeated his name with an icy edge. His hateful glare wasn't helping things any more than her threats to turn him into one of her cats.

"Fine," he said through gritted teeth.

Only once the elevator closed did she drop her arm. "Trouble, that one." She thrust her chin toward the elevator behind her. "You're no longer the fragile witch I took in. For all the pain he's caused, I hope you give him trouble in return before you accept him as a consort."

"The beacon," I said, not wanting to talk about Marcel. "Tell me about it . . . about the risks."

Señora Rosara sighed and turned to go back to the counter. Her nightgown swished along the concrete floor as her sandals slapped against it. She wasn't a large woman, but she wasn't petite, either. Her stature was short but curvy. She avoided the hard edges and cramped spaces of the crowded shop from familiarity alone.

"It'll call out to her soul, wherever it is, but the boy is right. It'll also call to anything *other*." She shrugged as she walked around the corner. I followed on her heels. "The room I've placed her in is warded, not just from the living, but from the dead as well. When I make the beacon, I can place a hole in that ward. A small one that only she should be able to get through."

"You're sure nothing else can follow?" I asked, sweeping the beads aside to reveal the hallway. No more than three feet of unimpeded walking space, and it would have made it a tight fit for the muscled men to carry Sasha through. Doubt washed over me, but I pushed it aside. Now wasn't the time.

"No," she admitted. "I don't deal in guarantees and promises. There's always a chance. I can make it more difficult for another spirit to follow, but I can't prevent it. That said, the more parameters I place to prevent someone else from entering the body—"

"The harder it will be for her to return to it as well," I finished softly, and I heard her softly hum in confirmation.

She stopped outside an unmarked door. By all accounts, it was inconspicuous. Plain white paint over what appeared to be wood. An ordinary knob that wouldn't be particularly effective against an intruder.

But the bone-chilling cold that radiated from it screamed *"turn back."*

I frowned, staring hard to try to see what magic came from it, but whatever had caused the immediate terror when I approached it . . . it couldn't be seen. I tried to shake off the ominous feeling.

"If we just preserve the vessel and don't do the beacon, what are the odds she'll find her body again?"

Her pinkish brown lips quirked in consideration. "I can't say none, because strange things happen all the time —but you will probably never see your friend. The veil destroys the minds of its inhabitants. We're on the clock now. The longer she is adrift from her body, the lower the odds of her returning to claim it before some other creature becomes aware and tries to take over."

My hands clenched into fists. I wanted to cry. I wanted her to be wrong, but I knew she wasn't. She had no reason to lie about this.

Before I could even think about how to push down my emotions, the beads rattled and my fear was overshadowed. I saw Sienna's light pink magic before her body came into view. Sienna rushed in, padding on bare feet in sweatpants and a P!nk T-shirt. Her unruly black hair was braided back, but the small hairs around her face were frizzy from sleep. Alarm made her vivid green eyes wide and alert.

"Where is she?" she choked out.

Señora Rosara sighed. "We don't have much time. The containment room will prevent another from stealing her form, but a decision must be made."

I bit my lip. "It's not mine to make. It should be hers." I looked at Sienna.

"Where's my sister?" she demanded. "Where's Sasha?"

Señora Rosara tilted her head, staring at me in expectation.

"In the veil," I answered, then shuddered at the heartbroken look on her face. It was visceral. Instant. Sasha was her twin, and I understood what it meant to lose one. All too well. Swallowing hard, I forced myself to look at her and not the ceiling. "Her body is still alive, but she didn't return to it at the end of the summoning. She's not dead . . . but she is dying."

I'd never forget the look on Sienna's face when I delivered the news, not in a year or fifty. The strange sort of devastation with sheer determination were at odds, but both telegraphed utterly in the set of her lips and pain in her eyes.

"Fix this," she said, but she didn't look at Señora Rosara. She looked at me. "You have to."

I took a deep breath and let it go. "There is a way, but it's risky. Señora can create a beacon—"

She took both my hands between hers, gripping them hard.

"Fix. This." Sienna shuddered. "I don't care about the risks. I don't care what has to happen. Just bring her back to me."

I released a pent-up breath, then nodded to Señora Rosara.

"Do it."

She dipped her chin, her shrewd gaze still on me. "To call her back to her body, I need whatever it is she holds most dear."

"That's me," Sienna said quietly.

"You're sure?" She slowly looked sideways. "If you're wrong, it could cost your twin her last chance at life."

Sienna shook even though she kept nodding, tension radiating from her body. Señora Rosara glanced back at me and lifted an eyebrow as if to ask for my confirmation. "Sasha took a blood oath for her so Piper would save Sienna's life. I can't see her doing that for anyone else except her niece." Especially not August. I knew that's why she was looking at me that way. My chest squeezed.

Silence spanned between the three of us. Then the señora reached into her skirt pocket and pulled out a bulb-shaped vial with five compartments.

"I can't offer you to the veil without killing you. To substitute, I will need your blood, sweat, spit, and urine. Leave the last one empty."

Sienna let go of my hands to take the vial, her trembling fingers wrapping around the glass. The señora shooed her off to collect what she'd asked for and Sienna didn't hesitate. Once she'd rounded the corner, avoiding Marcel as he stood near the doorway, the death witch turned to me.

In her callused fingers, she held another vial, extending it to me in silence.

I stared at it, knowing deep down what she was saying, but not wanting to take it.

"It's Sienna," I said quietly. "It has to be. Sasha may want him, but he isn't what she holds most dear."

The old witch smiled knowingly.

"It's for the ward. She's his mate. His magic will strengthen the ward while calling to her, but it will also recognize that bond and allow her to pass." She glanced down at the vial. "Blood, sweat, spit, urine . . . and for the beacon, his seed."

"His . . .?" I trailed off, hearing the slight quaver in my voice. She pressed her lips together and leveled me with a glare. I swallowed thickly, asking a question I wasn't sure I wanted to know the answer to. "Why?"

"To intensify the beacon's energy. To further its reach. She longs to be with her mate. Even if her mind starts to slip, this will draw her back. The bond magic within him will call to hers."

"Will it . . ." I cleared my throat. "Will it make their bond stronger?" I cursed myself for wanting to know. I hated that I wanted the answer to be no.

"Yes," she said, and I felt my chest constrict. "The only way to narrow the scope is by forcing his magic to allow only those it sees as either a mate or an aurae through."

My shoulders tensed, and my fingers wrapped around the cool glass. I held it in the palm of my hand.

"He may resist," I said quietly, trying to ignore Marcel from the corner he lurked in.

"He might. That's why I'm giving it to you." She smiled, without happiness or sympathy. "Ask nicely. You're good at that." My jaw went slack as she patted my cheek with something close to affection. "But this will come at a heavy price."

I knew it would. Nothing was free in this world, but I would pay anything to save my friends. Money was no object. "It doesn't matter as long as it brings her back. Whatever the cost, I'll take care of it."

She lifted a dark eyebrow, exhaustion lining her features. "Are you sure about that, child? I'm not certain your heart has the strength to."

I froze at her words. My limbs turned leaden as my heart slammed in my chest. "What do you mean?"

She gave me a sad smile, filled with pity—something she'd never shown me in all the years I'd known her. Trepidation swamped me.

"This spell won't just strengthen their bond, Nathalie. It will complete it."

My lips parted, and I felt like the breath had been forced out of my lungs as they burned. The pain of her words assaulted me, twisting my gut and making my ears ring. I couldn't speak. My mind raced, and my heart sank, breaking and shattering so deep within me I couldn't bear to give voice to it. I nodded, swallowing the lump that had formed in my dry throat.

Señora inhaled, taking a moment before dropping a last bomb on me. After a long pause, she said, "The moment Sasha's soul returns, they will become mates in every sense of the word . . . and his feelings for you, along with the aurae bond you share, will be forgotten."

Wrapping her hands around mine, she held them firm. "Are you still willing to pay it?"

No. I wasn't, but there was one irrefutable truth that made me nod my head anyways.

August was never mine. No matter what he thought, he was always meant to be hers.

"I'll see that it's done," I whispered.

To be continued...

acknowledgments

This story was a breath of fresh air.

For the first time, in five or so years, Kel actually fell in love with what she was writing and Aurelia finally found a male mc that she would totally lick if he were real. (Yes, it's August. She claimed him.)

From the very first chapter, Nat's story took a wild turn. We sat down expecting to write a trilogy about a witch and the devil she fell in love with. Instead, we stumbled across an incubus that was was supposed to be a one and done deal, but he lept off the page. Then we saw that she also had this deliciously disarming ex that wasn't going to let her go.

At that point, Kel called Aurelia and said, "I think we got a problem."

Turns out, we were writing a reverse harem about a smart and sassy witch who didn't have a hard time falling in love. She has a hard time with what comes after. Trusting them. Keeping them.

Nat is still very much on her journey, as are Lucifer, August, and Marcel. They've all got growing and maturing to do (except August) and we are so excited to be writing it.

Thank you for coming along on the journey with us. Nat's love story may not be a traditional one, but we promise it will be unforgettable.

Until next time in New Chicago.

- Kel and AJ

www.ingramcontent.com/pod-product-compliance
Lightning Source LLC
Chambersburg PA
CBHW030705190726
48286CB00001B/177